The Kindness of Witches

A Doctor William Gilbert Mystery

The Kindness of Witches

A DOCTOR WILLIAM GILBERT MYSTERY

LEONARD TOURNEY

LUME BOOKS

LUME BOOKS

This edition published in 2023 by Lume Books

Copyright © Leonard Tourney 2023

The right of Leonard Tourney to be identified as the author of this work has been asserted by them in accordance with the Copyright, Design and Patents Act, 1988.

ISBN 978-1-83901-481-9

Typeset using Atomik ePublisher from Easypress Technologies

www.lumebooks.co.uk

Arnaldus de Villanova fancies that the lodestone frees women from witchcraft and puts demons to flight... in such like follies and fables do philosophers of the vulgar sort take delight; with such-like do they cram readers a-hungered for things abstruse, and every ignorant gaper for nonsense.

William Gilbert, *de Magnete*, 1600

Prologue

Colchester, England. Year of Grace, 1574

The astrologer, who like others of his kind was also a prognosticator of the weather, had foretold the mildest of winters. The planets had so aligned, the astrologer claimed. It was with that assurance that the young doctor had set out from his father's house in Colchester, Essex, where he had been visiting for Christmas, to make the two-day journey to London, some sixty miles to the south and west, where he enjoyed a flourishing medical practice.

His father, a prudent man, had discouraged his son's plans. He had little faith in astrological forecasts. And besides, his father said, winter is winter. Foul weather is to be expected, especially in England, where even spring and summer weather could make traveling perilous given the lamentable state of the roads and bridges.

The doctor had not traveled far that day before he had reason to doubt the astrologer's prediction and suspect his father had been right. Over to the east the sky began to darken, an ominous gray hue. He reckoned he was now somewhere between Colchester and Chelmsford, the latter being a familiar stopping point for him, lying as it did near half-way between the beginning and the ending of his journey.

He rode a few miles more, not taking his eyes off the sky. Then suddenly the wind came up, blowing west. The wind became the fiercer, and then came rain, driven with such force that he was at pains to manage his horse, a two-year old gelding he had acquired from a local blacksmith but had only ridden once before.

The rain stung the doctor's beardless face, causing him to shield his eyes, pull his riding cloak more tightly around him, wish he had worn his fur cap, not the velvet one, which he was now at pains to keep upon his

1

head. Within minutes, the rain had turned to snow, the heaviest he had remembered. Within a few more minutes, the old Roman road that time out of mind connected Colchester and London was buried in it, and the air around him had become white, the sky and land dissolved into one.

Despite his cloak and heavy gloves, he was deathly cold, nearly blinded, and was no longer sure he and the horse still followed the road or had wandered off into the fens. He knew he had been wrong, not in setting out but in not turning back sooner. He had not expected the storm's suddenness or its fury.

He buried his face in the horse's thick mane. The poor creature was covered with ice crystals. The wind blew over him. His cloak, newly purchased in London a week before, provided little protection, although the man who had sold it to him swore it would resist the worst weather. Tailors' predictions were often no better than astrologers'.

The young doctor and his horse moved forward more slowly. Occasionally he could see the shadow of a tree or bush, but he might as well have been blind, he and his horse, for all they could see ahead. Suddenly the horse sprung sharply to the right, then stumbled, throwing the doctor headfirst into a snowbank.

He remembered later hitting his head, not on the soft cushion of snow but on a stone or rock, buried beneath. For a moment he lost consciousness. When he came to, he was alone, already half buried in the snow.

Once on his feet, he looked around him for his horse. He called out, hoping the animal would respond, but his call was lost in the wind. He was alone and, he now admitted to himself, quite lost.

It was only then that he understood the seriousness of his predicament. Before, the storm was an inconvenience, an impediment to his agenda, an annoying confirmation that his father had been right to caution him. Now he realized his life was threatened. He could no longer look to what the future might hold for him. He might have none. At least not beyond the next few hours, or perhaps even the next few minutes.

He knew he must keep going. What else could he do? He knew now that he would freeze to death were he to remain where he was. He might suffer the same fate were he to press on. But in pressing on he prayed he might find some refuge, if only a shepherd's hut or farmer's barn. A miserable outbuilding fit for pigs or poultry would be a palace to him under such circumstances.

The physical exertion of walking warmed his body somewhat but hardly enough, the cold penetrating his garments as though he walked naked. He was not sure whether he was traveling south-west as he intended, or his sense of direction was completely confused. No landmarks were visible to help him, and the snow was now deep enough to make walking difficult.

He realized he was moving through a forest. He had left the bare winter fields behind. He could see the trees rise up around him, the bare winter branches like arms reaching for him. Like ghosts or spirits. This was no road buried beneath snow and ice. He was wandering where no habitation likely was and therefore neither help nor hope.

He struggled on, the snow deeper and deeper. He could not think clearly. In truth, there was nothing for him to think about except for the necessity to push on, to somehow survive this calamity his own poor judgment had brought upon him.

After a while he felt his body falter. He was a healthy young man with a long stride who in dry weather could easily walk fifteen or twenty miles in a day. Now he struggled over uneven ground, slowed, holding his arms out in front of him like a blind man to ward off the threatening branches.

Soon he was not as cold as before – or did not seem so. His extremities, hands and feet, were beyond feeling. Then he suddenly realized he was not alone. Beside him walked another person. A woman, small, dressed in a gown he somehow remembered. He turned to look at the face. It was his mother, and for a moment he felt both a sense of relief and happiness. It was his mother, walking beside him, dressed for a summer day, not a winter's storm.

But then he remembered that she was dead, had been so for years. It gave him a moment of happiness in his struggle to move on, and now he wanted to stop. To sit down in the snow and let it envelop him, which seemed more delightsome a prospect than reaching some place of warmth, of safety.

But he knew what was happening to him. He recognized the symptoms. He was a doctor, and it was his business to know such things. The unnatural warmth, the hallucinations. He had never experienced these effects before, but he had spoken to those who had come near death by cold and lived to tell the tale, told their strange and improbable stories, how the body responding to the extreme and fatal cold conjured up false visions to comfort or deceive. When he remembered that, he turned to

3

the vision beside him, but his mother was gone. He struggled forward, found himself in a thicket, and then tripped and fell forward.

He was still conscious enough to see the shape moving toward him. It was not human but an animal. A creature of some kind. Low to the ground. Snarling at first, panting heavily. Was it a wolf? It looked like a wolf. Another delusion, he thought, before he slept.

His name was William Gilbert, or Gilberd as his father preferred, and he was always called William, never Will, by those who knew him. He was a tall, smooth-faced man of thirty, but already laden with distinctions, which he bore with what his associates thought admirable humility. He was skilled in the art of healing, knew the human body in all its parts and functions as if he, and not God, had created them. His father, Jerome Gilbert, was a lawyer and recorder in Colchester, the place of his birth, and he had grown up in his father's comfortable house, Tymperleys, which although he could not know it then, would stand for centuries after him into a time of wonders beyond his imagination.

His mother Elizabeth, now dead, had come from a good family, the Coggeshalls, who were gentry, well-established in the county. From his early youth he had shown curiosity and intellectual ability, had been sent to Cambridge when he was thirteen to study medicine and was now a practitioner of that art in London. But he was also a student of physics and natural science, especially the magnet—or the lodestone, as he preferred to call it.

The road to his success in his profession had not been smooth. He had earlier in his career been falsely accused of murder, had languished for a time in a dismal prison in Southwark, had narrowly escaped death at the hands of his enemies. And although all of that had passed like a dream in the night, he had never forgotten the pain of it, nor did he forget it while he wandered helplessly in the storm that struck the English coast in that year and seemed so ardent in its merciless clawing that the Devil must have been the author of it.

1

Before he could think again, he felt warmth, a warmth that he supposed, now conscious, he imagined. Like the illusory warmth he felt while freezing, his body succumbing to its end, himself preparing for it, like a condemned man reconciled to the stroke of the headsman's axe.

He was lying not in snow but enveloped in blankets. He could smell the damp wool, could smell also the smoke of a fire, not blazing but dying, yet still generating a restorative heat. Then to his nostrils came something else, an animal smell, strong, sour. He opened his eyes and the firelight showed himself within doors, lying by a fire, wrapped in blankets, yes, but not alone.

He slowly turned his head and saw the creature lying next to him, lying close like a wife or a lover. It was black, breathing softly, thickly furred. It stared at him out of canine eyes, a deep, penetrating gaze.

Suddenly his relief at somehow surviving the storm was replaced with a stark terror. If this wasn't a wolf by his side, he didn't know what else it might be. For it had every feature of wolf that he had ever learned, and despite their rare appearance in his part of England he knew these creatures still survived, not merely in local legend but in reality. He had seen one once, caged. At Colchester market. The beast had been injured and therefore helpless when captured by a poor farmer who was making his living showing it at fairs and fetes. A good living too, for the townspeople clamored to see it, regarding the creature with a mixture of horror and fascination. His people, the English, loved nothing better than novelty, some new thing to gawk at, to talk of, to dream about while they slept in ordinary houses and did ordinary things.

Had he been standing, able and ready to flee – armed even – he would have been no match for the wolf's attack. Prone as he was, his legs pulled up against his breast, and weakened by his ordeal in the storm, he was all the more vulnerable. By miracle, he had escaped an icy death, only now to be ripped to pieces. That was his fear.

He did not move, he hardly breathed. The wolf kept staring at him and then moved his long snout even closer to William's face, so man and beast could not be more than a hand's span apart and William could smell the wolf's hot, rancid breath.

Man and wolf lay side by side for what seemed to William to be hours, while the fire in the hearth died and became embers. At no time did the wolf sleep, but kept his eyes fixed on William, on William's face, his throat. William knew he was in a house – a farmstead, by the bare, rusticity of its furnishings. Someone must have found him in the snow, dragged his unconscious body in, placed him by the fire and wrapped him up so that he might revive.

But what of the wolf? Had he been superstitious, he might have supposed his unknown rescuer had changed his shape, turned into the black wolf. No mere animal, but a supernatural creature. A shapeshifter. Farmer by day, wolf by night. But William Gilbert was an educated man, a physician and scientist. Such tales of supernatural creatures he usually dismissed. But perhaps there was a core of truth in the old stories, something he had missed in his studies at Cambridge and was now about to discover through his own experience.

He tried to shake off these imaginings but at the moment, he could feel nothing else but the horror of his situation.

Somehow, later he must have fallen asleep. A sound woke him. Not a wolfish snarl or growl but a human voice; a woman's. He opened his eyes. No wolf now, at least. A woman peered down at him. She had long, dark hair streaked with gray, and dark eyes. By the lines around her eyes and mouth he thought she must be forty or fifty. A country woman by her homespun garments, a farmer's wife. "Are you well, sir?" she whispered; as though he still slept and she feared to wake him.

He took in the room beyond her. A spacious, high-ceilinged chamber, clearly built to be something other than a farmhouse kitchen. High, clerestory windows like a church, or his college at Cambridge. A generous hearth, dangling iron pots and ladles. A trestle table with benches, room for a dozen, perhaps more in a pinch. Against one wall a large, crudely made cupboard with shelves filled with wooden plates, bowls and cups.

No pewter, no glass, certainly no gleaming silver. No lord's kitchen this, a simple farmer's abode.

The wolf was nowhere. Behind the woman, morning light came in the windows, made more brilliant by the snow that must have shrouded the house as it had enveloped him along the road.

William answered the woman. He said he was well, which was hardly true. His body ached; his mind was yet to clear itself from the fear. "How did I come here?" He tried to escape his bedding, but lacked strength and fell back again.

"We found you lost at our doorstep," she said. "We thought you were dead."

"We?"

"My husband and I."

"You are alone here?"

The woman looked alarmed at the question. He thought maybe she feared he was a robber, his neediness a ruse. He said, "I mean, was it you who brought me in out of the storm, and bedded me down here?" He did not mention the wolf, which now he thought might have been a dream, or perhaps a hallucination induced by his closeness to death. Like the vision he had had of his dead mother. A ghost in the storm.

"My daughter found you. It took the three of us to bring you into the house."

"May I know your name?"

She hesitated, then said, "I am Mary Harkness. My husband is Jacob."

He told her his name, told her he was from Colchester, but was now a physician practicing in London. He told her he was on the way to that city when the storm came out of nowhere. He told her how he had been misled by the weather, thinking no storm was in the offing. He didn't tell her of the astrologer's prediction. He did not want to seem foolish for having believed it.

A man came into the room from outside. A sudden blast of frigid air chilled him to the bone. "This is my husband," the woman said.

A man looked down at William with a blank expression and made no response to his wife's introduction. She asked him where he had been.

"Cows must be milked," he said, curtly. "They care not that there's a storm."

William waved a hand and nodded at the man, tried to smile but his face still seemed frozen. The husband was tall, broad-shouldered, with a ragged black beard, broad forehead, and fierce-looking eyes. He took off his cap, revealing a shining bald pate that dominated the rest of the features on his face. He regarded William suspiciously.

"Where have you come from, sir?" he asked.

"Colchester," William said.

The man made a dismissive grunt.

"This is Doctor Gilbert," Mary Harkness said.

Jacob Harkness grunted again and peered down at William. William thought: *he's suspicious of me, thinks I may be armed and dangerous.*

"He was on his way to London and was caught up in the storm," Mary Harkness said.

Her husband snorted and walked toward the opposite side of the room. "What manner of fool travels in such weather?" Harkness asked no one in particular. He did not so much sit as collapse onto a stool, removed his heavy coat and wiped the snow off with his hands onto the stone floor.

"Thank you for finding me," William said.

"'T'wasn't I," the man said gruffly.

"'T'was our daughter," the woman said. "She found you, then called for me."

"Then I must thank her myself. For had she not, I would have been a dead man indeed."

"She's not here now. She's in another part of the house," the woman said. She looked over at her husband. "You need not be so rude, Jacob. The doctor here was in need. Our Lord calls us to Christian service, does he not? Like unto the Jewish man upon the road, whom the Samaritan gave aid to."

"And got little thanks for his effort, I warrant you," grumbled the husband. "Besides which, we are no Jews in this house, or Samaritans either."

The woman gave an exasperated sigh. At that point a young girl came into the room. Perhaps seventeen or eighteen. She was tall like her father. but whereas he was thick and stocky she was thin, almost bony, with a long pinched face and close-set eyes, a kind of boyish face, no softness in it but strong, well-defined lines. He could not imagine her ever eating, and if she did, then only sufficient to keep her alive.

The woman said, "This is our daughter, our only child. Ursula."

William nodded toward the girl. He struggled to stand but fell back again. His legs had not regained their strength, nor his arms. He realized his body had been injured by the cold and by the fall. He had faith he would recover, others had, but not at once and not because he willed it. He had been rescued by these people, he remained dependent on them, at least for the time being.

"Your mother said it was you that saved me," he said to the girl. "That must have been a heavy burden you bore. I'm sorry, I have no memory of it."

She smiled in response but said nothing.

He asked if there were a village nearby or a town. How far was he from Chelmsford, where he had hoped to spend the night?

"But ten miles or less," the woman said.

"But through the forest," the daughter quickly added. "There's a village closer, but there's hardly anything there. It sits beneath the castle."

"The castle?" William asked.

"It is called Mowbray Rise," the husband said, his eyes cold and distant as though he were viewing the place in his mind's eye. "Were you to view it, you should see, Doctor, why we in these parts call it the castle and not its proper name. It is the manor house of the Bascombes, God damn them. We live quite alone here."

"We live as we choose," the wife said.

"We live as we must," the husband said.

Husband and wife exchanged glances. William waited for further explanation as to the couple's hostility toward these Bascombes and their so-called castle, but none was forthcoming.

Outside, the wind wasn't letting up. It was shrill like a woman's scream, and he remembered tales from his boyhood about women lost in storms whose wailing could still be heard even after they were dead, frozen stiff, as he might have been had these Samaritans not taken him in, covered him with blankets, and placed him by the fire. He dismissed the wolf from his mind. It had been a delusion. Or a nightmare induced by his near-death state.

And then he heard a scratching on the door. Even above the howling wind he heard it. Ursula did, too. The girl turned and quickly walked toward it and in the next moment opened the door partly, holding her shoulder against the blast that invaded the room with a vengeance.

"Shut that cursed door," Jacob Harkness shouted above the wind.

William was momentarily blinded by the light. And then he saw the cause of the scratching.

It was the wolf of his nightmare.

2

The wolf moved softly across the stone floor and came to sit by the girl, who reached down and stroked its head. It kept his eyes fixed on William. None of the family expressed fear of the animal, but looked upon him as though he were but another creature they were used to having indoors, like a pet, like one of the spaniels fine ladies cradle in their arms and let sleep upon their feather beds.

But William didn't move, he could not. He didn't dare. Standing there, its teeth not bared but showing like knives, and then moving slowly toward him, the wolf looked huge – longer in leg and huskier than the one he had seen as a youth and found fearsome even then. Its black fur was wet from out of doors. William stifled a cry of alarm and drew back until he could feel the heat of the revived fire on his bare neck, and he knew he could retreat no farther.

Then laughter. Deep and derisive from the husband, then the wife, gentler, almost a chuckle. And finally, the daughter, a slight smile.

"Are you afraid of a mere dog, Doctor, that you turn deathly pale and pull away?" Jacob Harkness asked.

"Is that a dog indeed?"

"It is a dog, Doctor, as you can plainly see," Harkness said. "We would hardly have a wolf for a housemate, would we?"

"You are not the first to be deceived so," The wife said, looking down at William as though he were a child caught in a trap.

"It isn't a wolf?" William said, looking up, still not believing.

"It may be so – at least the half of him, that is," Ursula said.

"He's half wolf?"

"His name is Vulcan," she said.

She explained he was the whelp of her father's dog, whom he had loved.

11

The dog had run away, disappeared for a month or more. Then they had found her. Deep in a rocky crevice. Surrounded by her pups. Eight of them. All dead but one. "The bitch was dead, too."

"A wolf had tupped her, a big male," Harkness said. "I don't know what killed all the pups save him, or what killed my dog, who was as good a bitch as ever I had. But Vulcan lived and thrived, as you see."

"He's a good guard dog," the wife said. "Keeps strangers away from the house."

"Thank God, he didn't keep me away," William said.

The farmer's wife bent over a pot on the fire, stirring, singing to herself. It was a tune he had never heard before. Father and daughter were talking at the other end of the room in soft whispers. William couldn't hear, and he wondered if his ears were affected by the cold as his vision had been.

It was porridge the farmer's wife had prepared, savory and thick and spiced. She filled a bowl for her husband and daughter, who sat on a bench at the long trestle table. Then she brought one for him, along with a wooden spoon. When he could not hold it steady, she fed him, spoonful by spoonful as though he were a child. "There you are, Doctor. If you will be whole again, you must eat. That much I know of medicine, though I be taught only by my mother."

He had eaten porridge for breakfast all his life, but this was the best ever he tasted, and he told her so.

She smiled and nodded. "It will be a while before you will be able to continue to your destination, Doctor. The snow may stop, but it is piled high—and the road is eight miles or more from here, even if you were able to travel."

He was astonished. He hadn't thought to have wandered that far from the London road, but then he had been half delirious most of the time, fully so the rest. Perhaps he had even walked farther, going around in circles in the dense wood and coming upon this lonely farmstead by the grace of God and, now it seemed, a compassionate wolf that might otherwise have torn him to shreds.

"My family must know that I am alive," William said, ashamed suddenly that this was the first time he had thought of them at all. Of course, they would worry. But then he thought they might suppose he had arrived in London before the storm, while his servants and colleagues in the city might suppose he remained in Colchester. Yes, he decided, there was a good chance that no one was fretting over him. A weight lifted from him.

"You are welcome, Doctor, to stay with us until the snow melts and you are able to travel," the farmer's wife said.

Jacob Harkness looked at William with a steady gaze that made William a bit uncomfortable. He was unaccustomed to being scrutinized with such intensity by a virtual stranger. "You said, Doctor, that your name was Gilbert and you live in Colchester?"

"I did say," William answered. "Colchester is where my family is from. Now I live in London. I practice there."

"You practice?"

"I have my patients there, I mean."

"By some chance would you be some relation to Jerome Gilbert?" asked Harkness.

"He is my father," William answered proudly, for it ever gave him pleasure to learn how his father was known, not just in Colchester, but beyond.

"And a lawyer, I think?"

"Do you know my father?

"I know of him. When you return to Colchester, you may say to him that Jacob Harkness sends his regards and took his son in when there was none else to do it."

"Trust me, I shall," William said.

William looked at the farmer. He seemed less welcoming than his wife and daughter.

"I would not want to be a burden to you," William said.

Mary Harkness reached down and took his hands in hers. "You are the first stranger we have had in this house in ten years or more, Doctor. Vulcan found you, slept by you that you might be warmed again and live. Usually, he fends off strangers, protecting us. But he saved you. Is it not a sign, Doctor, from God, that you were meant to be here, to live rather than die of the cold? You are a blessing to this house, Doctor."

She moved away from him and walked toward a table where there were various bottles and jars. She took a cup, sprinkled something in it from one of half dozen bowls on the table. She filled it with water from a basin and then took a wooden spoon and stirred the concoction. She added other ingredients, stirred them in as well, and then walked back to where William was and handed the cup to him.

"Drink this," she said.

"What is it?"

"A restorative," she said. "We all drink it from time to time, and most especially when it's cold, as it is now."

She must have read the hesitancy on William's face.

"Don't be afraid, Doctor," the daughter said, laughing. "My mother knows more of herbs and simples than anyone else in our part of the county."

"I do what I have learned from my mother and her mother before her," the wife said. "Besides, that was long ago, before we came here."

William was still doubtful. He realized Mary Harkness was what was called a cunning woman. No licensed practitioner as he was, but a woman who had some skill in healing, learned from neighbors and family, even from experience and experiment. It was a type of healer he did not despise—unlike some of his London colleagues, who were obsessed with making their own healing art not only superior but exclusive.

William allowed that such persons, usually older women, sometimes applied their skill to good effect. On the other hand, he also knew that drinking the strange concoctions of country folk was always risky. Some were beneficial. Others caused sickness, even death. A woman in Colchester had treated her neighbors to a drink made of mulberry leaves and hemlock. Several had died; the others were so sick they wished they had. She said she had the recipe from her mother.

He looked at Mary Harkness's face; a comely, middle-aged face, open and guileless. She expected him to drink. He set caution aside. These people had saved his life. Were he to die from a homely remedy the irony would be delicious, although he would no longer be alive to enjoy it. He drank.

The liquid had a bitter taste, and he made a face of disgust despite himself.

Mary Harkness laughed. "I grant it wants something of sweetness, Doctor. Yet it is good for you, upon my oath. Drink it up, leave not a drop. My mother used to say, the worse it tastes the faster it heals."

He did what he was told, swallowing hard and hopeful the bitter aftertaste would quickly pass.

"Come, Doctor," the wife said. "I will show you your room where you shall have as much privacy as you desire while you reside with us. It will not be so fine as those bedchambers you are wont to sleep in, but it is clean, free of vermin, and none shall bother you there."

3

He had seen as soon as he had come to himself that he was in no ordinary farmer's dwelling. It clearly had been designed to house a community, not a single family.

"I see you're curious about our house," Mary Harkness said, leading him down a passage on each side of which were doors that reminded him of the prison in which he was once unhappily an inmate.

"It seems an unusual house for a farmstead," he said.

"It was once a priory, fallen into disuse in King Henry's time," Mary Harkness said. "When all such relics of papistry were torn down and priests and nuns and their like were sent packing."

She explained that a local knight had acquired it, then sold it several times over until the ruin and a portion of the original land was purchased by her husband.

"It is called the Old Priory, in town. My husband uses the chapel for a barn and stable, the refectory is our kitchen and parlour both. We are now in the wing of the house where the nuns lived. You shall have one of their rooms for your own, while here. There are two stories, or there were once. The upper floor caught fire."

"An accident, I assume." William said.

Mary Harkness laughed. "By design, I think. The nuns were not much liked around here, nor was the prioress who was then in charge of it all. When they were thrown out by Bishop Wolsey, the priory stood empty for a season, then was set alight by some drunken youth from Chelmsford who had little better to do."

The wife and daughter stopped at one of the doors. The dog trailed behind them. The wife opened it and led him inside. "This has a fireplace to warm you. Ursula will bring you things to make you a bed,

Doctor. You will eat with us while you are here."

It was a small, rectangular room of depressing austerity, the kind a pious postulant might have occupied and found sufficient, even inspiring. There was a small fireplace. Then came a knock. It was the daughter, carrying blankets in her arms.

He thought again what a strange looking girl she was. As tall and spindly as a boy with no sign of breasts at all and with long, straight brown hair that fell almost to her narrow waist. There was a wildness about her, as though, like the wolf dog at her heels, she was only partly tamed, perhaps only partly human. Her face wore a vacant expression as she made up his bed, as though he weren't there watching her do it, as though she were herself far off.

The wolf dog, who had remained when her mother had left as though his role now was no longer that of savior but guard, sat down and regarded William with a fixed canine intensity.

Ursula paid no attention to the creature. When she had finished, she looked at William and said, "There, sir, may it keep you warm and save you from whatever spirits abide here."

"What spirits do you mean?" he asked.

"This place was once inhabited by nuns who worshipped here," she said. "Though it is said that some kept not their vows, but did unspeakable things with the priests and bore children of them—and not wishing it to have it known, killed them and buried them in the graveyard yonder."

"Yonder?" William asked.

"You passed through it on your way to our door, Doctor."

Now William remembered some stones and rocks he had been dimly aware of before his collapse. He had not recognized them as gravestones, then. Just as well. At that moment his poor mind and body had enough to deal with.

"The Priory is old, sir," the girl continued. "Nigh unto two hundred or more years. They say it was first built when Henry III of that name was king and founded by a lady of the land who had been his mistress. She established it, 'tis said, to atone for her sins, since she was married to another man."

"Who cared not that she was the king's mistress?" William asked.

"Oh, he might have cared," the girl answered. "But his wife's lover was the king himself. What might the man do but accept what was? What would

16

you have done, Doctor, were you he? Challenge him whom God gave to rule over you? What we cannot change, we must endure, is that not so?"

The girl's strangeness extended to her manner of speaking. She told her tale slowly, in a voice almost without variation in tone. Indeed, it seemed to William more a recitation than what he would have expected from the daughter of a simple farmer living in the deep woods.

Ursula continued with other stories about the priory, stories she claimed she had heard from people in the town to which she had given no name, stories of the strict discipline of the prioress that seemed to him more torture than discipline, more obscene in its savagery than pious.

He asked her about the graves she had mentioned.

"The one not fifty yards from where we sit, sir. It's the graves they laid the nuns in when they died. The forest has covered most of it now, what was once an open space here." She then began to recount the names of species of trees that abounded in the surrounding woods. When she seemed to come at last to the end of her inventory, she did the same with the animals there, speaking affectionately of each of the species as if this knowledge were her only interest. She named the species but commented on the use of each, both for man and in the natural world.

"I know few learned men with such knowledge of the natural world," he said, "How did you come by it?"

His question was not idle curiosity, or even an effort to ingratiate himself with her, but he knew as a girl she would have little or no opportunity to educate herself, yet she had nonetheless acquired a good deal of knowledge.

"My grandfather, he that first lived here, was a scholar of sorts. He had studied to be a priest and knew well the world of books of which he possessed not a few. One of his books became mine on his death as directed in his will, because he knew I was quick to learn and had taught myself to read when I was very small."

"What book is it?"

"'Tis a book about plants and trees and animals, with drawings of some."

William thought he knew what book she meant.

"The book has descriptions of each variety of tree and each variety of animal that in England lives. Some are pictured there. When I was younger, I took the book with me on my travels around our land and noted where each tree and what kind stood here or there, what smaller plants grew at their feet and which animals ate of their leaves."

"Do you know herbs as well?"

"I do, Doctor, though not as much as some who claim they are cunning women and use their skill to treat the sick."

"So, you may turn cunning woman in due course," William said. "Like your mother – and take my patients from me."

"Oh, no, sir. I'd never do that," she protested, her eyes opening wide until she realized he was jesting.

He laughed to put her at ease. "Your father and mother are very generous to take me in."

"You are the first in many years. Not since I was a little child."

"You are very isolated here," he said, wanting to ask why but somehow feeling he shouldn't. These were charitable folk, but they were strange, he was not altogether comfortable with them, and given his helplessness, he dared not offend them.

"We live as it pleases us," she said. And then she said, "Have you a wife, sir?"

"I have no wife," he answered, surprised at how abruptly she had changed the subject and wondering to what end. He had always felt uncomfortable with direct personal questions, sensing an invasion of the privacy he was always at pains to protect. It was not that he had any great secrets—hidden vices, treasonous impulses, criminal designs—not at all. It was simply the way he was, reserved, ever looking outward rather than inward. In this respect he was much like his father, less like his mother, who had been a warm and open woman who made friends easily and loved to sing and to dance.

"You are a doctor, in London, are you not?"

"I am."

"You have patients who pay you well? I mean—you are not poor?"

William was not poor. His father was well-to-do in Colchester and William was his heir. Besides, for the last few years he had done quite well for himself. He had high-born patients. He was well regarded among his fellows at the College of Physicians. He had enlarged his circle of friends. But what was this strange girl driving at?

"I have sufficient for my needs. I want for little that I cannot afford."

"I thought you must therefore have a wife." she said.

It was a view shared by his father and stepmother in Colchester. It seemed inappropriate, however, for this girl to be inquiring into his personal life.

18

What business of hers was it whether he was married or no, whether he was rich or poor? He might have been offended by her curiosity in other circumstances, but her directness and innocence charmed him. Besides, she had saved his life; she and the wolf dog. He owed her, at the very least, patience.

He had no wife, indeed. He doubted he would ever be so yoked. There had been the Dutch girl, whom he had loved, whom he dreamed of still. And who he believed had loved him. But his hopes had been dashed. He still felt the pain of it like a wound that would not heal though it had been more than a year past.

"Tell me about this dog of yours," he asked. "His name is Vulcan, I understand. Vulcan is the god of smithies and fire."

"Is he, Doctor? I know nothing about gods, except of course He who reigns in heaven and made the earth and the creatures thereof."

"That would not be Vulcan," William said with a laugh, noticing that she had not crossed herself when speaking of deity. Adherents of the new religion, then; no papistry in the household, despite where they were living. Maybe *because* of where they were living.

"My father named the dog, not I," Ursula said with a shrug. "Don't ask me why he is called so. If it had been my choice, I would have called him some other name, a dog's name, no foreign god's name."

She reached down and patted Vulcan on the head. The dog lifted his nose and licked her hand with his long red tongue.

"He's a good dog, as dogs go," she said. "He comes when I say come. He sits when I so command. And he protects me as well. In faith, Doctor, I think he would kill anyone who tried to do me hurt."

William looked at the dog. He seemed tame enough now. But William still felt uneasy around him. The dog's dental work was impressive, his lineage uncertain. Humankind was unpredictable enough; animals named after pagan gods were more so.

After the girl left, he fell asleep, warmed by the blankets, and then awoke, finding the closed space and the fire had made his small room too hot. The room had a single unglazed window and the rough stone walls, designed he was sure to make the chamber as penitential as possible to the devotees who had once occupied it, acted to make him even more despondent. An alcove was cut into the wall where he suspected a religious image once stood. A rat sat in a corner of it, eying him suspiciously. When he swung his arm to frighten it, it didn't move for a moment, then darted past him into a hole in the wall. Rats and mice abounded in London, outnumbered humankind, even in his own house so he usually had little fear of them, but this one seemed particularly ominous. He shook off the feeling. He told himself he should be grateful he was alive, not downcast because his accommodations were so humble and severe.

He paced the room, gratified to find strength returning to his legs. He had no idea of what hour of the day it might be. He felt hungry and was relieved to be so. It was a good sign, a sign he was recovering. His body was returning to its usual state, demanding nourishment, expecting continuance.

Shortly thereafter, Ursula Harkness returned, the wolf dog at her heels. "Doctor, come. Sup with us in the refectory. My mother's a good cook. You will not go hungry while you are with us."

She led him back to the refectory and invited him to sit with them at a long trestle table with benches on each side.

The wife served. No one spoke. The husband, Jacob Harkness, presided at the table's end with frigid dignity. William thought it must be like unto the time when the nuns lived and ate here, observing a reverential silence, eating simple food, drinking not wine but water. But the Harknesses weren't religious observers, as far as he could tell. And this house, this former priory, had been refitted to secular purpose.

He wondered if the silence were for him, a way of warding him off, encouraging him to leave, despite the wife's insistence that he stay and the strange daughter's pleasant banter.

As to the daughter's silence at table, he did not know what to think. She, who was so voluble before, was now as mute as her parents. They even avoided his eyes, as though he were invisible to them, a translucent spirit, not flesh and blood. When they had finished, they stood and departed before him, leaving him alone in the refectory. Only the mother nodded to him, bidding him, he supposed, a good night in the little cell they had assigned him.

When he returned to his room, the rat was gone. He undressed down to his long shirt that came to his knees and lay down on the mat provided him. There was no pillow or bolster. He had slept on such conveniences before in his life; once when he had been briefly imprisoned for a crime he did not commit, once when he and his father had been forced to spend the night along the road because the weather had made it impassable. Another kindly husbandman had taken them in, provided a place in his barn. He had awakened the next morning with a cow licking his face and itching all over, bitten by some barnyard vermin in the night.

That night he dreamed he was back in Colchester at his father's house. But in the dream the house was empty. He walked from room to room, looking first for his father and stepmother, then his younger siblings. He felt a deep sadness as he searched, and then the sadness changed to fear. Fear for his family, fear for himself. Then, in the distance, he heard a baby's cry. It was far away. In his dream he looked all about him, commenced to search, but he could not find the source of the cry. His fear grew and awakened him, as fear often will.

He sat up in the bed and looked about him. All was blackness, his candle having burned out long ago, the fire out. But fully awake now, he heard the child again. And then all was quiet as before. He wasn't sure of whether what he heard was part of the dream or not.

When he awoke in the morning, he resolved to leave the Old Priory as soon as he could. He walked around his narrow cell, felt his legs and feet. All feeling was yet to be restored, but he thought he was perhaps fit enough to make it back to the road. That was, if he could find the road. Even half blinded by the storm, he knew it was rough, heavily wooded land that he passed over, one of the region's ancient forests. From there he would continue on foot to Chelmsford, stay in the inn he customarily used as a stopping place, procure a horse, and ride the rest of the way to London. The storm, the Old Priory, the wolf dog, the strange girl and her mother and father would all be like a dream.

Like the child's cry in the night. He would put them all behind him.

Surely, his disappearance would be remarked upon now. It had been three days since the storm. Three days of his confinement, for now he regarded it as such. The charity of the farmer and his family had turned cold, beginning with the husband's silence, then the mother's which seemed more out of compliance to her husband's wish than anything proceeding from herself for she had been the soul of courtesy upon his arrival, prevailing on her husband to take this distressed pilgrim in.

After that second day, he was no longer invited to the refectory. Ursula brought him food. Unlike her parents, she would talk to him, but often in short, clipped sentences as though she were confused, perhaps fearful. When she talked, she talked about her explorations in the woods, often about Vulcan, the wolf dog, who when indoors followed her from room to room and when outdoors never left her side, except for the creature's nightly rambling in search of food, the hare and squirrel and other small vulnerable creatures. He thought of the girl, Ursula. Her room, he guessed, was probably like unto the one he occupied, narrow and windowless like a coffin. She was a spirited girl. How could she stand it alone here, confined as much as he, with only her parents for company? Them, and her dog.

"I need to return to my family, to my patients," William said to her when she brought him breakfast the next day. He had not been out of the house since his arrival, but he thought surely the snow would have melted by now, the storm abated long before. "I have abused your parents' hospitality long enough."

"You have not abused it at all, Doctor," she said. "Besides which, you are the first person not of this family that has visited us for some time."

Her mother declared the same to him, and this was the second time Ursula had repeated it. As he understood it, the Harknesses lived a solitary existence by choice. No friends of the family were needed. No strangers need darken their door. He wondered why. Jacob Harkness was stern, even a little formidable. Yet so were many a man who made his living from the soil, worked from dawn to dusk, and spent more time with horses, cattle, sheep, and goats than mankind. His wife Mary was warm, accommodating. She reminded him of one of his father's sisters, and even of his stepmother on her cheerier days. As for the daughter – Ursula was a strange girl in manner and appearance, but he had known stranger. None were monsters or so different from the common run of mankind that they should seek such isolation, or have it thrust upon them by their neighbors.

"Are you so feared and hated in the town that no one dares approach you?" he asked, half jesting with her. Yet he had no sooner asked this, than he could read on her face that it was true. He had alarmed her with what she probably took as his ability to perceive beyond natural perception.

"How did you know?" she asked, a slight tremor in her voice.

"Know?"

"About how we are looked upon in the town…where you have said you never had been. You said you were a stranger here, had never been in our nearest village. You asked the name of it."

He saw that his question, meant innocently, had upset her, forced her to admit something that was true but frightening to her, or at least embarrassing. She had turned deathly pale. He looked for words to apologize for what he had asked, but could find none. Her eyes filled with tears, and she bade him goodnight abruptly before he could ask about leaving.

So, the family is feared. Perhaps, he thought, because of the dog. Perhaps, he suspected, because of where they lived, in a papistical ruin, doubtless thought to be haunted by dead nuns and their priestly lovers, an unsavory crew that could not help but morally contaminate the living.

He knew he would need a guide to find his way through the woods even if the snow had melted. Would it be her father, who wanted him gone? The mother because she had expressed sympathy for his plight? Perhaps even Ursula herself?

That night, he dreamed again. When he awoke, he could not remember the dream except again he heard the cry of a young child. And, awake, he could still hear it.

None of the family had said anything about an infant in the house. The farmer's wife was beyond child-bearing years. He decided that if this were a child and not merely a figment of his imagination, the mother must be Ursula.

The next day when the farmer's wife brought him his breakfast, he said, "I thank you so much for your charity, but I must return to the city. I would not abuse your hospitality more, but can I prevail on your husband to guide me back to the road? I remember how thick the woods were before you found me. I don't want to get lost a second time."

"I'll ask him," the wife said.

4

He ate in his room and waited throughout the morning for Mary Harkness to return to tell him what her husband had said, but she did not come. He decided to find the farmer and ask him directly. Harkness had been cold toward him since his first day at the priory. Surely, he would want his unwanted guest to leave as soon as possible.

William walked down the hall to the empty refectory and out the door into the yard. Snow still lay on the ground although the storm had obviously passed. To that point he had hardly left his cell, save for the first night when he slept by the refectory fire and then next when he was invited to join the family at table.

For the first time he could see the Old Priory from the outside and in the light of day. It was a sprawling ruin, surrendering itself to the encroaching forest. There was the chapel, used as a barn, the attached refectory used as a kitchen, and a longer wing including his cell and undoubtedly others the nuns had used for their quarters. The wing of the priory had originally had an upper story, he had been told, but this had been burned and only charred wood remained. Through the thick trees which he imagined had grown up where the nuns once planted their garden, he could see a few outbuildings reduced to rubble.

"Are you lost again, Doctor?"

Jacob Harkness had come up behind him – probably, William thought, from the chapel. Ursula had said her father spent most of his time there. He was closer to the man now than he had been before and although William was tall, he realized Harkness was the taller, perhaps by several inches.

The farmer's face wore the same stern expression he had shown William since he had regained consciousness. Since William had admitted his father was the lawyer, Jerome Gilbert. What that was about was a mystery to him and yet he had learned that the law bred enemies by its very nature. It imposed bounds and limits and penalties, infringed on personal liberty, and struck fear in hearts because of its power of life and death. Its symbol was not the gavel but the sword. His father had once told him that a lawyer would always have friends, but always more enemies than friends, whatever good he did. It was the nature of his profession, his father had said, in one of his more reflective moments.

Or maybe Harkness simply hated all lawyers. William had met more than one of that kind.

He decided to come to the point. "I must return to London. I think I can walk well enough to get back to the road, to get on to Chelmsford."

"You are still limping, Doctor, I watched you from the chapel," Harkness said.

"Yes, but I improve daily. I believe I am well enough to be on my way."

"And you're bound for Chelmsford, is it? You have friends there, people you know?"

"Only on the way to London. I know hardly anyone in Chelmsford. I might spend the night there, then continue on my way to the city."

"You wouldn't be telling tales there, would you?" Harkness asked suddenly, giving William a hard stare.

"Tales?"

"Of what you saw here, how we live," Harkness said.

"No, I would have no reason to. As I said, Chelmsford is but a break in my journey, a stopping place to make the ride less arduous. My work, my life, is far away in London."

Well, it was not that far away, but another thirty miles. A long day's ride for a good horseman and strong and healthy mount. William had exaggerated the distance to put Harkness at ease. No, he would have no reason to fear William's telling tales about a remote farmstead in an Essex forest. Not while he lay over in Chelmsford. Certainly not in London, whose inhabitants had much more compelling things to absorb them what with city crime and court gossip, rumors of war, and fears of pestilence.

Harkness expelled a breath as though relieved. Or at least that is how William read it; not exasperation but relief. "I ask because people are curious, you know," Harkness said. "And they will make things up, things that aren't true, because a good story is better than the truth you know, Doctor. They love a lie, better than they love the truth. Because it tickles their fancy and sharing it with their neighbors makes them feel like somebody better than they are."

The farmer's bitterness took William aback, but he knew what Harkness meant. He had observed the same tendency both in Colchester and in London, even among his medical colleagues. Truth rarely had the appeal of fiction with its flights of fancy, its dark conceits, its perversions of nature. He felt a surge of sympathy for Harkness, despite his fearsome appearance and rough manners, his suspiciousness and barely concealed hostility.

"I won't guide you to the road," Harkness said. "I cannot. I have my animals to look to and none to help me."

Before William could speak, the farmer went on, not looking at William but up at the gray sky above him, perhaps assessing the chances of another storm, or still meditating on his grievances, against gossips, against lawyers.

"I have too much to do here," he repeated. "I have no boy to help me, no son. As you have seen, a wife and a daughter, that's all. I must do everything that's out of doors. The girl can guide you, if she wishes. It's her choice. I think she knows these woods better than I."

"I am much obliged to you, then, Master Harkness," William said.

"You call a simple farmer, *Master*? You flatter me, Doctor. I know what I am and what I am not."

"No, I do not flatter," William said. "I was a stranger, and you took me in, sir. That is far more than the great mass of men would have done who entreat me to call them *master*."

Jacob Harkness nodded and looked down at the snow at his feet. He said, "By morning it will melt away, the snow. Not all, Doctor, but enough. Speak to my daughter. Guiding you out of here will give her something to do other than wander in the forest or dream of a husband whose family hates her and me as well."

He was happy that Harkness had offered his daughter's service as a guide. Better she than the farmer himself, with his sullen disposition, his bitterness. He believed he could trust Ursula, even if she brought the dog along as a companion. About her father, William wasn't sure. He spoke of Ursula's dream—of a husband, a family that hated her and her father as well. There was a story there, a story he had not heard from Ursula.

26

It piqued his curiosity, but not enough to invite Harkness to expand on the theme.

It was no business of his, anyway. In a day, God willing, he would be gone, never to return.

5

Before he could open the door of his room, he heard the infant's cry. It was long and anguished, and he found himself moving toward it, down the narrow passageway until he came to a half-closed door, driven by curiosity and even a little fear. Pushing it open, he saw Ursula sitting on a bed, suckling an infant at her small, white breast.

She started when she saw him, covered the baby's head and turned away her own as though ashamed of being found so. When she did not protest his intrusion and said nothing by way of explanation, he asked, "Is this child yours?"

She nodded.

He stepped into the room uninvited and looked down at the mother and child. Ursula looked up at him. She said, "This is my child and my burden."

"Why burden? Is it a boy or girl?"

"A boy," she said.

"How old?"

"Six months, or seven."

"May I see him?

She hesitated, then pulled the blanket aside.

Now he could see what she had tried to hide from him; the birthmark, spreading from the infant's forehead to right cheek and down to where the small lips formed a bow. It was a ruddy stain, as though the child had sucked wine, not milk, from Ursula's small breasts. By all appearances it was a healthy child, well-nourished for his age. Perfect, except for the mark.

William knew at once what caused the mother's hesitation, why no one in the house had spoken of the child. He knew how such marks were understood by his countrymen, not as some inexplicable accident of birth, but as a sign of something sinister, something unholy.

28

"Are you afraid of him?" she asked in almost a whisper.

"Why should I be afraid of an infant?"

He had seen such marks before. At least two of his acquaintances in Colchester had them, although neither was marked so conspicuously, neither upon the face, nor was the stain so extensive.

"Of the birthmark," she said. "Fearful of the birthmark. Some think it's a sign of the devil's claw, others that it's the mark of the wolf."

William thought of the wolf dog, Vulcan, that was the girl's constant companion and even now sat at her feet, protecting her and her child. Perhaps this explained the family's isolation, their suspicion of strangers who might tell tales, stir up trouble for them among neighbors. Country people were a superstitious lot, followers of an even older religion than those women who had given themselves to poverty and piety in King Henry's time and before.

"You're a doctor," she said. "Can you explain why my son is so marked?"

William said he could not. He told her such marks were accidents of birth. Sometimes they faded with age, even disappeared. Most times they did not, but remained as fixed, so that he who was so marked died marked, even as he had been born.

"Is your husband, the baby's father, dead?" he asked, thinking Ursula might be a young widow.

"I have no husband," she said. "I never did."

She covered her child's face again, taking more care in that than she had done in protecting her nakedness from William's eyes.

"What's his name, your child?"

"Thomas," she said.

"After the father?"

"Yes."

He decided not to probe further. But then she said, "You are an honorable man, Doctor. Can you keep secrets as well as cure bodies?"

He paused before answering, unsure of where any disclosures might lead. But she apparently assumed he agreed. Her baby, she said, was fathered by a young man in the neighborhood. She was a mere farmer's daughter, but he was the son and heir of a gentleman, a knight, an owner of much of the tract of land around the Old Priory. She said the Priory itself once was part of the whole estate, but it was not so now. It belonged to her family.

"He said he loved me and promised we would wed," she said, returning to the subject that preoccupied her.

It was an all too familiar story, William thought sadly, but did not say. It would have been too cruel to suggest that she had been deceived by her lover for what advantage his lie secured for him – a casual but consequential roll in the hay, or wherever they met in secret.

"But you did not marry?"

"His father forbade it."

"Was he not of age?"

'He is twenty-eight, I think. Maybe older."

"Then it was his decision not to marry?"

"It was his father's. He is an enemy to us, my family. When he learned of our love, he refused to allow his son to see me again, much less marry me. By that time, I was already with child."

William understood this. A son might be of age and still be bound to his father's wishes. A son who thought otherwise might well find himself disowned, deprived of an inheritance and an honest name, or merely locked up until he understood paternal authority.

The girl's eyes filled with tears. She clutched her baby close to her.

"Does Thomas's father know about the baby?"

She shook her head. "I told him not to tell his father."

"Why not? Knowing that he had a grandchild might have moved him to pity the both of you."

"It would have made all worse, Doctor. He might have wanted to see the child, then he would have hated the child and me, and his son as well. He's a hard man. I don't think he has a pitying bone in his body. His name is Sir Richard Bascombe."

"You said he was an enemy to your family. Why?"

"Because he would like to have the Old Priory for himself."

"He wants more land?"

"He wants the Priory."

"But why? If you will forgive me for saying so, it is a ruin, falling down around you save for the refectory and a few of the rooms the nuns once occupied. Were he to have it, will he rebuild the chapel, tend to the nun's graves, clear back the woods?"

She didn't answer. He wondered if it was that she didn't know, or that the Bascombes' motives were too awful to think of.

"And because he thinks I am a witch," she continued.

"What?"

"The other reason he hates us. His father thinks that I am a witch. Doctor, you are a learned man, are you not?"

"I do hope I am, for so my university degrees proclaim, and my colleagues affirm."

"Do you believe in witches?"

Her question surprised him. He was learned in physic, in anatomy. But witches and their doings belonged to a different realm, nothing he had studied, nothing he cared to study.

"You mean, do I believe that such creatures exist?"

"Yes, what do you think?"

"They may, or some may only claim to be so," he said. "I have known some women and fewer men who pretend to such powers, who work spells, who curse their neighbors, or poison their enemies, but whether these be witches, or just malignant souls, I cannot say."

The girl paused as though lost in thought. Then she looked at him directly. "Doctor, do you believe I am a witch, the kind of willful, malevolent creature you describe?"

He looked at the girl. She was no beauty, with her angular features and her tall, thin body, and he suspected as she grew older she would not flower, but her eyes were clear and honest. He said, "I don't know."

"You don't know?" Her face fell.

"I think it unlikely," he said. But then, seeing his affirmation fell short of what she had hoped for, he added, "Very unlikely," to put her more at ease.

She smiled thinly. It was a pleasant smile, a smile of gratitude, and it lightened her plain features until she was almost pretty.

He said, "you have not communicated with the dead, or familiar spirits, or applied charms that you might make others sick or bend to your will?"

"I have not," she said.

"No familiar spirit has suckled you?"

She shook her head and laughed a little. "As you have seen, doctor. I have small breasts and enough milk for my child only. As for my blood, I have none to give."

"Then speaking for myself, I don't believe you are a witch and see no reason why another would."

She leaned toward him, grasped his hands, and looked at him tearfully. "Oh, thank you," she said.

He was embarrassed by her expression of gratitude, which seemed excessive. He had told her what he believed of her, but she had taken it as a thought to be treasured, as a testimonial to be cited in her favor, like a medical opinion that casts out fear, or like one of his father's judgments at law, a verdict of innocence. He was no authority on witches and their craft. A common laborer or farmer like her father might have given the same assurance. Would Ursula have been equally grateful?

He wanted to know why some thought her to be a witch. First, she said, there was the dog. Some who had heard of it thought it to be her familiar. William knew whereof she spoke. The familiar, an innocent enough name, was a diabolical presence that influenced its human companion, an intermediary between the witch and Satan. Holy Writ spoke of them, witches, familiar spirits. How could they exist? Belief in such entities was deeply engrained in the minds of his countrymen. William knew this. He knew of no one bold enough to deny their existence, although he suspected some might have reservations in their secret hearts, which reservations they wisely kept to themselves.

He suggested she might have given up the dog, but by the look on her face he knew she would never consider such a thing. She loved the animal. He was her only companion, save her parents. "Besides," she said, "Vulcan is already known to be mine. Were he not here, yet he would be thought to be; invisible now, changed to some other creature – a cat, toad, bat, who could know? But still my familiar. Ridding myself of him would accomplish nothing, would make me look the worse as it would be seen as an admission of guilt. There is also my child."

"Your child?"

"Because my child is marked, as you have seen, Doctor. The midwife who helped me birth him saw the mark upon his face before I did, cried out, ran away like a mad woman. Flailing her arms like a devil herself. My parents told me about it, laughed at it. But it's no laughing matter. She told everyone in the village that I had given birth to the devil's spawn. That the mark proved it. That, and the dog. Since then, no one dares come here. It's not just that my father keeps them away. They fear me. They fear us all. They're terrified of a little baby God has painted a different color, at least on his face. And my father has welcomed no visitors. That is why we live as upon an island here. An island in the forest."

32

"I'm sorry this is so," he said. "But all this is the rankest superstition, offensive to God and to reason," William said.

"So it may be, Doctor, but if you ask anyone in the village nearest to us, or even farther off, in Chelmsford, say, they will dispute your learning. They will recite the scripture verses that affirm what you call their rank superstition. Their ministers of the Gospel will support their views, nurture their fears. And they will prevail, Doctor, because their belief is strong, stronger than your learning, older than your learning, sound though it may be."

He knew she was right. It was not only the unlearned of the countryside. Had not the late John Jewel, Bishop of Salisbury, denounced witchcraft in his volume, warning the very queen herself of what evil witches did in the country? How they caused deaths and other afflictions, killed cattle and horses, did the devil's work of every kind, maimed, destroyed, rendered healthy men impotent, their wives infertile?

And hadn't there been a great storm of witch-hunting in Chelmsford itself, the town where he had hoped to spend his night on the road, when Agnes Waterhouse and her sister had been denounced for witchcraft, tried, and sentenced? And she not the last in that town so to suffer?

"Nor does it help that this farm was once the home of papist nuns," Ursula continued. "For many of our distant neighbors papistry and witchcraft are of a piece, twin devils to plague the righteous and curse our neighbors."

"What do your father and mother think of all this?"

"They are afraid, afraid that all of us will be accused. Especially my father. He wants you to leave. He wants us to be alone here. He hopes the rumors and accusations will pass, that some other poor woman will draw the attention of the gossips and other malicious tongues. But Thomas' father stirs up such talk, and he is a powerful man."

"What's his name again?"

"Sir Richard."

"And his family name?"

"Bascombe."

William realized he knew the man, or at least knew of him, and thus how Jacob Harkness had known William's father. William's lawyer father had had some dealings with a Sir Richard Bascombe. William remembered the name, but not the matter. Some suit at law, some wrangle over property. He remembered his father complaining of the man's litigiousness.

33

The English were given to taking each other to court. The law had never appealed to William, who from his earliest years wanted to be a doctor and found the dry language and quibbles of the courts distasteful, much to his father's disappointment. Jerome Gilbert had wanted his son to follow in his footsteps, as eldest sons did by tradition and practice.

He looked down at her, this strange, thin girl who had turned out to be a mother and wondered that her body could have even borne the child she nurtured and claimed as her own. "I spoke to your father while I was out of doors."

"You were out? You can walk again?" An expression of happiness appeared on her face.

"Not as well as before, but each day my legs gain strength," he said. "I told your father I was ready to leave the Old Priory, to return to London. I asked him if he would guide me to the road. He said he could not, but that you might."

Ursula thought for a moment, then she looked up and smiled. "It has been a good thing to have you here, Doctor. But you have a life elsewhere, in London where I have never been. Yes, Doctor, I will guide you to the road. I and Vulcan."

She reached down and stroked the dog's huge head. He looked up at her adoringly. During their conversation the creature had seemed to sleep, but William knew he had been listening, listening for the odd human word or sound he understood, watching to see if the London doctor presented any threat to his mistress or her child.

William could see why the local population feared him. Vulcan – an odd name for a dog. The Roman God of fire, metalworking, and the forge. An ominous name for any kind of creature.

6

Ursula came in the morning before he had awakened and touched his shoulder lightly like a wife considerate of her husband's sleep, or afraid of his wrath if disturbed. William woke with a start.

She was dressed for the weather, bundled in a ragged cloak that hung upon her thin frame and must have been a cast off of her mother's. The sky, she said, threatened another storm although she thought it unlikely to prove as severe as the one before. The dog was at her heels, shaking himself and panting heavily, eager by all signs to be out of doors.

She left him to dress himself. He found her waiting at the doorstep, looking up at the gray morning sky. The snow about the Priory had only begun to melt but still blanketed almost everything, the earth, the trees, the nuns' cemetery. "Let's be off," she said, in a voice more command than invitation.

He followed behind her and the dog, which traveled between them within inches of her steps. Almost at once the forest closed around them. As they traveled, he wondered at her skill at finding her way in the dense growth of trees. They walked for an hour or more by his reckoning at a steady pace through a wood that upon his entering seemed almost impenetrable. There was no path that he could see, but she seemed instinctively to know where to step and where not to. A mariner with compass in hand could not have set a truer course. She found her way as he might have expected her to, she who knew so much of flora and fauna there, as familiar to her as her own garden. He knew that, had he been alone, he would have been lost at once, uncertain which direction he walked, or how he might return to the Priory if lost. It had not begun to snow again, but it was very cold. He would have faced death a second time within the week had he been on his own.

After a while she stopped and turned back to him. He was breathing heavily. Ordinarily, he would have kept apace of her, but he was still recovering, his legs still wobbly, an old man's legs on a young man's body. He could have used a staff or walking stick, but had not thought to ask for one.

"Here we can rest, Doctor, if you must."

The place she had chosen was a narrow stream, lacy with ice and bordered by rocks the pale sun had freed from snow. Ursula had brought with her a small bag, from which she now drew a flask and handed it to him. He drank. It was a sweet drink, made of berries of some sort, heavily sugared. She had also brought with her some goat's milk cheese and black bread wrapped in a cloth. "Eat," she said. "You'll need it if you're to make Chelmsford before dark."

They sat down on the stones. She began to talk about her baby's father. She said they had first met one day while she was looking for a lost calf and he was hunting with some of his friends. She said she knew she was unlike other girls her age, who dressed in fine garments, whereas she dressed in homespun garments that did nothing to make her attractive to men, much less to a gentleman, as her baby's father was. Yet, he had found her so. Attractive enough to arrange another meeting, and then another. In the woods, not far from where his father's land abutted that of her father. He had spoken sweetly to her. Whispered that he loved her and would always be faithful. She had had no suitors before him, and certainly no lovers. She had known no boys at all, she admitted. She was not used to such attention, such courtesy. In time, she yielded to his sweet words, his importunities. And then she found herself with child.

The girl was very frank in telling her story. She spoke without shame. She was, after all, a farm girl, used to the sight of animals mating; an ordinary, natural thing to her mind. She spoke even with a kind of satisfaction in having someone to tell her story to. He realized she had no one but her parents, no friends her own age, not in this isolated place full of spirits of the dead. It was not a love story she would have told her stern, disapproving father. Perhaps not even her more accommodating mother. But she told him.

That she should confide in him he found oddly flattering, but he was a doctor, accustomed to being the recipient of confidences. Perhaps, he thought, it was the physical intimacy of healing. The doctor's professional engagement in the patient's physical well-being implying at the same time

36

that he cared for the patient's mind and soul as well. He knew it was not always so. He had colleagues in his profession that spoke of their patients only with contempt, who thought first and foremost of their fees, who passed out medications on demand, careless of what the cost might be.

"Did he say he would marry you?"

"More than once, sir."

"And you believed him?"

"He swore by Christ, by his own head."

Her smile faded. She looked far away, perhaps toward the great house, the castle, her lover lived in. "He promised."

"And then?"

"As I told you, he spoke to his father. That was the end of it. He said his father had forbidden him to see me again, much less marry me."

"He said this to your face?"

"By message. A servant from the castle brought it to me."

She told her tale of lost love while sitting on the cold stones. William could see the tears run down her cheeks and seem to freeze there. She wiped them away, put on a braver face, and sat quietly staring into the bare trees, as though she expected her lover to emerge from them, say his father had changed his mind about the marriage and they could go ahead.

William ate most of the cheese, almost all of the bread. She nibbled at both. No wonder she was skin and bones, he thought. She told him more about Thomas Bascombe, what a good man he was, honorable, dutiful to his father. She said that except for the birthmark her baby was the very image of him, the same eyes, the same shape of nose, and high cheek bones.

He thought most women, having been abandoned as she was, would suspect the worst; that she had been used, abused, cast off, not by her lover's unfeeling father but by the lover himself. Having got what he wanted, he was done with her.

But William detected no suspicion of that sort. In Ursula's mind, her lover was pure and undefiled by selfish motives, by common lechery.

She stopped talking. They sat for a few more minutes in silence, a shared contemplation of what she had said. William wondered if the ground they sat one was also the place of their trysts and it was that which had inspired this flood of confession. It gave him an uneasy feeling, as though the place were haunted, not merely by her memories, but also by her absent lover. Was he watching, even as she told her tale? Was he watching even now, hidden somewhere amidst the trees, motionless like a tree himself, his arms, limbs of trees, his body a trunk?

He shook himself. Told himself to stop imagining things that were not.

He was almost relieved when they moved on, at her signal. The journey became harder. His legs protested, as though his muscles and ligaments were at odds. The snow-covered ground was uneven and stony, bare branches of trees threatened him at every step. It was just as he remembered, or at least as much as he could, like a nightmare recalled not as a complete narrative but in horrific fragments.

William wondered that he had traveled so far earlier, numb with cold and near blind, seeing ghosts.

She assured him there was not much farther to go, when they came upon his horse. It was lying in a kind of depression or hollow. Its body was stiff, the legs, one obviously broken, extended. A light dusting of snow had caused William almost to miss it. He felt a wave of grief, but as much for himself as for the poor animal. This might have been his fate, his body never found – or if found, not until spring when voracious beasts of the forest would have had their fill of him and left him a collection of bones.

Ursula took his hand and pulled him after her, as though reading his mind. Within minutes the trees gave way to an open field he recognized.

The much traveled London road was only beginning to reveal itself in a handful of places where the ruts of wheels and prints of horses' hooves showed themselves.

"Here you are, Doctor," she said. "Back where you started. You can make your way to Chelmsford from here."

He turned to look at her, but she and the dog were already moving away from him, back into the forest. He called out to her: "Give your father and mother my thanks again. And to you, as well."

His words seemed a poor offering after all they had done for him.

Now she was gone. She and her dog. Disappeared into the forest, as though she had been a figment of his imagination, like his own dead mother walking beside him in the storm.

He set out now with a will, confident as to his destination and the approximate time it would take him to arrive there. He reckoned there were a good three or four hours of daylight left to him. He still limped, his legs still protested, and although the farther he went the worse the

38

pain became by the time he saw the familiar church steeples that told him he was at Chelmsford he could feel only the bliss of his restored life. The Old Priory, the dismal forest, the frightening dog, the strange girl with her sad story of abandonment and witchcraft—all were behind him now.

7

Whenever he traveled to London, William always broke the journey at Chelmsford. And always at the same inn, the Blue Boar, where he knew the innkeeper and his wife and where he knew he would receive a warm welcome and a clean room. And so he did. Footsore and nearly exhausted, he stumbled into the inn to learn almost at once that his failure to arrive in London three days before had been noted, and a search of the road had commenced on that very day.

"Your father sent two men after you to see where you went. Your stepmother was beside herself with worry," the innkeeper said.

"Send word to them I'm safe and well," William said.

"They'll have it by the first post," the innkeeper said.

The innkeeper, a big, florid man named Rafe Tuttle, helped him up the narrow stairs to his room and laid a good fire there, while his wife, Martha, as rosy and big-boned as her husband, arrived with quilts and blankets to wrap William in.

The innkeeper's wife asked him if he wanted to eat and without awaiting an answer hurried down the stairs to the inn's kitchen.

The Blue Boar was a handsome house, tall, its second and third floors extending over the street below it and dwarfing the shops on either side, which were a candlemaker's and a weaver's. The street floor was given over to a tavern, an eating and drinking place open to all comers. It was a popular meeting place for the city fathers, sometimes even the local gentry. The food was good, as good as in a comparable place in London, so it was said in Chelmsford; but London visitors, and there were a few, sometimes expressed different opinions. William thought the food was excellent.

Rafe wanted to hear what had happened, the misadventures along the way. William gave him a short version, enough to make Rafe even more curious.

"You stayed at the Harkness farmstead, the Old Priory?" Rafe Tuttle said, as though he had not heard William's mention of the same clearly and needed it repeated.

"Three days, four counting the day I left, which is today," William said. The innkeeper's face bore an incredulous expression.

"Is there anything remarkable in that?" William asked.

"Remarkable, Doctor, that you were taken in," Rafe said. "No one that I know has set foot at the Old Priory for years, much less spent time there. Were it known here that you did that, you would be celebrated for your achievement—or condemned for your foolhardiness. Or converted."

"Converted?"

"To Rome."

"What are you saying, my friend?".

"Have you felt no papistical impulses?" Rafe Tuttle asked with a mischievous grin. "I mean the Old Priory, the very heart and core of papistry hereabouts. The ghosts of dead nuns."

"I was no papist before, and am not one now," William protested. "I was a guest there, no postulant. Their daughter, Ursula, told me that they rarely had guests."

"Well, that's saying too little, Doctor," Rafe Tuttle said, laughing. "None is welcomed there, and certainly not invited. What spell did you cast upon them, that they extended their hospitality to one such as you?"

"None," William answered. "As I have said, I became lost in the storm, near unto death, and awoke to find myself beside the fire and a dog that at first I feared was wolf come to devour me."

Rafe had heard of the dog. "It's more wolf than dog, I think, and may be purely wolf, though I have never seen the creature myself."

"My neighbor has seen the dog," the innkeeper's wife said. She had come back into the room, bringing with her a plate on which he could see and smell roasted duck. She handed William the plate, bid him eat his fill, and then continued her story, as he ate ravenously, even licking his fingers when his plate was clean.

"She told me that she once was picking berries in the wood and the girl and her dog came upon her," Martha Tuttle said. "She called out 'Jesu save me', when she saw the dog, for he was large and black, and she said she was always fearful of such creatures. She said she knew at once that it was no dog, but the devil, who she knew could take upon him what shape he pleased."

"Did the dog threaten her?" William asked, remembering his own terror when he awoke that first morning.

"I think not. When she saw it, she ran. She said she did not look back for fear if she would see it again, that seeing it would damn her soul."

"Did the girl try to restrain the dog?"

The innkeeper's wife said she didn't know. Her neighbor had not said. Martha Tuttle admitted the said neighbor was a notorious gossip but observed that even gossip was sometimes true.

"Well, they are people about whom much is said here in Chelmsford," Rafe Tuttle remarked.

William expected a recitation of what Ursula had told him about her being called a witch and was sorry he had revealed the identity of his rescuers. But it was not the same. What Rafe had to say was not about Ursula but about her father.

"I know the man's history," Rafe said, sitting down on the bed. "Did Harkness tell you how he came to have the place?"

William said he had not. And in truth, he was not sure he cared to learn, thinking that his experience at the Harkness farmstead was past, soon to be forgotten in the turmoil of his present career as a rising young physician. But he liked Rafe, who was given to story-telling and did not want to offend him. He decided to feign interest and shook off the exhaustion he felt.

"Jacob Harkness's father was a farmer, like him," Rafe said. "Of some means, in these very parts. He was the only son, the farmer's other children being girls. His father died from the sweating sickness that took his mother and all his sisters but one. He believed by this his land was cursed, losing so many of his family to the same illness."

"It's unlikely his land had anything to do with the deaths," William said. "Diseases and the fevers that attend them occur in towns and cities as in the countryside."

"It may be as you say, Doctor, but Jacob Harkness believed it. He buried his father, his sisters and after would not even look at the ground that was his. He sold the farmstead, his cows, and even more sheep, and sought a different place. He was not done with farming, you see, only with the ground upon which his family had died, believing it cursed."

42

"And the Old Priory? How did he come by that?"

"Ah," Rafe said, "That's the best of my story. Harkness married well. If you were at the Old Priory, you met her."

"His wife, Mary."

"She was the daughter of a well-to-do clothier of the town. She could not find a husband, until Harkness began courting her. Her father was anxious that she be wed and gave Harkness a dowry of one hundred pounds."

"A princely sum for a farmer's bride."

"Indeed, it was, and now he has the money from his family farm and his bride's dowry. He seeks as I have said, a better place, a place he can move into right away. He learns of this property for sale, a ruined priory long abandoned and land appertaining. A wealthy man, the father of a local knight, has fallen on hard times, largely due to his own mischief."

"Mischief? What mischief?"

"The usual vices of them who call themselves gentlemen and lords of the realm and bid us below to honor them. I do mean gambling and wenching. The man had more whores at his beck and call than the pope himself, or so it was said. He falls into great debt, and to save himself from ruin determines to sell off a moiety of the property."

"The Old Priory."

"The Old Priory indeed," Rafe Tuttle said. "His son, Richard, who inherited when the old lecher died, now grieves that the Priory is lost and has sued Harkness twice, arguing the sale of the property was invalid for lack of witnesses to the deed and because his father was incompetent when he sold it."

"How incompetent?"

"Addled, demented, methinks from the pox, syphilis."

"And I infer with no success, the lawsuits?"

"Most were threatened, never pursued beyond that. One judge said that were an addled brain justification for a bad contract of sale, half the transactions in England would be invalid." Rafe Tuttle threw his head back and laughed. His wife Martha joined in. William suspected it was a quip he had used before.

"Harkness's hold on the land is firm," Rafe Tuttle said. "There was a witness, nay two, servants of the old man whom his son pressured to deny their marks were upon the deed as witnesses, but who then recanted after the judge reminded them of what pain came to those who perjured themselves. But that has done nothing to abate the man's anger."

"Some of this I learned from Harkness's daughter," William said.

"That blighted maid?"

"Why blighted?"

"Well, you have seen her, Doctor, talked to her."

"I have."

"Did you not think her... unearthly?"

"Unearthly? No. Somewhat different from other maids, perhaps. Singular, I would have said."

"And there was something else."

"Something else?"

"You know the history of the farmstead, the Priory?"

"The daughter told me some tale of scandal, which I did not dispute knowing nothing of its history, but it seemed an antipapistical fantasy."

"No fantasy, Doctor, but a great scandal, a great disgrace," Mary Tuttle said, shaking her head. She had lingered in the room to hear her husband's story, although William suspected she had heard it many times before.

"Lecherous priests, murdered babies, moral corruption on a grand scale," William said. "I imagined her stories were just rumors to inflame passions against Catholics."

"Not rumors," Rafe Tuttle said, his eyes opening wide. "A true history, may God confound me if I lie. The prioress was a woman named Griselda, very proud and haughty. She ruled her roost with an iron fist that tolerated no disobedience. Even before the king closed the monasteries and priories, her conduct was questioned by the bishops and much complained of. Wolsey, he who was the great cardinal in those years, demanded the priory be closed, the nuns who remained sent off to other nunneries or just sent off. This was thirty or more years ago by my reckoning, long before our present queen."

"Then what Ursula Harkness said was true?"

Rafe nodded. "More than one of the nuns were big with child by the priests, or by others of the town. I think it was more brothel than priory, if you ask me."

"And the dead babes?" William asked, remembering Ursula's gruesome account.

44

"True as well. In the graves by the fallen church," Rafe said. "No one knows how many there were. Maybe some lived and walk among us here in Chelmsford or other towns. Children of wicked nuns and lascivious priests. There was also the matter of the treasure."

"What treasure?"

"The priory was not impoverished, Doctor, though the nuns there took their vows of poverty and chastity and so forth. The novices that came there brought with them dowries, which they gave up to the priory. And then in those days the priory had fields and flocks as well. While the nuns gave up the pleasures of this world, the priory gorged itself with the righteous offerings. When the priory was closed, the prioress left. It's thought she took much of the priory's treasure with her. I cannot say, nor can any other man, whether that be true or false."

"It is pleasant to think that somewhere in England this Griselda enjoys this world's goods without need of feigned righteousness," William said.

"Oh, Doctor, she is long dead and gone. She was a woman of middle age or more when the priory was closed. She'd be neigh on to ninety or even a hundred, were she still alive."

"And what of the treasure?"

Rafe shrugged and smiled wryly. "A tale for children now—and for fools that will ever be dreaming of wealth unearned by honest labor."

"Ursula said nothing of treasure."

"Well she wouldn't, would she? She has enough troubles of her own."

"You mean the witch matter?"

"Indeed," Rafe said. "It is ever on the brain of people in this county, ever since Mother Waterhouse."

William had heard of Agnes Waterhouse, the first of the Chelmsford witches.

"Mother Waterhouse wasn't from Chelmsford, though she was tried here and met her deserved end here," Rafe said. "She was from Hatfield Peverel, six or seven miles from here, a village of no consequence where she practiced her dark arts. This was..." Rafe Tuttle looked up at the ceiling as though there were a calendar written there "that would be 1565 or 6, if memory serves."

"I was at Cambridge then," William said. "I heard little of it other than her name."

"I knew the facts well, quite well," Rafe said, grinning. "Two other women were involved, an Elizabeth Francis and Joan Waterhouse. Sisters they were, and as deep in mischief as Agnes, though she was hanged and the others not. Agnes was accused of causing a mortal illness to William Prynne, a man I knew."

"By witchcraft?"

"Yes, by charms and the evil work of a certain familiar she had. It was a cat. She claimed it spoke to her in a strange, hollow voice."

"A talking cat, most improbable," William observed. "Save its discourse were all purrs and whimpers and the woman a most excellent translator."

All of them laughed at that.

"A spotted cat she called Satan," Rafe Tuttle continued, ignoring what William believed was a quite reasonable objection to the story.

"She might have chosen a better name for her familiar," William said. "At least if she wished to keep his evil nature to herself."

Rafe laughed. "Oh, she cared little about that, Doctor. She was as bold a witch as any member of your profession who inscribes his name upon a post or window to advertise his service to the public general."

"What motive had she for killing this Prynne?"

"Marriage."

"Marriage?"

"She would have him, but she was so homely he would not have her. He might also have been aware of certain detestable practices of hers, which no faithful man could abide. It was said she caused him who was her husband before to die also, though the malign agency of her familiar."

Rafe Tuttle took a breath, drained the cup he had brought with him, and continued. He described how Mother Waterhouse created her spells: "She told the cat what she wanted him to do, and he obliged her straightway, but demanded of her milk and bread."

"Not an unreasonable demand for a cat," William said.

"True, Doctor, but what is more he asked for a drop of her blood, which she freely gave him to seal the bargain."

"Which was?"

"Whatever advantage she sought to secure through his aid. Remember, she called this cat Satan. Does that not tell you, Doctor, whom she served?"

"A man might conclude that," William said.

Rafe went on, glad to have an audience for his account. He told William about the Queen's Bench trial, presided over by a Doctor Hale and Master Fescue and Justice John Southcote, learned and worthy gentlemen. He went into great detail about testimonies given, and most especially that of an eleven-year-old girl named Agnes Brown, who swore this same cat spoke to her and when the young girl asked who the cat's mistress was, the creature nodded toward Mother Waterhouse herself. This same cat had the power to change into a toad."

"A toad?" William exclaimed, suppressing a laugh.

"A toad, Doctor. So the girl testified under oath."

"But why a toad?"

"Well, Doctor, I know not," Rafe Tuttle said. "I'm a simple man when all is said and done. No great scholar of scriptures or such. But I do suspect this, that of God's creatures the toad is most hideous in his features, and poisonous in his capacity."

"I don't think toads are poisonous, although I admit their reputation is not good," William said.

Rafe Tuttle took a poker and stirred the fire, added another log. He said, "Our rector says the Devil has power to assume a pleasing shape. Might not he also assume an evil shape, thereby making his power the greater, and instill poison as well?"

"I suppose so," William said. "Your rector is not the first to claim the Devil's power is as you describe it."

William thought this tale was quite fantastical with its talking creatures and shapeshifting, but his innkeeper friend was so earnest in the telling of it that he hesitated to counter him. Yet There must have been something in William's face that suggested at least a moiety of incredulity, for Rafe Tuttle said, "You may well scoff at this story, Doctor, you who are so deep in your schooling, but all is true, as true as God is true."

"I will not dispute with you, Rafe, as to the truth of your account, much less the truth of God. After all, I was not there to hear the testimonies myself."

"Or her confession," Rafe Tuttle said. "For she confessed all said against her was true at trial's end. And admitted that when she prayed, she prayed in Latin, not in honest English as Her Majesty does commend and command."

Rafe Tuttle presented this fact as though it was the worst that could be said of the condemned witch. William had heard this allegation before. It was commonly believed that witches must pray in Latin, as their Catholic forbears, not in English as dictated by the queen and the bishops.

"You are blessed with a most excellent memory of the details of the case," William said to Rafe Tuttle.

"No wonder there, Doctor," Rafe said. "I was at the trial. I was one of the jurymen who condemned her. And if you ask me whether I sleep well of nights because of my verdict, my answer is that I sleep like a babe, despite my wife's shifting and snoring."

He grinned at his wife, who made a sour face and threatened to swat him.

"It is you who make such noises while asleep, husband, not I," she said.

Rafe Tuttle then went into detail about the execution itself, which he averred drew the greatest crowd that Chelmsford had ever seen. He told William how Mother Waterhouse pleased judges and jury alike with her repentance which, for all that, did her no good, save in the eyes of God, since she was hanged the day after the trial concluded.

"She was an old woman, as I have said, this Mother Waterhouse as she was called; sixty or so years and lumpy in her body so that when she was hanged, she died without squirming as do most folks who are hanged. But that was only the beginning of the witch trials in our town. I served on no other juries but attended a dozen or more trials and hangings until I came away fearing that every cat and dog on the streets of Chelmsford were the Devil's mouthpieces, familiars as we call them, and nearly every wasting death of husband, cow, or sheep the fruit of some Devil's bargain."

By the town clock it was ten before the innkeeper and his wife wished William goodnight. He had begun his day trudging through the forest uncertain whether his escape from the Priory would be successful or his guide trustworthy, then walking alone another two hours or more to Chelmsford. When he had arrived at the inn, he had practically fallen into the innkeeper's arms. He should after that have been too weary to think. A full stomach had restored him. Now he had time to mull over Rafe's story.

That the innkeeper had been a juryman and therefore heard the testimony of Agnes Waterhouse and the others, and had been a witness at the wretched woman's execution, he had no doubt. He had known Rafe Tuttle most of his life. His father on his occasional trips to London would himself stay at the Blue Boar. Rafe was a big, rough fellow but no fool, not the kind of man to be taken in. But the business of speaking cats and toads contradicted all William had observed in the natural world. And as for spells and curses, he believed there were such things, but that they proceeded from anything other than a troubled and malignant mind he seriously doubted. Tools of spite and envy, enmity and revenge were what he thought of them. Even the biblical authority for familiar spirits was questionable, for it was hard to know what the scriptures meant. Were they condemning the spirits as real, or only as imagined and thereby equally perverse delusions since they opposed God's power, infected the believer and the practitioner with evil, and created division and fear, sometimes even panic?

At Cambridge he had read of Arnaldus de Villanova, the Spanish physician and alchemist who believed the lodestone or magnet could relieve women from witchcraft. He had thought then it was an absurd notion, an aberrant conceit by a man otherwise well schooled in his own art of healing and worthy of praise. William had thought little of witches then, deep in his reading of the body and its parts, nostrums, and cures. Now, suddenly, he was enmeshed in witchery, in its myths and arcane practices.

Slowly, sleep began to overtake him. His thoughts drifted from images of witches and cats and black dogs to the matters of his real life. He had thought by reaching Chelmsford and the inn he would have crossed the border from the fantastical experience at the Old Priory to what he knew as real. But then Rafe Tuttle told his stories. They were troubling to him, disturbers of his comfortable universe, a reminder that in the hinterlands of his country there was a dark underbelly of superstition and myth.

Sleep came at last. After such a day, a gift.

8

In London, William dwelt in Wingfield House, a place he leased from his stepmother, Jane Wingfield, whom his father had married after the death of William's birth mother. William lived there as a contented bachelor, but with a dozen or so servants and frequent guests; often persons like him devoted to the study of the natural world. Some of these persons were from abroad, for these days he maintained a busy correspondence with like thinkers from Europe, men of intelligence and learning, curiosity and common sense.

It was a handsome house of several stories, with a dignified front and cobbled courtyard, a well-maintained garden in the rear. He had a good library, a competent Welsh woman as cook, a consulting room and library on the main floor, and a growing list of patients willing to put their trust in a physician who was still young and whose slender frame, smooth face, and ruddy cheeks made him appear even younger.

Upon his return he immediately sent messages to patients whose appointments he had missed during his sojourn at the Old Priory. He gave no explanation for his absence, other than to say there were circumstances beyond his control delaying his return. He decided that to explain fully his absence would take too much time. Besides, he didn't want to arouse idle curiosity about where he went and what he did. After all, his sojourn at the Old Priory was no one's business but his own, a bizarre episode in his life unlikely to be repeated.

He spent the first full day of his return attending to patients, some of whom came to his door and others, mostly members of the lesser nobility and higher gentry, he visited in their fine houses on the Strand or in some other respectable neighborhood in the city. William was a conscientious physician, generally liked by his patients and always willing to listen to their complaints. He was careful not to overprescribe, for he knew that some treatments and medications were worse for health than the conditions they supposedly remedied.

The most dubious of these, in William's view, was bloodletting, a practice based on an equally dubious theory of humors, basic bodily liquids that when out of balance were supposed to cause a multitude of ailments, mental and physical. It was a much-favored remedy, popular among his professional brethren and even more among patients, who often demanded it. Extracted by knife or leech, blood was drained from the body at various increments to restore a healthy balance of humors. William thought it was nonsense, the procedure futile and often dangerous.

The first patient of the day was the plump, rosy-faced wife of a wealthy sea captain who talked endlessly about the hardship of her abandonment by a man always at sea before she settled down to a specific complaint, that being recurrent pains in her abdomen that she said made her life miserable. William asked about her diet.

"I eat well enough, Doctor, the woman said. "My vexation is not what I eat but these pains in my belly."

"Which may proceed from what you consume," he said, but softly, trying not to offend.

Somewhat reluctantly, the woman gave an account of her typical meals. She ate, she said, four times a day and to William's way of thinking a prodigious amount at each sitting. She and her husband were not wealthy, but they had sufficient for their needs, as she put it. William noticed in her recitation of the fish, fowl, beef, and mutton she consumed enough daily intake to give even a normal belly an ache.

"And your drink?" he asked.

"Ale, beer, never water, malmsey on occasion."

"And the quantity?" William was taking notes.

"Of drink?"

"Yes."

"Is that important, Doctor?" the captain's wife asked. "I'faith, Doctor, I hardly keep an account, as I see you doing when I answer your questions. Writing down my answers in your book. What about my pain? Is there not some herb or ointment you could prescribe to relieve it?"

"Before we medicate, let us see what relief changing your diet might accomplish."

She regarded him skeptically. William had grown accustomed to such responses. He believed that good health practices led to good health, and disliked doctors whose first impulse was to send his patient to the apothecary for some new nostrum brought from the Indies or other remote clime and therefore in its exotic provenance thought superior to any homegrown remedy.

"Not more than three tankards of beer a day, a goblet or two of Spanish grape, and ale with each meal."

"How many cups or glasses?"

She shrugged, then said, two or three. I swear to you, Doctor, that I drink no more than my neighbors."

"I don't doubt it," William said. His belief was that his countrymen ate over much at their meals and often things that did little to promote a healthy digestion. He himself ate sparingly and drank very little, preferring wine to beer and clean, clear water if one could find it. Like other English, he avoided the water, which was so contaminated in the city that it was a danger to one's life to drink of it.

"Tell me, mistress, do you eat well when your husband is at sea?"

"Yes, always."

"More than when he's at home?"

She stopped to think about this. "I suppose I do. Eat more when he's abroad, I mean."

"Your meals, therefore, when you husband is at home are different?"

"My husband will eat neither fish nor fowl, but beef only, and then with all the fatty flesh cut off for he says he fares badly if he eats the fat."

"Fares badly. Meaning what?"

"Belly aches, he says, which his small diet does remedy."

"Ah," William said. "Follow your husband's example at table. Eat less, avoid fatty foods, and halve your drinking, most especially the malmsey. See what comes of this and then return to tell me. You should know what this change will bring within the week."

The captain's wife looked disappointed. "You will prescribe no remedy?"

"I have so prescribed," William said.

"I mean no medicament?"

William shook his head. "I have prescribed a change in your diet, reflected on your table and in your kitchen. If you find no relief, we will consider medicaments. If you do, then nothing more is needed."

"It seems too simple a solution," the captain's wife said doubtfully.

"Simple is not necessarily bad, Mistress. It is sometimes to be preferred when an available solution works."

During the afternoon, William attended to a lawyer with the gout, a courtier's butler with a broken arm and a lady in attendance to the aging wife of a bishop who wanted him to prescribe something to tighten the skin on her throat. This last patient took more delicate handling than the captain's wife, but William was typically diplomatic in his manner, and while occasionally a patient complained of him, most were pleased by his ministrations. He took one patient after another, without a rest and without a meal in between and then at the end of the day, he went out to supper with some colleagues in his profession.

Like almost all reputable physicians in London, William was a member of the Royal College of Physicians, which unlike his college at Cambridge, was not so much a collection of buildings as it was a licensing body, a guild that governed the education and conduct of its members. In that year, there were nearly sixty physicians so honored, and of them William was also an officer, called a censor. His duties, in that regard, were largely supervisory. He would interview each physician to verify their education and their practice, determine whether they had been complained of and why, whether their moral conduct was consistent with the standards set by the College, and in general elevate the reputation of the medical profession in the eyes of the public and – especially – of the court, upon whose patronage the College depended.

He met five of his colleagues at a tavern in Eastcheap, each prominent physicians in the city and each a member of a committee of which he was currently the head. They supped together in a private room at the head of the stairs, with the tavernkeeper under oath to keep both their meeting and their business secret. To someone unfamiliar with the College, they might have been viewed as plotters, meeting together to betray or undermine the State. But while there were political aspects of their work, their secrecy was not to undermine the court or government, but to keep their deliberations from their rivals in the city; the unlicensed practitioners, the assorted wise-women, conjurers, mountebanks, and quacks. And, in particular, the Barber-Surgeon Company, their chief rivals as medical providers. The Barber-Surgeons were ever wrangling with the College over which body had the privilege of providing which services for the sick and infirm.

But the conversation that followed was not about medicine or the profession but matters of court that the doctors present felt might impinge on their profession. It was only toward the end of the evening that William mentioned his time in the Old Priory. He did so because he was asked. Word of his ordeal in the storm had somehow gotten from the servants in his house to servants in the houses of his colleagues, so what was known was that he had nearly frozen to death, languished at some isolated farmstead for days, missed appointments, and had been strangely vague in describing what had happened. His colleagues, and especially one of the older doctors, were curious.

Why he had broken his vow not to speak of it, he hardly knew, except the truth was that he still thought of the Harknesses and their daughter and the fearsome wolf dog that had frightened him so. He also remembered every detail of his long conversation with Rafe Tuttle the innkeeper and the latter's lurid history of the Old Priory. All seemed to him now ever so much more arresting than idle talk of whom the queen presently preferred as her personal physician and whom she disliked.

"And what town was this, William?" one of his older colleagues asked.

"No town. An isolated papist priory turned farmstead. Not far from Chelmsford."

"Priory, you say?"

"Long abandoned, of course," William explained.

Another at table, about ten years William's senior, said, "Tell us then how you survived such a storm—and such a strange, ill-bred family?"

Suddenly William felt inclined to defend the Harknesses. They had, after all, saved his life. That he thought them strange and standoffish was one thing. That another, a haughty Londoner and rival physician should think so, should say so, offended him.

"They are decent Christians," William said. "Honest people."

"Yet they have no intercourse with their neighbors," the same doctor protested. "By your account, they are farmers but do not sell what they grow or raise. They do not go to the town or to the market. They live isolated by their own choice. Isn't this what you have told us, William?"

His colleague looked around at the others at table. There was general agreement that that was what William had told them and that there was something suspicious about it.

"They did not have to take me in," William said. "They might have left me, a stranger, in the snow to freeze, which almost I did despite their charity."

"Did they ask for payment for their hospitality?" another colleague asked.

"They did not."

"That's a wonder," the same colleague said. "They missed an opportunity there to profit from your calamity."

"They asked nothing of me for room or board. They are farmers, not innkeepers."

The conversation at table moved to pressing business; the Barber-Surgeons Company and their threat to certain prerogatives of the physicians, a scandal involving one of the members in Cheapside, the opposition of the bishops to certain new medical procedures which they claimed violated scriptural warrant. And, especially, the dangerous medical operations of one Valentine Russwerin, a German immigrant and Paracelsian practitioner who had recently set up shop in Bishopsgate Street and was drawing patients with his use of exotic chemicals to treat everything from cataracts to the French pox.

William and his colleagues regarded the German as an obvious quacksalver and fraud and had been busy compiling lists of those patients he had attended who had died as a consequence of his dubious treatments. That Russwerin was a foreigner was the first mark against him. That he competed with the licensed physicians of the College was another. Even William's patron, Lord Burghley, had sought out Russwerin's services, despite William's advice that the German's methods were untrustworthy.

Despite what would have ordinarily aroused his interest, William only half heard it, and had he heard all he would have added nothing to the conversation. He had said nothing about Ursula Harkness and the accusation of witchcraft. He had said nothing about her birthmarked infant, or her wolf dog and the part he had played in his rescue. But all of these things now occupied his thoughts. The truth was that he felt oddly bonded with the Harknesses, strangely invested in their fate. He knew the suspicion of their distant neighbors might well remain only that, a suspicion, and yet there was danger there. They knew it, and William knew it too.

As for the wolf dog, what farmer had no dogs? Indeed, what gentleman in the county did not boast a pack of slavering hounds and feed them often from the family table? The English loved dogs. Yet any canine could be thought a familiar spirit if he did no more than beg at table and lap up milk if offered him. Mother Waterhouse, after all, had a cat, a quite ordinary one from what Rafe had described. The cat was reputed to be her familiar. A cat that allegedly—and quite improbably in William's mind—turned into a toad.

He was brought from his reverie when he became aware that talking at table had ceased and everyone was looking at him. "We beg pardon, William, for boring you," one of his colleagues said. "You sit so silently pondering that we know no other explanation for your inattentiveness to concerns that touch upon us all. Do you not care that your service to Lord Burghley is being put aside as he gives ear to this German fraud?"

"I am concerned," he said. And he was indeed, but not so much in that particular moment.

William stood, excused himself, and bid his friends goodnight. He said he was still weary from his ordeal and needed to sleep, an excuse that by their sympathetic expressions they took at face value.

9

Winter ended, as in God's providence it must, much to William's relief since he still suffered dreams of his ordeal in the snowy woods and his fears of isolation and death. Spring, he supposed, would make it all better, and summer even more so.

Meanwhile in the city, William's busyness increased. William Cecil, the great Lord Burghley, with whom he had association a few years before and who had aided him when he was perilously close to spending years in prison for a false and malicious conspiracy against him, demanded more of his time in caring for members of his household. At the same time, his duties with the College of Physicians increased.

None of this busyness, however, bothered him. He thrived on activity. Indolence was his enemy. His life, he felt, was a fulfilling one for all the demands upon it. He was still young, barely thirty, yet he knew he had accomplished more than men twice his age, at least in the profession he had chosen.

Then, one day, all changed. He was at home in Wingfield House when a servant came to him, to say that a person was at the door asking for Doctor Gilbert.

"What person? A patient?"

"A roughly dressed man, a countryman I think, a farmer, sir, by the look and smell of him."

"Pray he does not have cow dung on his shoes then," William said, putting the book he was reading aside. "Fetch him in, but make sure he cleans his shoes. Did he give his name? Did he say what he wanted?"

William asked, although somehow, he knew.

"He said, Doctor, that his name is Jacob Harkness. He said you would remember who he was."

Of course, he remembered. He had thought of the man and his wife and his daughter and his dog every day since December last, despite the changing seasons, despite his work, despite wanting not to think of them.

In the commodious, well-furnished library of Wingfield House, Jacob Harkness seemed out of place, a stranger in a strange land. The burly husbandman looked about him at the books on the shelves, on the large table William used for his magnetic experiments, on the medical instruments, the tools of William's art, his very life and must have thought his coming there was a mistake and wondered how he might take himself off without offending the learned doctor, who was half Harkness's age, and nearly half his girth.

William noticed little changed in the man's appearance or manner. He had not changed clothes to come to the city, had not cleaned himself up, or trimmed his great black beard which looked as though it had never been combed or barbered. William could see the dirt beneath the man's fingernails, could smell the stink of sheep and cattle and dog.

If there was anything that was different in the man's manner, it was the look of desperation in his eyes. William knew it was not merely because Harkness was away from his farmstead, over which he was lord and master. Something had happened, something terrible. William sensed it, even before the man had opened his mouth.

When Harkness had taken the chair William directed him to, he had yet to speak of the reason for his visit. And once seated, he remained silent, as though his tongue had been cut out, or he feared plain English wasn't what was expected of him in so grand a house. Latin, perhaps, or even Greek. Harkness had looked around at the books, the gold lettering on their spines, the long incomprehensible titles. He would not have been able to read them, but he knew many were in no language he understood.

"Master Harkness, you have some sickness that has brought you to me?" Harkness looked surprised at the question. "I have no sickness, Doctor."

There was another silence. William wondered if the visit was for a less serious visit that he first feared. Perhaps Harkness had come to London to secure a reward for his hospitality, his charity to a man in distress. At the Priory, nothing had been said to him about that. Mary Harkness had made it clear that taking William in was to be an act of Christian compassion. Her daughter had certainly expressed no expectation of reward. Of course, that did not mean that Harkness himself had not since then conceived of some manner of restitution, both for the cost of William's food and lodging and for the inconvenience of having a stranger under his roof.

"I would like to thank you in more than words for saving me," William said, deciding it would be up to him to bring their conversation to the point. He stood, walked to his desk and found his purse. He undid it, took out what he estimated would be ten pounds or more and walked back to where Harkness sat, staring at him.

When the farmer appeared to realize what was about to be offered him, he held up his hand and said, "No, Doctor, I will take no money from you. You offered once, I said no. It is not for that I am come here."

"Then?" William sat back down.

"It's my daughter, sir. And my wife as well."

"Ursula and Mary."

"It is kind of you to remember their names."

"Not kind to remember," William said. "I could hardly forget them. Save for them and their mercy I would not have lived. Has something happened to them?"

"Two days ago, they were taken."

"Taken where?"

"Taken to Chelmsford, Doctor."

"You mean they were abducted, seized."

"Arrested, doctor," Harkness said. "The both of them. By him who is constable at Chelmsford. Master Samuel Pickney is his name."

"On what charge?"

"Witchcraft. Sorcery. Murder."

It took William a moment to take this in. Then: "These are grave charges, Master Harkness."

"They are indeed, Doctor," Harkness said, slumping in his chair.

"Who has accused them?" William asked, although he knew that too. It would have been the man who might, had he been more charitable, have become Ursula's father-in-law: Sir Richard Bascombe.

Harkness confirmed this. "It's Bascombe, Doctor, and his daughter as well, she who is sister to the son that's dead. The son that fathered the child upon Ursula. Her name is Lady Clara."

59

"But why now? Tell me what happened?"

Harkness explained slowly, and with some difficulty, the case against his wife and daughter. At least as he understood it, he said. "I am not a learned man, Doctor. I know nothing of books or things and less of the Scriptures. I wouldn't know a witch from a willow, but the constable had a warrant, as he called it, a piece of paper, and he read it out with a litany of things he claimed my wife did and my daughter did, and even what the dog was supposed to have done."

Harkness continued to tell how the constable and four of his men had come to the Priory. They were armed and treated his wife and daughter roughly, dragging them from the house and placing them together on a horse, binding them as though they were common felons, despite his protests, the dog's barking and snarling and raising such a commotion and the two women crying out that they had done nothing wrong, had harmed no one. They appealed to heaven and proclaimed their innocence. It made no difference to the constable.

"Nor could anything I say or threaten stay them. It was five against one, Doctor. Impossible odds. I tell you the man, he who calls himself constable, the man enjoyed what he did. I could see it in his ugly face. I wanted to kill him, every one of them. But there were more of them than me. The constable said they had been accused of witchcraft, of causing a death."

"Causing whose death?"

"Sir Richard Bascombe's son, Thomas. He had been long sick, wasting away. Nobody knew why. He was healthy before."

"Most are healthy before they are sick. Before what?"

"Before he forbade his son to see, much less marry, my daughter, which he had promised to do."

"Because he had fathered her child?"

"Bascombe says Ursula cast a spell upon his son, causing him to waste away, for he would not marry her as he said he would. He says our dog is her familiar."

"An absurd charge," William scoffed.

"Bascombe says that the dog is a wolf who speaks to her and suckles upon her as though she were his mother. He says the child—who if you have seen it, you know well enough—is marked, which mark proves that it is the Devil's child, not his son's, as she has falsely claimed."

"And the accusations against your wife?"

"That she furthered all, by teaching Ursula wicked practices. Like mother, like daughter, they do say, to make both evil."

At this, William thought about what his friend the innkeeper had said about the first of the Chelmsford witches, Agnes Waterhouse, how the mother had taught the daughter the secret of her devilish practices. The accusations against the Harkness women followed the same pattern, were a version of the same narrative. When the jurymen heard the case against the women, they would be well prepared to find them guilty, given the precedent of the Waterhouse case.

Harkness went on to say that the men had searched the Priory from top to bottom and claimed to find other things that incriminated his wife and daughter.

"What would these things be?"

"I asked them as well, Doctor. But they would not say, but only that all would be revealed when the women were tried."

"Where are your wife and daughter now?"

"Locked up in Chelmsford. I went there to see them, but Master Pickney, the constable that keeps them close, would not let me. He's a vile, meanspirited devil himself. A proud and ignorant fool who thinks, because he's been made constable, that he has become something beyond what he was before."

"What was he before?" William asked.

"A locksmith. And not a very good one. A tippler as well. He accused me of trying to help them, my wife and daughter, escape. But I was not."

Harkness looked down. Tears filled his eyes and ran down his cheeks into the thicket of his beard. His large body began to shudder, he whimpered, struggling to restrain his tears. William felt his throat tighten, the man's emotion somehow transferring to him. Whatever detachment he had achieved in treating patients, at keeping their suffering apart from himself that he might better serve them by his own cool rationality, he felt slipping from him, like water through a sieve.

Harkness's emotions had embarrassed him. He wiped his eyes with the sleeve of his coat and looked up at William again with soulful eyes. The swagger that had seemed earlier to William to be essential to the man's nature had been revealed as a façade. Beneath all of that, he was but a fellow sufferer, his happiness tied to those he loved, and desperate for help.

"And that's not all," Harkness said.

"What else?"

"They took Ursula's baby, as well."

"The baby? Surely the child is not suspected of witchcraft?"

"As evidence, Doctor. It's the mark on his face. You have seen it. You know what I mean, what they mean. They're saying it's the mark of the wolf."

"Preposterous," William said angrily. "It is nothing but a birthmark, a discoloration of the skin and nothing more. Most, if not all, are harmless. That the mark is on the infant's face is unfortunate, but has no supernatural significance, no significance of any kind. It is an accident of the child's birth. An anomaly."

"A what, Doctor?"

"An anomaly. Something out of the ordinary, unusual."

"They are saying that the mark is a wolf mark. They are saying that the baby proves my daughter is a witch. They are calling her the Wolf Maiden."

"Well," William said, "they might have chosen a worse name for your daughter. Still, she has fallen into the hands of religious fanatics and ignoramuses. Who would believe such a thing of an innocent babe?"

"Oh, there are many who do believe, Doctor," Harkness said. 'For the Devil puts such thoughts into their heads that they will believe anything if it does hurt to those they dislike or believe have done them wrong, their Christian profession notwithstanding. "

Harkness fell silent. He sat erect in his chair, fighting back tears and wringing his hands. His knuckles were white. William could not tell if it was anger or grief that prevailed within him. In light of the circumstances, perhaps it was both. The man was facing the loss of his wife, his daughter, his grandson, and probably his farmstead. He was fortunate not to have been accused himself. William supposed the man knew that, and that a vigorous defense of the women in his life would surely implicate him as well. His hold on the Old Priory was at risk of being confiscated by the Crown and them sold off to the highest bidder. William knew who that would be – Harkness's accusers, the powerful Bascombe family.

William looked for words. When he found them, he no sooner uttered them than he felt their emptiness, their absurdity. He had wanted to console the man, but this was hardly consolation, hardly qualified as help. His words offended even him. "I am very sorry that this has happened to you—to all of you."

For a few moments, Harkness did not respond. William thought about Mary Harkness, Ursula, the baby named after his dead father. He imagined them all imprisoned, as he had once been himself, but he was sure they were in worse straits. He had been helped by a powerful lord who had become his friend, Lord Burghley. Harkness was right. They had no one to help them. On the contrary, they had a powerful gentleman of the neighborhood as their accuser, as their worst enemy. They would receive little sympathy from the citizens of Chelmsford, long accustomed to the terror of witchcraft, ever since the trial and execution of Agnes Waterhouse. Doubtless, before it.

"I appreciate your words, Doctor," Harkness said bitterly. "But your sorrow will not save us. Not save my wife, nor my daughter, nor her child. The law is against us. The church is against us. Our rector gives sermons condemning us. He rails from the pulpit like a madman himself, drools with rage at witches, which he calls the blackest evil of the age. He says we are of a different kind than mankind is, and what he calls our kindness is of Satan. We have no help from man or God."

"What can I do?" William asked, almost fearful of Harkness's answer.

Harkness took a deep breath. An anguished look passed over his face. The softer side of the man reappeared, and William knew what was coming before Harkness said a word.

"I beg you to come to Chelmsford. Doctor. Speak for my wife and daughter. You're a learned man. Maybe they who judge my wife and daughter will listen to you. We practice no witchcraft in our house, not my wife, not my daughter. We are good Christians. At least, we try to be. We have no dealings with the Devil, with familiar spirits. We know nothing of curses or spells. We never have, nor would. I swear to you... that's God's truth."

William felt a sudden dizziness, as though his whole life as he knew it was tittering on an abyss. He got up from his chair and looked into the fire. Behind him, he could hear Jacob Harkness breathing heavily. He could almost hear him thinking, praying. Then he turned to look at the farmer. "I would, if I could," William said. "Believe me, Master Harkness. But I have many patients here that need me. I have a position with the College of Physicians. There's much to do now."

William recited more of his responsibilities, many of which he knew Harkness would not understand. Why should he? Harkness was a simple farmer. What did he know or care of licensure, William's professional obligations, warring schools of philosophical thought and medical practice? William was not just looking for an excuse. These were genuine responsibilities, he said to himself. He would be lying to Harkness if he told him otherwise, that he was at liberty to come to Chelmsford, to drop everything that was important in his life.

"I am very sorry," he said again. "It would be impossible."

Harkness didn't answer. He looked at William bleakly. As though he had heard nothing after William had said he would if he could. He nodded his head, mumbled some half-hearted thanks for the distinguished doctor's time, and rose to go. William reckoned Harkness was a man in his late fifties, but he might have been eighty or more as he struggled to his feet. It was as though the effort took all the man's strength.

William went to him, put his hand on Jacob Harkness's shoulder.

"Wait," William said. "Master Harkness...Jacob."

Harkness stopped but did not turn around. He stood, frozen.

"When is the trial?" William asked.

"At the next assizes, they are saying. Within the month."

"I am not confident I can do much in your family's defense, but I will do what I can."

Harkness turned around to face him. He still looked like a desperate man, a man who knew he himself was in jeopardy, being as he was husband and father to accused women.

"You will come then, Doctor?"

"I will come," William said. "It will take me a day or so to put my affairs in order. Then I'll come."

"Upon oath, Doctor?" Harkness asked, his face no longer despairing as when he entered only a quarter of an hour before. "You promise that you will come to Chelmsford? That you will speak for my women and my grandson?"

"Upon oath, Jacob. I'll speak for your dog, if necessary. After all, it was he that pulled me in from the storm and warmed me until I came to myself again."

When Jacob Harkness had gone, William sat down by the fire and mulled over what he had just committed himself to. The house was quiet now, the servants sent to bed. He was alone.

William was possessed of a methodical mind. Ordinarily he made his decisions with slow deliberation, weighing costs and benefits, considering consequences both unforeseen and unintended. Here he had acted on a sudden impulse, from emotion rather than reason. Yet he believed he had done the right thing, if not necessarily the most prudent thing. Most of the people he knew, including many who were educated, believed in witches. They believed in their existence, their power, and their prevalence, especially in the rural towns and villages where religion combined the teachings of the Christian church with the myths and legends of an even more remote age, an earlier time of magic and curses. Before the Normans, before the Saxons, before whatever peoples came before.

He did not really want to return to Chelmsford. As county towns went, it was not a bad place, but his life was full in London. He had his busy and increasingly successful practice, his duties with the College and a widening circle of interesting friends who, like him, were busy probing the secrets of the natural world, an activity that not only satisfied their curiosity but produced benefits for the country, economically and militarily. All of the foregoing he would have to put aside while he attended to a matter that had little to do with that for which he was trained, the healing of the sick.

Instead, he would be enmeshed in his father's business, the workings of the courts and the laws, a domain repellent to him. His role would be that of a character witness, and insofar as the jurymen at the trial gave credit to his education, a medical expert on birthmarks and their significance or lack thereof. But as uncomfortable as he was with these new roles, he realized Harkness had made a wise choice. After all, who else was there? Certainly, none in Chelmsford, where the family were considered strange and distant, and opinions were no doubt influenced by the dark history of the Old Priory and the precedent of the Waterhouse case.

He that lieth with dogs must rise up with fleas, his stepmother was wont to say. Were that the case, then he who lives in the house of papist nuns must likewise be infected with their evil. It was not a logic that William agreed with, but it was a logic he knew would be considered indisputable by the people of Chelmsford.

The guilt of the Harknesses would be a foregone conclusion based solely on the ground they occupied, the Old Priory with its cursed history of false doctrine, licentiousness, and infanticide.

10

William supped with his brethren of the College on Monday. On Tuesday, he had been visited by the beleaguered husbandman with his pathetic appeal for help. A week later, while he was preparing to leave for Chelmsford, his father made a surprise visit.

Jerome Gilbert came to London three or four times a year. When he did, he would stay with William at Wingfield House. William had told him earlier how he had been saved from freezing by a farmer and his family but had been sparing in detail. It wasn't a story he wanted to share with his father, who had advised him against traveling to London on the day of the unexpected storm. William did not relish the thought of being reminded of his folly, in preferring an astrologer's prediction over his father's counsel. William was now a grown man, a successful London physician, but his father's approval still meant something to him.

His lawyer father, William often thought, was an older version of himself, at least in body. Tall, lean, smooth-shaven, looking thereby younger than his fifty years. But father and son were different in temper. Jerome Gilbert was steady, rational to a fault, and had a quiet dignity that served him well in the execution of his civic duties. He was recorder for the borough, which is to say he was a judge of matters criminal and civil and was so involved in the town's affairs that he rarely had time for his growing family. William was more intellectually adventurous, emotive, and, at times, combative. Not physically, like some of his university friends who were given to brawling and dueling and marching off to war to invade France or Holland, but in the theatre of ideas where he was fond of contending with those who he believed were overly dependent on the wisdom of the ancients, who parroted old doctrines and beliefs, who were content with received ideas and unexamined premises.

"You never told me, William, that the farm you stayed at was the Old Priory," his father said, even before William had the opportunity to inquire as to the state of the family in Colchester or his father's present business in London.

They were seated in William's library. A fire burned brightly and warmed the space enough for his father to have removed his cloak and folded it neatly on his lap, like a large napkin.

"Who told you that?" William asked.

"You said only that it was a farm near Chelmsford," his father said.

"Which is true," William answered. "The farm was near Chelmsford. When the weather cleared, I walked out of the woods and then to Chelmsford, my horse having died in the storm. But where did you learn that it was the Old Priory where I stayed?"

"I met one of your colleagues on the Strand. Doctor Raphael Pierce. He told me you conveyed the full story of your rescue—and your rescuers."

"I didn't think it was important, the name of the family," William said. "You were very caught up in your business that day. Some suit of law you spoke of. Some judgment to render. I don't remember. To be honest, Father, I didn't think you would be interested."

A dry, mocking laugh came from his father. "I would have been interested had I known it was the Harkness Farm, the Old Priory, where you lodged."

And then William remembered how Jacob Harkness had reacted when William told him his father was Jerome Gilbert. Harkness knew William's father. Or at least knew of him. But Harkness hadn't said how or why he frowned when William told him his father's name. It had been one of the many mysteries surrounding his three days at the farmstead, a lesser mystery he had supposed. At least until now. But William could see that his father did indeed have a history with the Harknesses and having promised to help in their upcoming trial, William wanted to know it.

His father began a recital of facts, as he might have done in court when asked to summarize a case at law. "The land on which the Old Priory sits once belonged to the Bascombe family. Sir Arthur Bascombe is now deceased. His son Richard inherited after. Sir Arthur was a wastrel and womanizer and incurred such debts that he was about to lose all. In desperation he sold off the Old Priory and the land about it to meet the demands of his creditors. Sold it to Harkness, Jacob Harkness. Afterwards

Sir Arthur's son, Richard, regretted what his father had done and has moved heaven and earth to have the property again."

"All this I know," William said. "I learned of their dispute from our innkeeper friend Rafe Tuttle in Chelmsford. But why should Sir Richard want the Priory? The place is a ruin, half burned down, overrun with weeds and woods with oak and alder so thick one can hardly penetrate it. Do the Bascombes want land for some enterprise?"

"Sir Richard Bascombe wants it for pride's sake. It was his father's. Therefore, he feels it must be his, or if not he's less a man. It is not an impulse I completely understand, having sufficient land for myself."

His father scowled, going back in the conversation as if he had dropped something in the street and returned to fetch it. "You talked about this to Rafe, an innkeeper, but not to your own father?"

William could hear the reproach in his father's voice. But he was not inclined to apologize.

"As I said, I didn't think you would be interested."

"And did Rafe tell you that Sir Richard Bascombe pressed me to help him sue the Harknesses?"

"He said there were repeated suits. He said all failed. But he did not mention that you had done any legal business for the Bascombes."

"There were some of the suits that never proceeded to court," his father said. "They were absurd on their face, no wonder. No judge would have found for Bascombe. One of these was the one I was involved with. I know Richard Bascombe. We were friends, years before. He came to Colchester to find me. This was some years past, while you were away at Cambridge. He wanted to press a case. I don't even remember the grounds of the suit he contemplated. He told me about his earlier attempts. His failures enraged him."

"So he was not just angry?" William said.

"Beyond that, I do think," his father answered, shaking his head. He looked sad. "He was a different man when I first knew him. A good, honest, gentleman, well allowed among those of us who knew him and called him friend. Before I refused to be his lawyer, I went to the Old Priory myself. I talked to Harkness. It was not a pleasant meeting. When he found out who I was and why I was there, I thought he might kill me where I stood, or set the dog on me. He's a dangerous man, my son. You were more blessed by God in surviving his hospitality than the storm that drove you to it."

69

William thought of his meeting with Jacob Harkness. He had felt himself in no danger during it, even when William declined to help. He remembered the look of relief and gratitude on the farmer's face when William changed his mind.

"Harkness's wife and daughter have been accused of witchcraft," William said, thinking his father would have heard that too, having as he did friends and associates in Chelmsford. But William could tell that his father had not. "They've been imprisoned, and are awaiting trial at the next assizes."

"I am hardly surprised," his father said. "The wife is an odd piece of work. They tell stories of her. They have for years. The daughter is like unto her, a strange, homely girl. And then there's the dog. Vicious creature. More wolf than dog, although Harkness insists he's a good dog. All the time I talked with Harkness I feared that any minute he would set the beast on me."

"It was the dog that found me in the storm," William said. "Save for him, I would have died."

"Maybe that's just what you were told, son."

"I know it to be a fact," William said. "By the way, Jacob Harkness paid me a visit."

"When? Where?"

"Yesterday. Here at Wingfield House."

"He came all the way to London?"

"He begged me to help him... help *them*, his wife and daughter."

"You told him no, of course."

William shook his head. "I told him I would. I told him I would come to Chelmsford for the trial. I told him I would give what help I could."

"What help could you give?" his father asked, his voice full of disbelief.

"Character witness," William said. "I lived among them for three days. I observed their lives, experienced their Christian charity. And there's also evidence of a medical nature. Ursula Harkness has a child. The child has a port-wine stain upon his face. The prosecution will use that as evidence of the Devil's mark. They are calling Ursula the Wolf Maiden."

"Wolf Maiden?"

"Because of the dog," William said. "Because of the birthmark on the child's face. It means nothing. It is but an accident of birth. I have seen dozens of them on bodies I have examined. Of various sizes and shapes and colorations."

For a moment his father said nothing. He looked at William with an expression of incredulity. And then his expression turned darker. "The child with the mark... this is Ursula's child we're speaking of?"

"Yes, a son, about six months old, I think."

"She's married?"

"She's not. The father is, or was, Thomas Bascombe."

"Thomas? I remember him. A pleasant lad if I remember. He has a sister, a twin. Surely he did not rape Ursula, that she begot a son?"

"No, by Ursula's account they fell in love. Thomas promised to marry her, but his father forbade it. Then Thomas fell sick, languished for months. Finally died. Ursula is accused more particularly of putting a curse upon him for that he would not fulfill his promise."

"A likely story," his father said, shaking his head. "Ursula is no beauty that Thomas Bascombe should be charmed by her. I am sure you noted during your sojourn, unless by some miracle she's changed."

"I grant she's a plain girl," William said.

"That Thomas Bascombe should love her seems highly unlikely," his father said. "That someone of his blood and degree should take joy in her body even less so. It is more reasonable to suppose she gave herself to some farmer's son for a quick roll in the hay. Who could believe her story is otherwise than a tissue of falsehoods?"

William wanted to tell his logical father that love was not always reasonable, that it made strange bedfellows. But he knew such a response would be useless. His father, for all his legal learning, would not understand, could not understand.

"I believe Ursula, her story," William said.

"And?"

"I have promised to speak on her behalf, on her family's behalf, at the trial."

For a moment his father sat silent, stupefied, as William looked down at his hands, even as Jacob Harkness had done a week earlier, sitting in the same chair and beseeching William to help. Then his father spoke. In his eyes was more anger than mere disapproval.

"What would you say, son, were I to forbid it?"

"Forbid what?"

"Your testifying on behalf of these people, these witches."

"I think, father with all due respect I must make such decisions for myself. Tell me, would you find me a more worthy son, were I to surrender so readily my own agency to you, that you tell me what to do, where to go, what to say, whom to give aid to? Surely that is not the manner of a grown man, as I am. To demand submission is not the manner of a loving father who must respect his son's right to make his own decisions."

"Oh, you are too much caught up in this modern view of things," his father said, scowling and waving his hand away to dismiss the idea. "I was ruled by my own father until the day he died. Had I defied him, he would have beat me, even when I was a man."

"Times have changed," William said. "I do believe for the better."

They settled into an awkward silence. His father looked away from him, stared into the fire for what seemed a long time, although it could not have been so. Perhaps, William thought, his father was remembering happier times when William was a lad, easier to entreat because he was small and his father grown, because as a child he would have recognized his father's superior wisdom. William had been an obedient child, an easy child to rear, compliant, sweet tempered, an old soul in a young body. He had inherited his father's dislike of discord, his preference for accommodation and domestic tranquility. Father and son had rarely argued. Suddenly, it was different.

He turned back to William. "Then if you will not obey me, son, let us reason together. I cannot conceive of a more reckless undertaking. Tell me, I pray you, are you mad, son, or simply ignorant of what you do?"

"Neither mad nor ignorant," William said, assuming his calm voice again. "I have lived among the Harknesses, though briefly. I don't believe they practice witchcraft or any other devilish thing. Certainly, I saw no hint of such malignancy while I stayed with them. I would happily testify to their good character at their trial and feel obliged to do since but for their charity I would have died."

"Yes, you might well have done so, although all would have been avoided had you taken my advice and foregone your untimely return to London when a storm was brewing."

"A bad choice it may well have been, Father," William said, "but the choice was made and the consequence thereof I have suffered. I cannot rewrite the past, nor can I ignore its consequences. The fact is that I owe the Harknesses my very life. They took me in. They didn't have to. They warmed me by their fire, they fed me, and after three days their daughter Ursula led me through the woods back to the road so that I might sit here today by the fire and converse with you. For this, they asked nothing although I offered to pay them for their not letting me die of the cold."

"Harkness has bid you come to Chelmsford, come to a witch trial. I would say that is overpayment rather than just payment. You are like a man who owing a pound, repays his creditor two, nay a hundred. I trust you have not been bewitched by Ursula Harkness," his father said with a grimace.

"I have been bewitched by no one, and certainly not Ursula Harkness, but am doing naught else but repaying a just debt. And, perhaps, performing a charitable act."

William stood and looked down at his father, still seated and shaking his head.

"You call it a debt you feel obligated to pay," his father said more calmly now. "Have you considered how it will appear your defending accused witches? Witch trials rarely have a doubtful outcome. Their indictment and doubtless the cloud of witnesses eager to tell affirming stories of their malicious acts make their conviction sure. Trust me, I know these things."

William nodded. He would not contend with his father on that point.

His father continued; satisfied, William imagined, that he had won that point with his recalcitrant son. "To be accused is to be convicted in the public mind. In speaking on their behalf, you will but make yourself a figure of ridicule and scorn, not only in Chelmsford, but in London as well. Trust me, news of your participation will work its way back to the City, and what will your colleagues in the College think of you? "

William had a pretty good idea of what they'd think. He had already had a taste of their opinions at the meeting earlier that week.

"And what of your highborn patients? Lord Burghley. You, a physician, a graduate of Cambridge, even an officer in the College, consorting with witches, breaking bread with them in a cursed place, a foul nest of papistry, testifying of their good character in a court of law?"

William saw it all, even as his father was imagining it. A social disaster. A whirlwind of miserable outcomes.

73

His father stopped talking. He sat there looking at William, waiting for him to concede, His father's smooth face was flushed, but not by the heat of the fire.

William heard what his father was saying. In a way, he could not refute it. He was putting his reputation in jeopardy by agreeing to testify. It was as simple as that. Yet, strangely, his father's opposition made his own determination stronger. Was it mere stubbornness that he felt at this moment? A son's natural desire not so much to please his father as to insist on his own way that he might achieve a long-sought independence and establish himself as his own man, not merely another man's son and heir?

Jerome Gilbert must have realized his son's mind had wandered. He stood and grasped William's arm, the way he had when William was a child. "Listen, William. Hear me out. No good can come of this. You spent years at Cambridge, for which I paid a goodly sum. You have laid the groundwork for a career in this city. You may at some future year even become physician to the queen herself. All that lies before you. And all that may be ruined, a vanished dream, if your reputation is lost by this foolishness."

"It is not foolishness, father." William said, trying to keep calm. "Surely, you as an officer of the court should see that. Do the women not deserve a defense? Witnesses who can speak on their behalf? A physician such as myself who can dissuade some jury from convicting the innocent because of some superstitious views of witchcraft and the supposed signs thereof?"

He had become heated. He had said more to his father than he had intended, raised his voice in defiance of paternal authority. But having said it, done it, his resolve was the stronger.

"It is not that I deny them their defense," his father responded. "But must it be you who speaks for them? Let some other of their neighbors testify to their good works, some clergyman to swear they say the Creed and Paternoster in good English, not Latin. Not you, my son. I pray you reconsider. Counsel with your colleagues of the College before you act. A wise man secures the opinions of many before stepping into the dark, and believe me son, you are so doing in your resolve."

"I've promised Jacob Harkness. I've made an oath."

"In a court of law? Before God? Oaths otherwise can be broken."

"You fear for my soul, father?" William asked.

74

"Not your soul, son. Your career, perhaps your very life. I have seen it before in these trials. It's a kind of logic very difficult to refute."

"What logic is that?" William asked.

"One who defends a witch is one himself, else why should he defend whom God has condemned? You can call it guilt by association if you will and deride its premise, yet it will be credited. Trust me it will."

"Go to bed, father. You look tired."

His father sighed heavily. "I am worn out by your recalcitrance. How did I beget so difficult a son?"

"I got it from my mother, who is dead," William said, remembering the ghost that had appeared to him while freezing. He was weary himself. "Go to bed, father."

His father stood. "I think I shall, son. Same room as always?"

"Same room, Father. At the head of the stairs."

"Shall we speak again of this?" his father asked doubtfully, turning back to him.

"It will do no good, father. I am resolved."

Jerome Gilbert turned toward the door.

"Good night, son," he said over his shoulder. "God bless you."

"And you, father."

That night, William slept restlessly. He dreamed he was in the Old Priory again, making his way through the snowy woods with Ursula, the Wolf Maiden of the townspeople's imagination, just ahead of him. They were walking through the old cemetery where the nuns had buried their dead. The dog was there too, but in his dream the dog was larger than he remembered, his fangs longer and sharper. In the dream he was afraid of the both of them, the girl who had helped him and her dog who had crouched beside him on his first day at the Old Priory.

When he awoke, he wondered if the dream was his own mind trying to tell him something, perhaps that his father was right again. His father had warned William about the storm. Now he warned him about involving himself in a witch trial.

On Monday he supped with his physician colleagues. On Tuesday he had promised to testify at a witch trial. Within the week he defied his father's quite reasonable but ultimately unpersuasive argument that testifying at a witch trial would ruin his life. At least, his life as he had planned it.

The next day he set out early for Chelmsford, before cockcrow, before the servants were half awake. The weather was fair, no chance of a storm. He had consulted no astrologer this time and quite forgot about the dream that had disturbed him.

11

His usual room at the Blue Boar was taken by a sea captain, home from the sea. Rafe Tuttle was more than apologetic and assured William he would be given another room equally clean and commodious. It was not. The room was at the rear of the inn and its window looked down on a vacant lot filled with weeds and building rubble. He consoled himself by remembering that he was in Chelmsford for one purpose only; to give what aid he could to Ursula Harkness and her mother.

He thought it unlikely he should spend much time in his room, except to sleep, should he get any. His head was full of warring voices. Jacob Harkness's appeal for help, his father's warning that helping accused witches could ruin his life. He had thrown in his lot with the former, but his father's dire predictions still echoed in his head.

He had brought little with him—an extra shirt, a few books, and a few medical implements should his services as physician be called upon. It was as he was unpacking these and noticing the instruments that he came upon the way he should gain access to the two accused witches should he find, like Jacob Harkness, his way blocked by an over-zealous sheriff or constable concerned that a visitor to the women might aid in their escape. That fear had even prevented Jacob Harkness from seeing his family, a remarkably unfair and unwarranted precaution in William's mind.

William wasted no time in that effort. Rafe Tuttle told him upon his arrival that the women were confined to the house of the town constable, Samuel Pickney, a man Jacob Harkness had called an oaf, tippler, and an incompetent locksmith.

Rafe was surprised that William had heard about the arrests.

"London is not so far away that we are ignorant of what passes in

Chelmsford," William said. He had decided earlier to keep his meeting with Jacob Harkness to himself, at least for now.

"Most especially if it concerns witchcraft," Rafe added. "He keeps them shut up good in his own house, or at least in his stable."

"That's most hospitable of him," William said. "Although I suppose it's better than being shut up in the privy. You've seen this place?"

"I have seen it and would not be bedded there myself save it were the only bed in town, and perhaps not then. It is stinking foul, the animals dung removed at least once a year whether such removal is needed or not. Not even the beasts can abide it. A fitting place for those who practice the black arts and converse with the Devil, I say, but then what do I know? I am only an innkeeper, not a churchman to judge such matters."

"I will try to see the women," William said. "To find out how they do."

"Good luck with that," Rafe answered. "I heard Jacob Harkness tried to see his own family, but the constable in his wisdom forbade it. With all due respect, Doctor, why should you fare better?"

William shrugged. He had no answer. He let the matter drop. At least with the innkeeper. Rafe Tuttle was a good fellow, and William counted him as a friend, but he knew he would have to hold some things back.

It was late in the day, but not too late to visit the constable's shop. A helpful passerby directed him to it. He had been through Chelmsford many times, but while he knew the Blue Boar well, he knew little of the rest of the town, which consisted largely of the High Street, a wide space in the road where the Sessions House stood, and a few intersecting lanes with modest half-timbered houses, complete with thatched roofs and single chimneys. There was also, of course, the church, which stood on the edge of town, dominating the sky above it, its steeple pointing upward to heaven and thereby signifying the spiritual aspirations of the community.

The constable's shop was dusty and close, without windows. It smelled of lubricating oil. On the wall hung locks on pegs, more than William had ever seen. They were of every size and shape. Behind a bench littered with the constable's tools, stood the man himself, stout, sway-bellied, sandy-haired, about forty, William judged. He glanced up at William, then looked back at what he had been doing. When William realized Pickney was ignoring him, he introduced himself.

"I am William Gilbert, a doctor. In London. Here for a few days, perhaps a week or more," he told the constable, thinking he might establish his *bona fides* prior to requesting to see the women. The constable did not seem impressed, but looked at William confusedly, uncertain as to what he wanted, annoyed by the interruption of his work, which seemed repairing a lock fixed in a vice. The constable had some sort of tool in his hand, long, pointed, like a spike or pick. It reminded William of some surgical instrument he had seen.

William continued, "My father is Jerome Gilbert. He's the recorder and judge in Colchester, where I was born."

That information failed to move the constable, too. He stared at William as though William had said nothing at all. Finally, the constable spoke, proving his capacity therein to William's relief, for he had begun to suppose the man deaf and dumb, an odd sort of constable indeed.

"And what would you want here, Doctor? We have doctors a-plenty in Chelmsford, too many in my way of thinking."

"You have confined here a woman who is my patient," William said, thinking that the assertion was not really a lie, since should Ursula Harkness accept him as such then it was indeed true. But would she accept? The request for help had come from her father, not from Ursula or her mother. Perhaps they would feel differently about this London doctor butting into their business, as perilous a business as it was.

"And who might these women be, sir? I have a half dozen prisoners at this time who say they are female, and most appear to be so. But they're not at my house. Chelmsford may not be the size of London from whence you come, Doctor, yet it has enough malefactors to lock up that we have a jail and a good-sized one. I would be happy to show you the way there, if you are minded to see any of them."

"In fact, Constable, she I seek I am given to know is confined in your house, or at least in your stable."

For a moment the constable said nothing, then his expression changed. He looked at William suspiciously. "The witches, you mean?"

"I mean Ursula Harkness and her mother," William said. "Mary Harkness."

"They are not allowed visitors," the constable said.

"No visitors? But why not? I thought incarcerated persons frequently had visitors, from the clergy, from family, even from friends and other well-wishers. Surely a woman's doctor might reasonably visit her, to see how she does."

"That is true, Doctor, but with these women, it's different as night and day."

"How so?" William persisted.

"They are witches, Doctor," Pickney said, looking exasperated. "Not the ordinary run of criminal types, that is, good Christian folks gone astray."

"So, they are forbidden visitors by your own order?" William asked.

"Nay, Doctor, but by the order of Sir Richard Bascombe himself of Mowbray Rise. He is concerned that none aid in their escape."

"I have no intent to aid in your prisoner's escape," William said. "But I attended on Mistress Mary Harkness for a certain physical indisposition before her recent arrest and I have stopped in Chelmsford to determine the progress of my treatment."

"And what physical indisposition might that be, Doctor?" The constable did nothing to hide his disbelief, or perhaps it was merely perverse curiosity. William decided if it were the latter, he would do nothing to satisfy it.

"A not uncommon problem with women of a certain age," William said. "I could go into details, Constable, but it would require me to describe female privy parts, the names and operations of which are not generally known, at least to men."

"I care not for her privy parts, be they known or unknown," the constable declared, raising his voice a little. "But I, sir, am constable here and have a duty to my townsmen to enforce Her Majesty's laws and protect our citizenry from harm."

"From the witches?"

"Yes, sir, and their familiar."

"What familiar might that be?"

"Her wolf."

"You mean the Harkness dog?"

"Nay, Doctor, if I meant dog, I would have said dog," Pickney declared, bracing his legs and folding his arms in front of him. "But I said wolf, which is what I mean, Doctor. I may be only a town constable, no grand resident of London such as yourself, but I do know a hawk from a hound and a dog from a wolf. Have I and others not heard it howling of nights since the women's arrest? And one of our neighbors swears a great oath that she has seen its shadow moving through the High Street, whereupon she ran for her dear life and bolted her door against it."

William made no response but thought it unlikely the dog would have followed her mistress into the town. Under the circumstances, he was surprised Vulcan had not been killed at the time Ursula and her mother were taken. After all, wouldn't the constable and his men want the dog as evidence?

"You didn't capture the dog?"

The constable's face fell. "We couldn't catch him. But then I suppose since he is the Devil himself, it's no wonder. If it were easy to catch the Devil, Doctor Gilbert, we'd all live in a better world, should we not?"

"I suppose we should, Master Constable."

"I hope this condition you mentioned does not threaten Mother Harkness's life," the constable said after a pause. "It would be a shame were she to die before justice be done. Besides that, it would be a great disappointment to the town. They do love their hangings, Doctor, especially if it's witches that be hanged. With ordinary criminals it's different. Murderers, thieves, pickpockets, these are often their neighbors and sometimes family."

"Aren't the Harknesses neighbors?"

"I'd not call them so, if they are witches."

The constable asked again about the seriousness of Mary Harkness's condition.

"I think it's not life-threatening," William said.

"Well, then, perhaps she has no need of your attending upon her, but will mend herself."

"She may or may not," William said. "But the woman suffers— perhaps needlessly. I would very much like to see her and determine how she does."

"What suffering she or her daughter has may be alleviated, Doctor, by my good wife, who attends upon both. She is knowledgeable in herbs and other medicaments. Besides, sir, Mother Harkness may suffer more."

"How so?"

"At the assizes, in two weeks, her fate will be sealed. After that, I trust she will have no more complaints of the sort you have described, be they female complaints or men's complaints. I may not let you see her before that time."

"Before what time?"

"Why, before she is hanged, Doctor." The constable smiled grimly, looked to William to see whether he appreciated gallows humor.

"Surely, the assizes are a public tribunal."

"They are public, the whole town comes to see it, men, women, children too."

"And the woman's husband, the father?"

"Oh, Doctor, he came and wanted to see them, but he could not."

"And why not?"

"He wanted to help them escape."

"How do you know?" William asked. "He may have only wanted to console them in their affliction."

Pickney laughed. "Their affliction, Doctor, they have brought upon themselves. Jacob Harkness would have done better to comfort the family of him whom they cursed to death. The women are locked up where they can do no harm, Doctor. So I have been instructed. And they are guarded day and night else other of their kind snatch them away."

After that the constable continued to rail against witches. William heard the history of Agnes Waterhouse and her sister for the second or third time, with many elaborations obviously of the constable's own invention, for they seemed beyond fantastical. All this Pickney narrated with more pride than fear, relishing every detail, no matter its absurdity. It was clear to William that Chelmsford's role in the witch frenzy was a mark of pride for him. The more witches discovered and condemned the better seemed to be his philosophy. If Chelmsford had hanged more witches than Colchester that was all to the glory of Chelmsford, a proof of God's grace and the wisdom of the town's citizenry.

"I warrant you Colchester has as many witches as we," the constable said, remembering William had said he was from that place. "You only need to do better in ferreting them out."

"Perhaps we do need to do better," William allowed, not because he believed it but because he doubted he would get what he wanted by arguing with the constable further.

William learned that the Harknesses had at first been confined to the town jail, a building in the center of town originally used as a mill, but there was such an uproar from the prisoners objecting to being confined with witches that it was thought better for the cause of public order if the two women were confined elsewhere. "I have a stable out back but no horse. If they choke on dried dung and dust, it is no better than they deserve for what they've done and are. They are locked in there safe and sound, and I have two stout men guarding them every hour of the day, save when one of our local clergymen comes to warn them of the hellfire to come and urge them to confess their sins."

"What of the child... Ursula's child?"

"My wife cares for it," the constable said, grimacing as though the child were something to be thrown into the midden heap.

William imagined the constable's wife, a woman he had never seen. What must it be like caring for a child so marked as Ursula's child was and believing at the same time the mark was the Devil's signature?

"They have not confessed, the women?" William asked.

"They have not, yet they shall, Doctor, they shall. You may trust me in that."

William nodded approvingly, feeling that would put him in good graces with the constable.

"And you know what's more, Doctor? I have no doubt the child is so marked because the creature she harbors—I do mean her familiar—has not only sucked her blood but also planted his seed within her."

William tried to keep a straight face upon hearing so preposterous an idea, but he suspected the constable's conclusion might be shared by a good many of those who would attend the trial, including the judges and the jury as well. The very silliness of the idea would surely make it more appealing, stimulating as it did both the prurient imagination and fear of the unknown.

"I thought I heard the father was Master Bascombe's son who was dead, which was why the women cursed him for that the son would not marry her." William said. "Were the wolf the father, why should she protest a breached promise of matrimony?"

"Oh, I know not about that, Doctor. It may be so or no. I know only that the child is marked. I've seen him myself and the very sight of him chills the blood, it does. It chills the blood. Besides Master Thomas Bascombe may have abused her and yet not fathered the child. A woman may have two lovers, may she not?"

"It has happened, I think," William said.

"And one might be humankind, and the other animal kind."

William was about to say that such a coupling was impossible when his conversation with the constable was interrupted by the entrance of a narrow-faced, sharp-nosed man of about fifty, wearing a worn canvas jerkin and a soft cap too large for his head.

"I am come early, Master Pickney," the man said, nodding to the constable. "To relieve the watch."

"Then do so now, Parker." The constable said, waving the man off.

"Yes, sir, Master Pickney, as you say, sir."

William marked the man's face, the color of his flesh, the shape of his nose and mouth. He would remember the sound of his voice, the accent that was not from eastern England but somewhere to the north. He was sure this was one of the guards set to watch the stable where the women were.

He turned his eyes back to the constable who still regarded him suspiciously. He said, "If I cannot see my patient, Master Pickney, might you convey to her a message—unless of course that too is forbidden?"

"I suppose I might, unless it be a plan to help her escape. We shall have no escapes Doctor, not while I am constable here."

"I swear to you, Master Constable, I have no such intent and never did. I only want her to know that I am in Chelmsford and do hope her condition has not worsened since I saw her last."

"My wife can give her such a message. May I ask you again, Doctor, your name?"

William spelled out his name slowly. The constable made no move to write it down.

12

He had turned lurker and spy.

From the other side of the narrow street, William could see the stable the innkeeper had described, a ramshackle structure without windows and a barn door boarded up. Next to the door was another, an ordinary door. He could see it was locked with a large padlock of the kind William had seen in the constable's shop.

Parker, the constable's man, had already assumed his watch. He sat by the smaller door on a three-legged stool, his head fallen back against the wall, his eyes shut. He seemed to be sleeping, or perhaps praying for protection from the witches within.

Then he saw a plump, frowsy woman of middle age emerge from the shop and come around the corner. She carried a bowl covered with a cloth. The witches' dinner, whatever it was. Parker stood, said something to her, unlocked the door for her. She went in.

Of course, the women, the prisoners, would have to be fed. But what else? Examined? Questioned? Tortured? Forced to confess before the trial so matters might move smoothly toward what William's father had called their inevitable fate?

William was careful not to be noticed, pretending to pass by. William knew he was stalking, lurking—like a common thief or burglar—but for a good cause, yet he felt guilty in so doing. He was a law-abiding man, scrupulously so. The constable, though an ignorant lout, represented the law William's father had taught him to respect.

He continued to watch, furtively. Time passed. The woman, the constable's wife, came out. Parker closed the door behind her and locked it again. William watched the woman return to the house and enter into the constable's shop by its back door.

William waited and watched, concealed in a shadowy corner of an adjacent building. An hour or more passed. Another man came, Parker's relief. The two had some words William could not hear. Then Parker got to his feet and headed up the street, leaving his replacement to stand watch.

The new guard was hardly more diligent than Parker. He did not sleep, but he spent much of his time standing apart from the stable talking to a friend who had suddenly appeared. William was out of earshot. The conversation, begun amicably by all appearances, presently turned into some argument between them. The newcomer was threatening the guard, shaking his fist at him, then stomped off. If the stable door had been unlocked, the two women might have slipped out unobserved.

William returned to the Blue Boar, had an unsatisfying supper, and although disheartened by the constable's obdurate refusal and prejudgment of his prisoners, nonetheless determined to try another tack. He remembered the story of Pyramus and Thisbe from his Ovid, learned when he was a schoolboy. The two were lovers, forbidden by their parents to speak, but managing nonetheless to do so through a crack in a wall. He and Ursula Harkness were not lovers, but the locked, boarded up, windowless structure was as good as a wall. The question was whether he could find a crack in it. There would also be the constable's men to contend with, but if they were all as incompetent as Parker and his relief man, William might have a chance.

William knew that the proximity of the prisoners to the house of the constable and his wife made any close inspection of their place of confinement risky. Should the constable see him prowling about, he would immediately conclude that the London doctor's goal was the same he alleged against the husband of the accused women, an escape from the demands of justice. He knew that if he were seen again by the constable the man would remember his face, and if not that, his clothing, which was a cut above that of the average townsman. The ruff collar and silver buttoned doublet, the soft velvet cap signaling a gentleman, doubtless from the City.

Which left some manner of dress in between. He was not about to don a false beard to disguise himself, but he knew a different cap, a plain belted smock of the sort workmen wear, might at least upon distant view suggest someone other than himself and draw little suspicion. Besides, he had seen such laborers working on the construction of houses on the very street. Should he be taken as one of them he might get close enough to inspect the stable as he wanted.

It was nearly eight o'clock before he could get Rafe Tuttle aside to ask for his help.

"You are not satisfied with your clothes, Doctor? They seem most finely made to me and presentable as befits a man of your honor and attainment."

"They are well made and comfortable, right for London. But I'm in need of something less conspicuous. I have people to see in the town who would not be letting me in the door should they think I'm a magistrate or some uppity clerk with a summons or warrant."

Rafe laughed. "You want to dress like me, Doctor, an innkeeper?"

"Well, I was thinking of something less grand."

Both men laughed.

"Do you mind if the garments are used?" Rafe asked.

"By whom?'

"A dead man."

"Not hanged, I pray you, not murdered."

"No, this poor fellow died in his sleep. In this very inn. He had no one to come for his body—or for the things he had. Which things I have here."

"Here?"

"Wait. I will be but a minute or so, and you, Doctor, shall be outfitted as you please, though why you fear the attire you wear should alarm our citizenry in your ministrations escapes me quite."

Rafe left and was back almost at once, his arms full of clothing—shoes, hose, frayed shirt, jerkin, and a cap William wouldn't be seen dead wearing although before he knew it, it was on top of his head and he on his way downstairs, reclothed for the occasion.

Then his attention was drawn to the tavern bar, where a dozen or so men were gathered around a table, drinking and telling stories. He saw one of them was Parker. William walked over and took a seat at the end of the bar, where he would seem inconspicuous, and observed the group. Parker was holding forth loudly, telling some story that provoked much ribald laughter from his companions. Nothing to do with witchcraft or his appointed duties related thereto, as far as William could understand it, but something about a lascivious widow who had married five husbands and grown rich thereby. He could tell, however, from the guard's slurred speech and slovenly manner that the tankard of ale in front of him was by no means the first of the evening. After a while, Parker got up, begged the pardon of his friends, and announced quite loudly that duty called.

William watched as Parker walked out, then left himself, to follow the man. He could tell that Parker was more than a little drunk. He staggered as he walked, stopped once to relieve himself in an alley, and then proceeded until he came to the constable's stable. William continued to follow and waited as Parker and the man he relieved conversed briefly, then Parker took his station, sat down against the wall as he had done earlier, and as far as William could see fell asleep—as William had trusted he would.

William waited only a few moments before approaching the stable. Parker was already snoring softly, and William was fairly confident that the man would continue to do so. He walked toward the rear of the shop where the stable was and drew close to the wall and walked around to the other side, where earlier he had noticed a larger door for the animals to enter and leave. This was boarded up, but there were cracks between the boards, just as he hoped. One was larger than the others. William thought it was a terrible place to imprison any woman, be she witch or not, but he understood given the anger of the townspeople, it might be a safer place than Chelmsford's jail.

He put his ear to the loose slat. He could hear nothing. Not even a breath. He could smell the familiar aroma of a stable; horse, hay, dung. He whispered the names of the women. No response came. He called louder with the same result. His heart was pounding, and he could feel rivulets of sweat running down from the cap he wore onto his face.

He did not fear the constable's sudden appearance. He thought it more than likely the man and his wife were asleep, for he had heard the nine chimes of the town clock somewhat earlier. He reckoned now it was at least ten.

But there was Parker standing, or sitting, in his way. What if he awoke from his drunken stupor and saw William there? What would William say or do by way of explaining? The guard might even recognize William as the young gentleman the constable was conversing with earlier. William's disguise would only make him look more suspicious.

A third attempt to call attention to whoever was within met with the same result. He began to wonder if Ursula and her daughter were there at all. Perhaps they had been moved. Perhaps the constable feared the London doctor would cast some spell of his own and obtain their freedom. Perhaps he had moved his prisoners into his house.

He made what he decided would be his last attempt, after which he would return to the inn and abandon his effort, or at least this stage of it.

"Mistress Harkness, Ursula, It's William Gilbert, the doctor, whom you took in a while back."

He waited, repeated his name.

Then, at last, a response. It was a weak voice, a young woman's voice, hardly above a whisper. He recognized it as Ursula's. But it was a voice that expressed pain and fear. Ursula, but not the spirited girl he remembered during his stay at the Old Priory.

"Doctor, is that really you?"

"It is I, really."

"You look different."

He realized she could see him through the crack. Was she referring to his change of dress or something else, something in his face?

"What are you doing here?" she asked, her voice still tentative.

He imagined the girl on the other side of the wall, the strange, plain girl the townspeople were now calling the Wolf Maiden. William said, "Your father came to me in London. He asked me to come for the trial, he asked me to testify on your behalf, to tell the court how you had taken me in."

"My father?" she asked. "He has not visited us here, not since we were arrested."

"They wouldn't let him see you," William said. "He told me that. He came to see me in London, told me what had happened. The constable thought he might help you escape."

"Escape?"

"It's the constable's fear."

"We have no thought to escape, save to prove our innocence at the trial."

He could not tell her how difficult that might prove. His own father would have, unrestrained by any sympathy for their plight.

"How can I help you?" he asked, wanting now to hear it from Ursula's own words.

There was a silence, then her voice again.

"Can you tell them about my son, about his birthmark? What you told me about it? How it was an incident of birth, natural, no mark of

89

the Devil, no sign of the wolf? You're a learned man, a doctor, a graduate of the university. They'll listen to you."

She had the optimism of youth, and the naivete.

"I will do what I can," he said, not sure they, the jurors, would listen to him.

"They may hang me, Doctor," Ursula said. "Me and my mother. But I want my child to live, which he will not do if they believe he's cursed as much as I."

"I understand," he said. "Don't worry. I'll find a way to help the three of you."

Then he asked how she did, how her mother did.

"They have tried to make us confess," Ursula said, still whispering. "They have battered us with their accusations and questions. They have taken my child from me, and I know not where he is. They say I may see him again if I will admit Vulcan is my familiar, that he sucks blood from me, that he killed Thomas for me because he would not marry me."

Ursula recited again her story of how Thomas Bascombe's father Sir Richard forbade the marriage, indeed forbade any association. Nothing had changed in her account. "The fault was not Thomas's, but his father's, wherefore would I want the father of my child murdered?"

The girl began to weep. Softly at first. William wanted to see the girl's face, to see what they had done to her for himself. Somehow, he knew he would not see the same girl he had conversed with at the Old Priory. He knew suspected witches were regularly tortured. He knew what instruments were used, how applied and to what end—excruciating pain, a confession that might have no more meaning than the accused's desperate desire for a quick end. What God would be left to forgive was not the wickedness of the defendant, but the false confession of it.

"Would you do another thing for us?"

He said he would.

"Thomas has, had, a sister. Her name is Clara. She is our chief accuser."

"She grieves for her brother," William said.

"Yes, but more than that. It is not just her brother she blames us for, but has invented other wrongs we did, when in truth we did no such thing."

"What wrongs?"

"That we caused her father's cattle to die."

90

"Had you anything to do with her father's cattle?"

"No, nor did my mother, nor my father. Between our land and his is the forest. I swear before heaven that we never did. She also lays other crimes to our charge, that there is a sickness in the manor, that not only her brother but others have been sickened, though not unto death. All this she blames us for. The constable will not suffer my father to see his wife and daughter but will suffer Clara Bascombe to come to rail at us, that all in Chelmsford might know of our supposed wickedness, even before the trial."

"She came here?"

"She stood where you stand now, Doctor, and for an hour would proclaim to all that would listen that even the constable came to appease her so fearful he was that she would incite a riot in the town. She has visited the rector, four or five of the priests, the honorable justice of the peace and the Lord High Sheriff, and I knew not what other great ones of the town and county. All stand with her. None for us. But for you, Doctor, we are without help."

The girl's pleading had become almost childlike. It conveyed what for William was an unbearable desperation and neediness. He had earlier been moved by her father's appeal. It had caused him to defy his own father's counsel.

But this was worse. Her cry for help caused him pain whereas Jacob Harkness's appeal simply persuaded him intellectually that he owed a duty to the fly who had saved him from death. Yet he was wary of promising what he could not deliver. It would be too much like assuring a patient he would live when William knew death was inevitable and imminent. "I don't know what I can do to erase such enmity," William said.

"No," she said, "but perhaps you could find out its cause. That her brother is dead, her household sick. I grieve with her for such misfortune. But something more is behind her grievance against me, us, my family. You may be able to find out what it is and cure it."

"Cure it? I am a physician of the body, not the mind."

"If you were able to do that, Doctor, maybe she would withdraw her wild claims that have no truth in them."

"Perhaps she would," he said. But he had little hope. He did not know Clara Bascombe. He knew none of the Bascombes, at least personally. But they did not sound like a family easily moved, either by reason or pity.

"I will do what I can do," William said again, remembering that his father was known to the Bascombes. "Don't despair," he said to her, but got no response after. Within the stable all was as quiet as before.

"I'll be back. Have courage, and hope," he said.

She didn't answer. Silence only, the silence of despair, he thought.

He walked around to the side of the stable. Parker sat in a drunken stupor, his red, swollen face distorted, his eyelids batting, as though in a dream of furious activity, running from something.

Within minutes, William was back in his room at the Blue Boar. He removed the disguise he had worn and put it aside. They were a dead man's clothes, and he would not wear them again.

He began to think about Clara Bascombe, the sister of Ursula's dead lover. According to Ursula, Clara Bascombe had been most vocal in denouncing her neighbors at the Old Priory. William had spoken the truth to Ursula. He was a physician of the body, not the mind. He had no cure for the darker emotions of mankind: anger, jealousy, grief, rage. Even honest ignorance. But perhaps he could find a way to save the women, nonetheless.

Perhaps Clara Bascombe was that way. He knew that, even before he had any idea how he might approach her. He could wait until she made another appearance outside the stable. But she might not come again, and if she did, would she stop her invective long enough to listen to him, a man she didn't know, a man she did not care to know since he spoke on her enemies' behalf?

He did know where she lived. The Bascombes of Mowbray Rise. That was a start.

13

He went to sleep haunted by the girl's face, the face he hadn't seen. The girl whose weary and frightened voice he heard through the crack, but whose face he never saw.

His father had suggested he might be enamored of her, which was far from the truth. He was not attracted by her, at least not in that way, although he had admired her courage, her spirit, her steadfast devotion to her child, even her devotion to her dead lover. She was, as was her family, from a different world than his own. Their plight was a terrible one. They were, like the magnets that fascinated him, an attraction to every bit of malicious gossip and myth the human heart might conceive in its ignorance. And for that reason, too, he was more committed now than ever to save her, her mother, and the poor child so marked from birth that it was an invitation to all who saw him to infer some diabolical agency had been at work.

He rose the next morning, secured his horse, and having precise directions from his friend the innkeeper as to where Mowbray Rise lay, set out. Rafe had said the Rise was not far, might be reached within an hour in good weather or poor. "It is called the Rise because it sits upon one," Rafe had said, "the Mowbrays being the family that built it in ancient times."

"I'm told it's more castle than manor house," William said, remembering how Jacob Harkness had described it.

"You shall see and judge for yourself, Doctor," Rafe said with a laugh.

He had little thought as yet what his visit to the house of the Harknesses' enemies would accomplish. He could hardly ask Clara Bascombe directly about her motives, or how her brother died, even if he were privileged to speak to her and receive an honest answer untainted by enmity. Indeed, he felt the less he said about the witches the better, and certainly he did not want to introduce himself as a defender of the two women. That would raise the Bascombes' ire and undoubtedly get him thrown out before he could say his name or why he'd come.

He had conceived a plan. He would present himself as he was in fact, the eldest son of an old friend of Sir Richard, come to pay his respects and convey his father's good wishes. His appearance at the manor, though undoubtedly a surprise, would seem to any reasonable man, fitting. Yet for all that, William was unnerved by the prospect. Would the subject of the witch trial come up in casual conversation, entrapping him in some admission of his involvement? That was the risk he envisioned, and thus he felt more trepidation at this than he had the night before when he had defied the constable's order that he not speak or see the accused women upon pain of imprisonment himself.

At length he came to the village where Rafe had said the Bascombe manor was. Ursula had described the place as being of so little consequence that it barely had a name, and at once William could see why. There was a single uncobbled street, a cluster of wretched cottages, and a stone church of no architectural interest sitting at the head of the street. Above its thatched roofs rose a hill, upon which stood against the morning sky what he assumed was the manor house, although its twin towers and crenellated battlements gave more the impression of a Norman keep than a gentleman's home.

William took a deep breath, rode through the streets, drawing curious stares from the few passersby, and started up the road that led to the manor. Before he came to what was the main entrance, judging by its height and width, he paused, dismounted, and had no sooner done so, than two liveried servants came from the house and asked who he was and what he wanted.

It was not a courteous welcome, but William had not expected one, even though his dress indicated he was a gentleman, not merely a passing stranger looking for charity from the kitchen cook. To Sir Richard Bascombe and the family, he would be a stranger and to be warned off until he identified himself and, more importantly, invoked his father's name. And even then, William could not be sure his father would be remembered, or his own visit welcomed.

"I am Doctor William Gilbert. My father is an old friend of Sir Richard's. I am here to pay my respects to him and convey a message from my father."

There was, in fact, no such message. That was a lie, and as he spoke, he knew in his heart it would not be the only lie he would be telling during his visit, however long it might be. The servants looked at him as though William were a thief, come to steal the family silver. One went indoors while the other stood eyeing William suspiciously. Then within a few minutes a tall, dark-haired, well-dressed gentleman of about his father's years but of greater girth and with broader shoulders came out of the door and down the steps to where William stood. This was, by his fine coat and boots and his unmistakable look of authority, Sir Richard Bascombe. A black arm band suggested he was in mourning. The son that was dead, cursed by a witch. He looked at William and said: "You are Jerome Gilbert's son? The London doctor?"

"I am, sir."

Bascombe's face broke into a smile. He extended his arms and reached out to William to embrace him. The suspected thief had become the Prodigal Son. William breathed a sigh of relief and felt the man's powerful arms encompass him.

"You are most welcome, Doctor, to Mowbray Rise. Your father and I were friends in our youth and did some brief business together not too many years past. You were at Cambridge then, but he spoke well of you as a son a father could be proud of." He turned to one of the servants and said, "Phillip, see to Doctor Gilbert's horse. He shall not only be a visitor to Mowbray Rise but an honored guest."

Bascombe took William's arm and led him up a short flight of stairs to the door from which he had just emerged and from there into a narrow vestibule with dark paneled walls and portraits of what he assumed were Bascombe ancestors, given their solemn faces and older style clothing. They continued into a spacious and well-furnished drawing room.

Given the outward appearance of Mowbray Rise, William had expected the severity of cold stone floors and walls adorned with swords, pennants, and suits of armor. Instead, there was an assortment of chairs and tables, chests and cabinets in current styles, like those he had seen in fashionable London houses. The stone floor was well-carpeted, and against one wall was a table upon which were a variety of musical instruments; a lute, several flutes, and in a far corner were a harpsichord and spinet.

Bascombe said, "I see you are looking at the musical instruments, Doctor. I fear I have no talent in that way. All that is my daughter Clara's skill. You shall hear for yourself how gifted she is at each instrument, how sweetly she plays and sings."

"I will take much joy in it," William said, although music was not one of his favorite pastimes, nor a gift he had.

"You shall meet my daughter at supper, Doctor. And my wife and son as well." William noticed Bascombe said nothing about his recent loss. The omission was a relief. Surely any mention of the dead son would bring up the woman accused of causing the tragedy and drag William onto potentially dangerous ground.

Bascombe continued to talk about his daughter, Clara. She was twenty-two, he said, and though esteemed a great beauty and lauded for her talents, which went beyond musical skill, she had still to find a husband. "She is a young woman of refined tastes," Bascombe explained. "Several of our gallants in the county have sought her hand, but I would not force her upon one she had not chosen for herself. Do you think me too lenient a parent, Doctor?"

"Not so, Sir Richard. No man should find himself pleased to take the hand of a woman forced to marry him by parental demand." William pronounced this rule with great confidence, since he had recently seen what evil comes from a marriage arranged for the convenience of the parents.

The two men sat down on comfortable chairs arranged in front of the hearth that dominated the room and reminded him of a hearth he had seen in Amsterdam during a recent sojourn there. It was elaborately adorned with mythical figures, vines, and flowers. In itself a work of art.

"But tell me, young sir. You say you are a doctor in London. What has brought you to Chelmsford?"

It was the question William was waiting for, and he already had an answer prepared. "I have several patients in the town who, like yourself, Sir Richard, are old friends of my father and who therefore I have some obligation to attend to. But it's in London I do most of my work, and I am an officer of the College."

"College?"

"Of physicians."

"I have not heard of it. It sounds important," Bascombe said.

"Its purpose is to license those qualified by education and philosophy to heal the sick. To establish rules of best practice, and discipline those who break them to the hurt of the public. Our work is much approved by Her Majesty." William rattled this off with ease. He had often occasion to mention his affiliation with the College when he encountered new patients. Nor did it hurt to mention Her Majesty's sponsorship.

At the mention of the queen's name, Bascombe looked even more impressed than before. He may not have heard of the society to which William belonged, but he had heard of the queen and that was sufficient to put William's medical practice in a favorable light.

Several servants had come into the room during this conversation, glancing at William curiously. William noticed how solicitous they were. How they avoided looking at their master directly. Out of respect or fear or both, William couldn't tell.

He did not hesitate to explain to his host just how important the College was. That carried the conversation into a realm William felt comfortable talking about, for he had earlier discovered that the upper classes of England were generally more supportive of rules and standards in medicine than the lower, who because of ignorance or poverty tended to seek medical services from the village wise women and practitioners who learned their art from old wives' tales and outmoded practice. The poor cared little or nothing for medical licensure, although it was analogous to rules of admission and advancement of the numerous guilds into which tradesmen and their apprentices were organized.

Bascombe listened to all this without comment but with an approving smile, playing the gracious host. He offered William wine. A very select grape, Bascombe said, boasting of his cellars below the house. And it was a very good wine, William thought, very sweet and with no bitter aftertaste. But then the conversation took a different turn.

"Have you a wife, Doctor?" Bascombe asked suddenly. He leaned forward and eyed William curiously. The question brought William up short. Ursula Harkness had asked the same question. His father had played this theme, much to William's annoyance, but Bascombe was not his father. Did he wear his bachelorhood on his sleeve, that all he met wondered at his marriage state? Did they suppose if he had no wife at his age there was something wrong with him, or they should straightway find him one?

"No, Sir Richard, I have not yet had that honour."

"Do you seek a wife?" Bascombe said. The bluntness of this question also startled him, but he decided to answer forthrightly.

"I am at the present much occupied with my work." The question made him think of the Dutch girl whom he had loved and lost. He felt a sudden pain as well as a longing. Had he been successful in his suit, he might have a son or daughter by now and live comfortably in his London residence as a happy family man rather than as a bachelor. But she had married another, and by her father's account, had borne a son and died in doing it. All that remained to him were his memories of her and these were so interlaced with the tragic aspect of her history and his unintended part in it, that he could hardly think of her but there came to his mind the brutal consequences of their relationship.

William told Bascombe about his London patients without naming names or conditions, which he believed improper in a responsible physician, his charitable work at Bethlehem hospital, commonly and ironically called Bedlam, even about his interest in magnets and his desire to write a book someday reporting his experiments and conclusions. Bascombe showed an interest in these. He listened patiently while William explained his theory of the lodestone, its operation, and its relationship to the earth.

William could not help but speak long and passionately on this topic. While at Cambridge, his peculiar fascination had earned him the nickname of "Doctor Magnetic," a cognomen intended he learned afterwards to deride him and his hobby horse rather than praise him. He cared little about that now. His university days were past. His present life was too engaging and demanding to allow him time or interest to look behind him, either with pride or regret.

Bascombe's questions about this were courteous and seemingly sincere, but it soon became evident to William that his host was not a particularly learned man, although he was well spoken and, by Rafe Tuttle's word, was a prosperous if demanding landlord. His chief interest, insofar as William could tell, was the Bascombe estate and by other signs, hunting and shooting. This was consistent with what William's father had said about his old childhood friend, that his heart and soul were his property and its expansion.

While they talked, William took in the room around him, noticing the elegance of the furnishings, the finely crafted furniture, and the wall hangings that depicted rural scenes quite different from the Essex landscape he was accustomed to. They seemed more to suggest Italy or France, with vine-covered hills and trees of a variety he had not seen in his native land.

There were shepherds depicted as well, quaint, idealized villages, grazing cattle, sheep and goats. The hearth that dominated the room was rimmed with marble and the mantle looked made of the same material. All indicated that the master of Mowbray Rise had spared no expense in making his house a monument to his own wealth and stature in the neighborhood.

There were also the dogs, three of which were gathered around the chairs William and his host sat in, long-legged, sharp-nosed hounds, dozing mostly, occasionally raising their sleek heads to look at him. William thought of Ursula's dog. Vulcan. He would be a match for all of them, William thought, all at one time.

"What think you, Doctor, of Mowbray Rise? Do tell me your first impression," Bascombe asked, leaning toward William and smiling genially as though William had only been waiting an opportunity to praise his host's dwelling.

"I think, sir, it is a most excellent habitation, quite remarkable in its architecture."

"Remarkable, how?"

"Well, Sir Richard, when first I viewed it, I thought it not a manor house but a castle keep, built to repel invaders and defend the village below it."

Bascombe laughed. "You are not the first visitor here to answer my question thus, almost in the exact words. Indeed, it was what possessed my father to own it. He had been a soldier in the wars and all his idle talk was of battles he had fought and friends who had died around him. Had my mother not intervened, he would have turned the house into a fortress, stripped it bare, and made every bedchamber a barracks or redoubt. After supper, which I must press you to stay for, I will give you the grand tour. You shall see things you have but dreamed of and wish that every house had such conveniences. Speaking of which, where are you staying while you are in Chelmsford?"

"The Blue Boar," William said.

"Ah, I know it well. Rafe Tuttle is the innkeeper there. A good man of business, he."

"He is an old friend. When my father and I journey to London we stay there on the way."

"The Blue Boar is well-appointed as inns go, but I must prevail upon you to stay at the Rise while you are here. It is the least I can do to honor my friendship with your father that I should show courtesy to his son."

"I would not be such a burden to you, sir," William said.

"Nonsense," his host said, leaning forward and patting William on the knee. "You must stay with us."

"Then I shall accept your hospitality gladly, sir, and do thank you for the offer. My father has always spoken well of you."

Bascombe said a few more praising words about William's father, but it was clear from his comments that Jerome Gilbert and Sir Richard Bascombe had had little contact for the past twenty years. Bascombe knew his father was a lawyer but had not known of the death of Willliam's mother, his father's remarriage, or the status William's father presently enjoyed in Colchester. His memories were largely boyhood memories, and faint ones at that, in which one boyhood adventure is easily confused with another. He said nothing of having consulted his father more recently on a legal matter.

An old man in livery entered and, on Sir Richard's command, showed William where he was to lodge at the Rise. On the way upstairs, the servant, who looked about sixty, said in a confidential voice, "My master has few visitors these days, Doctor. That you are invited to stay the night is a rare privilege."

"I am honored then," William said. "Your master seems the soul of courtesy in every respect."

The old man chuckled, looked at William and winked. He continued to keep his voice low. "So he may seem, Doctor, at least for now, but I would take care, sir, were I you."

William asked why.

"My master is a man of many moods. It pleases him now to play the generous host, but I've seen him in other tempers where nothing pleases him nor could it ever. Indeed, sir, he is much like our English weather. If you like it not, wait. It will betimes change for the better, or for the worse."

They came to a door and William entered, to find a comfortably furnished bedchamber with one rather small window, more suited for an archer's bow than to let in light. He walked toward it and looked out. It gave an expansive view of the village below and the forest beyond, within which was the ruined priory Sir Richard Bascombe so much coveted and whose denizens the Bascombes now threatened.

"Will this do for you, Doctor?" the old servant asked.

William said it would.

The old man said his name was Sanderson and that he would be attending to the doctor's needs while he was at the Rise.

"Just Sanderson?" William asked. "You have no Christian name?"

"Just Sanderson, Doctor. If I ever had a first name, I have long ago forgotten it. And none in this house needs to know it to call me to my duty."

The old man left, and William went to the open window and looked out toward the village and the forest beyond. It was a bracing view. He filled his lungs with the country air, so much healthier than the smoke and fog of the city. Between the manor and the forest were stretches of open land, green pasture, but he saw no sheep, no cattle, no horses.

He turned away from the window, removed his shoes, flopped onto the bed, and looked up at the ceiling. There was a biblical scene painted there. Samson and Delilah, but a poor emaciated hero with close-cropped hair, in chains, his strength sapped by female betrayal. William was no judge of art, but the painting seemed poorly done, apprentice work, uninspired and somehow inappropriate for a bedchamber where an amorous couple might find a moral lesson not conducive to their love-making.

He appreciated this time alone. He needed time to collect his impressions, which were mixed and made more so by Sanderson's comment. Bascombe said the whole family would attend at supper. That meant Clara Bascombe as well. His host seemed a more complex man than he had first seemed. Would he find the knight's daughter equally complex?

When Bascombe had invited him to stay, William's first instinct was to decline politely, to make some plausible excuse. He was, after all, on dangerous ground. But he could not think of doing so. He had paid his visit to Mowbray Rise under false pretenses. He was not really there to give his father's regards to his old friend, or deliver an imagined message, but to act as a spy. He knew this, and his greatest fear was that Sir Richard would come to know it as well and this would undo his efforts to help in the trial.

It might also subject him to danger. He remembered the strength in his host's arms when he had embraced him. It was more than an embrace; it was vice-like. It sent a chill through him to think of it. But exposure and whatever followed was a risk William was prepared to take. He had made a promise to Jacob Harkness, reiterated it to his daughter. He had no thought of turning aside from either.

Nor was he deterred by Sanderson's warning about Bascombe's changing moods. For the moment, William was basking in his host's approval. Who knew but that, that moment of sunshine would last the duration of his visit, which would, after all, be short? When the weather changed, he would deal with whatever that change wrought.

Bascombe had sent another servant to Chelmsford to fetch William's things and to inform the innkeeper that his guest would not be returning for the next day or so. William wondered what Rafe would think. Would he suppose William had gone over to the other side, cozied up to the rich man in the neighborhood and abandoned the poor women? If that is what Rafe might think, William would set him straight later. At most, he believed, his stay at Rise would be but a few days. After that, he would return to Chelmsford, make another effort to see the Harkness women.

In the meantime, he would gain a better understanding of the wasting illness that had taken the life of Ursula's lover.

15

William remained in his room reading until he was fetched by Sanderson, the elderly servant who had escorted him there, and told him to be wary of his master's shifting moods. The old man spoke no more of this, only mentioned he had served at the Rise since he was a boy, knew well the old master, "him who nearly lost all through his profligacy."

Sanderson said he looked to die in service. "Some of us who serve here are buried on these very grounds, Doctor." Sanderson said this with evident satisfaction, as though he were looking forward to the event.

William was now led down the stairs to the same drawing room where he had visited earlier that day. When they arrived there, he found the family had gathered. There was a well-dressed older woman whom William assumed was Bascombe's lady wife, although she was not introduced as such, who seemed content to sit and smile at whatever was said and looked upon William once and then turned away, seemingly preoccupied with her own thoughts and indifferent to what was going on around her. A stocky young man of about twenty-five or six with a darker countenance, low brow, and a fringe of curly black beard was introduced as Bascombe's son, Julian. The surviving son and now, presumably, heir.

William bowed in acknowledgment of Julian Bascomb, but the young man hardly looked up. He sat downcast, as though he had just been disciplined by his father and enjoined to silence.

And finally, there was a young woman dressed elegantly in a green and silver silken gown and with fine yellow hair tucked within a bejeweled velvet cap. She was sitting in a straight back chair, looking very regal. She regarded him with a quizzical expression, her wide-set eyes and bow-shaped mouth set in a slight smile.

But the most notable feature of the girl was her coloring, or rather the lack of it. Her face, neck, and what he could see of her breasts, were startling white. Not the whiteness of an albino, a condition William had observed more than once in his countrymen, but an angelic whiteness, a purity, that suggested any red, tan, or brown was no mere attribute, but a stain. Even his Dutch girl had had no such complexion as this, and William found it both attractive and unsettling at the same time, as though the natural flesh he might have expected had been somehow exchanged for something unnatural.

William knew this could only be Clara Bascombe. And he realized the whiteness of her skin was a cosmetic. He guessed what the cosmetic was: Venetian ceruse, a concoction of white lead, water, and vinegar, painted onto the face and other body parts. He had seen it on women's faces in London, and on some men as well. It was a fashion and, to William's mind, a dangerous one, given the ingredients.

Bascombe gestured toward William and said, "Clara, this gentleman is William Gilbert, physician. He is a graduate of our great university at Cambridge. He lives and practices in London now, but is the son of my old friend, Jerome Gilbert, of whom you may have heard me speak. I do believe he has a brilliant future ahead of him, even at court."

Bascombe's praise seemed excessive to William, who while not without ambition was hardly aiming at so high a state. He found himself blushing furiously, a trait he detested in himself and for which he was sometimes mocked. It was clear from Clara Bascombe's expression that she had not heard her father ever speak of Jerome Gilbert, but she did not correct him, and nodded amiably.

"I am most happy to make your acquaintance, Doctor Gilbert," she said, with a slow bow of her head and half-closed eyes, almost as if she were drifting off to sleep. William thought she had a lovely smile that showed in her eyes as well as her mouth. "We rarely entertain visitors at Mowbray Rise. I do hope your stay with us is a benefit to you—and a pleasure, as well."

"I am sure it shall be, even as you say it, Lady Clara."

William's life up to this time had been largely a student's life. Only recently had he begun his practice, and learned the finer skills of social engagement that were expected of him in polite society, mingling as he did now not only with the rich but the high born. But he was a fast learner and was committed to the idea that his way in life would be the smoother if he practiced courtesy, with those above him and those below. Part of him disdained the conventions of rank and degree that characterized the society of England and every other country in the world he knew of, but he did not feel compelled to counter it with any revolutionary notions of social equality. He was gentry by virtue of his father's enjoying the same status in Colchester. That he was a physician and member of the College of Physicians strengthened that status. Lady Clara was the daughter of a knight. They were not quite equals, yet they were close, close enough for her father to suppose he might be a match for her, which William had concluded to be the reason for Bascombe asking about his marriage status.

A manservant entered to say that supper would be served presently. Bascombe suggested in the meantime everyone sit, which all did except for Julian Bascombe, who stood in the corner watching William warily. As for Clara, William noticed that she made an effort to sit opposite him rather than sitting near her mother, who if anything seemed unhappy with the presence of a stranger, as though his very arrival had disturbed a delicate balance in the Bascombe family comity.

The manservant who had announced the oncoming of supper now stoked the fire on the hearth to make it greater. John Bascombe admitted that though Mowbray Rise was well furnished within, it was a cold house and even in summertime there was cause to light fires in every chamber. Bascombe invited William to tell his story again, recount his birth, his education, his present vocation as a doctor. William did so, but omitted mention of the College. Through all this narrative Julian Bascombe said nothing. He seemed unimpressed by William's attainments and hardly seemed to pay attention to anyone in the room, William assumed that if Bascombe's younger son had any distinctions to note, his father would have cheerfully announced them.

But about his daughter Clara, Bascombe was effusive. Much of his praise repeated what he had told William earlier, if anything, enlarging on the earlier encomium, presenting her as a paragon of feminine virtues. He noted she was unmarried. This he presented not as a failure of opportunity, but a demonstration of her judgment and good sense. She had had suitors, he remarked, but they had not passed muster, at least in her father's estimation. He implied that Clara agreed.

Clara Bascombe sat through this discussion of her personal affairs with what William thought was extraordinary patience and equanimity. He could not have endured his father's praising him to another or rattling on about his love life, such as it was, with William sitting there, without embarrassment. But perhaps, he concluded, Clara was accustomed to it. He had already detected, beneath Sir Richard Bascombe's smiling exterior, a domineering spirit. His women, wife and daughter, knew their place.

"After supper, we shall have Clara play," Bascombe continued. "Her music, I mean."

"And what shall I play, father?" Clara asked in a voice as small and delicate as her body.

"Why, what you will, daughter. Doctor Gilbert is a lover of music, so he tells me. I am sure he will be pleased with whatever instrument you choose and were you to add your voice to it, his pleasure and my own would be increased thereby."

The girl nodded respectfully, first to her father, then to William, at whom she smiled. It was a small smile, perfectly decorous with a man she had just met and who had been presented to her as the son of her father's friend. Bascombe had said that she had had many suitors. William knew such assertions by parents were sometimes exaggerated, sometimes brazen lies, but William had no doubt there had been men interested in this woman with so white a face. She was young, but she had a mature composure belied by her delicate stature and what he imagined—since they were concealed by her garments—as her thin arms and limbs, and the small white hands and delicate wrists that he could see. Observing her and hearing her speaking later at table where a sumptuous feast was served, William could not help thinking of Ursula Harkness, Clara Bascombe's great enemy. How different the women were, one so cultured and refined, the other primitive and wild like the wolf dog thought to be her familiar.

Before supper, except for William's account of his background rendered by invitation of the head of the house, Bascombe had done most if not all the talking. William had the sense that this was typical of the Bascombe family polity: a strong, domineering father with subservient women and a son who by his sullen expression and wariness with strangers lived restive under the paternal thumb.

While everyone ate, Bascombe continued talking; talking about his tenant farmers and herders, his investments in London—which by his account had been more successful this year than the last—and his connections at court—a topic that seemed to give him particular pleasure. All this information about Bascombe's wealth his wife and children would surely know. But not the London doctor. He realized this was all for him. Implicit in all, was the size of Clara Bascombe's dowry. He was surprised that Bascombe had not already named the sum, flaunted it at table like a prize goose on a silver platter.

The rest of the family members listened. He was relieved that nothing was said by Bascombe or his children about the upcoming witch trial, or the Old Priory which he had been given to understand by Rafe Tuttle might be at the heart of the matter. Of these things, Bascombe said nothing.

After supper they returned to the drawing room, took chairs again, and Clara rose to take up one of the two lutes he had seen before. She sat upon a stool, cradled the instrument in her arms as though it were a child, and plucked the strings with a delicate touch. It was a sweet melody that William had heard before, but when Clara began to sing, he was captivated by her voice. It was, when she sang, surprisingly low for a woman, even husky, and William thought it thoroughly enchanting.

The song was a somber lament about two star-crossed lovers who run from their families to start a life together, only to have the girl die. Her young man then dies himself, of grief, at the song's conclusion. It was not a theme to instill cheer in the company or hope in love, but the family applauded when she finished, and her father beseeched her to sing again, which she did. She completed her evening's concert by playing the spinet. She had a sure, delicate control, and as little as William knew about music, he recognized that she had been well trained. He wondered what other skills she had. Could she read, could she cypher? Many women of her class could not; and cared not to learn. They were read to, their letters were written by secretaries, clerks, or ladies in waiting fortunate enough to have broadminded fathers who had been content for their daughters to have tutors. Did she have a curious mind? Would she appreciate his science, much less understand his passion for it?

And he wondered why he cared. He reminded himself of his mission. He had come to Mowbray Rise as a spy, not a suitor to its master's nubile daughter.

The evening ended. Clara excused herself, claiming that she found performance exhausting and had a devastating headache. He was not displeased when she turned before leaving the room and glanced once at him. It was indeed more than a glance, he thought. It was an inviting look coupled with a slight, almost mischievous, smile—as though she well knew what her father was about. Then her father and mother bid him goodnight, explaining that it was their custom to retire early.

"Good night, Doctor Gilbert. You are right welcome at the Rise, not only for your father's sake but for your own, sir."

Bascombe extended his arms and again embraced William, who for a moment half expected the gentleman would kiss him on the cheek. He felt his face flush with embarrassment and tried to think of something appropriate to say in response, but he had never been quick with words in awkward social situations, so he stood like a statue, staring at the door through which the master of the house and his lady had just passed.

Behind him, he heard a slight cough, a clearing of a throat. He turned back to the room. Unlike his father and mother, Julian Bascombe had not retired. He remained in place, propped up by the mantle of the fireplace, sneering at William. It was almost a malicious look, completely inexplicable to William's way of thinking since he could not imagine what he had done or said or was to so offend this young man.

"Good night, Master Bascombe," William said.

"Good night, Doctor," Julian said. And then, "A word before you go, if you please."

Julian took a chair, the one his father had occupied earlier, and bid William sit opposite him, in what struck William as more a command to sit than an invitation. William bristled but complied.

15

At supper, this thick-bodied, sullen young man had eaten little, said nothing to anyone, and ignored him, as if William were invisible. William had noticed the slight, but had made nothing of it, assuming Sir Richard's younger son was simply another discontented and idle youth, living off his father and spending his days in idleness, or in hunting and shooting, which to William amounted to the same thing. But now the two were alone, and he did not expect a warm embrace from Julian Bascombe, who he saw, despite his apparent indolence, wore a pearl-handled dagger at his side, doubtlessly in some sort of infantile show of manliness.

"So, you are a doctor, are you?" Julian said, looking at William up and down as though estimating the cost or fit of his doublet and hose.

William said he was, wondering that he should be asked such a question given that he was introduced as such earlier and his medical practice was commented on several times during the evening by Sir Richard in the midst of all the adulation of Clara.

"And live in London?"

"It is where I practice, therefore where I live."

"You must have patients who pay you well, for I have heard doctors demand great fees for their services in London."

"Some whom I attend are among the poorest of the city," William said. "Those I attend gratis. Others live quite well, and they pay no more than I deserve."

Julian Bascombe gave William an incredulous grin.

"Gratis, is it? What manner of doctor is it who provides his expertise for nothing?"

"One who believes charity is its own reward," William said.

"Are you Christian, then? I pray you are not a papist."

"I am of the queen's church, sir. I have no fealty to any foreign potentate, be he king or pope."

Julian looked relieved, or at least pretended to. He said, "I cannot abide papists, or those who suffer them. Now my brother Thomas was more tolerant than I, but then he's dead, as I think you've learned. He went down the wrong road and fell, at last, into a ditch. The house is in mourning for him, but you notice I wear no mourning band. He and I were never friends, though brothers. Do you think that strange, Doctor?"

"I have heard of it, between brothers," William said.

An awkward silence followed. William resolved to say good night and go to bed. The words were on his lips when Julian got up from the chair and said, "You doubtless wonder at my curiosity, Doctor. It is not idle curiosity, I assure you. We are a family of some wealth and distinction, as you have doubtless noticed."

"Your father made that plain at supper," William said.

"And my father has a daughter, and I a sister, of marriageable age. A certain kind of man might find that a bright prospect of increasing his own wealth."

William pretended he didn't know what Julian Bascombe was talking about.

"I mean by marrying up, marrying a rich man's daughter."

"I am not, sir, in the market for a wife," William said, finding the implication that he was a fortune hunter insulting. "Your sister is an attractive young woman, very amiable and talented as she has indeed shown this evening. But I'm not come to sue for her favors, as I said earlier, but to bring the regards of my father to his old friend. As for dowries, I am sure your sister's greatest dowry is her virtue and intelligence, which I do respect, but I have no aims beyond a friendship with your family appropriate to your station and the station of my family."

"And what station would that be? You are a doctor, well and good, but what of your family? My father says he knows yours, but in what respect? As a household servant, a school friend, or distant cousin?"

"My father is a judge, the recorder for the borough of Colchester. He is a man of some eminence in our town. My mother was kin to the Coggeshalls of Gosfield."

Julian made a face. "Never heard of it, the town you mention, nor the family."

"They are a family of some distinction."

"As I say, I have not heard either good or ill of these, what is the name?"

"Coggeshall."

"Yes, a strange name indeed. Is it English?"

"It is."

"I thought it might be foreign."

"It is a good English name," William said curtly. "There is a village not far from here so named. There have been Coggeshalls in Essex for centuries."

William was not prepared to give this rude young man a geography lesson, or explain how his father's social position in Colchester made him, and William by extension, gentry. He wondered that Julian Bascombe, so reticent to speak during the meal and after, should suddenly become so voluble—and insulting, as though throughout the night he had been storing up his suspicions and resentments only waiting for the moment when he and William might be alone, out of sight of parents and sister who would surely have disapproved of his being so discourteous to a guest his father had chosen to honor.

William felt himself heating up, an emotion he rarely experienced since he was by nature a diligent avoider of physical conflict, as zealous as he could be in pressing home ideas. He took a deep breath, then said, "I repeat, sir. I am not here to court your sister, to covet your father's money, or to offend you by my presence, which I have clearly done, else you would not have treated me with such rudeness."

"I, rude, Doctor?" Julian Bascombe said, wide-eyed with false amazement. "Why, you misunderstand me, sir. If I mistook your purpose here, I beg you forgive me. I thought you came to pay court to my dear sister. There have been so many suitors, you know, at least six or seven this past year."

William said, "Then your sister is fortunate to have so many eligible gentlemen to choose from."

"Oh, she may choose as she wills," Julian Bascombe said. "Yet she must find one who will choose her… after they get to know her."

"Then you insult your sister in thinking too little of her," William said. "She seems to me to be a most attractive young woman. I wonder that you should speak so ill of her."

"Do you, Doctor? Then we shall see… or I mean, you shall see soon enough."

Julian Bascombe said goodnight, leaving William to find his way up to his room, with no servant to escort him.

111

No matter, he knew the way.

His unpleasant conversation with Julian Bascombe had left a bad taste in his mouth which almost entirely spoiled his memory of the fine supper and Clara Bascombe's impromptu concert. He wondered that an exchange that could not have taken longer than a quarter of an hour so turned on its head any pleasure he had had. He wondered, too, not so much of Julian Bascombe's suspicious nature as his cruel dismissal of his sister's marriage prospects. William had a handful of siblings and half siblings from his father's two marriages. With these, he got along quite well. But he had seen enough in families to understand that blood ties, usually nurturing, were sometimes rife with rivalry and even hatred, so that the very name of family was mocked when applied to such discordant relationships.

As his candle burned low, he placed it by his bed, undressed and dressed again in a thin gown that was among the things Bascombe's servant had fetched from the inn. He walked to the window to open it. It resisted his effort and he had to give it several blows with the flat of his hand before it yielded. Like most of his countrymen, he was a staunch believer in the virtues of night air. Even if it often resulted in a chilly bedchamber and an occasional visiting bat.

He looked out over the village below the castle-like manor. He had to imagine where the village lay, for all was dark below. No lights to be seen, but then there would not be in so humble a place. Its denizens would go to bed with the coming of dark, rise with the dawn or before. All would be ruled by the sun, although William dreamed of some future day when it would be otherwise, when by some power, not magic but science, man would conquer the night, illuminate what he willed and when.

As for this present night itself, it was clear, the heavens spread open like a great map, and a round moon sailing like one of Her Majesty's great galleons through a sea of stars.

It was a bracing view of earthly beauty and heavenly, too. It was a testimony of the great design and of Him who designed it, for William, no religious zealot, was what he would have called an ordinary Christian of unexceptional virtue, even as he had declared to Julian Bascombe.

He returned to bed, blew out the light, and stretched his legs to enjoy the comfort of fresh-scented sheets and a down-filled pillow of extraordinary softness.

Almost at once, the image of Clara Bascombe came into his mind. He saw her form and face in every detail he remembered from the evening. He saw her slender arms and small, white hands, white but not as pale as her face. He remembered the glances she had given him when she had left for bed. But then he thought of her brother, an insolent, ill-tempered young man given to suspicious fantasies and armed with a dagger as if he needed to fend off enemies in his own house.

William resolved to avoid him so long as he stayed at the Rise, a visit he hoped would be brief.

William was on the cusp of sleep when he heard it; a prolonged, mournful howl. For a moment he thought he might be dreaming, but he sat up in bed and then heard the sound again. It was a single creature, not a pack. And it was the cry of a wolf, if he was not mistaken. Surely no dog or other creature could make such a sound, so dominate the otherwise silence of the night, so chill him.

And it was then that he remembered the women, the accused witches, the reason that he was at the Rise. Was the creature out in the night Ursula's dog, calling him back to his duty, away from distractions such as Sir Richard Bascombe's wealth and his appealing daughter? Or some random animal of the night, its soulful cry without clear meaning or purpose?

It was a fanciful notion of the sort to which he was not usually given. But he could not get it out of his head.

16

Upon waking, it took William more than a few minutes to remember where he was and even longer to recollect why. The night had turned cold. He rose from the bed and went to the window and closed it. He had not been able to see the houses of the village the night before. Now, he could see rooftops, and the steeple of the church and far beyond, the forest and within that, hidden from his sight, the Old Priory.

Two quick knocks at the door. Sanderson again, smiling benignly. Breakfast was served below. The family was awaiting their honored guest. The old man waited while William dressed.

The family breakfasted in the same spacious room where they had supped the night before. Sir Richard, his lady wife, and son, Julian, looked up as he entered. Bascombe greeted him. His wife and son said nothing. Evidently, Clara Bascombe had yet to come down. After inquiring how William spent the night, Bascombe said, "I owe you an apology, Doctor Gilbert. So taken were we all by my daughter's musical accomplishments I quite forget I had promised you a tour of the house. And, as bad luck would have it, this morning I have some matter of business to conduct with several of my tenants. I trust you will not be disappointed if my daughter Clara takes my place as your guide."

He was not disappointed. He remembered Jacob Harkness had assigned his daughter to guide him back to the London road. Now, another father was appointing his daughter as a guide. He was relieved Bascombe's substitute would not be his son. Julian had adopted the same sullen manner at breakfast as the night before and would surely have used the occasion to insult him the more, as soon as they were outside his father's hearing.

"The Lady Clara is out riding now," Bascombe said. "Her habit in the morning, for among her other attributes she is an excellent horsewoman. Do you ride, Doctor?"

"To get from one place to the other, Sir Richard. But for sport or pleasure, no." He joined the family at the table. A servant put food before him.

"Perhaps the Lady Clara can teach you, that you may enjoy the sport as much as she."

Her father no sooner said this, but the lady herself appeared, dressed smartly in a riding garb of forest green and close-fitting pantaloons that showed her slender hips and well-shaped calves. She still seemed out of breath from her exertion. There was a quick exchange of greetings and then Bascombe told his daughter she was to be guide to their visitor, for the promised tour of the house.

"I would not impose on you, Lady Clara," William said.

"No imposition, Doctor, I assure you. The pleasure will be mine. You see, unlike some who live in great houses I not only enjoy the conveniences of my habitation but also its peculiar history. I have an interest in things historical in general."

"Oh, do you?" he said, somewhat surprised by this new window to her character.

"You think that strange, that I, a woman, should take note of such things?"

"Not at all," he said. "Our queen does set an example of intellectual curiosity about a great many things, both in nature and in the actions of men."

Clara smiled and gave a little bow, which he returned. "I pray you wait for me. I need to change from this garb that smells I am sure of my horse and freshen myself. I shall not be long."

"I'll wait," he said, bowing.

He watched Clara Bascombe ascend the stairs, once stopping to turn and look back at him, then disappear around a corner. But no sooner had he lost sight of her than another woman appeared at the top of the stairs and began to descend slowly. This was a dark-haired, older woman, perhaps forty or even fifty, stern-faced and by her dress a higher servant, perhaps a personal maid to Clara or her mother. She came down the stairs and came up to William.

"You are the doctor from London," she said, after introducing herself as Lady Clara's secretary and companion. Agnes Robinson. "My lady has spoken much of you since your arrival. She refers to you as a most courteous gentleman."

"She does me too much honor, Mistress Robinson."

Agnes Robinson smiled. "Not so, sir, with all respect to yourself, Lady Clara is a shrewd judge of men, can distinguish a wise man from a fool, and a saint from a scoundrel, in the blink of an eye. She is young in years, but old in wisdom."

William said he had himself adjudged Clara to be a young woman of intelligence and judgment.

"To tell truth, sir, she has had already many young men come to Mowbray Rise to pay court to her and turned them flat away, seeing in them not what she desired in a suitor, much less a husband. When she marries, sir, she will marry well, if you know what I mean."

"You mean she will marry a man titled, not just a gentleman," William said.

Agnes Robinson closed her eyes for a moment as though to offer a quick prayer to deity, and then smiled again. "I see you are a man of discernment," she said. Then she bowed to him and said, "Should you need aught of me, Doctor Gilbert, I am at your disposal."

William watched her go into the back parts of the house. The woman walked with great dignity as though Mowbray Rise was hers as much as it was her mistress's. William realized he had just been warned off. Not as crudely as Clara's brother had done the night before with his personal insults and cynical disparagements. Agnes Robinson had been more subtle in her warning: Clara Bascombe was destined to become the wife of someone of stature, a lord or even someone higher, someone monied, pedigreed, connected. Definitely not the wife of a mere doctor in the city, regardless of what Sir Richard Bascombe had called William's potential. William might look if he chose, he might admire Agnes's mistress and imagine in his heart how he might win her and bed her, but ultimately his suit was hopeless.

London doctor, the lady is not for you.

That's what Agnes Robinson had said, in so many words.

17

It was near an hour before Clara Bascombe reappeared, during which time William was asked a dozen questions by her father about various physical ailments that either he or his wife suffered from, now or in the past. Both, it seemed, had been plagued during their adult years with illnesses minor and some serious, as had their three children. "God's beneficence preserved our lives until this hour but in the interim did not spare us physical conditions that warranted doctors' care and earnest prayer."

Then he mentioned his daughter.

"The Lady Clara is as healthy as a horse, of course. We look forward to equally healthy grandsons, in God's time."

William remembered that Clara Bascombe had excused herself the night before complaining of a headache. A not uncommon affliction, although if recurrent not necessarily a sign of radiant health. He decided the headache didn't necessarily contradict Bascombe's rosy assessment of his daughter's physical fitness, for childbirth or anything else. But then he was an indulgent father, marketing his marriageable daughter, not a physician.

Nonetheless, to Bascombe's account of his family's health, William listened carefully, as he was wont when a patient described his condition, answering what questions he could. He had a good understanding of the various diseases most common among his countrymen, the cures or mitigations most favored by his colleagues, and the less common conditions that remained a mystery as to cause or relief. Most of the foregoing he had had direct experience with. Others he knew only indirectly from his reading or the accounts of fellow practitioners.

Then William asked the question he had been waiting to ask. He said, "I understand your late son passed after a lengthy illness. Was he under a doctor's care at the time of his death?"

The question seemed innocent enough to William's ear, but Bascombe seemed uneasy with it. William could tell by the man's shifting in his chair and hesitant response.

"Actually, no," he said. "You see we always expected he would get well, that his aches and pains, his sufferings would pass. With all due respect to you who are a graduate of our esteemed university, Doctor Gilbert, most who provide for us in this region of the county are purveyors of old remedies and dubious cures. They have no proper training for their function. Some are but frauds and mountebanks preying on those of us in need. For the last several months of my son's illness he was cared for by his sister."

"Lady Clara."

"Yes."

"I am constantly amazed by your daughter's proficiencies," William said. "She is indeed an excellent lady."

"I am heartily glad you find her so," Bascombe said. "Every father wants to hear such words on a gentleman's lips, be they flattery or no."

"I swear I do not flatter, Sir Richard. It's not a skill I have."

Clara's father smiled genially. "She and her brother were very close. Twins, in fact, though fraternal, not identical, of course."

"His death must have caused her great grief," William said.

"She grieves still," Bascombe said. "Granted, she puts a brave face upon her sorrow and seems merry without when she grieves within. He is buried here at the manor. On your tour you will see his grave and how she adorns it with flowers each day in his memory. Of course, all in this house mourn for him, even the servants who waited upon him."

Bascombe paused and looked down. William wondered if Julian the malcontent surviving brother was among those who mourned. In his conversation with William, Julian had spoken scornfully of his brother, had shown even greater disregard for his sister except where it touched upon his own pride and position.

"So, no physician came to diagnose his condition, to give it a name or offer a remedy?" William asked.

"Well, a physician came, a physician of sorts. He did nothing, nothing that is that helped, though we think we know whereof my son died."

"And that was?"

"Do you believe in witches, Doctor?"

118

"I think there are some who believe themselves to be so and concoct spells and call upon the Father of Lies and evil spirits to further their ends."

"And deserve therefore to be punished for their crimes against man and God?" Bascombe asked.

"I think they deserve to be punished if proof is offered to justify their prosecution and punishment."

"Ah," said Bascombe. "But what manner of proof?"

William hesitated before answering. It was the conversation he had hoped to avoid, but now it was too late.

"Proof beyond the mere assertion of guilt by one who is a known enemy of the accused," William said. "Any man or woman can accuse another of whatever displeases them. Without evidence, how can the truth be known?"

"You make a thoughtful point, Doctor," Bascombe said. "Yet do you not ignore the fact that witchcraft in its very meaning deals with things above nature, touches upon the realms of spirit, the influence of the Evil One and, by correspondence, He who is all good. I mean, might God Himself not reveal by revelation the wicked source of another's power? We may be blind to the evil around us, but God is not blind. He sees within." Bascombe tapped his chest and repeated, "He sees within."

"I grant you, sir, God is not blind. But I am a doctor, sir, not a theologian. I must leave these mysteries to those who have spent their lives studying them. I am more an observer of nature, not a delver into the supernatural. I can tell you about the body and its parts, about minerals and the mechanisms of physics and such things, for these have come within the scope of my interest and diligent study, but as to witches and their works, familiar spirits, and devilish spells I must defer to one more studied in these matters than I."

William might have said more about his own beliefs, many of which he acknowledged to be out of the mainstream of thought of his contemporaries, but was prevented by the reappearance of Clara Bascombe. He was relieved. The last thing he wanted was to get into the thicket with his host over whether witches were or weren't. That was dangerous ground, and for more reasons than one.

18

William reckoned it had been nearly an hour since Clara Bascombe had gone, promising to be quick in changing. Now she appeared at the top of the stairs, fully gowned, her ceruse reapplied, her low bodice revealing a generous swath of her breasts, which were whitened like her face and throat. She came down the stairs from her rooms above laughing and, seeing him at once, began to apologize for the delay, though she immediately changed the topic to the dubious competence of her maid, who she said was a silly girl, as colorblind as she was deaf, and how her help to her was more hindrance than otherwise.

William assumed this description did not apply to the stern companion with whom he had spoken only minutes before. Agnes Robinson was no mere maid, no mere secretary and companion. She was evidently counselor and second mother to Clara. A woman to be reckoned with in the household.

Upon his daughter's arrival, Bascombe turned to William. "I promise you, Doctor, you will find in my daughter a most knowledgeable guide to this house. She knows its history better than I, and having lived here since her birth, she knows every dark corner and closet. She can also introduce you to the delights of the garden, some plantings in which have survived generations and still do bloom faithfully."

"I will put my trust in your daughter gladly," William said, bowing to the lady.

"And so you may, Doctor," his guide responded, taking his hand and leading him into the drawing room. "You may wonder at the appearance of this house, which seems built more for war than for comfort of those who dwell within," she began.

"Yes, I was surprised, although I have seen other houses in our part of England also fitted to repel invaders."

"To my knowledge this house has never been so used," she said. "Its builder was one of the knights of William, he who in our dusty history is called the Conqueror. This was hundreds of years before our time. This knight, whose name was Alain Mowbray, was said to have been given the whole grant of this land for services he rendered when William invaded and conquered at the great battle at Hastings. It is said that this knight wanted a house for himself and his family that would resemble those he had known in France, such houses that had indeed experienced the din and cry of battle. It was ten years in the building, from the foundation thereof to the highest battlement you have seen and on the day he completed it, Alain Mowbray died. He is buried in the chapel, beneath the floor. I'll show it to you. You shall see for yourself."

"So, his heirs were left to enjoy the fruit of his labor?" William said.

"And enjoy it they did, for they added to the land and because they were rich and devout, they gave money that a priory of righteous nuns might be built, both to praise God and atone for their sins, for they were worldly men, though devoted."

"Does the priory still stand?" William asked, as if he didn't know.

"It does, though most in ruins," she said, "and of course the nuns who lived there are long gone. Indeed, they were worldly nuns, who practiced black arts and unlawful relations with equally wicked and corrupt monks and priests. It is an unsavory story, Doctor. I could go on in detail, but modesty prevents me."

William asked if the Priory were to be part of the tour.

"Oh, no. Regrettably it is in other hands. At least for the time being, and my father has forbidden me and my brother to go there."

He noted that Clara Bascombe said nothing about the controversy over the ownership of the Old Priory, and he decided to say nothing about what he had learned from the Harknesses or Rafe Tuttle for fear this would offend and deter other revelations of the history.

"But now for your tour," she said with a radiant smile.

For the rest of the morning, she guided him from room to room, pointing out this wall hanging, this article of furniture, this stern-faced ancestor hanging in portraiture, commenting on the origin and often the cost of each. Those on the main floor of the house, the drawing room, the great hall, which he had not before seen, and the room in which they had supped the night before, and a well-equipped and spacious and high-ceilinged kitchen with a hearth large enough to roast an ox.

She had paid less attention to the weaponry, displayed almost everywhere. Spears, swords, pikes, knives, daggers like the one her brother wore at his side. He assumed these reflected her father's martial interests. "My father is a collector," she said when she saw him surveying the weaponry. "He collects weapons the way some men collect precious stones, Roman coins, old manuscripts, whatever. He loves weapons. He imagines himself defending the Rise from invading hordes, I think, but he is not himself a violent man."

"Your brother Julian seems to have inherited the same interest," William said.

"Oh, you mean his dagger?" she said with a short, derisive laugh.

"I was thinking of that."

"He likes to play the big man, but he's a coward at heart. I have warned him many times that if he isn't careful he'll stick himself with it. He doesn't like it when I say that. He doesn't like to be mocked, although I believe he is deserving of it."

She showed him the chapel. It was a small, intimate space, no larger than the room William had been given, furnished with altar, crucifix, several benches, and the smell of ancient piety. It was hard for him to imagine the Bascombes worshipping here, not together, perhaps not ever. The chapel was an architectural curiosity, like the battlements and the towers, but a standard feature of great houses where the rich and royal worshipped in privacy and often buried their dead beneath the floor.

They stayed but a minute. She had said the house's builder was buried there but she forgot to say where. Beneath the floor, he assumed.

"The Bascombes, my grandfather, came to own the house in king Henry VII's time. He was a chamberlain to that king and was rewarded accordingly. Some of the furnishings you see here come from that distant age. The chairs we sat upon in the great hall are over one hundred years old. There are other artefacts of antiquity I will show you presently that will interest you."

They climbed the stairs to the floor above, what she referred to as the dwelling chambers, and showed him a dozen or more rooms, including the one she occupied which, like his own, looked out upon the village below. Her own bedchamber, which she blushed to show him, was softly decorated with floral wall hangings, had a canopied bed that would have slept a half dozen, and one of the largest chests of drawers he had ever seen. A young girl of thirteen or fourteen, William supposed the poor creature Clara had abused as color-blind and forgetful, stood in the center of the room, William supposed for propriety's sake. For a young man and woman not married to be alone in a bedchamber might well be considered a scandal. Clara even alluded to this concern. She looked up at him and asked with a grin, "You have no fear of being alone with me here, do you Doctor?"

"We are not alone," William said, nodding his head toward the girl, who was blushing furiously. "Besides," he said, as a doctor I have often been alone with my patient, a woman without servant, parent or husband present."

"I'm sure you have," she said, laughing. "And seen more of her body than her own husband sees."

He admitted it was so. He was, after all, a doctor. The human body, male or female, was his business.

She explained there were two floors above, some with empty rooms and full of dust, haunts of bats, and owls, and strange birds whose names she didn't know. Others were occupied by household servants of whom she said there were twenty-four, if you included the stablemen, the gardeners, the grooms, the cooks and scullery maids. "I think none of those spaces will interest you," she said, "yet you must see what exists below us."

"Below us?" he said.

"In the cellars, the very foundation of Mowbray Rise. I promise you will find it most unusual and engaging. Something that you will not see every day of the week, Doctor. You are interested in history, aren't you?"

"I am, Lady Clara."

"Excellent, then. Shall we go down? We shall need a torch."

19

Sanderson fetched a torch. Clara insisted on bearing it herself. She told Sanderson to remain above.

His first impression was that this cellar was like other cellars in other houses, a necessity of construction, the footing for the more important floors above. It was dank and dark, low-ceilinged, so that a tall man like William ran the risk of braining himself. More cave than chamber, a repellant space to William despite his torch-bearing guide's assurance to the contrary.

Clara proceeded to show him various rooms there, the wine cellar, storage spaces, empty rooms without apparent function, and then she said, "You remember I said that the first owners of the house served the Norman king."

"Yes, William the Conqueror."

"Well, Doctor, he did conquer, but not easily, and he who built the house performed good services for his liege lord by confining in the cellar the king's enemies. I mean Saxon lords and lesser persons whom the Norman conqueror distrusted or feared. Some died here; *many* died here."

She said this with a kind of relish, as though the thought delighted her. He was a little taken aback. "You mean this was a dungeon," he said.

"Nothing less, Doctor." In the torchlight her face seemed even whiter and she a ghostly presence. Had he not known it was she, he would have shrunk from her. She smiled, noticing his dismay.

"Does that disturb you doctor, the idea of a dungeon in the house?"

"No, I have no fear of the dead, of ghosts."

"That's good," she said. "You know you are sleeping in my dead brother's chamber?"

The thought that Thomas Bascombe had died in the bed he lay upon wasn't so disturbing to William as the thought that he had suffered his

124

illness there, whatever that mysterious illness was. William lived in a time of plague and dozen other like afflictions that tormented the body and wasted it until there was nothing left to sustain life or hope. It seemed ironic to him that Thomas Bascombe's death must be explained by witchcraft, when there was such a plenty of diseases that might produce the same symptoms. Who, after all, needed the Devil's work to make human life more tentative and miserable, or increase its suffering?

But the tour of the cellars had not ended. She said the most arresting thing was yet to be shown and seemed to almost giggle with excitement. Clara took his hand and led him deeper into its bowels, for beneath the cellar they walked upon was another at an even deeper level. They came to yet another solid door, which Clara opened and holding her torch aloft revealed an almost empty interior except for some mechanical devices that at first William took for an iron bedstead, a sort of animal cage, and a what appeared to be a suit of armor like the ones he had seen in the great hall of the house. Along the walls he could see chains embedded in the limestone like little studs. At once he realized what he was being shown. This was no prisoner's cell. It was a torture chamber.

The metal cabinet shaped like a woman, she said was called the bird cage. In it, prisoners were encased behind a hinged door that opened to the front. Inside were spikes so that as the door was closed, these pierced the flesh of the naked imprisoned, tormenting them and causing ultimately death by exsanguination. What he thought first in the dim light to be an iron bedstead was the infamous rack, wherein a prisoner's sinews and bones were slowly stretched. There was another device as well. Something resembling a hat tree, though made of iron rather than wood.

God only knew what that was, but William assumed it would inflict unbearable pain.

Behind him, Clara said, "This Norman knight and his descendants were faithful to their king, as I have told you. They served him well and faithfully, imprisoning his enemies and drawing from them confessions they were loath to give. What you see here, Doctor, are what some may call implements of torture. I prefer to call them implements of justice, since it was justice the king sought, at least in the end."

"It's a wonder to me that your family kept them," William said. "I mean, after the Norman family was dead and gone and the Rise was no longer used as…" William looked for a word. Clara quickly supplied it.

"Prison house, you mean."

Then she laughed and pulled him by the arm back into the other room. "Come, Doctor, these are mementos of old time, of a time long passed. They have naught to do with us. As you have seen, the Rise is a much different place now. I would call it a happy house. Would you not, William?"

William would not have called Mowbray Rise a happy house, but he could hardly deny this woman her illusion, if that is what she thought. He said, "Yes, I think it must be happy, if those within believe it to be so. Happiness is a belief, is it not? Beyond proof?"

"You are too philosophical for me, William," she said, laughing. "But I will take it that you are in agreement with me."

"You may say that. I would not be so rude as to contend with you on any point."

"Shall we go up then? Perhaps you have seen enough of the Rise's dark secrets. The garden is next. It is as old as the house and has its own history, but I will spare you. We shall simply enjoy the flowers."

Above ground again, he tried to remember just when she began calling him by his Christian name. It was a sign, he was sure, an invitation, and he did not know quite how to respond to it. He was not prepared to call her Clara. Not yet. It still sounded too familiar to his ears.

He decided to wait and see what happened next.

20

Behind the manor house was a garden of several acres, but neglected. He remembered the magnificent garden of Theobalds, Lord Burghley's country house, manicured with such exquisite attention that it seemed the model for all natural things—well-ordered, flourishing, a microcosm of the ideal world, a golden age.

This garden was largely wild, with trees planted hither and yon and paths that were choked with weeds, and nestles and rocky hillocks and grottos that had collapsed with the weight of time. Indeed, there was little he saw there that pleased his eye, and he quickly understood that Clara's purpose in taking him there was not to display the gardener's skill, but to show him where her dead brother was buried, at the far end of the garden, in a shady corner beneath a yew tree, a decorous resting place. And didn't he agree? She asked him.

William noticed fresh flowers had been placed at the foot of the grave. Upon the top of a column was the figure of an angel, its wings furled, its head bent in an attitude of inconsolable grief. On the base of the monument was inscribed the name of her brother and the words *God keeps him who served in life.*

There were also dates of birth and death. By William's reckoning, Thomas Bascombe had been twenty-eight years old when he died. Clara Bascombe's age as well, since she and her brother were twins. William remembered that her father had said she was twenty-two. He thought it unlikely Bascombe had forgotten the age of his daughter. More likely he had made her younger to make her seem the more desirable. But then he would not be the first parent who had resorted to such a subterfuge to further the marriage interests of a child.

When he turned to Clara, he saw tears in her eyes, tears running down her cheeks. She looked up at him, drew close, and buried her face in his shoulder.

Her impulsive embrace startled him. He had not expected it and was not sure he wanted it. He felt her body convulse in her sorrow. Instinctively, he put his arms around her, not intending such intimacy but unable to withhold it. He could hardly have pushed her away from him. That would have been brutal, seeing as he did the fulness of her grief. He held her close, taken by the delicateness of her backbone, which he could feel beneath the velvet of her gown.

The embrace did not stir passion within him. He did not feel she was offering herself to him or inviting him to take her. Rather, the emotional moment was quite different from what he might have expected. He had occupied her brother's chamber, lain upon his bed, rested his head upon his pillow. Taken his place. He saw himself standing in for her dead brother, comforting his sister.

It was unlike anything he had known before, and his role in the scene displeased him, as though he were observing it from afar. He did not want to be a substitute for another, someone to play a part, someone that this pitiful woman could imagine to be someone other than himself. He knew the embrace was not for him, no more than her tears were.

Then she drew away. Her face flushed somehow, despite the cosmetic pallor that covered it.

"I do beg your pardon, William," she said, withdrawing from him. "It's just that..."

"I am not offended, Lady Clara."

"You may call me simply Clara," she said softly. "You are not my servant, Doctor."

"As you please, then... Clara."

She smiled warmly. "If I may call you William, or do you prefer to be called Doctor?" Somewhere in her attire she found a handkerchief, withdrew it, and dobbed the tears from her face.

"I am usually called William by my friends."

"Then I shall be a friend to you, William. I hope to know you better," she said.

They moved away from the grave. She took his arm and directed him back to the house.

"Your father told me how much you loved your brother and how deep was your grief," William said. "I have brothers and sisters of my own. And were I to lose them, my grief would have no end, in this life or the next."

"And so Thomas's death has done to me," she said, as they walked together. "I will mourn him to the end of my days. We were twins, you know. Born within a minute of each other. I was the elder, coming from my mother's womb first, then he after. When we were children, we were inseparable. We had no secrets from each other. When we grew older it was much the same. Without him, I feel lost in the world."

William said, 'It is well you have yet a brother to love."

She looked startled at the statement, as though it were totally unexpected, although William thought his remark, if anything, a stock consolation and felt half-embarrassed for having so little imagination to utter it. "Oh, you mean, Julian," she exclaimed.

She paused for a moment, then said with bitterness: "We share a mother and father, but that is all. You have met him, Doctor. There is little of him that is of merit, inwardly or outwardly. He says he seeks a wife, but he's as sullen as a toad and spends much of his time with women with little virtue to lose. His humor is unrelieved melancholy. What decent woman would want to come to his bed, bear his children, or suffer him in old age when the worst comes out in a man? You have doubtless seen that in him, even in the brief time you have been here."

"Really," he said, "I have had little opportunity to get to know him."

"When you do, you shall see I do not exaggerate his rudeness," Clara said.

He did not tell her about the wrangle he had had with her brother the night before. Telling it would mean he had to think about it again, and he did not want to. The conversation had been painful. "Your brother indeed has been somewhat cool toward me. I do think he questions the motive for my visit."

"How so?" she said, pausing in their walk.

"Well, he thinks I have come here as a jolly wooer of his sister. He thinks I have designs on your money or your father's money. But I do swear, Lady, that I do not."

"Have designs on me, William?" she said this with a pleasant laugh and immediately turned her face away so he could no longer see her eyes or what might be hidden in them.

He reminded her that his father and hers were friends from their youth.

He repeated what he had told her father, the lie about being in Chelmsford to see some patients. That said, he was suddenly afraid that she might ask who these patients were and from what illnesses they suffered, but her curiosity did not extend that far. He decided to change the subject, since he could see that his denial of being a wooer upset her. Why had he spoken so honestly about that when he had been content to lie about other things?

"Your father also told me you nursed Thomas during his final days," he said, as interested in changing the subject as securing information about her brother's last days.

"I did."

"You are a most caring sister," William said.

"He was my brother, what else could I do?" she said.

He wanted to ask her what treatment she had given the dying man, if any treatment at all. Surely, she would not have merely watched her brother languish, his life slipping from him, and then he remembered that her father had said they had hoped until the end he would recover.

"I was ever at his bedside from the time he first fell ill. He would have done the same for me, were I in his place," she said.

They came to the porch of the house and stood looking back from whence they had come. The day had begun fair and warm. Now it was turning cold and gray, like iron. To the east a storm was brewing. It would rain. Thankfully, it was too late in the year to snow. He remembered then the sudden storm that had confined him at the Old Priory and nearly killed him. He shuddered. Clara noticed.

"I hope, William, nothing I have shown you upsets you in any way, or that I have said or done anything that might make you uncomfortable or wish you had never come to Mowbray Rise. I would not be so inhospitable to my father's guest and the son of his old friend."

"Nothing you have shown me—or said to me—will disturb my sleep or my visit," he said.

William understood she was referring to the embrace they had shared but decided to not allude to that. "I understand the grief we feel for the death of those we love. I have witnessed much of it in my short life, for every patient does not survive the condition nor the cure. We physicians are left then to offer what comfort we can to those who live on."

"You are a very compassionate man, William."

"A doctor should be so," he answered.

130

She said then that she was very tired. She had ridden hard in the morning, had been up at dawn to do so because she enjoyed the morning light and the freshness of the air. "I hope to see you later, at supper, perhaps. You will be staying on until tomorrow at least?"

"Yes, I do think so—as long as I do not wear out my welcome."

"I assure you, William, you will not. You have been our guest for but a day and already my father speaks of you as if you, not your honorable father, is the old friend."

"Your father is a most generous host," William said.

He accompanied her up the stairs until she came to her room. She paused there and looked up at him.

"I thank you, Clara, for the tour," he said, remembering to use her Christian name although it still felt awkward on his lips. "You were an excellent guide."

"Thank you, William, the pleasure was all mine. We must do it again before you leave us. I do mean pass the time together, not prowl through dusty rooms and ancient histories."

And then he thought to ask, "By the way, last night while I looked out of my window, I thought I heard a wolf howl."

"A wolf," she said, laughing a little.

"Several times, not just once."

She shook her head. "Might it not have been a dream you had?"

"I was broad awake."

"There were wolves here in olden times," she said. "It must have been some other creature you heard."

He was on the verge of suggesting that the howling was Ursula's dog, but that would have revealed that he knew the Harkness women and the crimes with which they were charged. But the more he thought about it, the more he persuaded himself that it might be true. He had been told the dog had been searched for but not found. That the creature should be roaming beyond the woods, seeking out his mistress, was well within the realm of possibility.

He returned to his own room, the chamber that had been Thomas Bascombe's. As he entered, he felt a chill again. He had denied fearing ghosts to the dead man's sister, and it was not exactly a ghost he feared now. But he did sense a definite something in Thomas Bascombe's room; something unhealthy, something ominous, something unhallowed.

131

21

Clara having retired to her rooms and with her father abroad on some vaguely described duty, William was on his own until supper. He had brought two books with him. That was his custom when he traveled, regardless of the distance. One was a short treatise in Latin on the medicinal properties of herbs and plants, written by a German doctor with whom he had at sundry times corresponded. The other was a longer work, in English, by a countryman on metallurgy, a subject he studied deeply in connection with his experiments with magnets. In another time and place he would have found a kind of solace in either, not to mention valuable knowledge he might employ in his medical practice or experiments with magnets. But now he could not make his way beyond a few sentences in either. Instead, he thought of his next encounter with Clara Bascombe.

William had loved, and he had lost. The Dutch girl he had pursued and who, he believed, reciprocated his love, was now lost to him. She had married another, one of her own countrymen and a man of considerable wealth. And then she had died in childbirth, a sad fact he had learned from her father, a former mentor of his, who never truly understood the depth of William's affection for his daughter, or hers for him.

William had written back to express his sympathies, framing his condolences in the words of a friend, not a grief-stricken lover. Since that time, he had suffered a prolonged grief, a deep sadness underlying all he did. Also, a fear of loss that undermined his confidence, leaving him fearful that any future love would also be snatched from him.

But now he looked forward to supper when he would see Clara again. In this anticipation, he stood confused. His first impression of her—received not directly, but from Ursula Harkness's description of her as a railing termagant denouncing witches in the public square—was slowly being replaced by his direct knowledge of her as an attractive young woman, talented in music, compassionate in her care for her dead brother, welcoming his sympathetic embrace at her brother's grave. Even her use of his Christian name. Her invitation for him to use hers. All these gave evidence of receptivity on her part.

That is, if he was not beguiled by some spell, or his own vanity. True, he would prefer her natural visage to the ceruse. Still, he counted that as no great flaw in her, certainly not one of character. And he was yet to plumb the depths of her hatred for the Harknesses or determine whether she shared her father's acquisitiveness in which she held the Old Priory as hers and her family's by moral right, if not in law.

He sat musing on these things for some time. The chamber grew cold. Wood had been laid on the hearth and by it the means to ignite it. He might have summoned a servant of the house for such service, certainly his predecessor in the chamber would have done so, but he lighted it himself. He drew his chair in front of it, put the unread books aside, and watched the mounting flames, thinking of how Thomas Bascombe must have done likewise, at least until such time as he was too sick to rise from his bed.

As he did so, he relived his last encounter with Clara. He remembered the tears in her eyes, the deep sorrow in her voice, as they stood together looking down at her brother's grave. But principally he remembered touching her body, the delicate bones of her shoulders and back, as he comforted her. She had not resisted, not complained that he had presumed too much. And when he had denied being a suitor for her affections, she had seemed disappointed, almost offended by the denial.

The hearth was like almost all such hearths in his time not plain and merely functional but an opportunity for artistic expression. The ornate mantle, dark oak, sat atop a surround of black marble inlaid with intricate designs—flowers, trees, shrubs, leaves. The hearth itself was brick and looking upon it he suddenly noticed what he had not noticed before. One brick was slightly awry, unevenly placed, as though set by an incompetent bricklayer or his careless apprentice.

He got up from the chair and bent down to inspect it further. He prodded the brick. It moved a little as though that what precisely what it was designed to do. It yielded easily, revealing beneath a box-like cavity.

The cavity was not empty, but contained a sheaf of papers rolled up like a scroll. He hesitated for a moment, shy of intruding on another's property, which this surely was. The property of Thomas Bascombe. He lifted it from its cradle in the box and opened the papers to read what was written there.

These were letters, a dozen or so of them by a quick count, and in the same hand, written on the least expensive paper one could find. His eyes ran to the end of each before taking in the substance. They were from Ursula Harkness.

He had cast his learned texts aside, regardless of how immediate they were to his professional interests, but he could not help reading these missives. The person to whom they had been addressed, *Thomas, my beloved*, was dead. That they were private letters, not meant to be read by a stranger, was evident. But had William somehow secured an implicit permission, perhaps by the dead man himself? William occupied the dead man's chamber, sat in his chair, now warmed himself by his fire. He had felt uncomfortable in the garden when he sensed Clara's embrace was more for her dead brother than for him. But his feeling now was different. He was a defender of Ursula Harkness, the woman Thomas loved. Fate had made him privy to her letters. He determined that Ursula should have them back and know he to whom they had been written had prized them enough to keep them and conceal them from prying eyes.

Curiosity overwhelmed whatever scruples he had about invasion of privacy.

He began to read. The letters were written in a bold, almost masculine hand, but were quite legible. He found he could decipher every word. They were arranged by order of date, had been delivered to Thomas Bascombe to a servant at the manor who had acted as an intermediary and was not named. Together they chronicled the relationship, which began even as Ursula Harkness had said by a chance meeting in the forest on the borders of the two properties.

She alluded to their first embrace, embraces that became more intimate, more needy, deeper, she said—until her heart yearned for his body and she was satisfied. One of the letters made reference to her discovery that she was with child. All of this was to be kept secret, from his parents, from hers.

The last letter referred to his father's discovery of the affair. Nothing was said as to how the discovery was made, but the consequence of it was clear. He had told her that he was forbidden to see her again, she made reference to that and then in the last letter she said she was most sorry to hear that he was sick. She said she would offer prayers on his behalf.

It was largely the account that Ursula had given him while he was resident in the Old Priory. Thomas Bascombe had kept these letters. He had hidden them. That William and not some servant sweeping the hearth had discovered their hiding place was a wonder.

He read the letters over several times, feeling within himself a deep sadness. What might they have done, had Thomas Bascombe not fallen sick, yielded to his father's demand—would he have married Ursula, acknowledged his child?

They might well have ended up in London, happy in a new life, both of them free from Thomas Bascombe's domineering father. For London was where so many refugees from misfortune fled, not heaven on earth certainly, but a haven for the misused and abased.

And for the charges of witchcraft? They would not have been levied. Ursula would have had her husband to protect her from false accusations and public calumny.

He put the letters back where he had found them. Replaced the brick and adjusted it so that the crack that had caught his eye was less conspicuous. A knock came at the door.

It was Sanderson beckoning him to supper. William told him he would come down shortly. But then he asked the old servant to stay.

"Tell me, Mistress Bascombe has told me the chamber I occupy was before that of her brother."

"It was, Doctor."

"And I understand she attended her brother in his last sickness."

"She did, sir. And an able nurse she was although the result of her ministrations were not what we all had hoped."

"That sometimes is the case," William said. "But before his illness, was it you that attended him in his daily needs, or was it some other member of the household?"

"That would have been me, Doctor. I looked after him since he was a boy."

William would have liked to know whether the old man had been aware of his master's affair, or even if it were he who passed Ursula's letters to him. But he did not ask. If he were wrong, that would arouse the servant's suspicions, which then would be conveyed to Sir Richard himself. If he were right, what then? What questions would follow? William was already assured by the letters that Ursula's account of the relationship was an honest narrative, not a country girl's wishful thinking.

135

"I will be down presently. I know the way," William said.

He watched as Sanderson went down the stairs. He noticed the man's shoulders were bent over, as though he carried an invisible weight. William thought: *secrecy is not natural to a lover's mind. Nature prompts disclosure, an expression of feeling and expression sometime irrepressible. It must be shared with someone. Shared with a friend, or even perhaps with an old and trusted servant.*

22

The Bascombes set a rich and abundant table, with a dozen courses at each meal; foul, fish, beef, pork, and mutton, and a plenty of vegetables unrecognizable in thick and savory sauces. The chief cook, William had been told, was French. What was not eaten at table was passed to the servants and after to the master's dogs, who sprawled indolently at the feet of their master waiting for their share of the feast, and whom Sir Richard evidently considered as much of the family as his two surviving children and his silent and submissive wife.

William recognized that it was as much an exhibition as a meal, an exhibition for themselves if not for guests, comforting them in the belief that no one in the area enjoyed such wealth, for no healthy body needed so much to live or thrive. Whatever financial reversals had plagued the family during the grandfather's lifetime had clearly been resolved. The tenants' farms had had a plentiful harvest for several years, the herds of sheep had doubled in numbers and the price of wool risen as the demand increased, especially in London where it was no longer sufficient for a gentleman or lord to have a single suit of clothes, but he must change twice or thrice daily or be thought a pauper.

William learned all this at supper where Sir Richard Bascombe discoursed on his prosperity through most of the meal, while his little wife sat beside him close-mouthed, his son Julian maintained his wonted sullenness, and Clara smiled prettily, her lips slightly parted to show perfect teeth, a rare achievement for an Englishwoman of any social station. William could imagine her breath coming from her to his side of the table like an invisible influence, like an unspoken promise of things to come. Hovering servants completed the company and refilled William's glass after each sip. He had rarely been so hosted, even at Lord Burghley's magnificent house.

137

When the meal was done, William thought they all might be treated to another display of Clara's musical accomplishments, but it was not so. Instead, William was called aside by her father who said he wished to speak to him privily, as he put it. They proceeded into a kind of library or study, which William had been shown by Clara earlier in that day, but only by a look in at the door, since she had given him to know this was her father's private retreat into which neither she nor her mother were ever invited.

It was an intimate chamber, Bascombe's retreat, small and with dark panels making the space seem the smaller. There were few books, but another display of weaponry; in this case, knives, daggers, poniards, and stilettos, enough to arm a troop of robbers or assassins. The weapons hung upon the walls, framed and positioned as though they were family heirlooms, which William imagined they might be. There was a fire in the hearth and the room was overheated. Above the mantelpiece was the Bascombe family crest, a bar sinister with three crescents and some sort of creature at the helm, a stag or leopard. He could not tell what. He felt an unease in his stomach. This was more armory than library, and Bascombe's invitation to talk could not bode well. Had Bascombe discovered the real purpose of his visit? Was William now to be denounced as a spy, defender of witches and thereby an enemy of God, all good Christians, and more particularly, the Bascombe family?

William was offered a chair across from where Sir Richard Bascombe sat behind a very large and imposing desk piled with ledger books and papers. William wasn't sure what was about to come but he could tell on his host's face a certain expression he had not seen before, a heavy seriousness. To William, it was a little frightening.

"I trust my daughter was courteous to you in your tour of the manor?"

"She was the soul of courtesy, Sir Richard. I could not have asked for a better guide."

The older man nodded appreciatively and continued, "She is a good girl, talented as you have seen, and also... eligible."

"Eligible, sir?"

Bascombe gave him a long, searching look.

"Let me speak plainly, Doctor. She is of marriageable age, possessed of a handsome dowry to one who would take her hand."

Bascombe named the sum.

William was impressed. It was more than his income from all the years of his practice. More than double, triple. Even more. It would have bought a manor house and all land appertaining thereto.

Bascombe waited, studying William's face. William felt his cheeks redden.

"And open to proposals of marriage, should she deem one worthy of it," Bascombe continued. "I too would, of course, need to deem him worthy of marriage to her."

"One would not expect otherwise," William said, doing no more than acknowledging a father's right to govern his son or daughter's marriage choices—although William knew too that such a right was not always honoured. He knew a half dozen of his university friends who had defied tradition, scorned paternal authority, and eloped with their brides to the vexation of both families. He knew of an earl's daughter who had run off with her father's steward and enjoyed marital bliss, at least until the steward was apprehended and his new bride made abruptly and mysteriously a widow.

This was a conversation he was not prepared for, but it was not for him to stop it. Sir Richard had begun what the avid father could not himself stop, but he must press forward toward what William now understood to be the inevitable proposition of a marriage between Clara and him. As discomfited as William was by all this, he could hardly blame Clara's father. His daughter wasn't getting any younger. Were Bascombe to have grandchildren, at least legitimate ones, they must come from Clara. Her brother Julian's marital future was in grave doubt. Clara had said that, and she knew her brother best.

"My daughter finds you a worthy man, Doctor," Bascombe continued, in a thoughtful and deliberate voice. "Not unattractive to her in your manners, nor in your mind. Nor in your body. You are a young man but well educated and already distinguished in the world of medicine, an officer in the College of Physicians. You number some great ones of the city amongst your patients."

William was not displeased by this summary but wondered how Richard Bascombe knew this. Had he himself been spied upon, inquired of?

"Moreover, I know your family fairly well. I knew your mother, Elizabeth Coggeshall, a worthy woman of blessed memory. And, of course, I account your father to be one of my oldest friends. Indeed, on more than one occasion I took counsel of him as to matters of law."

"I trust, sir, you were satisfied with his counsel," William said, remembering the story Rafe Tuttle had told suggesting Sir Richard had been far from satisfied. He had, instead, been frustrated when Jerome Gilbert had encouraged him to abandon his suit. It seemed to William that Sir Richard's memory was faulty, or perhaps he was reinventing his own history for his daughter's marriage prospects.

"Quite, sir, quite satisfied," William said, deciding it would not be to his advantage to question his host's version of the story.

An awkward silence followed. Bascombe looked down at his hands that were folded neatly on his lap. His hands were small and well-manicured, but brown where Clara's had been made white with the ceruse.

"May I ask you, William, if I may call you that, how you see my daughter?"

"How I see her?"

"Whether you find her to your liking, attractive I would say. Do you find her witty, quick, charming?"

"She is a lovely young woman, sir, and I would hope to know her better and she me."

"I assure you she is a virgin, untouched, if that is of concern to you."

"I trust she is, sir," William said, unsure whether she was or not but not interested in making it a point of controversy by pointing out that many a so-called virgin bride was far from being so. He knew that she was a bold girl, not inhibited in expressing her feelings. But that was a quality he rather liked. As a wife she surely would not be like unto her mother, differential to the point of being habitually silent, acquiescent to her husband's every wish, a nonentity in her own house. But William would not have wanted that, either.

"Well, then I may say, Doctor Gilbert, that she would not be unresponsive to an offer of marriage, from you, that is, though I would hope the buds of love would bloom before the wedding day to the satisfaction of you both."

Bascombe paused to assess William's reaction, then went on.

"Love is of course not indispensable in a marriage, and when it exists before, it sometimes fades thereafter, as many have learned to their sorrow. Yet I do think the two of you would make a handsome couple, and she doubtless an asset to your professional standing."

William was not sure what to say next. The offer was on the table, coming from a solicitous father to what he perceived as an eligible suitor

140

for his daughter's hand. The offer demanded a response, a categorical answer—a yes or no that would either please his host or offend him to the heart. He remembered Julian Bascombe's remarks that his sister had had several marriage proposals, but all had failed to result in marriage. Had Sir Richard Bascombe been as direct with these earlier candidates as he was now, or was the knight simply growing more frustrated and anxious, more aggressive in looking for a suitable son-in-law?

He also recalled comments by Julian Bascombe and Clara's quondam governess and now companion, that Clara's proper destiny was to marry well. That is, with someone of a higher degree than he, a knight perhaps, even some lord. Her father's aim evidently was more modest. William was a gentleman by birth but had no title before his name, no Norman or Saxon lineage to boast of. He had an adequate income from his medical practice, and a sizable inheritance when his father passed. Still, he knew he was hardly one to support a wife of the evident expectations of Clara Bascombe, even with the proposed dowry.

And why had earlier attempts to find a proper husband for his daughter failed? The why of Clara's romantic history was more a mystery to him now, than it had been when he heard the slander from Julian Bascombe's cruel mouth. Was there something about this woman that he did not know, but should? Did his casual interest in her arise to the level of a budding love? And what of his original purpose in visiting the house, to discover how Thomas Bascombe really died, not from a witch's curse but from some natural illness that had a name and possibly a cure? Had he on such short acquaintance fallen in love, forsaken his purpose, his declared duty to his prospective bride's enemies?

In the firelight, the avid father waited an answer. His impatience was writ large on his face. William's head whirled. The pause had gone on long enough. William had to respond and respond quickly, to imagine an unoffensive middle ground. And so, he did.

"As I have said, sir. I hope to know your daughter better and she me. My father, who is the soul of prudence, has said often to me and to my younger brothers, a fool marries in haste and repents at leisure. I speak not about fears of your daughter's worthiness, but about what in me she may find shortly or in time disappointing. I am a busy doctor. My patients demand attention, often at ungodly hours of the night. In treating them I am exposed to every disease I diagnose or treat. Is it not wise that your daughter, as gracious and lovely as she is, should consider this before agreeing to marry one such as I?"

All this, William heard himself say and tried to read his host's mind. Had what he had just spoken secured some escape from a categorical answer, something that would foreclose nothing but not commit him either? Given the choice, he would have said no to Bascombe's proposal. He had known Clara but for two days, and he had not exaggerated his busyness as a doctor. But he was not prepared to attach himself to a woman he had known so briefly. Besides, the image of the Dutch girl, Katrina Weinmeer, still lingered in his mind. Maybe she always would, as an obstacle to any new love.

Sir Richard looked disappointed, but not angry. William was relieved. After a moment, Bascombe said, "I have always respected your father's wisdom. I would not have my daughter unhappy in marrying you, or any other who sued for her hand. Yet you may underestimate, Doctor Gilbert, her fortitude, her courage, her willingness to sacrifice even as you do in your profession. My daughter tended my dead son through the last months of his wasting, day and night. I think you know that. She did so without fear and without complaint. Surely such compassion and resolve give promise that she would not hesitate to marry one devoted to the healing of the sick and afflicted, even if it put her in some danger of contagion."

"Surely her history would lead one to think she might, Sir Richard, yet I would rather die than marry and disappoint my wife in such a way, to have her fear to touch me, to touch our children. To bring the sickness of others into the marriage bed."

Another silence fell between them. The mention of contagion seemed to have struck the appropriate chord. Sir Richard Bascombe might live in a castle armed to the teeth, but he feared plague and sweating sickness as much as any man. Then Bascombe asked, "How long may we hope to enjoy your company, Doctor?"

"I thought I might return to Chelmsford the day after tomorrow at the latest, sir. With your permission and an earnest desire not to abuse your generous hospitality. I have a patient there whose progress I must evaluate before prescribing him further medication."

"I pray you stay with us a week longer, Bascombe said. "During which time you may resolve your doubts as to your own worthiness and my daughter's capacity for self-sacrifice and Christian charity. You could go to Chelmsford, a mere hour's ride, and then return to us here. Tell the innkeeper to give your room there to another. It's Master Tuttle, is it not?"

William said it was.

"A good man, Tuttle. He will not lack guests to take your place, given the assizes are upon us. Consider this your home whilst you are here in this part of the county."

William accepted with thanks. He would stay for another week at least. Of the mystery of Thomas Bascombe's death he had but scratched the surface. He had yet to speak directly to Clara about her conviction that her brother had been murdered by witchcraft. He had not yet learned much of anything about his symptoms. Her father had spoken of aches and pains, the unrelieved suffering of his son. What manner of aches and pains, and in what regions of the body, of what duration? A doctor had come, done something, and been sent away. What had the doctor done and with what results, if any?

He needed to ask Clara. She had been her brother's nurse. She knew best what he had suffered.

22

When he returned to the great hall, Clara was gone. She had retired early, or so one of the servants informed him, busy cleaning up. William suspected she knew the topic of conversation William and her father were to have and decided to leave the men to it. It was, in a way, after all, their business, not hers. She was a woman, a pawn to be maneuvered on the marital chess board, at least to her father's way of thinking. He had bowed to her preference for the London doctor, but when it came down to it, Sir Richard Bascombe would decide, just as he decided everything else at Mowbray Rise.

William went up to his room, unescorted. No difficulty there, he knew the way by heart now. But when he opened the door and stepped into the shadowy interior he was overcome with a powerful scent. It was perfume, concocted of lavender if his nose didn't fail him. A figure stood by the open window.

The presence there, a shadowy form turned away from him and staring out into the darkness, caused him almost to drop the candle he had carried to light his way. He had let out a gasp that was near to a cry of alarm. Despite his disbelief in ghosts, William thought surely this must be one. The figure was garbed in a white dressing gown; silk, he thought from the way it draped the body like a winding sheet. It turned to him and whispered, "Shut the door behind you, William. Please don't cry out. It is I, Clara. No ghost."

He did what she asked, without thinking what her appearance in his room might mean.

"I'm sorry I startled you," she said, moving toward him. "I come here from night to night where my brother lay. Next to his grave, it is as close as I can get to him."

144

She started to move past him toward the door. He had not yet said anything, unsure as to what to say. Her long, fair hair hung to her narrow waist like a nun's veil. He was growing used to the perfume now. "Please forgive me for disturbing you. I thought you would be talking to my father longer. He is a great talker, as you saw at dinner, and doubtless bored you with his going on about whatever he was going on about." She laughed.

"I wasn't bored," William said, keeping his voice low. "This house is yours, Lady Clara, the host cannot trespass on her own property."

"Clara," she corrected.

"Clara, then."

He sounded like his father, the lawyer, dealing in legal quibbles, but the truth was he found her unexpected appearance in his chamber exciting, but also unsettling. Were they discovered, it would look like a lovers' tryst, an insult to his host, for surely her father's enthusiasm for a marriage would not extend to this, a private meeting without a chaperone, a compromising situation, a dishonorable act on William's part, even an attempt at seduction. His heart was racing. Yet he reached out to her to stop her from leaving, knowing that the movement might be a mistake, something he would regret, later if not sooner.

"Stay a while. The house is yours, this room. I'm only a guest here."

"If that is your wish," she said.

She paused, then said. "My father, what was he speaking to you about?"

"Oh, he spoke of you."

"Of me?" She looked surprised.

"He sang your praises, enumerated your virtues. You are blessed to have such a father, who thinks you have no faults."

She laughed lightly. "And what think you? I mean about me. Are you likewise beguiled by my... virtues?"

As she said this, she moved toward him, placed her hands on his shoulders, then pressed herself against him. He felt the breath go out of him.

"Am I being too bold, William?"

"Perhaps premature," he said, remembering the justification he had given her father for his hesitation. "You have known me for three days, no more. You don't know what manner of man I am."

"I know you are a good man," she said. "Else you would not be a doctor."

"Not all doctors are good men."

"But you are good. I know you are. My father says so. And he's a shrewd judge of men."

He moved her away from him, the way he might have moved a child. "I would not dishonor you, Mistress. I would not dishonor my host."

"There is an honorable way to satisfy your desires," she said. She moved back toward him and kissed him. Her lips were warm and the perfume on her body made him lightheaded. It was not what he would have called a chaste kiss, but then he would not have enjoyed that. He did enjoy this. He was about to kiss her again, this time initiating it himself.

Then he heard the wolf again, a long plaintiff howl.

He turned from her and went to the window. She came up from behind him, put her hand on his shoulder.

"What is it, William, what do you hear?"

"The cry of a wolf. I heard it before," he said, looking out into the dark.

"I heard nothing," she said. "I do think it is your imagination. Nothing more."

She pulled him away from the window. She drew her face up to his but stopped short of kissing him a second time.

Then she asked him if he rode. He said he did, but not for the simple joy of it. She laughed and said, "You must ride with me tomorrow. Promise me you will."

"I think tomorrow I must return to Chelmsford for the day," he said. "I have a patient there whom I must attend."

"Then we shall ride in the morning," she said. "You can see your patient in the afternoon. Besides, I have given you a tour of the Mowbray Rise, but have yet to show you our holdings beyond, the fields and the forest. We have more than a thousand acres of land, more if you include the Old Priory. My father may have spoken of it."

"He did."

"Oh, do come with me," she pleaded, and cast him a glance that he could not deny.

"Very well," William said. "I will ride with you. My horse needs the exercise."

"And you, Master London Doctor, need good country air. But you shall have another horse to ride, one from our stable. It's a fine stallion. My father bought it from a Spanish trader who in turn got it in Arabia when it was but a colt. He is well-trained, I assure you. He will show you what a horse of his blood can do."

She wished him goodnight and kissed him again. On the cheek this time, and it was not as good as before.

Alone again, William sat by the window, listening for the wolf he was sure he heard, although Clara had said she heard nothing. Was it his imagination, both this night and the night before? Clara had been confident in her denial, and he was unsure as to why she would deny it if it were true. He thought about her visit. He supposed her excuse for being in his bedchamber might have been true, given her devotion for her brother. But it had come too hard upon her father's offer of his daughter's hand in marriage to remove suspicion as to her motives.

Her lips had given him pleasure, as had the feel of her body next to his. He couldn't deny that. The bedchamber that had been her dead brother's, now seemed to be hers. Even he seemed to be hers.

Her perfume still filled the air.

23

In the stable, Clara introduced him to the stallion.

William had no doubt that the horse was stronger and prouder than the gelding he rode in on. And the one she had chosen for herself, her very own gift from an indulgent father, was also one a great gentleman might have bragged of. They had set out early, Clara dressed in the same riding cloak she had worn the day before. They had left before breakfast, when the sun was just beginning to rise and the light upon the fields and woods about the Rise glistened, a light rain having fallen during the night.

"Cook packed a bag for the both of us," she said. "First, we shall ride, then talk. I know a special place. It is a private place. You will like it too, William. I know you shall."

They rode at a gallop, William surprised that the unfamiliar horse answered to the most subtle of his commands. She led the way, heading out over open land. She rode with confidence and obvious delight, and William found himself enjoying it himself, although he held on for dear life while she seemed one with her mount. They stopped when they were breathless, leaving open fields behind them, at the edge of thick woodland, which he knew was not far from where Jacob Harkness's land began. Emerging from the thicket of trees and bushes was a small stream and a pleasant clearing. Here they tied up the horses and ate of what the cook had provided, a rich, creamy cheese, strawberries, black bread, and a Spanish grape Clara claimed was the finest in the wine cellars.

As they ate, she began talking about the lands about, how he her grandfather had purchased it at great cost and then nearly lost it from what she called unfortunate choices.

"Tell me about this Old Priory you spoke of," William said.

"Ah," she said. "That is a sore point with my father, as you may have heard."

"I've not heard," William said, thinking he might get more information and arouse less suspicion were he to claim to know nothing.

She took a deep breath and looked beyond him into the woods, where he knew the Old Priory lay. "It was—it is—part of our lands and was from the beginning."

"Beginning?"

"When Alain Mowbray built the Rise. He was given this land by the king, including where the Old Priory now stands. Those that occupy it now," she paused, made a face of disgust that he had not seen on her countenance before, "the Harknesses, those people claim they bought it from my grandfather, whilst in his distress. But my father says it is not so. My father says the land on which the Old Priory sits was never sold, or if it was, it was no legal sale and all documents asserting otherwise are false. For that reason, when I talk of it, when we—my father and I—talk of it, we claim it as our own."

"And you have had no help from the law?"

"None. There's evil there." She turned back to him, her eyes narrowing.

"Evil?" he asked.

"The Old Priory. It is a dreadful place, falling down upon itself. It is now possessed by witches, a mother and daughter, but most especially the daughter. It was she, the daughter, Ursula is her name, who cast a spell on my brother and brought him low and then to his deathbed."

William asked why Ursula Harkness would do this.

"Because he would not marry her," Clara said. "She bore a child... a creature, rather."

"What manner of creature?"

"A creature half human, half wolf. Which awful creature she claimed was fathered by my brother, but it is a lie. He never would have touched such a woman as she is, ill-favored, bones, not flesh, a whore looking for business. What man would have looked twice at her, want to bed her, want to touch her body?" She paused; her face contorted in disgust. "And he never would have sired such a thing as her son is."

William said nothing in response to this. He wanted to let her keep talking, to see where her anger might take her, take him. She had turned again to look at the woods, her eyes filled with loathing. He knew it was not directed at him, not about him. Still, he felt the effect of its intensity, as though her anger somehow enveloped him as well as the Harkness women. He was near to being afraid of her, he who the night before had enjoyed the touch of her lips, her body against his.

"She will suffer for what she has done," Clara said. "She and that mother of hers who, I have no doubt, taught her all she knew in the way of spells. Did I say she has a wolf as a companion, as a familiar?"

"A wolf, you say? No, you did not."

"On my oath, she has it. I have seen it with my own eyes and a more vicious creature you cannot imagine."

"Are you sure it is a familiar and not merely a dog resembling a wolf? I have seen such dogs and they are no more than that, dogs, big dogs, black dogs."

William thought it was a reasonable enough question, but Clara turned on him angrily, her eyes flashing. "It *is* a wolf, she cried. "I told you, I have seen it for myself. Do you think I lie? And it is her familiar. It speaks to her, does her bidding, sucks her blood. She is even now imprisoned in Chelmsford. Her body has been inspected. Inspected by good women. They have discovered the teats whereof the Devil has sucked, which all the world knows is proof positive of a witch's kind."

She searched his face—looking, he knew, for signs he agreed with her. She went on, more heated than before, "For this I hate her. She killed my brother, murdered him. She lied about her bastard, who never was my brother's child, and wanted him to marry her when in truth he hardly knew her. Why should he? She's nothing. She's not even a woman. If you were to see how ugly she is, how hard featured, why the idea that they should meet and mate and have children mocks reason and God Himself."

For the next few minutes Clara ranted on, her whitened face a mask of outrage, her eyes blazing. He had never seen her like this. She had been calm only minutes before. Now, she seemed a person possessed. The transformation had happened in an instant, and it was terrible to see, like a person seized and frothing.

He tried to calm her, but her anger was at a boil and would not be cooled. She was panting heavily as she spoke looking wildly about as though at any moment Ursula Harkness might appear before her, her wolf dog at her heels. She would fly at her, tear her to shreds, avenge her dead brother.

"She will hang, God willing," she hissed when she had caught her breath, her face still contorted with rage. "She and her mother. And if I have my way, her father, Jacob will hang as well."

"Why him? Why is he to blame?" William asked, thinking of the pitiful husband who had begged him to save his wife and daughter and grandchild.

"Man and wife are one flesh, are they not, William?"

"So I am told."

"Then Mary Harkness's guilt is her husband's as well. They cannot be separated, she guilty, he not."

William thought it was an absurd argument, hardly worth refuting. But he couldn't tell her that, not even if she were in a different state of mind.

"And then what will happen to the Old Priory?" William asked, thinking the question might distract her, restore her reason.

"The Crown will take it," she said defiantly. "We Bascombes will buy it back."

William had thought earlier that perhaps the witchcraft accusation was a mere device to secure the coveted property. But after Clara's intemperate diatribe he could see she was more bent on justice for her brother's death. The letters he had discovered, carefully concealed by her brother, gave evidence that his relationship with Ursula was genuine, despite Clara's denial.

When moments later, when she had come to herself, was breathing normally, and her features were those of the woman he'd kissed, he said, half afraid to do so: "Tell me about your brother's illness."

"He was cursed. As I have told you."

"Yes, but what symptoms did he have? How did his illness start?"

"You mean what course did the curse take?"

He said yes, encouraged her to go on.

"He was listless, complained of headaches, had pains in his gut, voided much, vomited often. Could not keep food down. This was at the beginning. Later, it got worse. His moods changed abruptly, he saw things that were not, visions."

"Had he ever suffered the same symptoms before?"

"He had such illnesses that children are given to. But in all, he was a healthy youth, strong and steady. And he was handsome, for which reason it is impossible that he should have loved Ursula Harkness."

"You tended him during his illness?"

151

"You know I did."

"What did you think at first? I mean, when he fell ill, what did you think was wrong with him? Did you think it a witch's curse or some natural malady? Something with a name. Something others suffer from."

She thought about this, then she said, "I thought it a natural thing. I thought he might have an imbalance of humors."

That Clara should know of this familiar diagnosis did not surprise him. Who did not? Getting oneself bled by knife or leech to cure or enhance this or that had become as much a fashion in London as Venetian ceruse, and to William's thinking it was no less dangerous.

"Did you seek a doctor for him?"

"Several came, one from Chelmsford. He bled my brother, three times."

"And with what results?"

He got worse, not better. I had no faith in the doctor. We let him go. But after that Agnes helped me."

"How?"

"She is more than a secretary and companion, William. She has been by my side since I was a child, my mother being as she is, somewhat distant from me and her other children. Agnes Robinson is a second mother to me, a counsellor. She is a wise woman and knows much of herbs and plants and what cures. She gave me... she gave me, it is called Venetian ceruse for my complexion, that my skin might be the fairer." She paused, embarrassed, he supposed, for having revealed to him the secret of her beauty. Agnes said the same substance would work to make my brother whole again. I painted his face, his throat and chest, even his legs."

"You painted him, painted his body?" William exclaimed. He could not keep the shock out of his voice.

"So Agnes instructed me. She said it would make him well."

"Good God in heaven, Clara, what made her think so?'

Clara didn't know. She trusted Agnes.

"And did it help, this painting of your brother's body?"

"No, he grew worse. I gave him more that he might improve and for a while he did, so that I gave him more, ceruse. Then one morning I came to where he lay and found him cold. He had died during the night."

She began sobbing at the memory. He held her close to him, afraid her hysteria would return, her rage be reignited by the memory of her brother's body. He wanted to comfort her in her distress, but he could think of nothing more than Thomas Bascombe covered with the leaden cosmetic. It was horrible to think of. It offended him as a doctor. It would have offended him had he *not* been a doctor.

She fell silent, he supposed still thinking of her dead brother. "Let's go back now," she said at length.

24

They rode slowly back to the Rise, as though they had all the time in the world, as though nothing had happened. Clara seemed to have forgotten the tempestuous emotions she had expressed earlier, the emotions that had alarmed him with their virulence. Now she chattered gaily about a variety of subjects. About her last visit to London, about her dancing master, about the difficulty of tuning her lute with its perverse number of strings, about the latest French fashion she admired.

Later, William could not remember what she said or how he answered her. He did remember that she had said nothing more about the Old Priory or its current inhabitants.

At the stable, she asked him if he had enjoyed his ride. He told her he had, looking into her eyes for some acknowledgment of what else had happened that morning, the tumult of emotion and anger against the Harknesses. Had she forgotten how she had exploded in rage? She had frightened him with her fit, not that he thought she would attack him physically but that her rage would overwhelm her reason, make her heart stop. He had heard of such cases, a sudden hemorrhage in the brain. And this, her anger, was what the Harkness women would have to contend with when Clara Bascombe testified at their trial, which she surely would, being their chief accuser.

At their parting, William reminded her he needed to ride into Chelmsford to see to a patient. It was the same lie he had told her father the day before, but he needed to get away from the Bascombes, if only for the afternoon.

And especially from Clara.

In Chelmsford, he went to the Blue Boar.

"Back so soon from the Rise?" Rafe said when he saw William.

154

"But for a few hours."

"And are they treating you well there, at the castle?"

"Like a prince."

Rafe laughed. "Ha, but do they know why you are here in Chelmsford, though?"

"They think I am paying a social visit, the son of Sir Richard's old friend."

Rafe nodded, laughed again. "Best they keep thinking that. You would hardly be welcome if they knew you were here to speak on behalf of the Harknesses."

"I would not be welcome. Therefore, my friend, please say nothing of that to anyone at the Rise, should they come to town. Servants included. They are the worst for gossip."

"You have my promise, Doctor."

Rafe made a motion suggesting his lips were sealed.

"Tell me, Rafe. Clara Bascombe told me several doctors attended on her brother at the beginning of his sickness, but she mentioned no names. She said one was from Chelmsford. Do you know who that might have been?"

The innkeeper shook his head. "It could have been a half dozen or so. If they were real doctors and not frauds, that drops to two or three."

"Let's say they were real doctors, not frauds or mountebanks," William said. "Can you give me their names?"

"With pleasure, Doctor. I'm always willing to name names—in a good cause, that is."

Of the three doctors mentioned by Rafe Tuttle, two had their houses and their places of business on the High Street within a short distance of each other. The third was farther out of the town but would have required of William but a quarter of an hour's walk.

The first two doctors were at home. William introduced himself as a visitor from London, said he was a friend of Sir Richard Bascombe, and asked if either had attended on the knight's son, Thomas. Both said they wished they had been so honored, but had not treated the young man and did not know who had.

Which left the third. This man William found not at his house, a modest thatched cottage, but in his garden adjacent to it, a pretty plot of land well planted and tended as if that was all he did. His name was Doctor Samuel Wilde, the innkeeper had told William. Wilde was an aged and stooped man with craggy face, white hair and a long, pointed beard that made him look more like a wizard than a physician.

Wilde seemed unimpressed when William said he was from Colchester and now practiced in London. He forsook his work of hoeing weeds and thistles and asked William curtly what he wanted in Chelmsford. William assured him that he was not a competitor for the Bascombes' medical needs.

"I am a friend of the family," William said. "Lady Clara was recalling the time when you assisted her brother and desired to know more of your thinking as to the sickness whereof he died."

"My thinking, Doctor?"

"About what caused his illness."

The old man shrugged. "Well, some may say the Devil, some may say God. I think it may have been both in concert, as it is in most cases. Tell me, Doctor, are you a religious man?"

"I am not irreligious," William answered. "I cannot claim to be pious, yet I honor the queen's church."

"No papist, then?"

"Not a bone in my body."

The old doctor nodded approvingly and leaned on his hoe. "God is the ultimate cause of all things, diseases included. More immediately though, setting aside religion for a moment, I would say nutrition, I think."

"Nutrition?"

"Or the lack of it. We are what we eat, are we not? The rich live well and die young because they stuff themselves, largely to show they can afford it. Meat, meat, meat. Of every kind and condition, some spoiled since they believe it improves the flavor. And the portions? Great God in heaven, sir. Each eats enough for two or three. So did Thomas Bascombe. It is no wonder he wasted away."

"I would have thought it would make him fatter," William said.

"In fact, he grew thinner," the old doctor declared, seemingly undisturbed by this contradiction in his theory.

"And that was what you diagnosed, no illness natural or supernatural?"

"I will be truthful with you, Doctor... I am sorry, I have forgotten your name."

"Gilbert," William said.

"Well, Doctor Gilbert, he may have had some transient thing, a cold or a loose stool that got out of hand, got worse, I mean. You know how

156

these things go. Today a condition seems mild, no more than an itch. Tomorrow, the man is buried. Or maybe he languished for love. I heard from his manservant Sanderson that the master had a woman somewhere in the countryside, but that his father forbade him to see her. That can be hard on a young man, full of juice and eager to propagate the race, as I am sure you know from your own experience."

William did know, but he didn't want to think about that now. "She said you bled him. Hardly a cure for love-sickness."

"Oh sir, she demanded it of me, and if you know Clara Bascombe you know she's a woman who will not be denied. I bled Thomas Bascombe twice, nay thrice, at her behest. She thought it might improve him. It didn't. After the last bleeding they didn't call me back. It was a handsome fee she paid for my services, so I regret that."

"And because the bleeding failed to cure, she let you go."

"Oh, in part, Doctor, but I believe it was really the influence of her secretary."

"Agnes Robinson?"

"The same. She took against me, wanted, I think, to take charge herself, though she has no more medical experience than an ass."

The old doctor again asked William why he wanted to know. William made something up, a skill he realized he was becoming good at. "So, some of the household have developed similar symptoms. Sir Richard's daughter wanted to know. She couldn't remember what you had said before."

The old doctor laughed. It was a merry laugh, rich in irony. "Why, sir, that's because no one pays attention to what doctors say, especially if it runs counter to their predispositions and pleasure. I heard she nursed her brother herself thereafter. Administered to him God knows what. Agnes Robinson plied her with ointments and salves, as well as advice on how to get what she wants when she wants it."

"Venetian ceruse."

"That's it, I think. You've seen her face. Lady Clara's as white as a ghost. The queen has nothing on her for hiding what God gave her."

William thanked the Chelmsford doctor for his help and turned to leave. Before he could, Wilde called him back and propped himself up on his hoe like a scarecrow.

"Lady Clara believes that a witch cursed him, doesn't she?" the old doctor asked.

"Her brother Thomas? Yes."

"So I've heard. But what think you, Doctor Gilbert?"

"I think the lady believes what she says," William answered.

"You know we in Chelmsford busy ourselves with the persecution of witches," the old doctor said, turning his attention again to his hoeing. "More than any other town in the realm. It's a peculiar distinction, is it not, Doctor? A town famous for rooting them out from amongst us. For trying them, parading them about, and hanging them."

William agreed it was.

"These wretches, most of whom happen by some strange quirk of fortune to be people against whom their accusers have some festering resentment that their own professed Christianity cannot assuage. Yet what better way to seek revenge than to peddle some idle and absurd tale of black dogs and chattering toads and see our old enemy squirm and at last face the rope. I do fear in time we shall have a dearth of old women and some old men as well, although women get the worst of it. All hanged and buried, Doctor, these so-called witches, to the great satisfaction of our city fathers, self-righteous hypocrites that they be. I tell you, sir, I fear for the safety of my aged wife. She's the best of women, but none's so good as to avoid calumny's tongue. Don't you agree, Doctor?"

"You sound skeptical, Doctor Wilde, in the matter of witchcraft, and you vilify the authorities of the town."

"I, a skeptic? A vilifier?" the old doctor laughed. The laugh ended in a kind of gag. When he recovered, he said, "On the contrary, sir, I am the most believing of men. I believe what my eyes see, and what they see is that malice lies beneath this witch-hunting frenzy. Though if you tell anyone in Chelmsford that I said that, I will deny it."

"They won't hear it from me," William said.

25

William returned to the Rise by suppertime, when he joined the family for another meal of that abundance the old Chelmsford doctor had condemned, but remembering Wilde's comments, William ate sparingly. Clara noticed first, then her father.

"Eat, Doctor, a man must eat to live," Sir Richard said, beaming at his potential son-in-law.

Clara also encouraged him. They had not talked since his return. But she had smiled at him constantly across the table, giving him knowing looks, as though there was something settled between them. He remembered the kiss, but it was quickly fading before more recent and much less pleasant memories.

He told them he had eaten heavily in Chelmsford at midday, a banquet hosted by friends. Then he received a letter, brought to him by one of Bascombe's servants.

"It came while you were in the town," the servant said, handing it to him while he was still at table. "Brought up along with a load of wood. It had your name upon it, see, Doctor, right here."

The letter was from his father. He recognized the handwriting. William excused himself from the table, not because he was tired but because he wanted to read the letter in private. He feared it was another effort on his father's part to discourage his participation in the witch trial to come.

He sat down on his bed, broke the seal, and opened the letter. By candlelight it was not easy for him to read his father's old-fashioned script, neat but eccentric as though written by some hoary ancestor. He read it quickly through, then a second time more slowly, already thinking how he was to respond or whether he should respond at all. It read:

Dearest William,

I am in receipt of a letter from my old friend Sir Richard Bascombe of Mowbray Rise, who tells me you have been his guest for these past several days. He tells me much of you, praises your learning, manners, and deportment while in his house. More importantly, he tells me that his daughter Clara is likewise impressed and that you and she have spent some pleasant time together. He has reason to believe, writes he, that you are likewise taken by his daughter.

My son, let me be plain with you. It is beyond time for you to take a wife, which thing will both ensure your posterity but likewise enhance your status among your friends and at court, for as you know a physician who is unmarried must ever be a source of suspicion of husbands concerned for the chastity of their wives and daughters. Besides the which, it is as you know a man's duty to marry. Both Reason and Holy Writ attest to this.

By all accounts, Clara Bascombe is a young woman much to be desired. She is said to be beauteous, fertile, and accomplished as a musician. She can read and write, a rarity in women of her class. Moreover, her father my dear friend has promised a handsome dowry, so you shall not want for money to set up housekeeping either in Colchester or London, as you choose.

The final paragraph of his father's letter, William read a third time:

Of course, if you pursue this end, marriage I mean, you must reconsider your support for the Chelmsford witches. As you may know, the Bascombes are their chief accuser and if you appear at their trial and speak well of the Harkness women it will put you at odds with the Bascombes. Your hopes, and mine, of marriage to the lovely Clara will be dashed.

Think, son, and consider my counsel.

Your loving father

William lay on the bed, still fully dressed, staring up at the muraled ceiling. Samson and Delilah again, the beguiled Samson still in dire straits. His father's counsel was very much what he would have expected from him, reasonable, practical, and lawyerly. William did not know how he felt about Clara Bascombe at the moment. Despite her lavish application of ceruse, she was an attractive woman. He had been taken aback by her explosive, almost violent anger on their ride together, discovering in her a person he had not seen before when her graciousness and her wit, even her bold amorousness, impressed him most. He could not deny it. He had enjoyed the kiss, the impulsive embrace, the sure knowledge that however he felt about her, she wanted him. The old Chelmsford doctor had said of her that she was a woman who got what she wanted when she wanted it. William felt like a target.

He was not averse to taking a wife, but neither was he desperate to find one. And he did not want to marry in haste and repent at leisure, as his father warned. Besides, he had made a promise to the Harknesses to help them in their trial. How could he break such a promise after they had saved his life?

To commit to Clara was to take her side in the trial, to adopt her shaky arguments, to accept her false premises, to collaborate in her anger and rage. It would defy reason, run counter to his science.

There was nothing in Clara's account of her brother's last months that convinced him that her brother's death had been wrought by supernatural means. The symptoms she described accorded with a dozen diagnoses, all made the worse by the damnable bloodletting, the fasting, the purging that would have gone with it, a malpractice that would have made a strong man weak; a weak man, weaker.

And most appalling, the painting of Thomas Bascombe's body with ceruse! What madness was there! Was not the absurdity of it, the potential risk of it, plain on its face? Even to one without medical knowledge?

How could Clara have consented to it, lest she was bewitched herself? Not by Ursula Harkness, but her own trusted servant.

26

His candle burned low, having been a puny stub to begin with. His room at the Rise was all shadows now, except for the open window. A hint of moonlight. He was removing his doublet and hose when a soft knock came at the door. His first thought was Clara. Another secretive visit? Another intimate exchange?

He felt a twinge of excitement. He hurried to dress himself again before telling his visitor to enter. When the visitor did, William saw it was not Clara.

"May I come in, Doctor?" Julian Bascombe said. "I trust I'm not intruding on anything."

William could hardly deny him, given he was his host's son and heir, although Julian was the last person he wished to see that night or any night.

Clara's brother looked about, as though he were searching for something. "I thought I might find my sister here."

"As you can see, sir, she's not here," William said, feeling a presentiment of what was to come. He felt his muscles tense up, his body like a spring.

"No, I can see that, but you wonder, Doctor, why I should think to find her here?"

"I have no idea," William said. "But I beg your pardon, sir. You must excuse me. It is very late. I'm tired. Can we not have this conversation in the morning?"

"No time like the present," Julian said. He advanced into the room and settled on to the bed as though it were his room and William the visitor. "Let me tell you, Doctor, that this is a big house but for all that, little passes here that is secret. For example, I know Clara was with you in this very room yesternight. And not just to stick her head in to bid you sweet dreams."

"Who told you that?"

"It makes no difference who told me, Doctor. I ask you if it's true."

"We did nothing improper, nothing dishonorable," William said.

"Dishonorable," Julian said. William could see visitor's face in the darkness. It wore a wry, incredulous grin. It suddenly occurred to him that were he to marry Clara, this rude cur would be his brother-in-law. The thought was more than distasteful to him. He marked it as yet another reason that this proposed marriage was a bad idea, a conspiracy of fathers to shape the lives of their children, ignorant of what they were about and whom they directed. A marriage was no mere yoking of individuals, it was a merger of families. The Bascombes and the Gilberts? It was unthinkable.

"Your protest, Doctor, would convince few of Clara's chastity," Julian said. "You were alone, in this very room. What might you do here alone together that does not offend God and stain my sister's reputation?"

"Your sister came here of her own accord, not of my bidding," William said, growing heated, his hands balled into fists now, quivering. "And we did but talk, nothing else that might not have been done in plain sight of her father, or of you for that matter."

William thought of the kiss Clara had given him. It was not exactly a chaste kiss. There was a quantum of passion in it, a promise of something even more intimate, but then she had initiated it, not he. No matter; he thought her brother had no business conducting such an interrogation as this was proving to be. Besides that, the truth was that they had passed time talking. She had not come to his bed, nor had he seduced her to it.

"She was here almost half an hour," Julian said.

"You spied upon us that you know so much?"

"It is my father's house, Julian said. "Since my brother's death, I am his heir. You have no privacy rights here, sir, regardless of my father's good opinion of you. Or my sister's."

"An opinion you have made clear to me you do not share," William said.

"To be plain, Doctor, no. I do not like you, sir. I see no reason I should. You are a presumptuous ass, sir. You are a doctor, not a gentleman. Your father is a common pettifogger, nothing more."

William let these insults pass, although the slur on his father's professional standing enraged him. He disliked dueling, which he regarded as a remnant of medieval bestiality and he knew he had just suffered an offense that for many would inevitably lead to the death of one of them, by sword or pistol. But although he detested Julian Bascombe, he was no more interested in his death than in his own, however God or fortune might dictate the outcome. This was, he knew, a time for a measured response. If Julian walked away thinking William was a coward for not answering his insults, then let him. He cared nothing of what Julian Bascombe thought, about him or about anything else. He could imagine the brother running off to tell his sister that the London doctor she had supposed a suitor for her favors was nothing more than a craven coward, not worth her love or respect, but if Clara bought into that, it only proved her less suitable for his wife.

"You say you talked," Julian continued, leering. "What of, pray? My lady's body parts and how delightsome they appeared in the dark? Did you explore her with your hands, sir? Examine her privities?" He made obscene motions with his hand and tongue.

"We talked, if you must know, about her brother whose bedchamber this was. I asked her how her brother died, what illness brought him to his end. I am a doctor. I am naturally concerned with such matters."

"And what did she say?"

"She said he lay abed much, weakened, then was bled. She said she nursed him until the end."

"True, but did she tell you how toward the end he became sometimes violent, had fits, delusions. How his brain was affected, not just his body, which to her and to me, sir, are right evidence of witchcraft, hardly the normal course of a physical disease. Would you say?"

"Many a disease affects body and mind," William said.

Julian laughed scornfully.

"If I tell my father that Clara came to your room last night, that you and she did the deed of darkness while the rest of us slept innocently in our beds, you'll have a cold breakfast in the morning. He will cast you forth with a good whipping, Doctor Gilbert. Your university attainments and London connections will mean nothing. You know that Mowbray Rise has a dungeon below stairs, in the cellars of this house."

"Your sister showed me."

"And told you about the cells there, and the curious instruments that remain."

William remembered.

"They might still be of use, those implements, though they be centuries old and rusty with disuse."

"Do you threaten me, sir? If you do, you must know that although I bear no weapon on my body, I can attain one easily enough and defend myself against you and any other who impugns my honor or name."

Julian looked startled by William's response, then burst out laughing. "Easy on, Doctor. You grow heated, which I am sure you know is bad for the digestion. I am not a duelist, as you seem to assume. I only tell you what I suspect, what appearances suggest."

"Things are not always what they seem," William said, his heart racing.

"If I tell my father you have stolen my sister's maidenhead and dishonored him in so doing, what do you think his response might be?"

"That would be a lie, sir," William retorted, no longer willing to keep his voice down. "A damnable lie, for I never did such a thing, nor would so offend my host or his daughter."

"You are very smooth, Doctor," Julian Bascombe said. "The accusation may be a lie—though I warrant you my sister is no vestal virgin as she claims—but yet it is a plausible lie, which is often as good as a truth. Take my advice, Doctor, leave Mowbray Rise. Leave tomorrow. Leave before it is too late."

Julian Bascombe rose from the bed, approached the door, pulled the door half open, and then paused, looking back at William. He smiled. "Oh, I almost forgot. The important thing. I also was in Chelmsford today. On a matter of business—at the house of a certain woman who is quite as fond of me as my sister is of you. I tell you this not to boast of my prowess, but to assure you that I know the game, have played it long and hard. They say that it takes one to know one, do they not?"

"I have heard that said, but cannot attest to it from my own experience," William said.

"While in town I happened to encounter a mutual friend. I mean someone you know and who knows you."

"Really, sir? And who might that be?" William asked.

"Chelmsford's constable, Master Pickney. You know him, I think?"

"We've met, yes."

"Well, he certainly knows you, Doctor."

"And if he does? What follows?"

"I like to make inquiries about my sister's suitors," Julian said, "and knowing that you stayed in Chelmsford on your way from London to Colchester, I thought I might get a character reference from the constable.

165

After all, he knows everyone in the town and most of those like yourself who patronize Chelmsford's inns and taverns."

William waited. So did Julian. The silence was heavy in the room. Then Julian continued. "He didn't remember your name. But he recognized you when I described you as a well-dressed London doctor, come nosing around."

"I did meet the constable several days ago, what of that? Certainly, it's no crime, is it?

"Oh, it is no crime to talk to a constable, but this constable told me that you had come to Chelmsford to see the witches. He said you wanted access to them, but he told you none were to see them by order of my father."

"So he did. I do not catch your drift, sir. Having heard of the upcoming trials at the inn I was staying at, I confess myself to be a curious sort. Who would not want to converse with a witch, to see such a creature with his own eyes?"

"He forbade you to see them because he suspected you might help them escape."

"That's a foolish notion,' William said, forcing a laugh.

"What? That you should help them escape their deserved punishment?"

"No, that I would aid them in such an effort."

"I spoke to my sister this afternoon," Julian declared with a note of triumph. "We talked of you. Indeed, she can talk of little else. She is, I regret to say, thoroughly smitten by your charms, such as they are. She said she had told you about the witches, but you had not said that you already knew of them, tried to visit them."

"With all due respect for your sister, I think her memory fails on this point. I am sure I mentioned to her not only that I had heard of the accused women but that out of curiosity I had endeavored to see them with my own eyes."

"I believe otherwise, Doctor. My sister has her faults, as you will soon come to know all too well if you continue in your suit of her. But one of them is not an imperfect memory.

Why, Doctor, believe it or not, she quotes you."

"Quotes me?"

"Chapter and verse. You might as well be Holy Writ so diligent she is in evoking your words."

"If true, I am much honored," William said.

"Honored, you may be. But know this, Doctor Gilbert. It is a brother's duty to look after the welfare of his sister. I am nothing if not diligent in that pursuit. Discovering that you were friend or partisan of the Harknesses, her worst enemies, would bring your pursuit of her love to a quick and disastrous end. Her loathing of them would easily transfer to yourself."

Julian waited for William's response to this, but William made no reply. Were he to argue with Clara's brother it would only provoke him to remain longer, the last thing he wanted. Besides, her brother was right. If Julian told Clara and her father what he had learned in the town, William would be tossed out on his ear.

"I wish you goodnight, Doctor. Sweet dreams, sir."

Julian disappeared into the passageway, laughing.

William walked to the door and bolted it. Had he been a priest, he would have cast holy water about the room to sanitize it, to rid it of the stench of Julian Bascombe's insults and threats. Better that Julian had died and not Thomas, William thought. Had fate so decreed, William wouldn't be in Chelmsford now. He would be in his own house, in his own bed, and with a quiet mind, and Ursula Harkness might have found the happiness she sought.

27

He took Julian Bascombe's threats seriously. He would be a fool to do otherwise. Before sleep, he had decided to leave the Rise, to leave in the morning as soon as possible, to leave without saying goodbye to either his host or his host's daughter.

Julian had wished him sweet dreams. But on that night, he had no dreams that were sweet. On the contrary, he had nightmares in which Sir Richard Bascombe and Clara appeared. Each took turns accusing him of betraying them, of going over to the enemy, despite the hospitality they had offered him, despite the affection Clara had shown him and he had, in some fashion, returned.

He would have dismissed these feelings of treason, but he believed them, even as Julian had, although William believed Julian's motives were something less than honorable. Julian was malicious. Julian was devious. William was convinced his guise of a defender of his sister's honor was a sham, hiding personal motives yet to be revealed. He had seemed to take pleasure in putting William into a vice, like the instruments of torture in the cellars of the Rise, and forcing him out and away from the life of his sister.

William had no doubt that Julian would carry out his threat if William did not leave Mowbray Rise forthwith. He had no doubt Julian would tell all even if William did leave. He had no choice, but to flee like a thief in the night, although he decided before cockcrow would be soon enough.

He awoke early, before dawn, dressed quickly, packed his few things in his travelling bag, and shut the door of his room quietly behind him. He knew in so doing he was breaking at the very least every rule of etiquette he knew, failing to announce his departure, give thanks to his hosts, stealing away without a word, an act that would surely condemn him in the eyes of Sir Richard and his daughter whether Julian told his story or not.

Descending the stairs, he met Sanderson coming up.

"Are you leaving us, Doctor?" the old man asked, noticing William's bag.

"I am. Pressing business in the town. I must be there by eight."

The servant nodded knowingly and chuckled. "I wager you've been talking to Master Julian."

William admitted he had.

Sanderson whispered. "I warned you, Doctor, did I not? Master Julian has ruined every relationship Lady Clara has enjoyed these past few years. Did he threaten you, sir? Offer you money to be done with you?"

William was not prepared to confide in Bascombe's servant and contribute to the manor gossip mill. He said, "Let's say, we agreed to disagree on some issues, and for that reason, God willing, we shall have no more to say to one another, neither in this life nor the next."

Sanderson chuckled. "Good luck to you, Doctor. May you find love elsewhere to your liking."

When he entered the stable, he found it already occupied by two men, the stableman and his son, the latter a thin lad of fourteen or fifteen William had seen on the day before when he had gone riding with Clara. The boy's father nodded to him and went about his work, but his son came up to him and asked whether it was his pleasure to ride and whether the lady would accompany him.

"I'm leaving today," William said. "I'll need my horse."

William stood in the open stable door watching the sunrise until the boy came back, leading not William's horse but another, a stronger and healthier looking one. It was the black stallion he had been allowed to ride before.

"That's not my horse," William said.

The boy, a sturdy, handsome youth, smiled and handed William the lead. "The Lady Clara said when you were ready to leave the Rise you should have this mount. It's a gift, Doctor, I think. A token of her esteem."

"That's very generous of your mistress," William said. "But overly generous, I think. I will not take it. I want the horse I rode in on."

The boy stood quietly for a moment, puzzled by the rejection of a gift of such value and wondering, doubtlessly, about the London doctor's inexplicable ingratitude. "Lady Clara's gentlemen rarely turn down her gifts," the boy said.

"Yet I must say no to this," William replied. He was not about to accept a valuable horse and make his ingratitude all the worse.

The boy shrugged and led the horse back to a rear stall. It was now broad daylight. The scent of horse and dung were pungent and not altogether unpleasant for William. Honest smells, better than those of a closed house and evil thoughts. The boy returned. His face was blank now, as though William wasn't there at all. He was only a stable boy, but William supposed he had taken the rejection of his mistress's gift as a personal affront. He reached into his purse, pulled out two coins and handed them to him. The boy bowed stiffly, muttered "Thank you, Doctor", and started to move away, when William noticed something on the boy's left hand.

"What have you done to your hand?" William asked. The boy's hand was covered with a milky salve. The salve extended from his knuckles to his wrist and disappeared into the sleeve of his shirt.

"May I see it?" William asked.

The boy rolled up the sleeve. William could see that the salve extended all the way to the boy's elbow. It had been applied like a paint and had hardened like a crust. "What is it?"

The boy shook his head. "It's a rash. It's plagued me since Michaelmas."

"Three months, then?"

"Near to."

"And what is the salve, this ointment, if that's what it is?"

"I don't know, Doctor. The rash itched me to death, sir, but since applying the salve I feel no itch at all."

"But who applied it? Was it a doctor?"

"Oh, no doctor, sir." The boy said, frowning. "We have little need of doctors at the Rise, begging your pardon, sir. I mean no disrespect, but we are country folk here and have women who know how to make things better."

"What women?" William asked, thinking it might have been the boy's mother.

"Mistress Robinson."

"She who attends on Lady Clara?"

"The same, Doctor."

William looked at the salve. He touched the boy's hand and took some of the salve on his fingers. He held it to his nose. It had a familiar smell. Like vinegar. The color he recognized too. It was the color of Venetian ceruse. The same thing Clara Bascombe used to whiten her face, here employed not as a cosmetic but a curative.

"Mistress Robinson knows much of salves and ointments. She is a cunning woman."

Cunning woman. William knew what the boy meant, not simply a clever woman but a woman with knowledge of herbs and simples, salves and ointments, knowledge learned not from schools or universities but from experience. Also from inheritance, knowledge sometimes passed down for generations. It was not William's brand of medicine, but he did not disrespect the possessors of it. In their ministrations they were often wrong, but sometimes right. He did not know which category to place this curious ointment into, but he suspected it was the former.

"I am glad the salve works, whatever it may be," William said.

"I am to apply it to my hands and arm for the month."

"That long?" William asked.

"She said it was used on her mistress's brother."

"On Julian?"

"No, sir, on Master Thomas, who is dead."

"Then it provided no cure."

"Yet it prolonged his life so that he did not die soon, but later," the boy said

William would have asked how this salve might have done so, but he knew the boy would not be able to say. He wondered if the woman from whom he had received it could. In his experience, cunning women might know a cure, but rarely could explain why the cure worked. It seemed to make no difference to them, whereas to William knowing the reason things worked was everything. If one knew how things worked, their utility could be amplified, extended to other things.

"Well, I wish you well with the cure," William said, wiping his finger on his own sleeve. Later, he would try to find out what it contained. It looked like Venetian ceruse. He was nearly sure that's what it was.

He thanked the stable boy again, mounted and rode out of the stable yard into the morning air. He pulled up suddenly when he saw Clara walking toward him. He was not sure what she had been told by her brother, but she was frowning, and he immediately feared the worst. Which was what? That she should rail at him, assault him, denounce him as a traitor and an atheist in denying the reality of witchcraft? Or that Julian having kept silent, she would break into tears at his parting?

He dismounted when she came toward him, not dressed for riding this time, even a little disheveled, half-dressed, her face unpainted.

"You're leaving us?" she asked.

"I am, a patient of mine needs me. He's in town, in Chelmsford."

She stared at him, her mouth set. "You mean *she*, do you not, Doctor?"

"I have a woman there I am attending," he said.

It was not a convincing evasion. It sounded like a lie even to his own ears.

"Two women I think," she continued. "Ursula Harkness and her mother. Each accused witches. Julian told me why you are really here, not to pay a call upon my father, certainly not to court me, but to spy upon us all that you may undermine our righteous prosecution and block our vengeance for my brother's death."

There was too much truth in what she said for William to deny it. Of course, he had come to Mowbray Rise for no other reason than to learn what really happened to Thomas Bascombe. And he still didn't know, although he was more convinced than ever that it had nothing to do with witchcraft. He stood there looking at her, as though he were deaf and dumb, not having heard a thing she said and therefore not able to respond. He was not surprised when she gave full throat to her fury. He had steeled himself for it.

"Liar, spy, scoundrel," she hissed. "I know not what other names to call you but to say you are worse than they. At least Ursula Harkness believes my brother did her wrong. What is your excuse for defending them? You have no excuse, Doctor. Don't tell me you do."

To her charge, William had an answer, but he knew it would be futile to give it. His reason proceeded from his gratitude for their saving his life, but it was more. His reason was that the whole prosecution of the Harkness women proceeded from a fundamental and dangerous error, rank superstition, seemingly in accord with true religion but in truth at variance from it.

"I don't believe your brother died because of Ursula Harkness's spells," he said. "I don't know why he languished, why he died, but no curse caused it. Your brother had an affliction of his own body, something

172

that has a name and possibly a cure. It was some natural thing, no work of the Devil."

"Some *natural thing*?" she hissed. "Is it natural that healthy young man, such as my brother was, should lie abed for months, his head aching, his strength gone, suffering I do not know what delusions and false visions? You do not know how he so changed from what he was despite all that I could do to make him well again. You know nothing of his sudden violent fits, where before he was as gentle in his demeanor as a lamb."

She dissolved in tears. Her slight body shook.

He did not dare move forward to comfort her. She had accepted, even welcomed, his comforting embrace before. She would not now.

"I hate you," she said, recovering for a moment. "I hate you so much, and if you speak on behalf of these women at their trial, I will not only hate you the more, but I will ruin you, here in Chelmsford, even in London, where my father has friends in high places. Never return to this house upon pain of death, for you will be seen as a trespasser, so says my father."

She fled from him as though she could hardly wait to get back into the house and bolt the door to him, as though he were some monstrous and dreadful thing threatening her and all she loved.

He had in his life seen people run from the plague in just that way. That was what he was to her now, a plague on all her house.

28

Back in Chelmsford, he went immediately to the nearest apothecary shop, showed the apothecary the white salve he had a smeared upon his sleeve and asked the apothecary what it was. The apothecary, a cheerful young man named Adam Hawkins, of about William's age, looked at it carefully, smelled it for a long time, then looked up at William. He grinned triumphantly.

"Why it is ceruse, sir. It is ceruse without doubt. Do I not recognize the color? Cannot I smell the vinegar in the concoction? Some fine ladies of the court and others paint their faces with it though they be as white as ghosts before. Others do it to hide blemishes, pockmarks, blotches, wrinkles even if they be old enough to have them. Look, sir, I sell it by the bottle. I do make it myself. Yes, sir, it is what they call Venetian ceruse."

The apothecary wanted to know it the gentleman who had inquired desired to purchase a bottle of the substance, perhaps for his wife or his intended, or his… *whore* was what the man was probably thinking, but did not say out of respect for the well-dressed gentleman. Willliam said no, but he did ask if the apothecary had heard of the substance being used as a salve for itchy rash.

"Oh, I think not, sir," the apothecary laughed. "Rashes, no. It's more likely to cause one than cure it, given what's in it. But then people will try almost anything if their need is great. Desperation moves mountains, as they say. Isn't that so, sir?"

William said it was so.

"Do you sell much of it?"

"Ceruse, no. I have but one customer, but she is regular, as regular as sun rise and set."

William asked who it was, but he was sure he already knew. It would not be Clara Bascombe. She would not stoop to enter an apothecary's shop like a common housewife or servant.

It would be Agnes Robinson.

"She comes on Wednesdays like clockwork," the apothecary said. "She buys ceruse and she buys ratsbane."

"Ratsbane?"

"For rats in the kitchens, she says."

"What hour does she come?" William asked.

"Near ten in the morning. Sometimes a little later."

The apothecary asked him again if he didn't want to take a bottle of the ceruse with him. William said he did not.

"Then some ratsbane. I can offer you the best price in town."

"No, Master Apothecary. I have no need."

"No rats?"

"I have a cat," William said, and thanked the apothecary for his time.

Back at the inn, William spent the evening thinking about Venetian ceruse and its properties. But more particularly about lead, its principal ingredient. The mineral was mined extensively in England, especially in its northern parts, even in Roman times. In William's time, lead was one of the principal exports of his country, supplying half of Europe with its material for building roofs and casting balls for pistols and canon. He had once met a man who had claimed to have mined it. William had been doing charitable work, as many physicians in the College did, in St. Bartholomew's Hospital. The man had been found dying in the streets. William had pieced together that the man had been a lead miner in the north-east of England. He was sick and had sought William's help.

Now that he remembered it, the man had many of the symptoms Clara Bascombe had described in her brother before his death; severe headaches, loose bowels, vomiting, general malaise, even mental disorders, irascibility, mood shifts. Although a critic of the ancients, William was a zealous student of their writings and conceded that they were not always wrong. He knew from his studies that a certain Greek physician named Nikander had written of the dangerous effects of lead poisoning, several centuries before Christ. And Galen, the Roman physician, who most of his colleagues thought was the last word in every aspect of medicine,

175

had likewise proclaimed it as dangerous, both to the body and the mind, producing delusions and eventually death. Clearly, if it were as dangerous as belladonna or other noxious poisons, it would have killed anyone who dug for the mineral or ate off pewter plates. But that did not mean it was not dangerous, because not always fatal.

The man William had treated eventually recovered. But what of prolonged use, as in the case of Thomas Bascombe? What of having one's body coated with it?

He would have liked to ask Clara directly. But the idea of talking to Clara now seemed impossible. She had declared her hatred of him, a hatred he knew was born not only by his support of the Harknesses, but of his rejection of her love. Perhaps, to Clara, the last offense was the worst.

But he knew the cause of Thomas Bascombe's death was central to the case against the Harkness women. Surely, that case would fail if it could be shown that in her endeavor to save her brother, Clara, not some witch's curse, had unknowingly poisoned him.

He knew the very suggestion would inflict Clara with great pain, perhaps even unto death given her devotion to her brother, and the thought of making the argument did not set well with him. Clara might hate him, but he did not hate her. She might be herself cruel, as he had now suspected, but William was not. He had been manipulated by her—and by her father—and nearly seduced by her charms. But did she deserve such devastating news? It seemed almost too cruel, if indeed what William suspected was true.

But his theory of Thomas Bascombe's death was only that. He needed something more. If he could not talk to Clara, perhaps he could talk to Agnes Robinson. The apothecary had said the woman obtained her ceruse from him. He said she came there once a week. On Wednesdays—tomorrow—around mid-morning.

29

It was late morning before Agnes Robinson appeared at the apothecary's shop on the High Street, carrying a basket.

William had waited almost two hours and had been almost ready to give up. But now here she was, just as the apothecary had said. He watched as she entered the shop. After a few minutes she reappeared, basket in hand. That basket would contain the ceruse, and perhaps the ratsbane, too.

William followed her until she came to the end of the town. Then he called out to her. She turned around, recognized him, and continued on as if she had never seen him at all.

"Mistress Robinson?"

"I mustn't speak to you, Doctor," the woman called back, over her shoulder.

She continued on her way, picking up speed. He caught up with her, matched her stride. She was breathing heavily.

"Did your mistress forbid you to speak to me?"

She shook her head. "No, she said nothing about you, but I know she would disapprove were she to know. She is greatly offended, Doctor."

"I know she is," William said. "And for that I am heartily sorry."

"Then I will wish you good day, Doctor. I have to get back to the Rise before noon."

"Please, wait." He reached out to take her arm. She shook his hand off and glared at him.

"Don't touch me, Doctor. If you touch me, I swear to God I'll fetch the constable."

"I don't mean to alarm you, Mistress Robinson. I ask only a moment of your time."

"What, sir, to use me as a means to restore yourself in my lady's good graces?" She looked at him with contempt, another in the household convinced William was no more than a fortune-hunting scoundrel, a dastardly spy to boot. He wondered if she had been talking to Julian Bascombe.

"I think that unlikely now," William said. "No, Mistress Robinson, that is not my desire. I only want to talk to you about your own practice."

She had been moving on to this point. Now she stopped and faced him. Her expression was still hard and her eyes full of suspicion. But he could see what he had just said to her surprised her. "What do you mean, my practice?"

"As a cunning woman," he said. "I have heard you called such."

"Called by whom?"

"Well, the stable boy for one."

"He has a name, Doctor. His name is Peter Simmons," Agnes said. "I know those of us in service in great houses are near invisible to such as you, who have titles before your names and are raised above us as gentry, but the boy does have a name, as do I. I pray you use it in talking of him. He is a good, honest lad."

"Very well, Peter, Peter Simmons. He told me you gave him ceruse to apply to a rash on his arm. As a doctor, I am always alert to new medications."

"Even if they come from what you call a cunning woman, as you call me?" she asked skeptically.

"Yes, Mistress Robinson. Even if they come from a cunning woman. The natural world is full of things that our modern thinkers and practitioners have yet to discover. I mean things that might heal and invigorate, save lives, promote health, even save from death."

She was a hard nut to crack, with her class sensitivities, but she seemed to soften at this. Then she said, "My legs ache from the walk, and I have miles yet to go. May we sit, Doctor?"

By the road was a fringe of green grass, sloping upwards and giving a pleasant view of the valley and in the distance, Mowbray Rise; its stone protuberance an anomaly in the otherwise wooded landscape. She walked over and sat down heavily, stretching out her legs before her, careful to cover her hose-clad limbs with her skirt. William joined her. She was a large woman of middle-age. She might once have been beautiful, he thought, with her dark coloring, her hair thick like a rope and graying underneath a woolen cap. There was perspiration on her forehead, and she was breathing heavily from the walk from Mowbray Rise to the town, and perhaps from anticipation of the uphill walk to return.

"Tell me how you learned your skill?" he asked.

"My skill?"

"Your knowledge of herbs and simples, ointments, and such."

"From my mother, naturally."

"And the ceruse?'

"Ceruse?"

"What you have in your bottle."

"We call it something else. Angel white," she said.

"Angel white?"

She nodded. "Which is what my mother called it."

"You gave it to your mistress?"

"When she was but a child, she suffered the smallpox, which illness left her face with some imperfections. A pitiful thing for a child to suffer. I gave it her to cover her blemishes. To make her face whole again, that she should be beautiful as before. She was a beautiful child, sir."

"I'm sure she was," William said. "And you gave it to her brother Thomas?"

"She gave it to him, painted him with it."

"But to what end?"

"Why, that it should heal him of his sickness," she exclaimed. "That it should save his life."

William said, "It is made of white lead, vinegar, water. That is what the apothecary said. I know it as Venetian ceruse. It is used by many ladies of the court, even the queen is said to apply it that her face. Some men at court as well."

"I don't know what it contains, only that it covers my mistress's blemishes, that it cures Peter's rash, that we call it angel white, although Master Hawkins, the apothecary gives it a different, fancier name. That my mother used it to heal me when I was sick."

"Sick of what?"

"Some disorder of my bowels. She gave it to me to drink, and I did drink it up and then was well again."

The very thought of drinking a liquid with lead as one of its ingredients horrified William, but he did not say so to her. He would not do that now. But he wondered that the woman survived it. He recalled again Galen's warning. Lead is poisonous to the body, and to the mind. The miner he had treated in the hospital had survived, but barely. How might it have affected Thomas Bascombe? How might it still affect Clara, who like her brother displayed unusual swings of mood and frequent headaches. If the ceruse was the cause, was it already too late for her?

He told Agnes he had a horse and offered her a ride back to the Rise. She wouldn't have to make the long, uphill walk. He thought the offer might assuage her anger, although at the same time he knew it was a ridiculous idea, he and Agnes mounted together, showing up at the very place he had been forbidden to return to.

"Walking is good for the soul, Doctor. I must decline your offer."

She asked him what he thought of what she had called Angel White.

"I think it does what cosmetics do, cover blemishes, scars, pits. But in the long run it may do harm."

She scoffed and asked what harm he meant.

"Does your mistress use more of the ceruse than she used before, lay it on more thickly?"

"She applies as much as she needs, as much as she desires. It is her choice, not mine."

"She applies it more heavily because the natural skin beneath is being damaged," William said.

"I advise my lady, I do not control her actions. That isn't my place."

"Did you advise your mistress to apply the ceruse to her brother's body?"

"The idea was hers, not mine. She's used it for years with no harm done to her."

"It's dangerous, Agnes."

"You are wrong, Doctor. You are plainly wrong."

She got to her feet with surprising agility and glared down at him with contempt. He knew that whatever ground he had gained with her the past few minutes he had lost. His rejection of her preferred remedy she took as a personal insult. He was back to where they had started: enemies.

She spat out her words: "You doctors think you know so much, but you know nothing but how to collect your fees and make money off the poor and them that are below you. Mountebanks, the lot of you."

She strode off, up the hill, mumbling to herself. And then he couldn't see her anymore.

He thought it likely that he would never see her again. Yet William was not sorry he had warned her of the dangers of what she had called angel white. He could have done no less, for he was a doctor and had sworn an oath to do no harm.

But he knew he had no power over her or her convictions, and less power now over Clara, who he feared would become the next to fall victim of so dangerous a concoction.

30

Back at the inn, Rafe Tuttle told him he had a visitor, a distinguished visitor, no common fellow or somebody's toady with cap in hand. Rafe's oath upon it.

William was too tired to be impressed, but he did get Rafe to say who his visitor was. "It's Doctor Junius Culpeper."

"Doctor Culpeper? Do I know him? Is he another physician?"

"Not that kind of doctor," Rafe said. "A churchman. I have sent him up to your room. He wanted to talk to you privately."

"Privately, why?"

Rafe shrugged and grinned. "Maybe to call you to repentance, or to ask you to increase your tithes and offerings. You'll have to ask the learned doctor yourself."

Doctor Junius Culpeper was standing looking out the window when William entered. He turned slowly, revealing himself as a portly man, dressed in clerical collar and cassock with gray hair and a round, ruddy face like an aged, overstuffed cherub.

"You are Doctor Gilbert?"

"I am, sir."

"I beg your pardon for this intrusion. The innkeeper showed me up and let me in. I am Doctor Junius Culpeper, rector of St. Peter's."

William had had much experience with clergymen in his relatively short life. Like most of his countrymen and certainly persons of his class, he had been christened shortly after his birth. He had attended his parish church in Colchester as custom and the law required, and at Cambridge priests of the queen's religion were as common as crows and attendance at sermons, sometimes dry-as-dust, was mandatory. Ordinarily, therefore he would have found nothing threatening in this smiling, seemingly affable cleric, but the place and time, and the request for privacy, made him apprehensive. A few of the encounters he had experienced since arriving in Chelmsford had been pleasant, most had been threatening. He wasn't sure which one this would be.

"And to what do I owe the honor of this visit, sir?"

"I bring you a message from Sir Richard Bascombe," Culpeper said, drawing from a pocket a piece of paper which he proceeded to refer to by dropping his eyes to it intermittently as though it were the text of a sermon he had only half memorized. "Sir Richard expressly wishes you not to return to the Rise and advises you to leave Chelmsford and return to London or to Colchester, whichever you prefer."

"May I ask why Sir Richard asked you to deliver this message? Why did he not deliver it himself? Or have his son or daughter, or a servant do it?"

"It is of a very sensitive nature," the rector said. "Besides, Sir Richard and I are old friends."

"Then, sir, you must tell me what it is, this message. I do perceive you have more to tell me than just let me know of my banishment."

The rector took a deep breath and proceeded.

"I must speak plainly."

"Pray do so," William said.

"Sir Richard says you assaulted his daughter, more than once."

For a moment, William was too astonished to speak. His expulsion from Mowbray rise was to be expected, but this outrageous charge quite took his breath away with its audacity.

"*Assaulted his daughter?*" William exclaimed. "I never did, nor would think of doing so."

"Nonetheless, so the Lady Clara charges you. She says you seduced her to come to your room at the Rise, where you forced yourself upon her, kissing her upon the mouth when she denied you such a privilege and suggesting she spend the night with you."

"Not true," William cried, growing alarmed by these charges, which went far beyond Clara's earlier complaint that he had rejected her love.

"And, moreover," Culpeper said, warming to his theme, "that you are in conspiracy with these people, the Harknesses, mother and daughter, now awaiting trial for witchcraft, and that your purpose in coming to the Rise was not to pay your respects to your father's friend, Sir Richard, but to spy upon the house and gather evidence to support these notorious women."

For William it made more sense to deny all of this, even though these allegations were at least in part true, than try to separate truth from fiction. "I came to Mowbray Rise to visit my father's old friend. I made no improper advances upon the Lady Clara, forced no kiss upon her, nor invited her to my bed. I don't know where Sir Richard got his information. I doubt from the lady herself, for I think too much of her to believe she would so falsely characterize our time together. But I would assure him, were he here, that these allegations are false."

"Sir Richard has proof of each charge."

"Has he? Then he should bring such proof forth," William shot back, turning away from his visitor and stalking toward the door. He held it open, motioning to his visitor to get out.

"It is the word of Lady Clara herself," Culpeper said, his round, fleshy face beetroot red.

"I would prefer to hear these charges from her own lips, not from some writing in your hand, Doctor Culpeper, which for all I know may be the work of your own imagination."

At this, the rector's face lost its benign expression. By candlelight, he looked almost devilish. "I do protest, Doctor, such an implication. By God, sir, these are the words of Sir Richard. Not mine, I assure you. And it is he, not I, who has the power to bring you to account for your misdeeds."

Culpeper gave William a withering look, of the type that he might have given some miscreant who stole from the sacristy.

William said, "Is that Sir Richard's intent? As to the last charge, that I spied upon his household, I know enough law to know that is no crime in England, now or before, even had I done so, which I deny. As for my supposed assault upon his daughter, I think that since these things alleged were done behind closed door and without a witness, it will be my word against hers."

"She is a lady, the daughter of a knight," the Rector declared, his jaws quivering with indignation and as though that fact settled the issue.

"I grant you that, sir, but I am someone as well who has a certain amount of credibility."

"Besides which, there was a witness," the Rector said, departing from his notes at last.

"Pray, who?"

"Indeed, two witnesses." Culpeper said.

William waited.

"Master Julian, her brother, and her ladyship's companion, Agnes Robinson."

"And these listened at the door, peeked in the window?" William asked incredulously.

"They listened at the door."

"The two of them?"

"So they will attest, Doctor."

"And heard me force the lady despite her protests but did not enter to rescue her from my lascivious advances?" William laughed. "Oh, Rector, these charges defy belief."

"They will testify to what they have heard," the rector said. "And what they saw."

"They saw what?"

"Saw you with the lady, in the garden where you did press her to your chest."

"I did so to comfort her. We were at her brother's grave. She was mourning her dead brother, weeping uncontrollably. Besides which, it was she who pressed her face against me."

"Nonetheless you did take advantage of her state of grief," Culpeper said.

"I did what I would hope any decent man would do to give solace to another. You are a professor of the faith, sir. As a good Christian, would you not have done the same? It was she who wanted me to see her brother's grave. She practically dragged me there."

The rector scowled. "I see you are unrepentant, Doctor."

"I cannot and will not repent of what I did not do," William said. "The lady Clara showed me many courtesies while I stayed at the Rise, for which I am truly grateful. I think she did mistake my own response as being that of a suitor rather than merely a friend. For that I am sorry. But at no time did I assault her or anything of the like. You may tell her that, and you may tell her father, Sir Richard Bascombe, likewise."

The Rector went to the window and looked out at the night. Silence followed. Then Culpepper turned suddenly back to William. "Sir Richard is prepared not to press charges against you, Doctor."

"Oh, is he? And why not if they are as serious as he claims? What, a father has evidence of an assault upon his own daughter yet is prepared to make no charge against the vile fellow who did it? And for what, Doctor Culpeper? Are there terms here yet to be disclosed?"

"I have prevailed upon him to allow for a misunderstanding," Culpeper said.

"Really, sir. A misunderstanding?"

"As you say, Doctor, the lady has one view of your conduct, you another."

"A moment before there was but one view, Rector. And it was the Bascombes' and evidently your own."

"If you leave Chelmsford forthwith, Sir Richard will show you mercy."

"Leave Chelmsford? Wherefore should I do so? Is it not enough he has forbidden me to darken the door of the Rise again?"

"It is not enough," Culpeper said.

There was another silence. The two men fixed their eyes on each other, as though waiting to see which would turn away first. It was the rector of St. Peter's.

"All this scandalous matter is about the trial, isn't?" William said.

The rector didn't answer, but as his lawyer father might have said, quoting Plato, silence gave consent.

William continued: "The trial of the witches, or supposed witches, I should say. Sir Richard doesn't want me to testify for them."

"He does not want you to testify, Culpeper said. "The wretched women are guilty as sin. I have questioned each of them myself. I have considered the evidence."

"Gossip and superstition," William murmured.

"Sir Richard told me you were an unbeliever," Culpeper said.

"I am not an unbeliever, Rector, but I do think I know the difference between sound doctrine and claptrap."

"Sound doctrine is what the clergy says it is, Doctor Gilbert, not you. Sacred Writ speaks of witches. It would not do so were they not... a thing. The sooner these women are dispatched, the better."

"I do not believe they're guilty," William declared. "Further dispute is futile. I will not leave Chelmsford, until I have done what I came to do."

"You know that Sir Richard will be one of the men who presides over the trial?"

"It makes no difference to me who presides," William answered with a wave of his hand. He was growing heated, he knew it. He could feel the blood rush to his head, and he could not for the life of him unclench his fists.

186

"I think, Doctor, you will find it makes a great deal of difference. I am another."

"Another what?"

"One who will preside. We have power to depose witnesses. We also can exclude your testimony, whatever it may be."

William tried to calm himself. It had been a long time since anger so possessed him. He had an almost uncontrollable desire to throw himself at this impudent cleric and stuff his threats down his throat. Culpeper was a large man, soft-bellied, with enough muscle to move arms and legs but little else, he suspected. He would be unarmed. William might have done it, throttled him and enjoyed the experience.

But murdering the town's religious leader would hardly recommend him as a witness at a trial. He took a deep breath to calm himself. Finally, he said: "You may show forth your power, Doctor Culpeper, you and Sir Richard, and I will answer it as I am able in a court of law. My father is a lawyer in Colchester. He can advise me as to how I might best respond to these charges and threats."

"You'll need more than a father's advice, Doctor Gilbert. You do not know who you are dealing with," the rector said, with a practiced solemnity he must have employed a thousand times in his sermons.

"I do not, sir? But I *do* know, I know very well. I am dealing with you, sir. And with Sir Richard Bascombe."

"You are dealing with God!" Culpeper bellowed with such force that William drew back from him. "Offending the very powers of heaven with your atheism, your recalcitrance, your refusal to be reasonable. Out of the goodness of his heart, Sir Richard has made an offer of conciliation, damn you, Doctor. All that is required of you is that you leave Chelmsford and the business of its witches to us to whom that business properly belongs. Don't be a fool, Doctor. Accept the offer and save your soul."

"I would lose my soul were I to accept such an offer," William said. "It is corrupt to its core."

He opened the door and bowed stiffly to his visitor.

The rector scowled and left without another word. He didn't look back.

Alone, William imagined Culpeper shaking the dust from his feet outside his door. Well, he could shake what part of his clerical anatomy he willed,

William would not be intimidated, either by a knight in his castle or a rector in his pulpit.

Later, falling asleep, he wondered if Sir Richard had written to his father complaining about his alleged assault. What would his father think? He would be disappointed in the failure of William to pursue Clara Bascombe. But would he also believe the lies Sir Richard was prepared to tell about his conduct there? The thought that his father might believe them disturbed him more than the not-so-veiled threats of the Rector of St. Peter's.

31

For the next few days William stayed in his room, having his meals brought up to him and telling Rafe he was not open to any more visitors, no matter how distinguished. He had been told that the assizes were but a week away, and in the meantime, he had no desire to encounter any of the Bascombes or their household on the streets for fear of having another unpleasant encounter such as he had endured with the Reverend Doctor Culpeper, whom he now listed among his enemies.

Despite what he believed was his own strong defense of his honor, Culpeper's threats had rattled William. He reviewed the scene in his mind a thousand times, revising his responses to an imagined Culpeper, who grew more hypocritical and mendacious at each version as William became more articulate and cogent. The whole accusation of assault was bogus, he knew. A manipulative contrivance to get him out of town. But he would have a hard time defending himself if the Bascombes carried through with it.

Clara Bascombe would be seen as a pitiful victim of his lust and avarice, her brother Julian as a heroic defender of his sister's honor. He knew both of them could play their parts ably, especially if their performance was before local citizens, much beholden to the lord of the manor and naturally suspicious of outsiders of whom they would believe capable of any enormity, especially if he were seen as defenders of witches.

But even were he able to avoid the strictures of the law, his reputation would be ruined. What husband or father would trust him with their wife or daughter? And there would no question of the whole sordid business not getting back to London. Clara herself had threatened that it would, through her father's connections at court. He would be expelled from the College of Physicians by its own rules. Even the queen might hear of it, by direct report or court gossip.

Rafe had told him that he had seen both Sir Richard and his son Julian about the town, another reason for him to stay indoors.

"Doing what?" William had asked.

"Why I suppose tampering with the jury," Rafe answered with a cynical laugh.

"A jury not yet selected?"

"Well, it will be in due course, will it not, Doctor? I see it this way, not every man in Chelmsford is likely to be chosen for the jury. Rather it will be solid citizens."

"Like yourself," William said.

Rafe made a comical bow and flourish with his hand. "Shopkeepers, tradesmen, yeomen, clerks, an honest farmer or two. Julian and his father will make the rounds, I guarantee it. And if they do not pad the purses of potential jurors in this case, they will at least fire up the town to such a temperature that those who are finally chosen to sit in judgment will not dare to find innocent them who so many of the town are pleased to see hanged. Why, even I may be called to serve a second time."

"Would that please you?"

"Yes," he said, after a moment's thought. "It's good notice for the inn."

William had not thought of this, but of course Rafe was right. If the innkeeper did serve, how would he decide? Would he answer as he had with Mother Waterhouse, condemning her to the gallows? Or would he find something in the Harkness case to give him pause? William could not answer. The Harkness case had yet to be laid out. Thus far it had all been fragments, this accusation, this charge. A frenzy of malicious gossip that would under the rule of law be reduced to a formal indictment and series of charges, numbered like a grocery list. He knew it would not be until the trial itself when the chief prosecutor, the queen's attorney, laid out the indictment and the evidence that the case would be clear. Only then would he know what he and they would be up against.

Both Sir Richard and the rector had threatened William, in a bid to exclude him as a witness for the Harknesses. That was a concern. But he wasn't sure the threat carried much force. He wished he knew more about the law. He would have secured his father's help in that, but now that source of information seemed cut off by what his father would surely call William's insufferable obstinacy, if not direct disobedience. To his father, William was prepared to sacrifice his profession. And he was guilty of a

190

new crime against paternal authority, ruining his chances for a marriage with the beauteous, if possibly mad, Clara Bascombe. Besides, even if his relationship with his father were smoother, William's pride would not send him to his father to know how to proceed as a witness in a witch trial, despite what he had told Culpeper. That door was shut, and William had bolted it firmly himself.

He was on his own.

So, as he had done at Cambridge when examinations loomed before him, he resolved to prepare himself. To do so he resorted to his characteristic habit of mind. He was a reader. Before he was a physician and scientist, he was a student. From a bookshop on the High Street, Rafe had acquired for him a pamphlet detailing the trial of Agnes Waterhouse, the first woman hanged for witchcraft in England, eight years earlier. This he read over a dozen times, taking, as was his custom, copious notes both to fix the facts of the case in his mind and because such practice was habitual with him. He could hardly read without a pen in his hand, without a notebook to record impressions and observations, imagining arguments and developing counter arguments. He knew that in any trial in his country, the defendant was always at a disadvantage. The legal experts all worked for the prosecution. No defendant had a lawyer to speak on his behalf, no power to call witnesses. The defendant stood naked before the majesty of the law, or the caprice of the jury of the defendant's peers, often the defendant's worst enemies and more than happy to find them guilty. Judicial corruption was taken for granted. Juries were easily swayed by arguments that were consistent with prevailing views in the town where the trial was held, and often, William knew, those views were primitive indeed, if not barbaric. As he saw it, England was not a single land, but a layered world of peoples at various stages of civilization. One did not have to travel far outside the cities before one found himself in the older world of myth and superstition and practices that to a person like himself, educated and traveled, were well established before the Romans came and thrived in dark corners of the nation still, in little pockets of rank barbarity.

William also read an account of witches written by the illustrious Bishop of Norfolk, that had sold ever so many copies. It was dry reading, full of obvious errors, hysterical prophesies, self-congratulation, and tormented scriptural exegesis, but he could see why it commanded so wide an audience both among the upper and the lower classes. Witchcraft explained the largely inexplicable. It made sense of misfortune, accident, illnesses for which there was no diagnosis or apparent cause. Religion put everything in the hands of God. Witchcraft gave power to man, at least to some men and mostly women, helped along of course by God's mighty opposite, Satan, Belial, the Devil. Call the old fellow what you will. Like God, He had a hundred names. But at last, it was the same dark force of evil given a local habitation and a name.

He had filled his notebook with pages of notes. Then he was interrupted by a knock at the door. It was not Rafe bringing him his supper. It was Rafe bringing him word of another visitor.

"No visitors, Rafe. I told you," William said, annoyed. "For pity's sake. the last—your most Reverend Doctor Culpeper—left me with threats of prison and hell save I gave over any effort to defend the Harknesses. Of such bullying and extortion, I have had my fill."

"This person will not threaten you. He comes as a friend."

"Do I have friends in Chelmsford other than yourself and your good wife?"

"One whom you do not know, but I think will benefit from," Rafe said. "I know him fairly well, more than by mere reputation let's say. He is Master Jeremy Winton."

"What is he, this Master Winton that I should care what he has to say to me?"

"He's a boon companion of Julian Bascombe. They drink together, play cards together, and if you will forgive the vulgarity, Doctor, they go awhoring together."

William remembered Julian Bascombe's boasting of his visits to women while he was in Chelmsford. He assumed then, as he did now, that these women were less than reputable sorts. "Then I should think he is of the Bascombe party, which makes me believe his visit will do me little good but rather give me more nightmares of the fate awaiting me if I open my mouth at the trial."

The innkeeper was silent for a moment, then said, "Trust me, Doctor. You will find it much otherwise. If I am wrong, then damn me to hell. But I am confident that you will benefit and have reason to thank me after."

William looked at the innkeeper and saw no sign of guile in the man's eyes. "Oh, very well, Rafe. Let him come up if he wishes. But

I tell you, I will throw him out if he preaches to me, threatens me, offers me a bribe. I will throw him out with all the strength I have."

Rafe looked pleased. Then he said, "You will have no need to throw him out."

"Why not? Is he not here?"

"He does not want to come here," Rafe said.

"What, your inn is too disreputable a place for his honor?"

"It's not that, Doctor. He says the inn is being watched and he wishes his conversation with you to be private, not known to the Bascombes or any of their friends."

"Then he wishes to converse with me where? Must I come to him?"

"Yes," Rafe said.

"And where shall I find this person, this Master Winton as you call him?"

"There is a house across the river named Cobb's End," Rafe said. "It is a kind of low tavern with some rooms above it that, to be blunt, Doctor, are used from time to time for lewd and unsavory purposes, if you know what I mean." Rafe winked.

William said he did.

"Tell me again of this Master Winton. He is a gentleman, I presume, if he keeps company with Julian Bascombe."

"He is a gentry through and through. Like Master Bascombe he is son and heir, lives large in a manor house in Gosfield, if you know that village."

"I know it," William said. "My mother had relatives in that area, Coggeshalls."

"Before the death of Thomas Bascombe, the three gentlemen were bosom companions, hunting, riding and so forth."

"And after?"

"There was a falling-out betwixt them, and they were not so friendly as before, but still conversed, I think, played cards, boozed, wenched, raised hell where they could. They cannot walk down High Street without offending some ordinance of the town but the constable, Master Pickney, is deep in their pocket and will do nothing to stop them."

"You seem to know their history well," William said, smiling.

"Servants from both houses come to Chelmsford on market day," Rafe said, raising his hands in mock defense. Rafe was well allowed to be a faithful husband to his wife, though she was no great beauty and somewhat of a scold. "And servants will talk," William said, knowing well that it was true. It was a rare household, great or small, that could keep secrets from servants or keep them from gossiping about the vices and frailties of those God had put above them. Rafe saw it as a kind of revenge of the oppressed. Lords and lordlings might rule, but servants would talk.

Rafe said there was something more, something that would put the icing on the cake.

William smiled at Rafe's phrase, which he had not heard before but whose meaning was plain enough. "And the icing is?"

"Master Winton was once betrothed to Julian's sister."

"The Lady Clara?"

"The same, Doctor."

William was impressed. He had not said much to Rafe about his brief association with Clara Bascombe, and certainly nothing about its amorous encounters such as they had been, but it was clear from Rafe's expression that he had learned of it, possibly from this Master Winton who was friends with Clara's brother. That same brother had been bold enough to tell William that his sister had had other suitors, suitors of name and title. William thought then it might be a lie, a clumsy effort to humiliate him, or to advance the prestige of his sister. But perhaps it was true. There *had* been others before him to whom Clara had offered herself. But what had happened? He was not merely curious. Somewhere inside him he thought this knowledge might be useful, perhaps even essential, to defending Ursula and her mother.

Now he was interested in meeting this Master Winton, even if he had to meet secretly in a place that sounded more like a brothel than a tavern. Even if there was still a chance that this clandestine meeting afforded another opportunity for the Bascombes to intimidate him, or perhaps even attack him.

And even if it was all some kind of trap, to lure him from the relative safety of the inn to a loathsome den where he might simply and unaccountably disappear.

He wondered, was his imagination running wild? No, he decided. He needed to consider all possibilities, as grim as they might be, and then act.

"What hour did you say?"

"Hour?"

"When I should meet your Master Winton."

"He said after dark. Say, ten or eleven."

"That late?"

"No one goes to bed much before at Cobb's End," the innkeeper said, looking down. "Well, they do go to bed, but not to sleep or pray."

Rafe's laughter ended in a coughing fit.

32

At nine o'clock, William set out for Cobb's End, as directed. That night the weather was clear, the moon luminous, the heavens opened in such a way that William made his way boldly. He walked confidently, fearlessly, already anticipating his conversation with Clara Bascombe's previous suitor and what he might have to say.

He had no trouble finding Cobb's End. Rafe Tuttle had been most exact in his directions.

Sitting off from the road in a little wood of oak and ash, the roof of Cobb's End could be seen even in the dark. William thought it must have been a farmstead in its time. It had that look, not of a gentleman's house but that of a prosperous farmer to whom some disaster had befallen, fields gone fallow, animals all dead or sold, just a house, a tavern as Rafe had called it. But it had no sign dangling from its front door, and William imagined that its customers learned of its sordid function by word of mouth. It was that kind of house.

As he approached, he heard the sound of loud, raucous voices from within, and upon entering—he did not bother to knock—he found himself in a poorly lit room furnished with several trestle tables and benches, and a handful of customers talking and drinking. Some were playing cards or throwing dice, others were chatting with some women at the end of the room who by their dress and demeanor seemed what his rigidly moralistic father would have called ladies of ill-repute. One of these, a fat girl with a round, rouged face, insolent smirk and breasts overflowing her bodice, came up to him to ask him if he were the doctor from London come to meet a certain gentleman.

William said he was and had. She took his hand and pulled him after her.

At the end of the room were stairs and he followed her up them, uncertain of what was to happen next. He was partly relieved to have been recognized but at the same time his earlier fears for his physical safety came flooding back. Cobb's End was indeed a disreputable place, and by all appearances a brothel, given the unsavory women he had thus far seen.

They proceeded down a dark and narrow passageway off which were several doors. From within these, he could hear laughter, whispers, occasional grunting and groaning of both males and females.

At last, he was brought to a door at the end of the passage. His guide knocked twice. William heard a man's voice say "enter", and then his guide shoved him in, slamming the door behind her. He could hear her giggling beyond the door.

Within, he saw two persons sprawled on a filthy mattress, one a man of about his own years, dressed only in his shirt, and a younger black-haired woman wearing nothing but what she was born with. At his entrance, she sprang up from the bed where she had been lying, hastily threw a robe around her bare shoulders and breasts while the man shouted at her to get out, saying he had some serious business with the gentleman and she was no longer wanted.

The girl said something under her breath that William could not understand, in a foreign language, maybe Portuguese, gave William a quick look of disdain, and hurried out the door. William stood aside as she left.

"You're the London doctor," the reclining man said when they were alone.

"I am."

"And I, Doctor, am Jeremy Winton. Rafe Tuttle told you about me, I trust."

William nodded. Winton pointed to a stool beside the bed. Winton himself did not rise or even sit up. He had been lying on his back when William entered. He apparently saw no reason to change his posture for his guest, to pull on more than the shirt he wore.

Winton was a thick-chested man with a full head of fair hair and thin, almost indistinguishable, eyebrows. His mouth was what William would have called cruel. It was large and his lips were likewise thick, giving an impression of sensuality and avarice. His eyes were small and wide set, his cheeks sallow. William's physician's eye marked the man as anemic, probably from drink.

"You wanted to see me, Master Winton?"

"You may call me Jeremy, if you like, Doctor. There's no reason to stand on ceremony here. A place like this makes all men equal, don't you think?"

"I suppose it does, if they be not so already."

Winton gave out a laugh. It was surprisingly high pitched, like the cry of some bird.

"I have heard much of you, Doctor," Winton said when he had recovered from his hilarity.

"From whom?"

"From Julian, Julian Bascombe. He tells me you and his sister are betrothed, or practically so. Ready to post the banns. It was a status I enjoyed until recently, when at some cost to me—well, to my father to be honest about it—the engagement was broken. I am afraid I left the lady heartbroken, but in truth I had myself to look out for. I was most glad to hear I had a successor for her affections. I did not want to marry the lady, but neither did I hate her so much as to want her to die an old maid."

"I am not betrothed to her," William said. "I made no suit to her."

Winton looked at William skeptically, shifted himself in the bed, but still did not sit up or make to dress himself. "I heard something different from Julian, who told me that his sister was promised to a successful London doctor by the name of William Gilbert and that I had missed my opportunity. He taunted me with it. Julian and I are old friends and have spent many happy hours together. My ending my relationship with his sister put a damper on our joy, as you can imagine. He hoped to have me as his brother-in-law, a position I might have enjoyed until I came to know the lady better. But you say you are not betrothed?"

"I am not. If Julian told you otherwise, he was misinformed, or more likely, lied outright."

Winton laughed. "You are plainspoken for a doctor, sir. Accusing another gentleman of lying. Don't you fear his wrath, should he discover you giving him the lie?"

"I would prefer to speak plainly," William said.

"You did not pursue her, ask for her favors, bed her, or otherwise act in such a way to give her hope?"

"I did not," William said, annoyed that he should need to continue defending himself on that point. He wondered if Winton had heard the trumped-up accusations of his assault. Since Winton had said nothing of that, at least had not as yet, he assumed that Winton had not or he would have mentioned it already, William's lechery a fact, not merely alleged.

Winton breathed a sigh and laughed again. "So, in sum, the lady remains a virgin, unspoken for."

"For all I know she does,' William said. "It is not a question that concerns me now or did while I was in her father's house. I was there to make a social call, not find a wife. If you want to know how she feels about me, you must ask her yourself."

"Oh, Doctor, I don't think I dare do that. When I broke our engagement, she said she would kill me. I doubt she's changed her mind about that."

William said, "May I ask you, Master Winton—"

"Please, Doctor, *Jeremy*."

"Jeremy, why you ended your betrothal?"

'You may ask, and in so doing bring me to the very point of our meeting."

"Which is?"

"I wanted to warn you."

"Warn me, of what?"

"Of her, of course, what else? You see, Doctor, I am what our more righteous citizens call a worldly man. Were I not burdened with public duties—my father is a magistrate—I should become a permanent denizen of this wretched place, spending all my time playing cards and proving myself a great whoremaster in the eyes of the righteous. Are you one of the righteous, Doctor Gilbert?"

"I do not call myself such," William said.

"But you don't condemn me for my, what shall I call it, style of living?"

"I do not condemn you. You live as you choose, as do I. I am a doctor, not your judge."

"Well then, perhaps you will believe me if I say that despite what you see of me here, luxuriating upon this flea-infested bed, I am not without a charitable impulse. And when Julian bragged to me that his sister had found another and better candidate for her affections, I thought to myself, poor miserable wretch, to fall into the clutches of such as Clara Bascombe."

"You make the lady sound like a harridan or a wolfish creature," William said, suddenly finding himself defending a woman who hated him.

"I tell you doctor, she is neither, for those qualities implied in those words simply make her sound like a woman. Neither better nor worse. I am sorry to sound so bitter and cynical, but you see I am not without experience in love, or its counterfeit, lust. And while my father is a magistrate and is honored publicly thereby, my mother rules at home and has made him miserable every day of his life with her demands and demeaning commentary on his alleged failures. Yet compared to Clara Bascombe, my mother is the Virgin Mary."

"That's hard to believe," William said. "I observed the lady to have many admirable qualities."

Jeremy Winton shouted, "Don't tell me about her musical accomplishments, or that damned paint she paints her face with to make her seem as white as snow. Clara Bascombe is mad."

"You mean angry?"

"No, Doctor, I mean mad, in the clinical sense of the word, deranged, demented... use what word for it you will. I think you know my meaning."

"I think I do, sir," William said, remembering Clara's outbursts, her sudden change of moods, the virulence of her emotions.

Jeremy Winton continued to talk about Clara, telling stories of her explosiveness, how at one moment she would be calm, her mind composed, all sweetness and light, and then, of a sudden change as though she were possessed of some demon, seeing things that were not, fearing what was not to be feared, and then possessed of a terrible jealousy, railing at her attendants, the chambermaids and the kitchen maids, threatening violence against them, and finally against him.

"Her father made a stink when I said we would not go through with the marriage. He threatened to sue me for breach of promise. At first, I told him to do so, and the devil take him and his daughter, but then was advised by wiser heads it would be better to settle. I learned all this had happened before."

"What do you mean, before?" William asked.

"I mean there had been others, other suitors, other engagements. At least two. I found out from her former governess; her secretary, she calls herself, though I doubt the woman can read or write."

"You mean Agnes Robinson."

"Yes, a hideous woman and bad influence on Clara, if you ask me. I had the information from her, of course. The price of her loyalty to her mistress was two pounds. She knows what side her bread is buttered on. She spent the better part of an hour regaling me with stories of Clara's disastrous love affairs. Some proceeded to engagements, such as in my case. The luckier gentlemen broke off before it came to that extreme and thereby avoided legal entanglements such as I suffered."

"Were you then sued for breach of promise?"

"My father bought her father off. But nothing would allay the rejected lady's feelings about me."

"So you wanted to warn me?" William said, still suspicious of Winton's motives. "An act of what you call Christian charity."

"Not Christian, necessarily. I reckon that even a stone-cold atheist may find within himself some desire to help a fellow sufferer. But since the story of your betrothal is false, my charitable impulse has been misspent."

"Not necessarily," William said. "The truth is, I am still involved in some respect with the lady. Like you, I am hated where before I was loved, But the scope of her hatred goes beyond my rejecting her. Clara Bascombe hates me because she learned I stand with the women she accuses of causing her brother's death."

"You mean the witches of the Old Priory?"

"You have heard of the case?"

"Who has not? Chelmsford talks of nothing else."

"Master Winton, Jeremy, I would know more about this madness you say afflicted the lady."

"Why? Are you not done with her, sir?"

"I am a doctor. I heal the body, but sometimes I address the illness of the mind. You might say I have a professional interest in her."

"Very well, then," Winton said. "I give you a case in point. While you were at the Rise, did she ever show you the dungeon beneath the house?"

"The cells, the implements of torture. She did."

"Well, she would," Winton said. "If you ask me, Clara has a morbid fascination with the history of that medieval pile she lives in. Loves to go on and on about the old days, about what went on in the cellars. Don't you think, Doctor, with your professional interests, that such fascination is beyond strange, even perverse? I mean, especially in a woman?"

"I suppose so," William said. "She once gave me a tour of the house."

"She took me three times, nay, four. And the last of the times, she said she would kiss me long and hard and give me liberty of her body should I place myself within those iron constraints. I said no and left forthwith. I would gladly have taken her, but not at that price."

201

"A lady of unusual tastes," William said, unsure of whether Winton was telling the truth or merely inventing a salacious story to defame his subject. "What do you suppose she intended?"

"I fear to think, Doctor, what she intended. A sane man may not know. And I'll tell you another thing. Her brother who is dead—"

"Thomas Bascombe."

"You know they were twins, do you not?"

"I do," William said.

"I knew Thomas well. It was through him and Julian that I met Clara, came to know her and early in my suit was attracted to her—until I learned her true nature. As for Thomas, he was a good companion. Not like my relationship with Julian, which has always been up and down."

"Did you know about Thomas's relationship with Ursula Harkness?"

"Ursula who?"

"Harkness. The girl who lives at the Old Priory. She who is accused of being a witch. Thomas met her in the woods, said he loved her, got her with child. According to Clara that is why she put a curse upon him, because he would not marry her."

"I have never heard of it, this girl, or any child begotten by Thomas. Although I must say Thomas was different from us, Julian and me."

"How different?"

"Well, we take our pleasures where we find them. Julian and I like women. If it's a sin so to do, then what can I say? If we are made by God, then He has made us what we are, and the fault is therefore His. It wasn't that Thomas did not like women, only that he refused to join us here at Cobb's End. Is this Ursula you speak of a great beauty, that he should be drawn to her?"

"No great beauty. She is thought by nearly all who see her as plain. Did you ever see Thomas after he fell ill?"

"Numerous times, at first. It was then that I was courting his sister."

"You saw how she ministered to him when he was sick?"

"Oh, I did. I saw it daily during those first months when all had hope he might recover."

"Did she ever say to you that her brother was cursed?"

"I suppose so. I never thought about that. Is it a medicine, this ceruse?"

"No, Master Winton, it definitely is not."

There was a period of silence. From a neighboring room, William heard a sharp cry, whether of pleasure or pain he could not tell. It was a dark house and noisy, full of cries and whispers.

"It would seem, Doctor, that I have summoned you here for nothing."

"For nothing?"

"Well, since you are not betrothed to the lady, my warning is without purpose."

"By no means, Master Winton. You have been most helpful, in the way of my medical interests. I will take my leave of you now, but many thanks. I wish you joy of your evening."

"Ah, and you of yours, Doctor."

William thought of the young woman who had been Winton's companion before his arrival. Would she return when he left? Or would she be replaced by another? Perhaps the frowzy wench who led him up the stairs and laughed beyond the door, cackling like a witch.

33

William reckoned he had spent an hour or more with Master Jeremy Winton. But it was worth it, despite the unsavory venue and the company of a man he did not like. He had learned more about Clara Bascombe's erratic behavior. He had also confirmed what Clara had said, that her belief that her brother was cursed was a later development in his long illness, that at first, she believed he languished for natural causes, then found another explanation, or the explanation was found for her. Perhaps by her father, who had his own motives for wanting the Harknesses condemned and evicted. Perhaps by Agnes Robinson, who seemed to be her chief advisor in medical matters. Agnes had said the choice of using the ceruse was Clara's. But William knew she might have been lying. He doubted Clara did anything before consulting the woman she had called her second mother.

He left Cobb's End, eager to get back to the inn. The moon now was obscured by clouds He walked hurriedly and was almost to the bridge when he saw two figures approaching him. When they drew nearer, he could see two men, both townsmen from what he could see of their dress. One large, heavy-set, the other thin and taller. The larger man hailed him in a gruff voice and asked the way to Cobb's End. William pointed the way and hurried on.

He was starting across the bridge when he heard the sound of muffled voices behind him. He turned to look. The two men who had asked directions were now following him. Suddenly he was alarmed, although the two had made no threatening move. He walked faster. He heard the footsteps behind him. The men were catching up.

Then he broke into a run. His pursuers followed. He could hear the accelerating beat of their shoes on the cobbles, heavy breathing, one urging the other to run faster.

He had made it almost to the bottom of High Street when he was hit hard from behind, shoved forward to the ground.

At once, one of the men, the thinner, was atop him, twisting his arms behind him and pressing his face into the cobbles. He felt terrible pain, he gasped for breath. He felt his purse snatched from his belt and then a rain of blows on his head and shoulders of such viciousness it took his breath away.

Later, he was grateful that it was only fists the two men used. He would not have survived cudgels or staffs. He lost consciousness, but it must have been a brief loss for when he came to himself again, he was aware one of the men, the thinner of the two, still straddled him, his knees pressed against his shoulders, pinning him down. William's nose ran with blood and into his mouth. He could taste the blood, his blood. The men were laughing, and talking about him, calling him vile names, bidding him wake up, stand up. Don't be a coward, fight back.

And then he recognized one of the voices. Where had he heard it before? He struggled to move under the knees of his assailant and succeeded enough to turn his head to see the face of the man.

Since leaving Cobb's End, the clouds had passed and for a brief moment light shone on the thinner man's face. Now, he put both face and voice together.

The man straddling him got to his feet. The last blow he received was from the man's boot. It struck the soft tissue beneath his rib cage. William heard the rib crack. Then one of the men, the man William had recognized, said to him hoarsely, "Leave town, Doctor, or you'll receive worse."

Suddenly the men were gone, and William still lay face down on the cobbled street. His shoulders and back ached with pain, so did his side and head. He thought he couldn't rise, wouldn't have the strength, but then he did, pushed himself up and got to his feet. For a moment he thought he might faint again. He staggered like a drunken man, his vision blurred. He leaned against a shop door and felt a wave of nausea sweep over him.

He was alone in the street. He supposed it was nearly midnight. No one to help him. No one to help even if he were to cry out. His desperate plea would more likely invoke fear and bolted doors than invite aid.

He stood there for some time, trying to get his bearings. The nausea passed. Then he made his way toward the inn, slowly, the pain in his side and the lacerations on his face now achieving their full effect, blood streaming down his face, blurring his vision. His assailants had disappeared. He was alone on the empty street. If he was lucky, the porter at the Blue Boar would still be awake. He would recognize William and let him in.

The porter was there, although asleep on a stool. When William touched his shoulder to wake him, the man looked up at William's bloody face, torn clothing, and muttered "Jesu, what happened to you, sir?"

William told him he had been robbed.

"Here in Chelmsford, sir?" the porter asked incredulously, wide-eyed.

"Just down the street. This side of the bridge." He could hardly talk.

The porter let him in. "Would you be needing something, sir."

"A good doctor, I think."

He struggled up to his room, entered, and flung himself onto the bed without disrobing. Within a minute he was asleep, or perhaps unconscious again.

He had arranged with Rafe to have his breakfast brought up to him no later than seven o'clock, but this time the deliverer was not the kitchen boy as before, but Rafe himself. The porter had told Rafe of William's bloody face, his difficulty in walking, and had assumed William was drunken and abused in some brawl. Apparently, the porter had said nothing William's claim that he was robbed. He had reported it to Rafe in the morning.

When Rafe entered, he said, "My God, Doctor, what have you done to yourself?"

Half awake, William answered, "Not to myself, but to me by others."

Rafe's wife appeared in the open doorway. She looked in and muffled a scream. Rafe told her to fetch hot water and towels and cloths that could be used for bandages. When they were alone again, Rafe asked, "Did this happen to you at Cobb's End?"

"After I left," William said, groaning, feeling now the full effect of his injuries. His whole body ached, not just the cracked rib or his skinned nose and bruised mouth.

"Then I am heartily sorry I ever gave you the message to go there."

William shook his head. "No, Rafe, it was good, the meeting with Wilton. He's no better a man than you said he was, yet I gathered information from him that I can use to good effect."

"But who did this to you?" Rafe asked, pointing toward William's bruised face.

Two men fell upon me as I walked home. They snatched my purse like common robbers, but I think they had something else in mind."

"You're a stranger in town. You probably didn't recognize them."

"I did, at least one of the villains."

"Who?"

"One of your constable's men, Timothy Parker. He was at the constable's shop on my first day in Chelmsford. He is one of the men guarding the Harknesses. I remembered his face, his voice."

"I know Timothy Parker, a vile fellow who were he not the constable's man would be unemployed, for none would have him. He's no better than them he hauls away at the constable's behest, as is often the case of those who are hired to enforce the law."

"That's a cynical view, my friend," William said.

"Then a cynic I am, for that is indeed my view. Oh, Doctor, I could tell you stories of what has happened in this town. But you said Parker and his companion aimed at more than cutting your purse from you."

"After my beating, I lost consciousness for a space. When I awoke, I knew not where I was or why. But, in a moment, all came clear to me again. I looked up; by moonlight I could see the man's face as clearly as I can see yours now. He was looking down at me, grinning devilishly, told me to get myself from Chelmsford or worse would befall me. I think the money he stole was his pay."

"Pay from?"

"Pay from him who put the two up to it."

"Who might that be do you think?"

"The Bascombes, Sir Richard or his son, Julian. Maybe even your distinguished cleric, Doctor Culpeper. For all his professed sanctity, I think he's a violent man. They all conspire to be rid of me, and this attack, which might have killed me, proves their seriousness."

"What are you going to do, Doctor? Will you go back to London as they bid you, or perhaps home to Colchester?"

"Neither. I'm resolved to stay, despite Parker's threats," William said. "And moreover, I will report his actions to the constable himself and demand he arrest Parker and discover the name of his friend, the one who made mincemeat of my face."

For a while, Rafe looked at William without saying anything. Rafe's wife returned with a basin of hot water and a towel. She bathed William's face and said he was a poor soul and what a pity it was that a doctor should need mending and have none but a common person as she was for a nurse. She asked him where else upon his body he hurt.

"I have a cracked rib, I suspect, but it must heal itself with time. I can sit up well enough and walk as well, despite what my attackers did to me."

"They are Satan's imps," she said, shaking her head. "May they burn in hell."

When she left again, Rafe said, "I don't think it is wise to complain of what happened to you, Doctor, if you want my humble opinion."

"What, not report a robbery, an assault and battery as well?"

"Assuming you're right about Parker being one of them, I think it likely the constable will rather defend his man than protect your right to your money and your freedom to walk of nights."

"Then he is a scoundrel himself," William cried.

"Which is what I was saying before my wife came in, Doctor. I tell you, I would rather trust a wolf in the sheepfold than a constable, for what power is vested in him he will abuse to his own advantage. The constable's corruption the town will come to know in due time, but for now he holds the advantage over you. Your complaint will come to naught and may well work to your hurt."

"I am well hurt now," William said. "I cannot believe that in England a man can be attacked in the street, complain to the law, and have that complaint set aside."

"Stranger things have happened in this England that is nowadays," the innkeeper said.

Rafe asked if William wanted anything from the bar below. He said good strong ale often helped a bruised body—or a cracked rib. At the very least, he said, it dulled the pain whatever else it might do and that was no small thing.

William stood up and tried his legs. He could walk, but when he did so his side ached where he had been kicked. He resolved to go that afternoon to the constable, complain of the robbery, and accuse the constable's man of being one of the robbers. He thought he might get his money back at least, but—more important to him—he might see a wrong made right.

34

William had no mirror to see the bruises on his face, but supposed that Mary Tuttle's cry of dismay when she saw him indicated that they were unsightly, if not alarming. His cheeks and chin were tender to his touch. All the better, he thought. His battered face would testify to the truthfulness of his report, the viciousness of the assault.

He found Constable Pickney in, sitting at a table poring over some papers, the first evidence William had seen that Pickney could read and write. The constable looked up when William entered, looked him over, but said nothing about the bruises, didn't look twice at his battered face as though he knew what he would see before William even entered. The constable did not bother to rise from the stool he sat upon.

William said he wanted to report a crime.

"A crime, Doctor, what manner of crime?"

"A robbery, an assault, a threat against my life."

"And when did this happen, Doctor?" Pickney was preoccupied with the task at hand, whatever the task was. He looked frustrated, distracted, half listening.

"Last night, about eleven o'clock."

"And where?"

"At the end of High Street, north of the bridge."

"You witnessed this crime?"

"It was done to me. I was the victim," William said, growing increasingly impatient. He noticed that the constable was writing nothing down.

"You were the victim?"

"That is what I said, Constable Pickney. I was the victim. I was beaten and robbed and threatened."

Pickney looked up. For the first time the constable seemed to notice the bruises on William's face. He looked at William with squinty pig eyes and smiled. "I see you had a nasty fall, Doctor."

"I didn't fall," William said. "I was assaulted. By two men. I was beaten and robbed."

He looked at the constable to see his response. The man's face was blank. William might have complained about the weather for all that what had been done to him registered in the constable's face.

"And what do you claim was taken from you?"

"My purse, small change. And it is no claim, but fact, Constable."

"No great loss, then?"

"It was a loss to me. I understand enough of our law to know that any amount constitutes an illegal taking, in this case a robbery since force was involved."

"Are you a lawyer, sir, as well as a physician, that you know the law so well?"

"My father is a lawyer," William said. "He's a judge in Colchester. I know myself as much law as any man knows, and any man knows that a theft is a theft, be the sum taken great or small. It's a hanging offense."

"Yes, it is a hanging offense, amongst a great many others," the Constable said casually. "Yet it must be proven, Doctor, if you know the law you must indeed know that. Were there any witnesses?"

"There were no witnesses but heaven," William said.

"Unfortunately, Doctor, as you must also know, in the law heaven is not sufficient to bring the accused to trial."

"I know what I experienced, Master Constable. I bear the marks of it on my face, as you can plainly see."

"Yes," the Constable said. "I do see the marks, but the marks of what, sir? Are you sure that's what happened to you, Doctor, I mean a robbery, an assault, and you mentioned threats against your person? You said you were out late, eleven o'clock. That's a time decent folks are lying abed, or on their knees at prayer. What were you doing out at that hour may I be so bold to ask, exposing yourself to accident?"

"It was no accident," William insisted.

"Had you been drinking, Doctor? I know of no other honest reasons for being out so late at night when decent folks sleep the sleep of the just."

"I had not been drinking," William said, raising his voice for emphasis.

210

The constable made a gesture suggesting that William had spoken too loudly and inappropriately.

Then William said, "There's a certain house at that end of town. Cobb's End. Do you know of it?"

"I have heard tell of it. It has a bad reputation."

"I'm sure it does, for to give it its right name, it is a brothel, Constable."

"Oh, we in Chelmsford don't like that word," the constable answered. "Let's just say it is a house where things happen out of the course of the everyday."

Now it was William's turn to laugh. He had rarely heard such a candying-over of corruption. A house where things happen, indeed. Out of the course of every day, indeed. But the constable had not laughed. He regarded William suspiciously, as though he were the criminal, not the victim.

William suddenly regretted admitting he knew of Cobb's End. The constable was obviously a fool, one step up from the village idiot, but shrewd in his own way, and adept at words. Maybe the Constable's obtuseness was a façade, a trap for the unwary. William needed to watch where he stepped, lest he find himself in trouble.

"Well, Doctor Gilbert, were you paying a visit to Cobb's End last night, tasting of the local product?"

"Product?"

"I think, Doctor, you know my meaning," the constable said, shifting himself on his stool as though he were preparing to leap at William. "And where there's whoring there's drinking, as my own father used to say and is affirmed by our learned clergy who tie both neatly together in every other sermon."

"I was doing neither, Constable," William said dryly, although realising that his denial would do nothing to convince the constable otherwise.

"But you do admit, sir, you were at Cobb's End?"

"I went there at the invitation of a gentleman," William said, thinking it was useless to deny it since he had been seen by several of the patrons there, not to mention the women who accommodated them. None would have reason to protect his reputation.

"And this gentleman's name is—?"

"That I cannot say," William said. 'He is a man of name in this county, and he would not want his presence there to be known."

211

The constable laughed. "Indeed, Doctor, I am sure he would not. No man at Cobb's End wants his name to be known, and more especially by her who is his wife or mistress, if you know what I mean."

"I also recognized one of the robbers," William said.

The constable looked up quickly, apparently registered what William had said, and then asked, "And who do you imagine that to have been?"

William's assertion had been enough to cause the constable to rise from his stool. The man had the chest of a weightlifter and sturdy thighs. William felt a tinge of fear.

At that moment, the door of the shop opened, and Parker walked in. William looked at Parker and Parker at him, and for a moment neither spoke. Parker stared at William's face and smiled thinly, as though he were admiring his handywork, as William suspected he indeed was. William said, looking at Parker accusingly, "One of my attackers was this man standing before you. I believe he is your assistant, Constable. His name is Timothy Parker, if memory serves. I recognized him because I noted his face and voice on my first day in Chelmsford. I met him in this very shop, and as God is my witness, he was one of two men who beat me last night and robbed me as well. I demand you arrest him."

Parker showed no surprise at William's accusation. He laughed and said, "This is a jest, is it not, concocted betwixt you to make game of a simple man such as I am?"

"You are laughing, not I," William retorted. He turned from Parker and looked at the constable. The constable was smiling thinly. William looked back to Parker.

"You and a companion rushed upon me, thrust me to the cobbles, sat upon my shoulders that I could not move and snatched my purse. I observed your face, recognized your voice from when we first met in this very place. This is no jest. My battered face bears witness of that, sir."

"I am falsely accused, Master Constable," Parker said in a whining voice, opening his hands in a gesture of appeal. "For as God is my witness, I never did such a thing, nor would I. And I wonder that the doctor here can recall me with such accuracy, being that we met but once before. It was night, was it not, and late? It is not always easy to tell one man from another in the dark."

"How did you know it was night, fellow, and not broad day? I never said, nor did the constable, or were you listening at the door before you came in?"

212

"Well, Doctor, I supposed since it was a robbery you complained of the natural time of such events is nighttime, is it not? I suppose robberies and purse snatches happen in daytime, but I would say the nighttime is to be preferred."

"You were the one, you and your companion," William said.

"And where did it happen?" Parker asked.

"You know very well where it happened, since you were there."

"The Doctor says it was just beyond the bridge. He says he was down at Cobb's End about eleven o'clock."

"At Cobb's End, was he?" Parker laughed. "Then I am surprised he had any money left in his purse, for she who is mistress there is more than capable of taking a man's every last penny, leaving him with nothing but his shirt, if that."

Both the constable and Parker laughed at this, then the constable said, "Well, Doctor Gilbert, with all due respect to you, sir, it would seem it is one man's word against another. If one man calls the other a robber and the man accused says he is not and there are no other witnesses to come forth, it stands to reason that there is naught to be done but to throw up one's hands, or maybe draw straws. But that's not how the law works, as I suspect you know. I have known Timothy Parker here since he was lad. He has never done such a thing that you accuse him of."

"Nor would I do so, so help me God," Parker said, looking piously up to the ceiling as though heaven were overhearing his oath.

"I see you will do nothing, then, Constable," William said, finding it increasingly difficult to manage his frustration. Rafe Tuttle had been right, at least about the Chelmsford constabulary. He suspected the constable knew very well what his assistant had done, perhaps even had encouraged the act.

"Doctor Gilbert?"

"Yes?"

The constable walked toward him and pressed his arm. It was an odd gesture, under the circumstances, being as it was more a gesture of comfort than a threat. "Consider this, Doctor. You were at Cobb's End. You admit as much. We are all men here, though our station in life be different, and we all have our needs, men's needs. Our clergy may condemn those needs, pretend they don't have them themselves. Yet they do. That cemetery out at the Old Priory is full of the spawn of priests who made merry with the nuns there. These were so-called men of God, papists all, yet I trust the clergy that we have now are no more strict in their observance of God's laws against whoredom than the papists."

"What are you talking about, Constable?" William asked, thinking now that he had best leave, before he said something that he would regret later. One beating in a day was enough, he thought. He didn't need another from these two.

"I am saying, Doctor, that perhaps this is what happened. You were paying a visit to Cobb's End to scratch an itch, drank overmuch as part of the play, then staggered home, fell into a ditch or over a dead dog, and knocked yourself out. Awakening from a dream, say, you imagined yourself assaulted. You remembered Master Parker here from when you two met and imagined him there."

"And my purse?" William asked. "I imagined it cut from my belt?" He did not try to hide his contempt for the lie the constable was weaving.

"Lost, lost along the road, or mayhaps before, snatched at Cobb's End. You know the women there aren't the most honest in the county. My father always said that a wench that will sell her body for sixpence will steal a purse for penny."

"I see, Master Constable, that your father was full of wise counsel," William said, sneering.

"Oh, he was, Doctor. I do swear it before God and His angels."

"I see I have come here for nothing, Master Constable," William said. He turned to go.

"Oh, Doctor, wait for a moment, will you?"

"What?"

"You said you were beaten, robbed, threatened?"

"All three," William said.

"And what threat was made against you, Doctor? That is, if such a threat was indeed made and you can remember what it was."

"I was told, that is, your man here, Parker, told me that I should leave Chelmsford, or worse would befall me."

"Did he?"

"I said no such thing," Parker said.

The constable and his man exchanged knowing glances, and William realized that Parker might be the constable's subordinate, but he was also his friend. He suspected they drank together, shared a past, anticipated some future in which each would benefit from knowing the other. William's suspicion that the two men were conspirators became even stronger and that his plea for justice was futile. Did he have defeat written on his face, that they could see how he was failing in his arguments? William sensed it must be. Both constable and his man now seemed at ease, watching him as though he were some kind of entertainer, whose failure to prevail was essentially comic. As though they could hardly suppress their outright contempt for him, for his unsustainable complaint that he had been attacked and robbed.

The constable said, "Again, it's one man's word against another, though one be a learned doctor and the other a, well, a simple man of no great city such as London be. On the other hand, Doctor, if this threat was made against you, then mayhaps you should consider the wisdom therein. Chelmsford can be a dangerous place of nights and sad to say there are thieves and robbers and other malefactors amongst us who think little of giving a man a beating or slitting his throat. And all for a mere pittance. And you know what is more, Doctor?"

William said nothing, not really caring to know more but confident he was going to hear it.

"We have witches in this town, and they have powers you and your learning know not of. But we of Chelmsford know what powers they have. We have dealt with demons before, and we are determined that they will not go unpunished."

William glared at the two men, who looked back, both smiling pleasantly as though some agreement between the three of them had been reached, a happy consensus.

35

William hurried back to the inn, his gut roiling with anger. He avoided Rafe Tuttle, whom he saw working in the taproom, and slipped upstairs. At the moment, he wanted no company.

Rafe had been right, and William had no stomach for any chiding about his naivete in believing the constable would help him secure justice. At least not now. Now he needed to rest, and he needed to think. He bolted the door. During his time at the constable's shop, he had nearly forgotten his aches and pains. The contention there had been a distraction, almost a blessing. Now the pain came back to him in a wave. His rib ached where they'd kicked him, but worse was the pain in his gut. He knew what that was. Nothing that had happened to him in the dead of night. It was raw fear for his life.

He sat on the edge of his bed, sat without moving, as though in a trance. From below stairs, he could hear music and singing and occasional bursts of laughter. How apart he felt from that world of simple pleasures and concerns. He thought back to the time before he knew the Harknesses, before he had any reason to be in Chelmsford. How simple his life had been then, how uncluttered with fears and anxieties. It was different now. This, at least for the time being, was his life. He knew he must bolt doors behind him, be constantly vigilant, avoid walking abroad of nights, and believing anything he was told. The mocking laughter of the constable and his man still rang in his ears.

The pain subsided. He had some bread and cheese left over from the breakfast brought to him that morning. He ate of it, but not much. He had little appetite, although he knew he needed to eat.

When Rafe did come up later and knocked, William could hardly keep him out.

Rafe asked him how he did. The innkeeper didn't mention the constable. William told him what had happened.

Rafe shook his head. "I would have been surprised if Pickney had done aught else. He would hardly be happy to acknowledge that his assistant was a robber. How would that make him look? Already half the town thinks he's corrupt. Admitting his assistant roughed you up would convert the rest to the same opinion."

"He said there were no witnesses. It was my word against Parker's."

"Well, he would say that, wouldn't he?"

"He accused me of being drunk, made much of my being at Cobb's End. He suggested I went there for venery's sake, got blind drunk, my purse snatched there, fell down on my way back and imagined the rest."

"Well, that is a plausible tale," Rafe allowed.

"But false, false every word of it," William said. "My oath upon it."

Rafe nodded. "I believe you, Doctor, and you need not swear oaths for me to take your word before the constable's or his assistant's."

"It was worse than that,' William said. "He threatened me, just as Parker had done."

"In the same words?"

"To the same effect, that Chelmsford was a dangerous place. That there were thieves and robbers around, some quite willing to take a life along with an honest man's purse."

"About that he was exaggerating," Rafe said. "Chelmsford is no worse than any other town in this part of England. The average person in this town is honest, goes to church, gives to the poor and needy, says his prayers, loves the queen. He commits no thefts, robberies, murders, or other outrages. And as for venery as you call it, which we simple folk call whoring around here, well there's many a man who puts money in the poor box but goes down to help Cobb's End turn a profit."

"I'm sure that's true, "William said. "The constable said I should leave Chelmsford, for my own good. The threat was clear. He and Parker and the Bascombes are all of the same mind."

"I'm afraid the whole town is of the same mind, should the question be put to them," Rafe said. "They're hell-bent on hanging witches in this town, whether they be guilty or no. It's a form of local recreation."

"And what of you, Rafe, are you among them?"

"Among them?"

"Among those who believe I should get out of Chelmsford."

Rafe laughed. "No Doctor. I am not among them. After all, sir, you are a paying customer of long standing here. I'd never say to a paying customer, get thee hence. It would be bad business, wouldn't it?"

"And about the witches, what of them?"

"Well, that's what the trial is about, is it not? To find out whether they be guilty or no. When I was juryman for Mother Waterhouse's trial, hers and her sister's, the judge said to us all that we were there to determine what was true and what not. That was to be our charge, our duty. He called us the finder of the facts. I'll always remember that, Doctor, *the finder of the facts*. That's a strange phrase, is it not, Doctor? As though facts were things that got lost like in a hay pile or in a laundry basket and it was for us to ferret them out."

"I suppose it is, Rafe. The law is full of strange phrases that no one uses but he who is learned in that dry subject."

Rafe continued, "I suppose the jury in the Harkness case will have the same charge. Find the facts. As for you, Doctor, I do think you are in Chelmsford for the same purpose, and because you are learned then you will help all understand what the facts are and what the fictions are, what the truth is and what the old wives' tales do declare."

"I pray I may do that," William said.

"God bless you, Doctor, in that effort," Rafe said, and then wished William a good night and asked again if he wanted something from below to make him sleep.

This time, William did not refuse the offer.

36

Mary Tuttle had fetched something from the apothecary that William knew was effective in treating bruised and swollen flesh. This he made into a poultice and applied it to his cheeks, eyes, and forehead. He stayed abed through most of the next day, not so much for safety's sake as to rest his cracked rib, which he knew nothing but time would heal.

But by the end of the day his convalescence had become tedious. His eyes were tired from reading. Hungry, he decided to go down to the tavern where he knew he might find both good food and enough company to make another assault upon him unlikely if not impossible, despite the constable's dire warnings.

He was seated in the back of the low-ceilinged room at a little table where the server, who recognized him, looked at his bruised and swollen face but did not remark upon it. For this, William was grateful. He had a good appetite for supper, but not for explaining how he came to be in such a state.

William ordered and quickly he had his supper before him, a plump chicken thigh, a duck's breast, and some other smaller winged creatures he could not readily identify covered with a savory sauce. There was a half-decent pudding, as well. He was given ale in a pewter tankard, not so fine as the implements he had observed at Mowbray Rise, but handsome enough. He sat back to enjoy his food and observe the company, feeling relatively safe.

It was in large part a mix of tradesmen and laborers, all men, and like other times he had patronized the inn's tavern the patrons were a boisterous bunch with loud laughter and occasional bursts of song. He had nearly finished and had motioned to the server for his account, when William became aware of two men approaching him. One was Timothy

Parker. The other was a larger man with a scraggly beard and bulbous nose. William recognized him as the other constable's man set to guard the Harkness women. He thought it likely he was the other man who had assaulted him, the big man.

Parker strode up to William and announced loudly enough for half the room to hear. "Doctor William Gilbert, you must come with us. A complaint has been laid against you for housebreaking and theft."

Before William could respond to this, Parker reached down and pulled him to his feet.

This move drew even more attention from those present. Suddenly the buzz of conversation ended, and all eyes were fixed on William. Parker seemed aware of this and made his voice louder, looked about him eagerly, as though he were an actor commanding the stage and the attention of an audience.

"I have done neither," William protested, struggling to free himself from Parker's grip.

"I have here the proof," Parker said in the same stentorian voice. He pulled from within his leather jerkin a silver cup and held it up for all to see. "This cup belongs to my friend here, Daniel Smythe, who declared you broke into his house to steal it. It was found in your room here at the inn."

"That's ridiculous," William said. "I've never seen that particular cup before in my life, and I certainly did not break into this fellow's house to steal it. As for it being in my room above that is not true. It was never there. And I have not left my room—until now—since Wednesday."

"It was there indeed," Parker cried. "Did we not find it beneath your bed there? Come now, Doctor, you must perforce come with us."

"I will not go with you, Master Parker. This is more of your trumpery, an abuse of your office, and an offence to me and to the law itself."

"Stop that officer. Release that man."

Everyone turned to the direction of the new voice.

He who said this was a white-bearded gentleman whom William had observed earlier sitting at a nearby table. The man, about sixty, William reckoned, was well dressed and seemed by his demeanor to be someone of authority in the town; although when Parker demanded angrily to know what business this gentleman had in interfering with officers of the law, William concluded he was as much a stranger in town as William.

"Leave me to do my duty," Parker cried, "or I will take you into custody, sir, for obstruction of justice, as well as this malefactor, and you must suffer each other's company in our jail."

The white-bearded gentleman responded to this threat quite calmly. He looked Parker in the eye and said, "I am Justice Sir John Southcote, and here with me is the queen's attorney, Master Anthony Poole. We are both here for the assizes." Southcote gestured toward his companion at the table, a sallow-faced, beardless man who looked more like a cleric than a lawyer. "I don't think we shall sleep this night in your jail, Constable. Not if there is any law in England."

Parker evidently knew these names, even though he did not know the men by face, for he quickly complied with Southcote's order.

"I beg your pardon, Master Justice, I did not recognize you, my lord," Parker said with an awkward bow.

"Evidently you did not, sirrah, or you would not have threatened a justice of the queen's court with arrest," Southcote said.

"I was but doing my duty, my lord," Parker said, looking frightened now. "Apprehending this malefactor."

Southcote regarded William and then turned back to the constable. "He whom you are arresting hardly looks like a housebreaker, Constable, but rather an honest gentleman, although one who by his battered face seems more deserving of charity than wild accusation. What evidence have you against him?"

"Why, my lord, this silver cup, which belongs to Master Woodard here." Parker turned to look at his companion. Woodard was white-faced and trembling.

"It is a prized family possession, most prized, and it has been in my family since my grandfather's time," Woodard said.

"What other evidence is there to warrant an arrest?" Southcote asked Parker.

"None my lord, save the cup itself, which I did find in this man's room above."

"And how came you to search it in the first place?" Southcote asked. "Was the so-called thief observed in the act? You said there was a house-breaking. Was there a witness to this?"

"There may have been, my Lord. Master Woodard lives but at the end of High Street. Many pass by his house daily."

"And these witnesses? Are any present?"

'No, my lord, they are yet to be discovered."

"I do think you'll have a better case when they are, sir. But as for now, you have no credible case. And how does this Master Woodard live?" Justice Southcote asked as if Woodard were not standing there and could not answer for himself.

"Why Master Woodard is a tailor, my lord."

"And owns a silver cup?" Southcote asked.

The constable answered nothing. Southcote looked back to Parker. "Let me see the cup," Southcote said. The tailor handed it to him. Southcote examined it, turned it around several time, and looked at the base, then said, "I see there's an inscription on the rim of the cup. It is in Latin. Do you read that language, Master Tailor?"

"I do not, my Lord," Woodard answered, visibly shaking. "Nor would I since it be a papist tongue and I am wholly Christian."

"*Omnia vincit amor*, it says. You never noticed the inscription, Master Tailor?"

"Marry, I never did, my Lord."

"And yet you claim it has been in your family for years. You claim it as your family's most prized position."

The tailor said nothing.

Southcote gave the cup back to the tailor. "I put it to you, Master Woodard, that the cup is not yours but some other's, and therefore you have no standing to complain of theft. Would you like then to reconsider your testimony against this man? Did you find it under this doctor's bed as you claim or was it given you by another?"

Woodard hesitated for a moment, then said, "I do think I was mistaken, my lord."

"How mistaken?"

"In where I did find it. I swear, my lord, it is mine, but I misplaced it."

"You misplaced it?" Southcote said with an ironic grin. "Then given its value and your negligence in handling it, I suggest you get yourself to your house and lock it up and do so at this instant."

"Yes, my lord, I will." Woodard turned and pushed through the crowd of spectators, looking back once at Parker. As he did so, those around observing the scene broke into laughter. It was clear that neither Parker nor Woodard, both constable's men, were popular among those in the room.

"I'm afraid you do not have much of a case here, Master Constable's Assistant, to warrant arrest of this gentlemen or upsetting so many here in attendance."

Then Southcote addressed William. "And you, young sir, what is your name again? I'm sorry, your name was announced to all here, but I have quite forgot it. Your face, what I can discern of it through all the black and blue, seems familiar to me, but I cannot place you."

"I am William Gilbert."

"Of this place?"

"No, my Lord. I live in London now, but before in Colchester."

Southcote nodded. "And what do you in London?"

"I am a doctor and an officer in the College of Physicians."

Southcote nodded approvingly. "And whom do you treat, Doctor?"

"I am a personal physician to Lord Burghley, my Lord. Or at least one of his physicians, for he has several."

"That is no less an honor if you must share it with others," Southcote said. "I know Lord Burghley well. Should I inquire of his knowledge of you, I should not find that you have spoken falsely in claiming to know him?"

"Absolutely not, my Lord," William said. "As God is my witness."

Southcote was quiet for a minute. Then he said, "You claim to be from Colchester."

"I do, my lord."

"I know Colchester. I also know a judge there named Gilbert. Jerome Gilbert. You would not be related to him, by any chance?"

"He is my father, my lord."

Southcote broke into a smile, "Ah, you do resemble him, or at least as he was when he and I first met. I remember once he came to London to see me on a matter of law, something to do with a contended will, if I remember it. He had with him his young son, who occupied himself with a book from my library while his father and I conversed in Latin over some subtle point of law."

William said, "I cannot remember such an occasion, my lord, but that young son would have been I, for among my brothers only I have had the honor of accompanying my father on his London excursions."

"And now you are a man—and a physician?"

"As you see, my lord." William swept his cap from his head and made a short bow.

"You did not choose to follow in your father's footsteps?"

"They were not shoes that it was my fate to fill," William said. "My mind took another turn that led me to mysteries of the body and also of natural laws."

"Where did you study medicine?"

"At St. John's College, at Cambridge."

Southcote nodded approvingly and said he had studied law at Oxford, but would have preferred Cambridge, for the more learned faculty and the better air. Then he turned to Parker who had been standing all this while in mortified and fearful silence. He was the same man who had attacked William, mocked him the day before. He did not seem so audacious and brave as he was then, nor did his friend Woodard, standing behind him, his face frozen in fear.

"Master Constable, you have performed as much of your duty as the law and good sense dictate. You have no case against Doctor Gilbert, and so for that I wish you goodnight and better sense than to create such a public uproar over a bogus charge. This tailor, this what's his name?" Southcote pointed to Woodard.

"Woodard, my lord."

"Yes, Woodard the tailor. The man has no credible claim here. I doubt the cup is even his, and am even more doubtful that you found it in Doctor Gilbert's room, for why would you have searched for it there in the first place? Were I at leisure, which I am not since the assises begin tomorrow and there are graver matters pending, I would ask for an inquiry into your conduct, both Woodard's part in it, as well as your own. Go now and obey the law you have sworn to uphold. Go now, before I change my mind."

By this time Parker's courage had failed him. He now had been reduced to a quivering thing, like a chastised kitchen boy. He seemed struck dumb, and William was surprised that he could move. But move he did, making as awkward a bow to Southcote as William had ever seen in a grown man, and departing the tavern where he received more than one abusive comment from those who had witnessed the scene and were glad to see the constable's man so put down by the white-bearded gentleman, whoever he was.

"Come, Doctor Gilbert," Southcote said, taking William's arm. Join us at table, for I desire to know why you are here in Chelmsford and to hear word of your father, whom I consider both a colleague in my profession and also a friend."

37

William was now seated at the best table in the room; the table in a quiet corner where gentlemen of name or rank staying at the inn ate and enjoyed the privilege of the best service and the best prepared dishes. The table where there were chairs, not stools or benches, hard enough on the backside to discourage lingering.

Southcote did all the talking at first; even Master Poole, the Queen's attorney, was quiet. While stern with the constable's man and the constable man's witness, Southcote was affable and good humored now that the commotion had passed, and William was no sooner seated than he was listening to one anecdote after the other in which his father played a leading part.

Most of these stories William had never heard; some he had reason to believe were true at the core but so wrapped up in whole cloth of rumor as to be incredible. In this discussion, Master Poole, the Queen's Attorney, also participated. He did not know William's father, but he had heard of him, since Jerome Gilbert had served from time to time as a judge in the assizes. Since this learned justice knew his father and Bascombe knew his father, William wondered whether Bascombe and Southcote knew each other. As it turned out, they did not, except by name. As presiding judge, Southcote already had been given the facts of the case, but all parties, he declared, were virtual strangers to him. "I have heard of this knight, but certainly not of the defendants, living as they are reputed to do in the middle of nowhere. Which is just as well, for I shall be the better judge if I have no interest in one party or the other."

And with that pronouncement, Southcote turned to the case at hand not realizing, William was sure, what part William might play in it.

"And so, Doctor, what has lured you from our beloved London to the countryside?"

He told him flatly it was for the assizes.

"What, you have a peculiar interest in the law, in our perversely complicated judicial system?"

"No, my lord, I know the defendants in the Crown's case."

"And the complainants?"

"I know them, too."

"And have you likewise felt their curse upon you, these witches? I trust and hope that you are not sick unto death like unto Master Bascombe, who is dead."

"No, my lord, if anything, I shall speak on their behalf, if I am permitted to do so."

"Why should you not be permitted?" Southcote asked.

Then for the next hour William related his experience at the Old Priory and at Mowbray Rise. As he did so, the company in the room dwindled and finally left just the three men, huddled at the table like conspirators. He told the justice how the Bascombes had discovered his acquaintanceship with the Harknesses and how their friendship had turned to hate and threats if he did not leave town. He also told him about the attack upon him by Parker and another man, he thought Woodard.

"The constable's man, this base fellow you sent off, was one of my assailants. I recognized him by moonlight. It was he who beat me about the head and shoulders, pushed my face into the cobles, and later denied he did it."

"As I suppose he would," Southcote said. "From what I have learned of your constable, I have no doubt his assistant is as corrupt as he. But why should they so want you to leave the town, Doctor. What did you do to offend them?

"I think they are in the pay of Sir Richard Bascombe, my lord. It is his daughter, the lady Clara, who made complaint against Mother Harkness and her daughter. She is her dead brother's twin, and so devoted to him in life and in death that she can think of little else but revenge against those who she believed cursed him to die."

"I wondered how you received those bruises on your face, Doctor. I trust you have no need for a doctor to see to your own wounds."

"No, my lord. They look worse than they are."

"I am glad to hear it," Southcote said. "Now, tell me what information you might provide the court and the jury who will judge the women."

"The Harknesses saved my life, my lord. They took me in, warmed me back to life, fed me, gave me a bed to sleep in. During that time, I saw no behavior on the part of any of the three, husband, wife, daughter, that would suggest some satanic influence or malign intent. Ursula Harkness spoke of Thomas Bascombe, but lovingly. She would have married him had his father not forbidden it, or so he told her."

Up to this point, Anthony Poole, the Crown's attorney and prosecutor in the case, had been content to let Southcote carry the conversation. It was as if he was not even there at table, but William could tell he was, listening, assessing, judging William as a potential witness for the defense. But now he spoke.

"You saw the black dog? The child with the marked visage?" Poole asked.

"I did, Master Poole. The family saved me, but first it was the dog. who discovered my distress and called his master to my need. Without him, I would have frozen to death. The town calls him a wolf and I must admit that I first thought him so myself. But he is but a dog, though I grant he may have some wolf in him."

"Ah, what dog worthy of the name does not?" Southcote said.

"And the child?" Poole asked.

"The child has a birthmark, a port wine stain upon his cheek. It is an uncommon thing but scarcely unheard of, although usually found upon another body part."

"It has been cited as evidence of the wolf's influence," Southcote said. "Some say the wolf is her familiar, or that it fathered the child and that the mark itself resembles a wolf's snout."

"Nonsense," William said, speaking now with more confidence. "Whoever says that has never seen the babe. The stain looks no more like a wolf's head than it does a bird spreading its wings or an angel taking flight. A birthmark is no more than an imperfection in the skin. That the child's face is so marred is an unfortunate incident of birth, not a manifestation of some moral flaw or diabolical influence."

"That is not what is commonly thought," Poole said.

"I would agree, Master Poole, yet what is commonly thought is not always true. I could provide you with hundred ideas that are commonly thought and show to your satisfaction that they have no more substance than a dream."

"So you will speak, if permitted, in their defense?" Southcote said.

"My lord, I hope to serve as a witness, to bring my medical knowledge to the case, and whether that works to exonerate or incriminate I leave you and the jury to decide."

"Medical knowledge? Not spiritual knowledge, or legal knowledge?" Southcote said. "I must say Doctor, I have presided over more than one witch trial. Indeed, I was the presiding judge in this very place when Mother Waterhouse and her sister were tried and condemned, eight years ago. I have tried others since, and never has medical knowledge been regarded as relevant to such a case. As witnesses we have had doctors of law and doctors of theology aplenty, but no doctors of physic."

Poole agreed. He said he could not see what value medical knowledge might have in the trial. After all, he said, witchcraft was hardly a medical condition.

"I would agree," William said, "unless by medical we include what a twisted mind might conceive. Not just the witches, but they who accuse them. Thomas Bascombe died after a prolonged illness."

"Because he was cursed," Southcote said.

"Perhaps my lord, or perhaps not. What if Thomas Bascombe's illness was a disease that has a name, a disease that has a cure, but none was applied. What if a cure were applied, and the supposed cure did him more harm than good? I mean, my lord, what if no supernatural force is at work here, but only a lamentable ailment of the body, or the fumbling of those who tried to help? Some cures have been worse than their afflictions, and many died thereof."

"Ah, Doctor, that is for the jury to decide, not you, nor I for that matter," Justice Southcote said. "Will you have evidence to give the jury that Thomas Bascombe died of natural means, not supernatural ones?"

"I believe I shall, my lord."

Southcote thought for a moment, then said, "Doctor, I will speak truly. I do not know if these women be witches are not. I shall not prejudge them until I have myself heard the evidence like all others in the court, but I promise you this: the women shall be fairly tried and fairly judged by a jury. If they are found guilty, they will hang, if acquitted, they will go free."

William asked when the trial would begin.

"Tomorrow. At nine o'clock. The women will be arraigned, the jury selected, after which Master Poole here will read out the charges and present witnesses. All will be done as it is always done, as it has been done during my lifetime, and I suppose will continue to be."

"And how will the jury be selected?"

"It will be drawn from a list of citizens of the town who by their reputation are known as honest and responsible subjects of Her Majesty. These will be men of good judgment and sound mind, decent Christians," Poole said.

"It is to be hoped the jury has these characteristics you describe, Master Poole," Southcote said, turning aside to his younger companion. "But I fear the jury you conceive is composed of angels, not mere men, and is more to be wished for than to be seen. Nonetheless, we must do what the law dictates and find the best jury that we can."

Then Southcote turned to William and said, "The law, as you know, provides for no counsellor to argue the defendant's case. But I will hear your testimony, your science, not for your father's sake, but for the sake of justice, that it may be done, even in Chelmsford."

"I can hope for little more, my lord," William said.

38

Once, when William was six years old, he had asked his lawyer father what "assizes" were. It was a strange word, he thought in his young mind, and his father had used it to explain how he had to travel four times a year to Chelmsford, the chief town of the county, and leave him and his mother for several days.

His father had laughed when he realized William thought assizes was a person. "No, son," his father had said, "assizes is no person at all. It is an old French word made English by use, meaning a seat, or session, or court of law."

"Why then do they not use a good English word?" William had asked in his innocence. "Since there are English words that mean the same thing and might as well be used. Are there not words enough that English must steal from other languages to make it whole."

"Ah," replied his father, laughing. "You ask a very good question, my son, yet one to which there is no ready answer. The law likes old things and ways, thinking them sounder and safer because proven by use. It is like unto a display of ancient usage, loved because of its antiquity, not because of its utility."

William thought of his father's words while he stood in the High Street the next morning, shortly before nine o'clock, and looked up the road to see the Sessions House, a squarish stone building the ground floor of which he had been told by Rafe Tuttle was used as a corn exchange with the floor above a spacious assembly hall used for quarter sessions among other things. From where he stood, he could already see a large crowd gathered at the door.

He hurried forward. As he did so, he heard his name called out. It was Anthony Poole, the queen's counsel who would act as prosecutor, robed in black and carrying a sheaf of papers beneath his arm like a college tutor.

"Come, Doctor Gilbert. Come with me," Poole said. "We will be fortunate to find a place in the trial chamber, and I'm he without whom the case cannot proceed. But you shall have a good seat, even as Justice Southcote promised. There's a section of the courtroom roped off for the gentry, such as yourself, that you don't need to sit with the common herd."

William thanked the prosecutor for his courtesy. He did not think of the citizens of Chelmsford as a herd, but he did not look forward to being jammed in shoulder to shoulder as he anticipated the crowd to be.

"It will be an interesting trial, Doctor, you shall see."

"How interesting, Master Poole?"

"Why, the women have not yet confessed," Poole answered as they walked. "We shall have to push them to it in the trial itself. A very usual situation in a witch trial. Yet it will make the case all the more absorbing. You shall see for yourself."

As they approached, the crowd saw Poole, guessed by his dress and demeanour he was one to whom deference must be paid, and gave way. William followed him in.

Inside, the stairs to the upper floor were full of people, making their way up or lingering for friends who were late in coming. William could see that the crowd included persons of both sexes and of every state or condition. He saw young children as well, grasping their mother's hands, and a number of old men and women who seemed hardly able to walk but were pushing through the multitude like the younger folk. William realised the trial of the Harknesses was doubtless the most entertaining event the citizenry of Chelmsford would experience since the trial of Mother Waterhouse. Indeed, he realized that the Waterhouse trial was but a preparation for this even more outrageous case of satanic possession and murder, involving as it did not merely some common person but one of the county's wealthiest families.

The inside of the upper chamber was spacious and high-ceilinged but already uncomfortably warm, because it was summer and because of the press of bodies. William saw that at the far end of the chamber were a dais and podium like a pulpit; the long table behind it he assumed was for Justice Southcote and other officials, and to the right were two rows of stools. These were presently empty. He assumed they were for the jury, when it should be chosen.

The spectators took what benches or stools they could find while many stood or leaned against the walls, struggling to see or be seen, calling out to their friends and neighbours and exchanging views about the two women to be tried. There was a great din of chattering voices and occasional bursts of raucous laughter by some men who despite the hour were already drunk and seemed little prepared for the solemn occasion to follow.

The section reserved for the gentry consisted of a row of benches toward the front. And this was nearly full already. He sat himself down and then noticed, with a sudden shock, in the row in front, Clara Bascombe and her brother, Julian, sitting together companionably as though all their mutual enmity had passed. They had not seen him, at least he had thought they hadn't, and if he were lucky, they wouldn't, although he knew it was only a matter of time before they did.

And what then? Another wild diatribe against him? It was a public place. Surely that would restrain their anger at seeing him, recognizing as they must their efforts to drive him from the town had failed. He wondered what Clara Bascombe would think of his wounds, still visible although already beginning to fade. Would she pity him, or feel that he had gotten what he deserved for his betrayal of her affections?

In no time at all, despite the multitude of faces, William had spotted Sir Richard Bascombe. He came in scowling under his bejeweled velvet cap, nodded to his son and daughter, and took his place at the table on the dais along with Doctor Culpeper, the rector. The Reverend Doctor had made a great show in entering, wearing his full ecclesiastical regalia and greeting on each side his parishioners as if they had come to hear him preach, not to hear evidence against the accused women. The defendants were yet to be brought in.

Then, William caught Clara's eye. She nudged her brother, and both of them sent him a killing glance, Clara's so baleful that he wondered that for even a moment he might ever have found her attractive.

At the stroke of nine from the town clock, Sir John Southcote and prisoners had yet to appear, and the crowd was growing unruly like an audience for a play when the performance is delayed. Some in the room began to clap their hands or stamp their feet, others cried out, demanding that the witches be brought forth. William saw Constable Pickney come in along with half a dozen other men, obviously recruited for the occasion. All were big, burly men, all armed with clubs as the sole symbol of their authority and regarding the crowd with the happy anticipation of quelling any untoward disorder by beating the brains out of the offenders.

William wasn't surprised to see Timothy Parker among them. The constable's good friend, Timothy Parker. He would not be discharged for merely bearing a false witness against William at the inn or humiliating himself before Justice Southcote. At last, Southcote entered the chamber. Many stood out of respect for the court, but most, unaccustomed to the decorum of the courtroom, kept chattering like monkeys until the vast chamber was called to order by a bewhiskered bailiff pounding the floor with his staff.

Order restored, Southcote warned the crowd that each person present was obliged to keep the peace, or they would be forcefully removed and fined. These threats did little to calm the crowd, especially the drunken men in the back of the chamber who were loudest in complaining they had nowhere to sit or they could not see what was going on, even before there was anything to be seen or anything happening except confusion and loud talking.

"You shall sit in the stocks if you don't keep silent," Southcote called out to them, but the threat fell on deaf ears for some present, who continued to talk to their friends as though the event were a village fete, not a trial.

It took, by William's estimation, close to a quarter of an hour before order was achieved and yet another quarter after Ursula and her mother had been brought into the chamber in manacles.

The women were pale with fright, especially Mary Harkness, who clung to her daughter despite the restraints. Ursula looked the calmer of the two, either because she was the more hopeful or because the more resigned to her fate. Dressed in black, both women appeared haggard, their drawn faces drawn and pale, like two ambulatory corpses. William could see they had been roughly treated while confined, possibly tortured. But he had already learned from Poole that they had yet to confess and would plead not guilty to the charges against them.

At the appearance of the defendants there was a great explosion of anger from every quarter of the room. If the Harknesses had friends among those assembled, they were wisely silent since it was clear whoever they were they were a despised minority. Those who had been sitting before stood and railed against the defendants, a great clamor of accusation and invective, name-calling and obscene slurs.

The black garb, William suspected, was Pickney's idea. He had never seen the women so dressed during his stay at the Old Priory, and he surmised they had been dressed in black to satisfy public expectation. They were witches. What else might be expected but that they should be garbed in the color of evil? He was surprised they had not been equipped with broomsticks, or leashes for their familiars, the great black dog or some flea-bitten and scabby cat, trailing behind them as conclusive evidence of their guilt.

During his time in London, William had witnessed a handful of public executions. He disliked these events and even more the behavior of the spectators. This was very much like. It was also clear that the audience had no other expectation that the two defendants would be hanged, perhaps even on that very day. There was an atmosphere of excited expectation in the room, not suspense, which implied an unpredictable outcome. William could feel it himself.

Again, a stout jowly man, the bailiff of the court, ordered silence in a loud booming voice, but the audience was slow to comply as before, and William began to wonder if there should be any trial at all, but Ursula and her mother dragged from the court and torn apart in the streets by a howling mob.

Finally, there was enough quiet for Southcote to announce that a jury was to be chosen. "These twelve men have been chosen from among citizens of Chelmsford, known to be good and true subjects of the queen. The list has been prepared by Sir Richard Bascombe and the Reverend Doctor Culpeper, two gentlemen I believe are known and respected by you all."

At this announcement, a number of the spectators applauded. William was unsure whether this was a sign of approval of the two gentlemen selecting or merely satisfaction that the proceeding was at last to begin. In either case he thought this was a bad sign. After Bascombe's attempt to drive him from town, he thought it unlikely that he had not also selected jurymen who would be persuaded to see the defendants as Bascombe and his daughter saw them. It would be a handpicked jury, thereby refuting Prosecutor Poole's rosy assessment of English jurymen.

Then the bailiff was handed the list of names by the judge and each man's name was called, along with a description of his calling or vocation.

The first two called were tradesmen, a clothier and a tailor—but not Andrew Woodard, the tailor who had falsely accused William of having stolen the silver cup. Then there was a silversmith, a grocer, a butcher, and a joiner.

At the announcement of each name there was a response from the crowd, usually a cheer from that person's family or friends, although Chelmsford being the small town that it was, it was clear to William that everyone was known by all. The next four men were all husbandmen, whose farmsteads were in smaller villages nearby. They wore for the occasion the simple garb of their calling, yet seemed not to be intimidated by being thrown together with better-dressed folk from the town, as William might have expected.

There was Adam Hawkins, the apothecary whom William had visited to ask about the ceruse, and there was William's friend, the innkeeper, Rafe Tuttle, a veteran juryman of witch trials.

It was odd to him that Bascombe had numbered Rafe among the jurymen, knowing that Rafe was William's friend. Bascombe would have discovered that, surely, as the man had discovered so much more about his business. And yet perhaps learning that Rafe had voted to convict Mother Waterhouse, Bascombe believed he would do likewise on this occasion. William had read enough about the earlier trial to know that the evidence against the Harknesses was far more damning than that against Agnes Waterhouse, Agnes' confession notwithstanding.

The final juror was another tailor, whom William recognized. It was Woodard, the man who had falsely accused William of stealing the silver cup, the man whom Justice Southcote had berated and exposed as a liar. Roger Woodard, a friend of Timothy Parker. Like the others on the jury, he was to sit in judgement of Ursula and Mary Harkness. The tailor, a man without principle, a man anxious to please, a man undoubtedly bought and paid for as he had been in falsely accusing William of theft.

The jurymen were now seated on their stools, six to each row, and most looking pleased with themselves to be so honoured, especially the lying tailor who positively beamed and at once point threw a

236

malicious glance at William as much as to say, "see, Doctor, this is how I avenge myself."

They were sworn in by the bailiff, after which all knowing each other and some friends as well as fellow townsmen, they chatted amiably among themselves as though sitting outdoors in the sun on market day. By this time the town clock had struck eleven, and the air and heat in the assembly hall, made worse by the closed door and the press of sweating bodies and unwashed garments, was almost unbearable, yet no one moved to leave for all the discomfort, or seemed disposed to. William observed all this with increasing apprehension. Nothing he had seen thus far promised justice for the defendants.

The bailiff stood and ordered silence for the third time that morning, but the audience, trusting now that the trial was indeed ready to proceed, responded. No one wanted to miss anything, now that there would be something to miss. Even the drunks in the back of the room quieted themselves, leaning against the wall, staring not at the officers of the court but at the defendants, both repelled and fascinated by them. Was it possible that a witch could cast a spell on an entire town, cursing them all, bringing death and destruction to them all?

The fear must have been in the minds of many, William thought.

Prosecutor Poole rose to read out the indictment against the defendants.

The official charges were couched in a legal language that made it not altogether clear what the women were accused of doing, but afterwards William would remember the gist of it. Ursula Harkness was accused of murdering Master Thomas Bascombe of Mowbray Rise, "for that he failed to keep his promise to marry her after begetting a child upon her body." She was accused of keeping a familiar, to wit: a wolf, or at least a large dog resembling one. Her mother, Mary Harkness was accused of being a co-conspirator in this crime, the indictment affirming that "Mother Harkness did teach her daughter all she knew of the Devil and his works, tutored her in casting spells and causing other misfortunes in the town too numerous to mention in the indictment, but to be revealed in due course."

Ursula Harkness was also said to have given birth to a child, marked upon his face to suggest he was in truth fathered by the wolf dog, her familiar, rather than Master Thomas Bascombe, who was declared to be innocent of any impropriety or misconduct in the case.

"My son committed no fornication with that woman," Bascombe declared after the indictment was read, standing and pointing to Ursula, causing Justice Southcote to issue a stern reproof.

"Sir Richard Bascombe, you have no voice in this court at this time. Your son's conduct has no relevance to the matter at hand. his innocence is declared in the indictment. So be pleased, sir, to keep silent unless you later are asked to give testimony."

Reluctantly, Bascombe sat back down and flashed an angry glance at William as though he had issued the reproof and not Southcote. After this interruption Southcote asked the two defendants how they pled to the charges.

Both mother and daughter cried in one voice, "Not guilty, my lord. Not guilty."

Their denial brought another round of jeers and catcalls, but it quickly subsided. William wondered that the two women had the strength to express their innocence so forcefully, so wretched they looked, so besieged by the hatred of their fellow townsmen.

William knew that in the witch trials he had read a not guilty plea was unusual, even as the prosecutor had said, and that generally by the time of arraignment the supposed witches had confessed, either having seen the error of their ways or shrewdly concluding that a guilty plea offered best hope of leniency and ultimate salvation in this life and the next. At that point too, William imagined torture would have made a guilty plea a safer road to a speedy death than the obstinacy associated with a profession of innocence.

But he looked at the faces of the two women, mother and daughter. There was no doubt there of what they were or were not guilty of. Mary Harkness, though weary and worn, stood straight and tall, looking her accusers in the face as though daring them to give her the lie. Her daughter Ursula did likewise, although she of the two was at most peril, having been accused of murder. William remembered these were the women who had saved his life. But for them, he would not be here. But for them, he would not be anywhere.

At the conclusion of the charges there was another uproar from the spectators, some calling out for the two women to be hanged without further ado, and even some calling for the hanging of Ursula's child, although he was not on trial and was by William's reckoning still under a year in age.

It was now past noon, but it was clear that Southcote was annoyed by the delay and had no intent to pause in the proceedings. He told the queen's counsel to present the first of the witnesses. Willliam thought this might be Clara Bascombe herself, since she was the chief complainant, but it was a woman named Joan Berkeley, of whom he'd never heard.

39

This first witness was a woman of middle-age, dressed plainly in a grey homespun gown and old-fashioned wimple, with a round, florid face, a conspicuous goitre, and large, bulging eyes. When she stood up, she was no taller than a child. She came up to the witness box, which was no box at all, but simply a spot upon the platform where she was told to stand, which she obediently did. She was handed a Bible by the bailiff, asked to place her hand upon it, swear to tell the truth or face eternal damnation. All this she did, trembling as though she herself were on trial and about to receive judgement, not just of a jury of her peers but of God Himself.

"Your name, Mistress?" Poole asked.

"Joan Berkeley, my Lord."

"Your occupation?"

"I am my husband's wife, my children's mother."

Her response drew a sprinkling of laughter. It was clear that this woman was a known person in the town. William had seen more than a few in the audience wave to her as she stood there.

The prosecutor said impatiently, "I mean, what is it you do in the town? Why are you here?"

"I am midwife, my lord. I have been so for thirty years or more."

"A midwife. An honorable calling, Mistress Berkeley. And how do you know the defendants?"

"I helped birth the defendant's child, my Lord."

"You mean Ursula Harkness's child?"

"The same, my Lord."

"And when the child was born did you experience anything usual pertaining to it?"

"To the child, my lord?"

"Yes, to the child or anything unusual in the birth chamber?"

"T'was no chamber, my lord. Hardly so much as a corner of the kitchen."

The prosecutor breathed a sigh of exasperation. A titter of laughter went around the courtroom, but Southcote did nothing to restrain it. After the earlier outbursts, William supposed Southcote was grateful that the crowd at this moment was no more unruly.

"Were there any manifestations? Flames of fire? Ghostly presences? Was the defendant's dog in the room?" Poole asked, facing the jury, although the question was obviously directed at the witness.

"I don't remember, my lord. About the dog, I mean. As for the other things you said about flames and ghosts and…" She hesitated, searching for the word.

"Manifestations," Poole said.

"No, my Lord. There was nothing of that that I remember. No ghosts, no flames, no… manifestations."

Poole seemed disappointed at this response but pressed on.

"And when the child was born, what did you see upon the infant's face?"

"I saw a dreadful mark, my Lord. It seemed to me to resemble the face of the great dog she had, the dog that was like unto a wolf."

At this there were expressions of horror from the audience, and then a stirring of restlessness, as though the midwife's very words presented a danger to them all. William knew those present would have heard all of this before the trial, but somehow hearing it from a witness in the court itself made the birthmark all the more alarming.

"And when you saw it upon the infant's face, what did you think, Mistress Berkeley?"

"I thought, my Lord, nay, I knew, that it was the devil's mark."

"And then what did you do?"

"I fled, my Lord. I never wanted to go to the Old Priory in the first place."

"Why not, Mistress Berkeley, are you not paid for your service? Is it not what you do, aid in the birthing of infants?"

"It is what I do, but the Old Priory is a fearful place."

The midwife began to explain her fears of the Old Priory. She said she feared the place because of them who had once lived there and done unspeakable things. It was the same account of debauchery and infanticide he had heard from Clara Bascombe, even the same account he had heard earlier from Ursula Harkness herself. Yet the Harknesses held on to their farmstead

241

as though it were all they had. He knew from Sir Richard Bascombe that to regain the property was his dearest hope. Yet everyone apparently believed it was cursed, haunted, malevolent. William thought this very strange. Why would someone covet such a place, want to make it his own?

"You mean the nuns." The prosecutor said.

"Yes, my Lord. The papists."

The audience stirred at this too. William knew there might be papists in Chelmsford, but he supposed they would be few and would be wisely concealing their faith, given the local antipathy and strictures imposed by Parliament and the queen. It was clear to him that where the Harknesses lived was a detriment to any defense of their innocence, but only confirmed to the townspeople's deep-seated suspicions. How could they *not* be witches, living where they did, drinking from the spring the nuns had drunk from, living near the cemetery where they and their bastard children were buried?

The atmosphere was poisonous.

"You say you fled upon seeing the child's face?"

"I did, my lord. It frightened me so."

"Did you ever see the child another time, perhaps when his mother brought him to town?"

"To my knowledge, my lord, the woman never brought her child to town, nor did she come, either." She paused, looked at Ursula in the prisoner's box, and said with an accusing finger, "She wouldn't dare."

Here the queen's counsel paused, turned to the defendants, and stared at them with a look of incredulity and distaste.

"And you never had occasion to return to the Old Priory?" Poole asked, turning his attention again to Joan Berkeley.

"I would not dare, my lord. I am a Christian woman."

"I will ask you one final question, Mistress Berkeley."

"And I will answer truthfully, my lord."

"Is it your belief, based on your knowledge of these two defendants, that they are guilty as charged?"

"I do believe it, my lord. I believe it with all my heart, for I also have had a dream confirming the same."

"And what was that dream, Mistress Berkeley?"

"I saw the two of them, Mary Harkness and her daughter, burning in flames and heard a voice say to me, 'a fit end to those who practice witchcraft against the righteous.'"

The midwife stepped down and the courtroom buzzed with talk about the testimony and especially about Joan Berkeley's dream. On the dais the officials were conferring, about some point of law or perhaps the order of witnesses to follow. In any event, the trial proceeded without recess, although William could see persons getting up from their places and making their way toward the doors. Others were coming back in after being outside, having answered calls of nature, there being no privies or chamber pots available within, nor discreet places to use them.

The next witness was called: Lady Clara Bascombe.

40

It was what William had dreaded, what he knew must come. He had watched Clara's face during the midwife's testimony. It was a face cold and hard as steel, her jaw stiff as if immovable. She had listened attentively to Joan Berkeley's testimony and William did not doubt she believed every word of it, including the woman's reported dream, evidence beyond any possible verification.

The midwife was a single voice, but it was not a voice crying in the wilderness. Joan Berkeley, humble creature that she was, would be speaking for the town, fear and hatred of Catholics, a suspicion of people who kept to themselves, who kept a strange and terrifying dog more like a wolf than a dog. It was a wonder to him that Ursula and her mother had not been accused before. Their way of living, their isolation, made them ripe for gossip and a great black dog, especially one with wolfish features, was a better candidate for a familiar than the ordinary housecat with its whimpering and meowing and preoccupation with mice.

But now there was Clara Bascombe, not a simple townsperson, but a knight's daughter, a person the jurymen would listen to, believe, no doubt without question. She was dressed finely, more finely than he had seen her dressed before, so that no other woman in the room could rival her. Her whitened face, so different from the faces of the others in the assembly, made her glow in the unlit chamber and seem almost other-worldly, much as the queen's majesty appeared in her frequent public appearances, when she was adored by her subjects, not merely honored as their queen. Now, the gravamen of the case would be presented, the murder of Thomas Bascombe.

He watched her come up from where she had been seated next to her brother, to stand before the court. She moved slowly and deliberately, obviously conscious of how she must appear, radiant, her father's wealth on her back like a badge. She took the same oath that the midwife had taken, but to William it was different. The midwife trembled as she lay her hand upon the sacred book, fearful he had no doubt, of divine wrath should she tell a lie. But Clara touched the same book lightly, casually, as though the very Bascombe name was a guarantee of her truthfulness and she required no greater support than that, certainly no divine mandate that she speak truth.

Anthony Poole rose from his place at the table and approached her, bowed before he addressed her. It was a practiced gesture, but William had no doubt it was genuine. He had already noticed Poole eyeing his chief witness, even before she was called. Poole would treat her with kid gloves, anxious not to offend, eager to show he was on her side, on the side of the rich and powerful. Irony and sarcasm he would save for simple souls like the poor midwife.

"Lady Clara Bascombe?" Clara nodded but did not answer. Justice Southcote told her that she must speak. It was for the record, he said.

She hesitated, and then did. When her testimony began, she resumed her haughty air, an attitude that William thought might have offended the jury and the spectators, but he saw no sign that it did. It was, after all, what they expected of a knight's daughter. They would have been disappointed were she otherwise, perhaps even unbelieving that she was who she claimed to be.

"Lady Clara, the prosecutor began, "you have charged these women, and more particularly Ursula Harkness, with casting a spell on your brother so that he languished for months before his death where before he was a healthy man."

"I do, sir," she said.

"Madam, you must refer to the Queen's Attorney as "my lord," for he is deserving of that honor," Southcote interrupted.

Clara looked at Southcote, nodded her head, and then turned back to the prosecutor. William thought, *she is contemptuous of the court, even though she uses it to get what she wants, contemptuous of the jury, upon whom she won't deign to cast an eye.*

"I do... my lord. I make that complaint of this vicious woman." She pointed a finger at Ursula Harkness. "She did kill my brother with her spells, which I have no doubt she learned from her mother and from the cursed soil where both lived."

"And she did so because your brother, Thomas, would not marry her, having fathered a child upon her?" the prosecutor said, reading from a sheaf of papers in his hand.

Clara paused for a moment, then lifted her face and glared at Poole. "My brother, my lord, would not have given Ursula Harkness a second look. Her child has another father, not my brother, I swear it. If she says otherwise, she is deluded, or she lies outright for reasons of her own. That she might have wanted Thomas for a husband, I do not doubt it. Many a woman would, given his qualities and station. But that he wanted her at any time defies belief. She is lying. What else would you expect of a witch? You only have to look upon her, skin and bones as she is, as hideous as she is."

Clara paused again—for effect, William thought—and gave Ursula a withering look. "My brother was a handsome man. He might have had any woman of position he wished. Wherefore should he stoop to abuse Ursula Harkness, of all people?"

When Clara said this there was a murmur of agreement in the chamber, and William noticed that her father and the learned rector also were nodding their heads. Clara had given the full-throated denunciation of Ursula that William had expected, and Ursula herself had seemed to shrink from the charge, her eyes cast down in deepest humiliation. William felt pity for her, not just because she was on trial for her life, but because the public abuse must have been in itself a little death. She was a girl who had, by the world's standards, little to offer a man. Clara's condemnation had subtracted even from that.

"And how can you be sure, madam, that your brother did not merely abuse her, that is, take his pleasure of her body, because it was offered him?

Clara glared at the prosecutor. Held fire for a moment, and then screamed, startling the court, "I said, that you must look at that wretched woman. What pleasure could any man have in that, that?" Again, she pointed her finger at Ursula Harkness, who so attacked seemed whiter in her face than Clara. "A man might better copulate with a skeleton for all the pleasure she would give."

Clara's language and bitterness had startled everyone, including several of the jurors who had seemed half asleep before. The bailiff cried out for order in the courtroom, and in a moment, silence was restored. William looked at Clara. She seemed unperturbed now, as though she could not remember her screaming at the prosecutor, or even the reaction it had provoked among the spectators, who might now have reasonably a somewhat different opinion of the lady or, William thought, have found her outburst alarming.

Her outburst had affected the queen's counsel. Poole seemed at a loss for words. He looked nervously through the sheaf of papers he held in his hand, as though he were searching for something. He cleared his throat. Finally, he said:

"Lady Clara, will you tell the court about your brother's illness?"

Clara paused before answering, as though the prosecutor's question surprised her. Then she said, "He at first lay abed without strength in him, slept much of the time but not to his rest. His muscles and joints ached. He had no appetite, and what little he ate he could not keep down. He grew worse. At no time did he improve. Then he died."

"Did a doctor attend him?"

"Doctor Fields from this town,"

"And what did he do for your brother?"

"He bled him; twice, I think. No, three times. He said my brother had an excess of bile within him. But the treatment did no good. We dismissed the doctor. My brother's condition grew worse."

"When was it you concluded he had been cursed?"

"He told me some woman had falsely claimed he had fathered her child. It was he, my brother, who suggested it was witchcraft."

"Your brother believed he was cursed by a witch?"

"Yes, my lord, he truly did."

"And he told you this woman was Ursula Harkness?"

"My lord, my brother didn't even know her name. He referred to her as the whore who lived in the Old Priory. Who else could he mean but the defendant, Ursula Harkness? It is she who lives there, who gave birth to this monstrous child, which is, I attest, another reason my brother could not have fathered it."

William remembered that, in Clara's account of her brother's illness, she never said that the charge of witchcraft had originally come from him. On the contrary, she had said he was unaware of the cause of his sickness. That he was a victim of a witch's spell had been her idea, or Agnes Robinson's. The man who had carefully preserved Ursula's letters could not have been unaware of his lover's name. And he certainly would not have believed she wished him dead. Clara's testimony was a tissue of self-serving lies.

"Other than Doctor Fields, you had no other to attend to him?"

"Only myself, my lord. Heaven knows I rarely left his side until the day he died."

"You are to be commended for your charity, madam," the prosecutor said, obviously charmed by her, despite her earlier fiery comments. "Not every sister would have been so accommodating, given the severity and duration of his illness."

"Christ calls us to such service, my lord. I could have done no less." She cast her eyes down, in modest acceptance of Poole's compliment.

"Then, my lady, it is your testimony that Ursula Harkness murdered your brother and that her mother, Mary Harkness, was her confederate therein in advising her as to how that might be done?"

"That is my testimony, my lord."

Clara was excused and returned to where her brother sat. Southcote announced that there would be one more witness to be heard for the day. This brought a groan of disappointment from the spectators, who evidently were eager to see a verdict given and the witches condemned.

But William was relieved. Clara had perjured herself, he was certain of it, and her testimony, a tissue of lies, would have its effect. But William was determined to counter it.

Southcote had promised to let him speak.

41

The last witness of the day was Julian. This younger Bascombe came up to the place where his sister had just stood with a confidence and arrogance that matched every ill impression William had had of him during their several encounters at Mowbray Rise. For a moment, they locked eyes, and then Julian's lips curled up into what was almost a snarl as he announced his name.

"Master Julian Bascombe of Mowbray Rise."

He was sworn in by the bailiff, and showed the same haughtiness his sister had displayed in looking over the court room. Like Clara, Julian had dressed for the occasion. He looked more like a creature of the court than a country squire. He had combed his hair, trimmed his beard, and struck a kind of pose of magisterial authority that William found almost laughable, knowing what a lout he truly was.

"You are the brother of the late Thomas Bascombe?" Poole began absently, obviously not as interested in this witness as in his sister.

"I am, my lord. He was my elder brother by several years, my beloved brother I might add."

"And what evidence have you to give against these defendants?" the prosecutor asked. It was a question William had in his own mind. On the several occasions he had spoken to Julian, Clara's brother had said little more than what his sister had just testified to, although he had said nothing about Thomas having been first to blame his illness on witchcraft.

"I have evidence against the character of the defendant, Ursula Harkness," Julian announced, imitating the tone he had been hearing from Southcote.

"And what evidence would that be?" the prosecutor said.

"That she is a whore, my lord, a very whore, for she has more than once accosted me while I rode around my land and inquired of me if I would be pleased to lie with her."

"Lie with her? You mean, have carnal relations with her?"

"That is what I mean, my lord. And her mother is another of the same ilk."

Ursula, who had stood silent during the previous testimonies, now cried out, "That is a lie, my lords. That is a very lie. I have never as much spoken to the man. He lies, my lords, who says such a thing. As God is my witness."

Mary Harkness joined in her daughter's protest since she had also been defamed. Their response caused another uproar in the courtroom. William had been in courtrooms before, but never had he seen such discord and disorder, such disrespect for legal authority or unruliness in those who came to testify or serve in juries.

Southcote, very red in the face, stood up from his seat, and ordered the prisoners to be silent, then tried to quiet the spectators, who were stirred up again by the accusation and chattering among themselves as though they were out of doors. William could overhear some of the talk, the voices were echoing the testimony they had just heard—there were comments about the appearance of the women, vulgar comments about their faces, estimates of their attractiveness or lack of it. Some of it was rude humor, bawdy. Some deeply malicious and obscene as though those who uttered it hated the defendants for reasons too personal to disclose.

When it was silent again, Julian continued. "And I have it of certain companions of mine who have ridden in the same region of the forest that she likewise accosted them with the same proposition."

Since the charge of prostitution had not been included in the indictment there was now a hurried discussion among the judges on the bench as to how this new allegation was to be received. After some deliberation, Southcote said, "We have not heard this before, but since it goes to the moral character of the defendant and calls into question her assertion that Thomas Bascombe fathered her child rather than some other she lay with, we will accept it."

Southcote told Poole, who seemed at this point almost beside himself with glee as to the trial's outcome, to continue. He wore a foolish smile on his face and William noticed he kept nodding at Clara as though they were part of a conspiracy.

"Will you now tell us the names of these other gentlemen who were propositioned, Master Bascombe?

Clara's brother thought for a moment then said, "I would rather not, my lord, for fear it would put their reputations in doubt."

"Why should it, Master Bascombe?" the prosecutor returned. "I presume these friends of yours didn't succumb to Ursula Harkness's wiles?"

"Several did, my lord, for which they have since felt shame—and deservedly so."

"As they properly should, Master Bascombe," Poole said. "Think you one of the unnamed gentlemen may have been the father of her child?"

"I think, my lord, it might be so. But I do here swear before God it was not my brother."

"And why not, Master Bascombe?"

"It is as my sister has testified, my lord, my brother was a discerning man, a handsome man. He could have any woman he wanted. Why should he condescend to some strumpet who knows only how to keep cows and a familiar, as ignorant as she is filthy. I say he never tupped her, never promised to marry her as she claims and, her desires frustrated, she cast a spell upon him, which art she learned from her mother."

"Then you believe, Master Bascombe, that Ursula Harkness's story is false?"

"It is false as hell, my Lord. Upon my honor it is."

"Why do you think she picked your brother out for her false tale?"

Julian gave a short, scornful laugh. "Why, is it not obvious, my lord? My brother was my father's eldest son and heir. We are a family of means, of honorable reputation. What an advantage that would give her to marry such a one as my brother was, a chance to escape the miserable life she led at the Old Priory, the devil's domain if there ever was one."

William looked around the courtroom. As far as he could tell, Julian Bascombe's theory of Ursula's motivation was generally received as being sound. There seemed little sense in the courtroom that this case was about lost love rather than personal advantage. Also, William knew the Bascombe's estimation of Ursula's beauties or lack of them would accord with the town's. Thus far, there seemed to be no weakness in the prosecution's case, or no easy way to undermine the testimony so far given. Those who knew Julian Bascombe might doubt he refused Ursula's offer of her body, but not that she offered it, if he said she did.

Julian ended his testimony with more drama. He declared his great fear that the town was besieged by witches and demons, and it was every man's duty to suppress evil wherever it was found and that should the women not be found guilty the judgment of God would fall on them all. He gave the jurymen a searching look, as though he were challenging each to deny the truth of his statements. Then he stalked back to his chair and sat down heavily in it as though his testimony had sapped all his strength. William saw Clara put a hand on Julian's shoulder, a gesture of support for a brother she heretofore had despised and mocked.

To William, and he hoped at least to a few others in the courtroom who knew of Julian Bascombe's reputation as a wastrel, it was a disgusting performance. William believed he had never heard such hypocrisy or mendacity from a witness, and all an affront to the oath Julian had taken. He remembered Julian's boast of wenching and whoring during one of their unpleasant encounters at the Rise. Julian's friend Winton had confirmed, both being frequent patrons of Cobb's End. And here he falsely condemned Ursula.

The court was adjourned. Although there had been some signs of disappointment that the verdict would thereby be delayed, it was evident now that adjournment was coming as a relief to most in the audience. The session had lasted nearly eight hours. No pause had been made to see to the needs of audience, or jury. Many of the spectators had been standing the whole while for want of place to sit, and were thereby stiff-legged and bone-weary. None had eaten or drunk in all that time and as the company dismissed there was an evident desire to go home to eat, to escape the stifling and odiferous courtroom, and to share with those unfortunate enough not to be present the scandalous testimony of the witnesses.

Rafe Tuttle caught up with William as he was heading back to the Blue Boar.

"What think you, Doctor, of the first day? Some choice entertainment, is it not?"

"It would be, Rafe, were the stakes not so high," William said, a little annoyed at Rafe's flippant tone. "You and the other jurymen are dealing with the lives of these two women."

"With the Bascombes' testimony their conviction is sure," Rafe said.

"I pray it is not so," William said. "There is still more testimony to hear. I have been promised by Justice Southcote an opportunity to speak, and will do so to controvert much of what has been said today. Julian Bascombe's testimony was a tissue of lies. His sister's true only in part, and she has left much out relevant to the case."

"It will be like unto pushing a great rock up a slippery slope, Doctor."

"Like Sisyphus, you mean?"

"Sisyphus, Doctor? A patient of yours?"

William laughed. "An old story, a legend or myth, Greek."

"I know no legends, Greek or otherwise, yet still I say it's a slippery slope."

"So it may be, Rafe, yet I will push the rock, though my heart break of it."

Back in his chamber he thought to write to his father. To report the proceedings of the trial, in which his father would surely be interested. But then he decided against it. He had in his actions cut himself off from Jerome Gilbert, who, having a quite different view of Clara Bascombe, her father, and William's own responsibility to the Harknesses, would surely hesitate to respond in any way useful to William and only begin another round of futile recriminations.

He decided to retire early, unable to eat, and given what testimony he intended to give on the next day, unable to sleep as well. He tossed and turned in his bed with its lumpy mattress, dreamed once of being in London with his colleagues at the College, and woke at dawn abruptly when he imagined Clara Bascombe sharing his bed. Or was it Ursula Harkness? Or was it the Dutch girl he had loved and lost?

42

They wanted to see the baby, to see with their own eyes the wolfish stain. *They* being almost the entire courtroom, judging by the resounding and insistent demand, including the jury who were most insistent of all. Justice Southcote had heard of the birthmark, the audience had heard of it, but only a few of the earlier examiners of the two women, the Reverend Culpeper, and Constable Pickney had actually seen the child. It had been the prosecutor's suggestion, and the suggestion had quickly grown into demand. Was the marked face not evidence? And should it not be shown to all and sundry? The indisputable proof, as if the court didn't have that already.

The queen's counsel said he would have the dog itself brought forth if it could be found. Julian Bascombe claimed he had set out to find it, kill it. He said he had seen it once, but it suddenly vanished, another sign that it was no dog, but the Devil himself. Few had seen it and thus the imagination of the town had made it larger, more ferocious, and more satanic than it was or could be.

The child had been in the keeping of the constable's wife, who had complained sorely of the duty and feared some manner of contamination as a result of feeding it, holding it perforce, having it within the precincts of the family's living quarters above the shop on the High Street. Pickney had sent for his wife to bring the child to court.

The constable's wife returned, holding Ursula's baby away from her chest as far as she could, as though the squealing infant were some filthy thing, threatening to soil Mistress Pickney's apron or poison the milk in her breasts.

"This, my lords, is the infant of Ursula Harkness, the defendant," the queen's counsel intoned, pointing to the child, who stopped his protest and turned to look not to the judges or the jurymen but to the audience, all of whom were on their feet and pushing and shoving to see the it. No child, but some strange thing, some marvel of nature, or in this case of hell, some major attraction of a freak show.

"The child itself is a witness," the queen's counsel continued. "For though he cannot speak, his very countenance gives sure testimony to the evil of her who bore and suckled him."

The presentation of the child put the chamber in an uproar, for the birthmark was clearly visible and even to William, who was sitting a good dozen feet from it, the discoloration seemed to be ruddier and more conspicuous than he had remembered. What was more, rather than express alarm at the crowd's cries of horror, the child quieted and seemed to smile at them as though he were glad to have the attention of such a multitude. By their horrified reaction, the crowd considered the infant's smile even more sinister and disturbing than his squeals and William heard some of those present exclaim that the witch's child was possessed, and that he should be snatched from the hands of the constable's wife and drowned or burned.

For William, it was a dark and ominous beginning for the second day of the trial, and to William's mind a clear victory for the prosecution. He knew that for most of the audience, perhaps for all, nothing proved Ursula's guilt more than the disfigured child, if not the mark of the wolf, at least a mark that signified some abnormal and therefore sinister influence, reflecting on her who had given the baby life even more than on the child himself.

The judge ordered the baby to be removed from the courtroom, but since it was evident that not everyone had had a chance to see the birthmark, and most especially the jury, there was a scramble among them to be first. The jurymen left their stools and came around to the front of the court to see for themselves, elbowing each other to come closest to Ursula's baby. Mistress Pickney was simply unable to move from her place to comply with Southcote's command.

Justice Southcote cried for order again and threatened to clear the courtroom. This threat, even more than arrests for riot, had the effect of bringing some semblance of order, for the trial to this point had satisfied everyone's expectations of an entertaining spectacle, far above a dog fight, bear baiting or hanging. The constable's wife removed the child, who filled the restored quiet with a new round of screams as he was taken from the chamber. The view of the infant's face had caused at least three women in the audience to faint and need to be carried out.

Everyone who had a bench or stool or place against a wall returned to it, William sat on his stool and craned his neck to see over a large woman who had taken a place in front of him and obscured his view of the dais and the court officials. He was about to ask her to move over, when she did so anyway, leaving him with enough of a view to see the witness stand. William wanted to see everything, and he knew the layout of the chamber would always prevent that. But he knew it was even more important to hear what was said. It was that to which he would presently have to respond.

43

Justice Southcote called for the next witness, and the Reverend Doctor Culpeper rose like the sun from his place at the table and marched to the witness stand. He was sworn in, and even before the prosecutor had opened his mouth to ask him to identify himself and his vocation, Culpeper spoke in a deep, resonant voice to announce that he was the Reverend Doctor Junius Culpeper of St. Peter's Church, Chelmsford.

Some in the audience cheered at this, anticipating, William supposed, that the rector's pronouncement of the women's guilt would be the final word. He was, after all, the representative of spiritual authority in Chelmsford, well recognized as an expert in all matters religious of which, of course, the practice of witchcraft was a dimension.

That Culpeper would be called as witness was no surprise to William. In his short and unhappy conversation with the man, Culpeper had declared his intention to present evidence against the accused women. Now, he and the court were to learn what evidence this was.

"And Doctor Culpeper, will you tell this court how you came to know of the guilt of the defendants?" Poole the queen's counsel asked, turning away from the witness and looking at the audience.

"I examined Ursula Harkness and her mother, both, my lord."

"You examined their bodies?"

"Mistress Pickney did examine them, she and Mistress Willoughby."

"Mistress Willoughby?"

"My housekeeper," Culpeper said.

"And what did they find, Doctor?"

"They did find witches' teats upon the both of them, my lord."

Culpeper's statement set the audience in motion again—expressions of horror, cries of "hang the witches", demands that the defendants be

257

stripped so that the teats could be seen by all. William had learned from his reading about witches that physical evidence such as this had in earlier trials been dispositive in establishing guilt, although such teats, as they were called, had often been nothing more than moles or wens, minor imperfections of flesh that might mark the body of the most innocent of souls.

"And where were these teats, these witches' teats, found?"

"Upon the body of Mary Harkness, my lord. Behind her left ear there was a mark. She claimed falsely it was but a scar where she had been bitten by a dog when she was a child. Whereupon I said to her, 'yea verily, Mother Harkness, you might well say it was a dog who bit you for that mark is where the great black dog who is your familiar has sucked your blood.'"

"And what did Mother Harkness say to that, Doctor?"

"She denied it, my lord."

"What of her daughter Ursula?"

"She had a round mole upon her left breast, as black as night, just above the nipple where the wolf did suck her blood for which the same familiar did then perform those things Ursula Harkness desired of it."

"Which were?"

"A curse upon Thomas Bascombe because she believed he loved her, begot a child upon her, and would not marry her. Even as has been declared by earlier testimony."

"Thomas' father, sister, and brother all deny that Thomas had anything to do with Ursula Harkness," the prosecutor said.

"I am sure that is true, my lord. For as all here can see with their own eyes, she is an ill-favored wench, given to lewd behavior as Master Julian Bascombe has testified, and not to be believed in any matter, though she swear on a dozen Bibles. I asked her to say the Lord's Prayer in English, but she said it in Latin instead, which as all know, is ample proof of Satan's grip upon her."

William was confident the business of the prayer was a lie. Ursula had made it clear to him at the Old Priory that she had no affection for papist practices, nor particular knowledge of them. An older person alive before the recent reforms of worship might have prayed in Latin out of mere habit. But Ursula was born after. No matter how much the Harknesses were out of step with the people of Chelmsford, they were with them in matters of religion, as far as William could tell. He knew in past trials the inability of the defendant to say the paternoster in English was evidence of satanic influence, just as the insistence of the defendant to say the prayer in Latin made one conclude the same, but it had as much effect upon the court as the discovery of suspicious marks upon Ursula's body.

Justice Southcote said, "Master Prosecutor, will these two women be called to affirm what Doctor Culpeper testified, I mean Mistresses Pickney and Willoughby?"

"I thought not, my lord, to call them, since I am sure there is none in this court that would not take Doctor Culpeper's word for what they reported to him."

"No, my lord prosecutor, I do wish the testimony to be heard myself, inspecting the defendant's bodies in their own words. It is not that Doctor Culpeper's testimony is not to be trusted, but since both of these women are here in the courtroom, I see no reason they should not speak for themselves."

The judge told the prosecutor to continue his questioning of the Reverend. "We shall have the testimony of the women after," the judge said.

"Doctor, will you tell this honorable court and worthy jurymen what the church teaches with respect to witches?"

"I will, and gladly, my lord." Culpeper turned from the prosecutor and addressed the courtroom as though it were his congregation using, William was sure, his sermon voice, his sermonic gestures.

"The scriptures are clear, my lords, and leave no room for doubt. *Thou shalt not suffer a witch to live*, we read in the Book of Exodus, chapter twenty-two and in the eighteenth verse thereof. Were there no witches, wherefore would God have condemned them? Moreover, my lords and all within my voice, do you not remember Saul and the Witch of Endor when that same wicked creature summoned from the dead the prophet Samuel that he might take counsel in the day of battle against the Philistines? The scriptures be no fiction, no child's tale. God's word on every point must be accepted as true, or all is false. He who disputes the existence of such baleful creatures in the world is no better than an atheist, for he does deny God's word, the existence of the Devil, and where there is no Devil, there can be no God."

It was an argument William had heard before. Culpeper himself had evoked it when he had come to William's room at the Blue Boar and tried to persuade him to leave Chelmsford and forsake the Harkness women. And the logic of it was one of the dangers he knew he faced in giving testimony, when he should be allowed to do so. His defense of the two women might easily be seen to be an atheistical affirmation, which would not only destroy his credibility with the jury but put himself in jeopardy.

The prosecutor continued, "Doctor Culpeper, can you tell us what the baleful influence of a witch can do to this entire town?"

"I can, my lord prosecutor, and many thanks to you and this court for giving me the opportunity so to do. A witch is of a different kind than humankind. Their kind, their species, if I may use that word, is of the Devil, not of God. We, my lords, are God's children, and therefore His kind. But the witch is of the Devil. He is their father. They are *his* kind."

Culpeper stopped to take a breath, or perhaps to see how his comments were being taken. Then he continued. "A witch may curse an individual. If she is successful in so doing, that is, if he or she whom she curses suffers death or other misfortune, the witch is emboldened thereby. She will not stop there but proceed to curse others. Everyone within the sound of my voice, every man, woman, or child, has reason to fear these two women. Master Thomas Bascombe is dead because he would not yield to the petitions of this creature, this creature of the Evil One."

Culpeper paused, pointing an accusing finger at Ursula. She did not react, too stunned by the defamation to do more than just stare. Culpeper went on.

"Who amongst us shall be the next? What honorable man? What virtuous wife? What innocent child? The beasts of the field are not immune to witchcraft."

Saying this, Culpeper paused again, to catch his breath. William thought he might have concluded his testimony, but the real climax was yet to come. Culpeper held his head high and looked around the chamber. He pointed his finger at this person or that in the audience in a way an actor might do upon the stage. "Will it be you?" he asked of a woman sitting among the gentry. "Or will it be you?" he asked of a man toward the rear of the assembly.

William expected yet another outburst from the audience condemning the defendants but instead there was a dreadful silence, presumably as each person considered what a threat the women were to himself or herself, a loved one, an innocent child, a fruitful orchard, a beast in the field. Any or all blasted.

The queen's counsel let the silence in the chamber have its full effect. At last, Justice Southcote asked the reverend if he had anything more to say. William knew he would. The man seemed to have an inexhaustible supply of words and know instinctively how they would play in the minds of his audience.

He concluded with a dreadful warning.

"I say this, my lords and good men of the jury, if you do not find these women guilty of such wickedness, then God's judgment will fall upon us. God will not be mocked, my lords. He expects each of us to do our duty. And the scriptures are clear as to what that duty is. *Thou shall not suffer a witch to live.*"

Culpeper stopped and cast his eye toward the ceiling. He held the pose as if it were not the ceiling he viewed but beyond it, in the heavens, the very throne of God to whom he looked to validate his dreadful warning.

A man sitting next to William said. "The man speaks with the voice of an angel, don't you think, sir?"

William held his peace.

44

The reverend doctor resumed his place at the table among the other officials and received the commendations of those around him—particularly, William noticed, Sir Richard Bascombe and the justice of the peace, the father of Julian Bascombe's friend, Adrian Winton. Then, the two examiners Culpeper had alluded to returned to the stand, the constable's wife and a Mistress Martha Willoughby, the latter identified only by her name but presumably some woman of respectability and well-allowed virtue.

Culpeper had referred to her as his housekeeper; William thought it highly unlikely that her testimony would contradict that of her employer.

Their testimony was brief and was largely what Culpeper had reported, that devil's teats had been discovered on the bodies of both women, although they reported that one of these was found upon Ursula Harkness's private parts, which the reverend had not mentioned, out of the indelicacy of it, although it was clear to William that this added information had a great effect on men of the jury and the spectators as well, since it suggested an even greater depth of depravity.

"And what did the women, the defendants, say when you noticed these teats?" the queen's counsel asked. He asked this of the constable's wife, but Culpeper's housekeeper answered.

"Why, they denied it. Most strenuously, my lord. They said the marks were naught but what they had had for years upon their bodies. They denied beasts had sucked upon them, but I knew, my lord, that both lied in their teeth."

"How did you know that?"

"Because I know the devil's teats when I see them," the housekeeper said, and turned to look at her employer, Culpeper, who beamed with approval.

"You know them when you see them?" the queen's counsel said. "And precisely how?"

She did not hesitate to answer. It was if she had been prepared for the question, as William suspected she had been, doubtless by the Reverend himself. "My mother taught me how to recognize these marks. She was gifted with the power of discernment. She could merely look at a woman and tell whether she was possessed or not, possessed of some spirit not of this earth. She needed not to examine the woman naked so to discern."

To William the testimony of the two women had proved nothing more than the credulity of them both, and perhaps the housekeeper's absolute devotion to Culpeper in that it was clear she would say anything to please him. In a way, the presence of some imperfection in the flesh was the weakest evidence of witchcraft, yet William had learned from his reading that it was regularly resorted to its prosecutions, perhaps because, as William knew as a doctor, a flawless skin didn't exist, at least among normal mortals. Yet it was often seen as conclusive physical evidence, something that could be seen and touched, marveled at, and feared.

The queen's counsel now turned his attention to the constable's wife, who being unused to public appearances, quivered as she stood, her face flushed with embarrassment.

"You have been their caretakers while they were imprisoned in your husband's stable, is that not true, Mistress Pickney?"

"I brought them food, once daily."

"And did you ever observe any private communications between them?"

"Well, my lord, they are mother and daughter. That they should.... commune with each other was natural."

"Of what did they speak?"

"Of the trial, of the Old Priory."

"Ever of the dog? Or of the child?"

"Of the child, my lord."

"And said what of it?"

"Wondered how it did, my lord, and lamented that they could not care for it themselves."

"The child was in your custody, was it not?"

"It was, my lord. Though I was much afeared of it. My husband, the constable, insisted that I keep it."

"You said they did not speak of the dog?"

"Not that I overheard, my lord. They may have done so while my back was turned."

263

"While your back was turned, they spoke of it?"

"I know not what they spoke of while my back was turned, my lord.",

Poole looked down at his notes, then turned to the jury. "By the way, Mistress Stickney, what was the dog's name?"

"They never said, my lord. They did not speak anything about the dog, at least not when I was in the stable with them. But I have heard since his name is Vulcan."

"They named their dog after a pagan god," the queen's counsel declared, his voice registering amazement, as if he did not already know the dog's name and how it might affect the jury.

"So I have been told, my lord."

"And why should they have done this? Are there not Christian names enough for dogs but they must resort to the names of the godless heathens?"

"I have no idea, my lord."

"And the child's name?"

"Thomas, I believe."

"After the imputed father. Did they ever speak of any other wickedness?"

"Wickedness, my lord?"

"Something they might have complotted while imprisoned in the stable."

"Once Ursula Harkness said she hoped my husband—"

"The constable?"

"Yes, my lord."

"Your husband what?"

"Might break his neck, my lord."

There was some tittering laughter in the courtroom at this, quickly hushed since everyone was eager to hear more.

"She cursed him to that effect?" Poole asked.

"I suppose you might say she did, my lord. You might say a wish is close cousin to a curse, at least in my way of thinking."

"One might suppose that," the queen's counsel remarked, exuding confidence. He gave the jury a knowing look and dismissed the two witnesses.

45

It was now beyond noon. Justice Southcote ordered a recess until two o'clock. This announcement was well received, even in some quarters of the courtroom with applause.

William was relieved, too. The previous day without a break had been exhausting, and were there to another of such duration he feared it would impact negatively on his own testimony, if and when it should be heard. Besides, as before the closeness within the room had again been unbearable. There were windows in the courtroom, but they had not been opened, perhaps for fear the prisoners at the bar would escape through them, or that evil spirits might enter to give the defendants aid.

Outside the Sessions House wine sellers and grocers, bakers and farmers had set up booths, anticipating the break in the proceedings and selling drink, pastries, and other delicacies at inflated prices. William thought it was very much like market day, both in what was provided and in spirit. It now seemed clear that with the reverend doctor's powerful discourse the trial was drawing to its inevitable conclusion. The atmosphere was festive rather than fearful, despite the reverend's warning about the serious dangers witches presented to all and sundry.

William walked over to one of the booths and purchased a slice of a pigeon pie wrapped in paper. He ate a bit of the pie and threw away the rest, deciding he wasn't as hungry as he thought.

"Enjoying the trial, Doctor?"

William turned to see the apothecary Hawkins approaching him.

"I might ask you the same, Master Hawkins."

"Oh, yes, I do enjoy doing my civic duty as juryman," Hawkins said chuckling. "Besides, it makes me better known in the town. A man of business can always use more of it."

"I should think you were well enough known as is," William said.

"Oh, a man cannot have too many customers," the apothecary said. "Wouldn't you agree, Doctor?"

William didn't respond. He hated the implication that as a physician he was just another businessman, hawking his wares, collecting fees for services rendered.

"I understand that you yourself will give testimony," the apothecary said.

"Who told you so?

"Oh, Mistress Robinson from the Rise, she who comes once a week to have her ceruse of me and of course other things."

"You're a juryman, is it proper that you discuss the case with one who is not?"

The apothecary shrugged. "I know not, Doctor. I know little of the rules of law and care less. Besides, Doctor, we're not really discussing the case against the witches, are we? I haven't even mentioned the word—or the Harknesses. But I would hope you would say nothing about Mistress Robinson should you testify. She is a very good customer, as I told you. It's not only the ceruse she buys of me, but other things as well. Should you mention her she might get in trouble with her mistress and in so doing find fault with me for telling you of her."

"Ah, and patronize another apothecary," William said.

"Well, there are others in Chelmsford," the apothecary returned. "A man must make a living."

"So he must, though one hopes it be an honest one," William said. "By the way, sir, did Mistress Robinson ask you to speak to me on her behalf, that her purchases might be kept secret from the court?"

"Well, she did put a word in my ear to that effect. But for no other reason than her name might not be dragged into the proceedings and sullied thereby. She's a good woman, sir, a discreet woman, a good customer. I should be sorry to lose her. I thought I might do her a favor in speaking to you."

"I'll keep that in mind, Master Hawkins," William said. "Though I can promise nothing. I will surely be examined by Master Prosecutor. He may ask me questions I am under oath to answer truthfully. Some may pertain to Mistress Robinson."

"Surely, I would not want you to do otherwise, Doctor. I pray you do not think I was asking you to lie."

"The thought never crossed my mind, Master Hawkins."

46

William continued walking despite the unnatural heat down High Street almost to the bridge where a few days before he had been attacked and robbed. His bruises had faded, his side remained sore but was tolerable. He was mending fast because he was young and healthy, for which he thanked God. He could do no less. It was the second time in twelve months that his life had been spared. By divine intervention, or dumb luck, who could know? Thanks were due in either case.

He turned around and started back. The sun was hot, but it was better than the closeness of the sessions house and heavy odor of sweat and fear. At least one could breathe out of doors, one could think.

His brief conversation with the apothecary had been unsettling. Agnes Robinson had asked him to speak to William, prevail upon him not to mention her name in court. He'd said she didn't want her name sullied. Was that her reason or something more sinister? Agnes supplied her mistress with the ceruse, the ceruse that was endangering Clara's health and which he now was convinced might have been responsible for her brother's death. The symptoms reported by Julian and by Clara herself, the languor, the mental confusion, the fits of irascibility suggesting that the lead in the ceruse was undoing the brain as well as the body. But was the ceruse enough to cause it, even if Clara had applied it to her brother lavishly. Or was there something else added? Something like ratsbane...

He should have thought of it before. Why didn't he? Perhaps because his mind was focused elsewhere, on Clara, on her living brother, on her domineering and powerful father. Sometimes, he had learned from his scientific inquiries, focus was everything. If you looked to the right, you ignored the left. If you looked up, you couldn't see below you. If you looked behind, you missed what was right in front of you, sitting there waiting to be noticed, to be understood, to be corrected, to be feared.

But if it were ratsbane—arsenic—added to the ceruse, not by the apothecary, but by Agnes Robinson or even Clara herself, for what reason would either woman do it? Both women might misapply the ceruse, thinking it harmless, but neither would have supposed ratsbane to be so. What would be either woman's motive? Clara, William was convinced, would never kill her brother. If there was one thing he was sure about it was Clara's near worship of her twin.

But what of her former governess and long-time companion and counsellor, Agnes Robinson? What reason might she have for wanting her master's eldest son dead? One thing William was sure of. Murderers acted with purpose, unless of course they were mad, insane. Clara Bascombe was unstable; she could at times flirt with insanity in her outbursts. But Agnes Robinson, though misinformed and arrogant, gave no evidence of being out of her mind. She seemed, rather, a shrewd, calculating woman, controlled and dedicated to the advancement of her mistress in the social scene.

He saw the crowd returning to the Sessions House and started in that direction. He had prepared to defend the witches, to tell his story of their rescuing him, to explain to the jury the significance of the birthmark, or its lack of significance, and to at least raise doubts as to the cause of Thomas Bascombe's death. But now as to the latter he was less certain than before, and he was certainly not prepared to accuse either Agnes Robinson or her mistress of poisoning Thomas Bascombe.

Or was he?

"Doctor Gilbert?"

William turned to the voice. It was queen's counsel, catching up with him.

William did not particularly like Anthony Poole, and he was sure the feeling was mutual. He knew Poole wanted a conviction. Successful prosecutions added to his prestige, promised advancement in his profession, perhaps at court. Justice Southcote had referred to the prosecutor as a rising star. That meant money and power and promotion. William's testimony would hardly help in that effort if it worked on the defendants' behalf.

"You are next up, Doctor. Justice Southcote has asked that it be so."

"I'm ready," William said.

"But I must warn you, sir."

"Warn me?"

"That whatever you say in defense of these women will surely contradict Doctor Culpeper's testimony, which even you must agree was a powerful indictment of witchcraft and of the women. It must also contradict the Lady Clara Bascombe's testimony, and in so doing inflame the passions of those who have heard them speak."

"I seek not to inflame passions of any man, or woman, Master Prosecutor," William said, as calmly as he could, "but rather provide information that may be either of benefit to the defendants or to the prosecution. It is for the jury to decide, is it not?"

"It is," Poole said, "but the trial has run long as it is. Isn't it possible, Doctor, to limit your testimony to, say, a half hour or less?"

"I think that is possible, Master Poole."

"I pray you make the effort, Doctor. It is, after all, for your benefit as well as the court's."

"And how to my benefit?"

"As I have said, Doctor, for all intents and purposes, the trial is over. Nothing can overcome the strong testimonies already given. We lack only the jury to announce its verdict, a mere formality. I know juries, Doctor, as you know, I think, the body and its workings. I know which way the wind blows with them, and it blows against anyone who would contradict what has already been sworn to. It will blow mightily against you to your detriment. I say this to you because I like you, Doctor. You are a pleasant enough fellow, and I am sure competent enough in your medical practice. But we are dealing her with matters of greater pitch and circumstance, satanic possession, curses, deviltry. I pray you be ruled by me. Say your piece, be brief, and then be gone."

The prosecutor turned and without another word walked toward the Sessions House. William followed. Of the warning he had received from various persons since his arrival in Chelmsford, Poole's admonition troubled him the least. He'd gotten used to threats. They touched him like a soft prod, not a heavy blow, and in Poole's case he found laughable the admonition that he keep his testimony short.

He resolved to take as much time as the court would allow him, and Poole be damned. The Reverend Culpeper had turned his testimony into an hour's sermon. Clara Bascombe and her brother had been allowed all the time they needed while prosecutor Poole paid sycophantic deference to both. Poole had seemed charmed by Clara, even after her venomous rant that surely would have put any sensible man on notice that there was a darker side to her, something to be wary of—a troubled mind, if not a perverse will.

Undoubtedly both.

No, he would not curtail his testimony for the convenience of the prosecution. The defendants deserved more than that.

And so did he.

47

"We have a final testimony," Poole announced when the court had been seated again.

A great sigh of relief came up from the audience. William imagined he could read the thoughts of those around him. It was collective disappointment. Expectations were that the case would be delivered now to the jury and they would render a verdict straightway. What more was needed to convict? The guilt of the women was plain on its face.

William was called, at last. He looked out over the audience. The other witnesses they knew or at least had heard of. William was a stranger, except of course to the Bascombes, father, daughter and son, whose eyes were turned on him, not with the idle curiosity, nor the personal hatred of before, but with what looked more like apprehension, as though they now feared what he might say. It gave him confidence.

William took the oath.

"You have something to offer, Doctor Gilbert? The court is happy to hear from the learned physician. From London, are you not?" Poole said, adopting an amicable manner, but William knew already preparing to discard anything William might say as an irrelevant footnote to the testimonies already given.

"I practice in London, my lord prosecutor. I am originally from Colchester."

"What do you know, then, of these defendants? You who are from Colchester and practice in London. What can you say of them that has not been said by Lady Clara Bascombe or by the Reverend Culpeper, whose mighty commentary upon witches all of us heard in this court and must surely remember and respect."

"I spent three days at the Harkness farmstead, the Old Priory," William began, "Six months past in the dead of winter and during the great storm."

There was a stirring of interest in the audience. William knew what occasioned it. Although a stranger in the town, he claimed to have an experience that none present had had, not even the Bascombes. He had been at the Old Priory, breathed the tainted air, slept over in a fetid bed, whereas they had only heard rumors of it.

"You were at the Old Priory for three days? There with the witches and their familiar?"

The prosecutor asked, his tone of incredulity implying that William was making this all up, a good story to tell by the fire on a winter's night, a desperate fiction to absolve the obviously guilty.

"I do swear I was, my lord. As God is my witness."

"God *is* a witness to your testimony, Doctor. You must not lie."

"I swear it is the truth," William said.

"Tell us then what you saw and did, consorting with witches as you claim you were," the prosecutor said.

"First, my lord, I must explain why I was there, which I do believe will make it clear why I am here this day."

At this William recounted his story. He told how he became lost in the storm, came close to death but was saved by the Harkness dog who alerted his master and mistress to his plight. He told how he was revived by the two women, nourished back to health, and finally aided in finding his way back to the road and to Chelmsford.

"And pray what Doctor did you observe while among these women?"

"I observed Christian charity for a wayfarer, my lord, religion pure and undefiled."

At this, there was a roar of protest from the spectators, the jury, and the three Bascombes. Had William denied the Holy Trinity, the resurrection of the dead, or the superiority of men to women, there could have hardly been greater outrage.

Sir Richard Bascombe leaped from his seat. "My Lord Justice Southcote, I do protest this man's false testimony. It is nothing but a monstrous lie. That he was ever at the Old Priory I strongly doubt, but has made all this up because he made suit to my daughter and she would not have him."

"Let him speak. Master Prosecutor, continue," Justice Southcote said. "We shall hear the doctor's experience from his own mouth and judge whether he lies or tells truth."

273

The uproar subsided, and looking over the crowded room, he realized that not all present wished him to be silent. He had at least aroused curiosity in the room, if only because Sir Richard Bascombe's accusation introduced a new element to the ongoing drama, an allegedly spurned lover. It gave him courage to go on.

"Doctor Gilbert, you say the defendant's dog saved you?"

"So he did. When I awoke, I found myself alone by a dying fire. But not alone. The dog nestled against me. At first, I thought it was a wolf and was fearful that he should attack me."

"Fearful that he should attack you, Doctor? Poole said. "Was that because you realized that it was no mere dog you lay with, but an evil spirit, a familiar, an embodiment of the Devil in animal form? We all know the devil has the power to assume a pleasing shape. May not the Prince of Darkness thereby assume any shape he pleases?"

"You must inquire of him yourself, my lord," William said. "I know nothing of devils or familiars."

A titter of laughter passed around the room at this. Poole, flushed, looked at William sternly. Southcote admonished William to avoid levity in his responses. William said he would endeavor to do so, but in a tone suggesting it would not be easy.

"I see, Doctor, your face is bruised. Did you fall afoul of some door or fence post?"

Hearing the question, William knew Poole has been talking to the constable, and he suddenly had a feeling of vulnerability. He knew where this line of questioning was going. But he resolved to tell the truth, whatever the consequences.

"I was attacked, my lord. And I was robbed."

"And where did that occur, this assault and robbery?"

"Here in Chelmsford."

"Precisely where in Chelmsford? Remember, Doctor, you are under oath."

"On the outskirts of the town, at the bottom of the High Street."

"Was it not, rather, at the place known as Cobb's End, Doctor? And was it not a robbery but a brawl in which you participated, occasioned by a quarrel over the reckoning there?"

William was about to answer, to deny the accusation, but Poole spoke over him. "And is not Cobb's End a notorious bawdy house?"

274

"I was in no brawl, my lord, nor did the event occur at the place you describe as a bawdy house. It may be that indeed, but you perhaps know better than I what manner of house it is."

For a moment Poole paused, taken aback by William's sharp response, which drew peals of laughter in the court. His face reddened with embarrassment. Justice Southcote said, "Doctor Gilbert, I admonish you a second time to do no more than answer the question put to you. This is a court of law, not a sparring match. Humorous jibes from either side have no place here."

"I am most sorry, my lord, I meant no disrespect to the queen's counsel, Master Poole."

"Then render none, Doctor," Southcote said—hiding a smile, William thought.

Poole turned to the jury. "The jurors may decide for themselves if your testimony on this point, Doctor, is true or false, and what it may imply as to your conduct and testimony on behalf of Ursula Harkness's character."

Then Poole returned to the wolf. William felt relief, but he also knew the damage had been done. The jury would look on him not as a distinguished physician but a hypocritical whoremaster, unfit to render judgment on the moral character of anyone, much less two women accused of witchcraft.

"It was a dog, my lord prosecutor," William said. "Nothing more nor less. I allow he looks more like wolf than dog, yet he is a dog, sir, and never while I was there did he manifest himself in any other way. No wolf would have behaved as he did."

"I say you are deceived, Doctor, or deluded," Poole shot back.

'Neither deceived nor deluded, my lord. I say but what I observed while there, nothing more nor less—in expectation that it should be of interest to this honorable court."

"And what of Ursula Harkness? What had you to do with her?" the prosecutor asked.

"Nothing unseemly, my lord, if that's what you're implying."

"I imply nothing, Doctor," Poole said. "I am only asking a question, a quite reasonable one in light of Master Julian Bascombe's earlier testimony of Ursula Harkness's character, and your own admission to being a patron of Cobb's End."

"I made no such admission," William said, barely containing his anger. "She and her mother fed me, gave me a bed to sleep in," William continued. "Ursula Harkness guided me back to the road. Without her

275

I should never have found my way. I was still weak. The snow still lay heavy upon the ground and the woods were thick."

The prosecutor paused and turned from him to look at the jury. "Doctor, we have heard strong testimony to the effect that Ursula Harkness is naught but a whore, a slattern. Master Julian Bascombe testified as such. Yet you want us to see her as a saint."

"A saint? I think not, my lord, no saint, only an honest woman who acted charitably toward me and for which thing I owe her and her family a debt of gratitude."

"And what of Thomas Bascombe, whom she cursed and who died thereof? We have heard firm testimony of that." The prosecutor asked.

"I do think it more likely he was poisoned." William said.

He might have expected an uproar at this declaration, but instead there was absolute silence in the room. Either because of amazement at this new twist in the proceedings, or intense curiosity as to whether the London doctor could prove what he had just said. But the queen's counsel leaped to his feet.

"*Poisoned?* Poisoned, indeed, Doctor, by the woman you see before you."

The prosecutor pointed at Ursula Harkness. She did not look at the prosecutor, but fixed her eyes on William. Her face was white; whiter than Clara Bascombe's face, if that were possible. Her expression did not make beautiful which never was, but it was a noble countenance, defiant in its insistence of innocence, its protest against the injustice of the proceedings and the slander of herself and her mother.

"I use no metaphor, my lord. But poison in the literal sense."

"What proof, sir?"

"I will presently give it," William said. "The defendants, my lord, are falsely accused. Ursula Harkness loved Thomas Bascombe. She loves him still. I'm convinced of it. And would have done him no harm although he breached his promise to her."

"He made no promise, my lords, my son made no promise to that whore," Sir John cried out as though he were leading troops into battle. Clara Bascombe and her brother joined the chorus and for a few minutes all that could be heard in the courtroom were protests from the Bascombes. They were shrill and explosive. It was a while before Southcote's orders could silence them and William's testimony could proceed.

When he did continue, William adopted a softer voice. "I have said, my lord, that Master Thomas Bascombe was poisoned. I would like to explain, if I may."

The prosecutor hesitated, but his hesitation was overridden by Justice Southcote who said, "I would very much like to hear your explanation, Doctor."

"By several accounts, including the Lady Clara, her brother's treatment was what is called Venetian ceruse, whose primary use is as a cosmetic to make the skin appear white and smooth. Ceruse is made of lead, my lords, a substance that the ancients have declared to be poisonous with prolonged use. Galen, for example, the famous Roman physician. noted this as have others over the years. The effects thereof touch upon the body but also, my lords, upon the brain itself, producing in him who is poisoned lassitude and strange shifts of mood and behavior and may ultimately lead to death."

As he concluded this William stopped to take a breath, noticing at the time Clara Bascombe's flash of anger directed at him and her abrupt exit from a side door of the chamber, her brother Julian trailing after.

"Surely, Doctor, you are not suggesting that Thomas Bascombe painted his face with this this ceruse?"

"No, he did not, but his sister applied it to his face and body, thinking it would cure him, Regrettably, it did not. It could only have made his condition worse."

"You are saying then, Doctor Gilbert, that it was not witchcraft that killed Thomas Bascombe, but the cure conceived by his sister," Southcote said.

"Conceived by her and by her companion and counsellor, Agnes Robinson. It was Agnes Robinson who obtained ceruse from apothecary Hawkins, he who sits upon the jury before us and who, I am sure, will confirm what I say is true. Agnes Robinson encouraged her in this use."

"My lord justice," the prosecutor said angrily, "I must point out that her majesty is said to use ceruse upon her own face, as do many another great lady of the court and several gentlemen thereof and none, I believe, has suffered death as a consequence, or even failing health. What Doctor Gilbert offers us here is a preposterous and baseless theory motivated by his desire to clear these defendants from blame. Where is the proof of this? He is saying that Lady Clara killed her own brother. This is an outrageous and monstrous accusation, a defamation for which Lady Clara might reasonably seek compensation in court, and her brother and father satisfaction in the field."

"I say not, my lords, that Lady Clara acted with malice, but with ignorance," William said. "Surely she did not mean to harm her brother but to make him well again."

"Nonsense, wicked nonsense," cried the reverend.

Sir Richard Bascombe joined in condemning the very idea.

This exchange had now drawn the attention of everyone in the room, even the scattering of children who might not have understood the issue discussed but were well aware that tempers were rising on all sides. Many of those present obviously knew Agnes Robinson. It was clear to William that some in Chelmsford liked her, and some did not, and the prospect of her being involved in the death of the Bascombe heir provoked outcries of support and condemnation from every side.

When this contention subsided and order was restored, Justice Southcote spoke.

"Doctor Gilbert, you have made indeed a serious accusation against Lady Clara and have alluded to information you obtained supporting it. What proof indeed have you?"

"I would have the apothecary Master Hawkins called to testify."

William was excused but told he would be asked to return. The prosecutor, with some reluctance, called the apothecary up from where he sat among the jurymen to the witness stand. Hawkins gave William a quick look of dismay.

The apothecary was sworn in.

"Master Hawkins, Doctor Gilbert has said you provided this ceruse to Agnes Robinson. Say if that is true or not," Anthony Poole said.

The apothecary, clearly surprised by his summons as a witness, seemed confused and fearful. He glared at William, although William had never said he would keep Agnes Robinson's name out of his testimony. Hawkins paused, as though trying to decide what answer would serve him better. "Yes," he said finally. "Mistress Robinson comes to my shop. She buys the ceruse."

"And it is your understanding she buys this for her mistress, the Lady Clara."

"Yes, my lord, she has told me so."

278

"Did she ever tell you that she was using the ceruse as a curative, as something that might be applied to make a man well again?"

"No, my lord she did not."

"Is it your opinion as an apothecary that ceruse contains lead?"

"It does, my lord. White lead—and vinegar and water."

"And do you also believe this substance lead can poison the body and the mind?"

"I have no such knowledge, my lord," Hawkins said, glancing toward William. "I eat upon pewter plates which are made in part of the same substance and suffer no ill effect. My wife tells me I am of sound mind and as healthy as a horse."

"Then as to the harmfulness of lead, a mineral God created, you and the good Doctor here disagree?"

"Yes, my lord. I think we do disagree on that point."

William said, "Justice Southcote, may I ask a question of Master Hawkins?"

"Proceed, Doctor, one question only."

William asked the apothecary if Agnes Robinson bought anything else for her mistress.

"Ratsbane," Hawkins said.

"And for what purpose?"

"Why, Doctor, for that purpose for which God made it. To kill rats."

48

The apothecary was excused, giving William a reproachful look before he resumed his place among the jurymen. Then the prosecutor said he would like to recall the Lady Clara Bascombe to the stand. Since she had been defamed by the doctor, he said, she deserved the right to respond to such defamations. The other gentlemen sitting on the bench agreed, and Sir Richard Bascombe most vociferously. "She will put this fraud in his place," he declared shaking his fist at William.

As it happened, Clara and Julian Bascombe had not gone far from the Sessions House. They were found nearby and presently brought back into the court, although under protest on Clara's part.

She took the stand, took the oath again, although Southcote told her that it wasn't needed. She was still under oath, he said, from before, but she insisted, "that all would know she told the truth and nothing but in face of lies that had been spread about her." Her face was hard, her eyes cold. William knew she was deliberately avoiding him now, but he had no doubt she hated him more than ever. He had humiliated her in court, called public attention to her face, caused her to be summoned a second time when the first appearance had been mortifying enough.

The queen's counsel began by asking her forgiveness. Recalling her to the stand had not been his idea, he wanted her to know. Justice Southcote ordered him to proceed.

"Lady Clara, the doctor, has said that you applied ceruse to your brother in an effort to heal him."

"I used several ointments and salves in that effort," Clara said, flashing yet another angry glance at William. "Doctor Gilbert has little honor in declaring what I revealed to him in private."

"Then you did tell him that you used ceruse—among other things," Justice Southcote asked.

"Yes, my lord, I did. And what if I did? The doctor I secured for my brother did nothing to help. What was I to do?"

"Did you get the notion of using ceruse from your companion, Agnes Robinson?"

"Agnes Robinson is wise in the ways of medicine, your lordship. She has been with me since my birth. She has cured me of many ailments in my life. I trust her knowledge implicitly."

"May I ask the lady a question, Justice Southcote?" William asked, rising.

"My lord, this doctor may give testimony, but by what authority may he question another witness?" Poole said.

"I suppose by my authority, Master Prosecutor," Southcote said. "If it leads to greater understanding of what transpired here, let us set aside what is customary." Southcote asked William to proceed.

"Lady Clara, did your maid, your companion, Agnes, tell you that applying ceruse to your brother would cure him of his illness."

"Yes, she did," Clara replied coldly.

"And did you find it effective?"

Clara hesitated, then said, "No, he grew worse."

"And as he grew worse you applied more ceruse, as Agnes Robinson directed?"

"Yes, I did. I trusted her."

"Lady Clara, tell me what symptoms your brother had as he became the sicker."

Clara Bascombe fought back tears. "He became weaker, so weak he could not hold a book or a cup. It was the witch's curse."

"Did the illness disturb his mind?"

"His mind?"

"Yes, was he not only different physically but mentally as well, confused, sometimes angry, threatening? Did he have visions, delusions?"

She paused as though declining to answer.

"You told me once he did," William said. "Were you lying?"

"I do not lie, Doctor," she said icily. "Unlike some here present."

"Then your brother did, in his last days, see things that were not?"

She admitted he did, but insisted that they too were part of the curse.

"He saw strange creatures, animals with human faces, sometimes heard voices, rumbling sounds in his room."

"Are you aware, Lady Clara, that what you have described are symptoms of lead poisoning, in an advanced state, and that no supernatural means are required to explain what happened to your brother?"

"The learned prosecutor has said that her majesty uses ceruse on her face and yet does not die of it, nor do I hear she hallucinates, as you call it."

"She may not," William said, "But you applied a great deal more of the ceruse than does the queen. You covered your brother's body with it, by your own account."

For a moment, Clara Bascombe seemed to choke, suddenly she began to sob uncontrollably. Her father leapt from his seat and ran to her. He cried out, "She has given her testimony, my lords, I will not have my daughter abused the further." He shook his fist at William. "Damn you, Doctor, damn you to hell. I rue the day I opened my door to you. I'd rather see you hanged than these two women here, witches though they be."

Justice Southcote said the witness was dismissed. Clara Bascombe was escorted out of the chamber, her father on one side, her brother Julian on the other. She was weeping copiously, hardly able to walk. There was a great buzzing of talk in the courtroom. Southcote called for order, but William's testimony had taken the trial in a different direction. When quiet was restored, Southcote said, "Doctor, have you aught else to say regarding this case?"

"I do, my lord, one thing alone. The Reverend Doctor Culpeper has called me an atheist for my defense of these two women. Before God I swear I am not so. I am not here to dispute the existence of witches, but only to affirm that not all who are so accused are guilty. I believe Thomas Bascombe's death resulted from a misapplication of substance that in most uses is harmless, or at least causes little harm unless used over a long period. I do not accuse Lady Clara of murdering her brother. Murder implies intent, and certain it is that she had no intent to harm him but to save him rather."

"In sum, you believe her brother's death was accidental?" Justice Southcote said.

"I do, my lord, there is much in the earth that is beneficial to man, herbs and minerals, plants and animals, and other, but also some that are harmful. We are still learning, my lords, which is which, what benefits and what harms. The wisest of us in these matters is ignorant when we understand how much there is to know."

William paused and then said, "And if I may say something else as well. Much has been made here by Master Poole and others of a birthmark on Ursula's child's face. The child and the mark were displayed here for all to see. We marveled at it, imagined it as depicting one thing or another. It has been argued by the Reverend Culpeper and others that the mark signifies the baleful influence of Satan. But birthmarks elsewhere upon the body are not uncommon. I would hazard a guess that on every other person here, be he male or female, there is an imperfection in the flesh that is an accident of birth. On most it is hidden away on some less visible part. Ursula's child, unfortunately, is marked on that part that is most visible. That is a pity, my lord, not to be condemned or made the matter of false accusations, ridicule and scorn, or evidence of evil within."

William sat down, exhausted and depressed in spirits. He had said what he wanted to say but was unsure as to whether it would convince the jury. To save the Harkness women, he had to show that Clara Bascombe had killed her brother unwittingly. Her breakdown at the end of her testimony, her heart wrenching sobs, suggested that she feared he was right about the cause of her brother's death. He was not in love with Clara, although he had flirted with it briefly at the Rise, but he realized that to save the Harkness women he would need to put the blame elsewhere. Clara would blame herself forever.

He found no joy in contemplating her suffering, which surely would not pass quickly, devoted as she had been to her brother.

It was now late in the afternoon. Justice Southcote said the trial would continue the next day, when the jury would render its verdict.

49

William took his supper at the inn but had little appetite and less hope. His alternative explanation for Thomas Bascombe's death he knew was more than plausible, and should have put a reasonable doubt in the minds of the jury as to whether some curse had been placed on Thomas Bascombe by Ursula Harkness or her mother. And yet he knew for them it did not accord with the general hostility of the town toward the Harkness family. His scientific explanation lacked the drama of the witch narrative and its moral seriousness, its appeal to deep-seated fear. Chelmsfordians didn't worry about being poisoned by chemicals, although maybe they should have, he thought. They worried about being bewitched.

Eating alone, he was aware that he was being observed and talked about by everyone else in the tavern. Only a few hours before, he was a complete stranger to almost everyone in Chelmsford. Now his testimony and audacious defense of the witches had made him known and doubtlessly hated. His accusations against Clara Bascombe had made it worse. He was an outsider. He had disrupted the flow of evidence that previously had moved inexorably toward conviction. He had delayed what the town wanted over and done with.

He had thereby made even more enemies. But he was determined not to hide out in his chamber like a fugitive. He had been insulted, assaulted, and falsely accused of theft and atheism, sexual assault, brawling, whoring, and base jealousy. His reputation was in shreds, at least in Chelmsford. The Bascombes despised him. He could only guess which of them—father, son, or daughter—despised him more. An unholy trinity indeed. He was feeling the burden of all this and the sense of failure when he was aware of someone standing over him.

He was a thin, beardless man with a long, serious face, wearing a flat cap and a dark gray doublet, a little frayed. William had seen this same person in the courtroom, not far from him. He had noticed the man not because of any unusual feature of form or face but because he had had a notebook on his lap and during the proceedings had busily been writing as though recording the testimonies given. He had been particularly busy at writing during William's testimony.

"Doctor Gilbert, my name is Matthew Spaulding. I am a printer by trade, although I also am what I believe is now called a pamphleteer."

Without invitation, Spaulding took a stool opposite William.

"A pamphleteer. And what is your subject?" William asked.

"Crime, Doctor," Spaulding said. "The more lurid the better. I write of murders, assaults, rapes, infanticide, what you will. In this my only competition for readership is sacred writ. These are true accounts, Doctor, not fictions. May I borrow some of your—no doubt invaluable—time?"

"If you want to abuse me because of my testimony or defense of the women," William said, "I would prefer not to talk to you. Since coming to Chelmsford, I have been constantly harassed and threatened. Little you could say, Master Spaulding, could move my mind to another position than that I have taken. I do not believe Thomas Bascombe died of a witch's curse. Any effort to persuade me otherwise is futile."

"I assure you, Doctor, that isn't my intent," Spaulding said, smiling pleasantly. "Rather, I would like to tell you my story; parts of which, if not all, may aid you in your cause."

Spaulding carried a worn satchel by his side, reached in it, pulled out a sheaf of papers and handed all to William. William read the title page. It was an anonymous account of the trial of Mother Waterhouse and her sister, an account of the 1566 Chelmsford trial that he had read over several times in the last few days and which he had admired for its detail and relative objectivity.

"I have read this," William said dismissively.

"I imagine you have," Spaulding said. "It has been read by many."

"Therefore, I need not waste my time by reading it again," William said, handing it back to him.

"But I wrote it," Spaulding said.

* * *

The man who had identified himself as Matthew Spaulding told William he had been born in Chelmsford, lived there until he was nearly thirty, and had since lived in London where he owned a printing shop on Broad Street, and also sold books, including pamphlets he had written himself. Printing earned him a good living, he said, but writing was his passion.

"I see you do not identify yourself as author," William said, taking the pamphlet back and searching the title page.

"No, I don't," Spaulding said. "Usually, my readers don't care who wrote the pamphlet and at first in my career I found identifying myself brought me more enemies than admirers. Remember, these are true stories, Doctor. The people mentioned therein are still alive, save those of course who have met evil ends or brought about those ends in others. Few are happy to end up characters in what I write and were they to find me out I might end up in some alley with a dagger in my back."

"You have chosen a dangerous profession, or passion as you call it," William said.

"True."

"And will you write a pamphlet about this case when it's done?"

"I hope so to do. The pamphlet before you sold many a copy and does yet. The English public cannot get enough of witches or murders it would seem. And they are of interest to every class, the scullery maid and the lord of the manor. I wrote a pamphlet describing a ghastly murder in Cheapside that I am given to understand the queen herself commended."

"And are you enriched by your writings?"

"I wish it were so, Doctor; yet I feed myself, my wife, and our three children and we own the London house we dwell in."

"You said you had something to tell me that would advance my defense of the Harknesses," William said, hoping this enterprising fellow would soon come to the point of his visit.

"I did and do," Spaulding said.

Spaulding explained that while he lived in Chelmsford he had come to know the Bascombes well, through a serving girl he once loved. "This was before my marriage, you understand. Her name was Lucilla. She was a lovely girl but more gossipy than ten old widows and there was little that happened at Mowbray Rise that she did not know of."

How much of what she related to Spaulding while they kept company was true, rather than invented, he wasn't sure, but there was one thing he was told that Spaulding thought William might find interesting. Even important.

"Lady Bascombe, she who is wife of Sir Richard, is not the natural mother of Julian, whom I think you must know, since you have been a guest at the Rise I understand and of course he testified at the trial."

"And lied his head off. I know him more than I want to know him, for he is a despicable person," William said, thinking of the many insults and threats he had suffered from Clara's younger brother. "So, are you saying that this maid you once courted told you Julian is a bastard?"

"A bastard indeed," Spaulding said. "In the technical sense."

"And every other," William could not help but add.

"Lucilla, told me many things I had reason to doubt, being that some were too fantastical to be easily credited, but I believe she told the truth in this. Lady Clara and her twin brother Thomas are the natural children of Sir Richard and Lady Margaret Bascombe, but the youngest had another mother."

"And who might that have been?"

"Guess, Doctor."

"I cannot."

"Agnes, Agnes Robinson."

William's first impulse was to dismiss this story as malicious speculation. He looked hard at Spaulding. The man seemed deadly serious. The question was, if this were true what might it have to do the witch trial or Clara Bascombe?

"How did she know when apparently no one else did?" William asked.

Spaulding leaned close to William. His voice dropped to a husky whisper. "Because she once overheard the two of them, Agnes and Julian, chattering between themselves and Julian called her mother and Agnes called him son and prayed he would look after her when she was old and decrepit, and he said he would, because it was a son's duty to look after his mother."

"She heard this?"

"Maids have big ears."

"And vivid imaginations," William said.

287

"Perhaps, Doctor, but I think her report is true. I don't know why she would make this up."

William didn't know either. "So, say this is true, what this maid reported. Then we must think Lady Margaret Bascombe suffered this in her house, her husband's bastard by his daughter's governess, as Agnes was then, to abide there and present himself as her own child?" William said, skeptical still.

"Have you met Lady Margaret?" Spaulding said.

William recalled the quiet, submissive woman who seemed more afraid of her husband than devoted to him. He remembered that while at Mowbray Rise she had not once spoken to him, although he had addressed her more than once. Indeed, he remembered wondering if she had a tongue, so timorous she was, or if she might be demented, although she did not seem that old.

"If true, I wonder if Clara and her brother knew that they had different mothers than Julian?" William said.

"I think not," Spaulding said. 'I don't know if Sir Richard and Agnes are secret lovers still, but the fire once burned hotly, things fell out as they will in such cases, and Julian was the consequence. For all anyone else knows, the three Bascombe children are all of the same parentage."

"Julian Bascombe now presents himself as the heir apparent of the house when his father's dead," William said. "How can that be, if he's a bastard? Surely it should be Clara who inherits by default, not her bastard brother."

"Ah, there's the thing," Spaulding said. "Some legal document regarding the Bascombe family ordains that only sons inherit, be they legitimate or not. Agnes is ambitious for her son and surely was not displeased when the legitimate heir passed to his reward, which he now has."

"You're saying that she had more interest in seeing Thomas dead than saving his life, despite what she may have told Clara and seemed to have done on Thomas's behalf."

"I am, Doctor."

"It would be difficult to prove what you say is true, Master Spaulding. Science knows no method of proving parentage, and calling one a bastard is so common an insult that it means no more than you detest a man. I grant Julian does not resemble Clara, and therefore not Thomas Bascombe her twin. "

288

"I remember Thomas Bascombe well," Spaulding said, "He was a tall and fair-haired youth, and you are right. He was nothing like Julian, neither in stature nor feature. Julian resembles Agnes. Think about it."

William did. He had had no reason so to do before, not thinking there might be shared blood, but Julian and Agnes had the same broad forehead, the lower brow. The same colored eyes, more green than blue, more deeply set in the skull, and Spaulding was right. Both were short and dark, darker than the English, more Spanish or Italian. He tried to remember if he had seen any exchange between Agnes and Sir John during his three days at the Rise, any amorous glances or knowing looks.

He had not, but then perhaps as Spaulding had said the mating of master and maid may have been more happenstance, a single adulterous embrace, rather than a prolonged love affair. It might even have been a rape. Almost anything was possible, especially in a great house where the master ruled almost without constriction and those who served them suffered indignities with patient endurance and little recourse to the law and less to the church.

"The physical resemblance would not be enough to prove Agnes is Julian's mother," William said. "It would only be put down as another attempt to defame the family. I have already been threatened with a suit for slander. The risk would be too great. Besides, wouldn't the twins, Clara and her brother, be aware that their mother, Mary, was not the mother of Julian?"

"A point well taken, Doctor," Spaulding said. "But do consider this. There are many ways to conceal a pregnancy from young children who know little if anything of life, that see a bulge in a woman's waist and think it mere fat, or fail to notice it at all beneath heavy worsted. Remember the twins would have been but two or three when Julian was born. And as for Lady Margaret, she is a simple creature who might gladly have suffered her husband's adultery to keep the peace at home or the beast at bay. She would hardly have been the first wife to tolerate, even condone, a violation of the marriage bed. He might have confessed all and repented and she, being of a forgiving nature, accepted what could not be undone."

"Sir Richard doesn't seem the repenting sort," William said.

"Or he might simply have told her that unless she accepted his bastard as her own child, she should find entertainment in that dungeon of the

289

Rise. Lucilla told me about that, too. She was full of such stories of disobedient servants tortured."

"Was this maid you speak of ever tortured herself?"

Spaulding shrugged. "She never spoke of it. I imagine she would, had it happened."

"But all this is about family scandal," William said. "I am not interested in Bascombe secrets and indiscretions but about saving those who saved me, the Harknesses."

"It might prove that the poisoning you speak of was no accident," Spaulding said. "Clara might have innocently and foolishly followed Agnes Robinson's counsel, but Agnes may have had reasons of her own to see Thomas Bascombe displaced by her own son."

William thought about this and quickly saw the direction the conversation was heading. Spaulding had supplied what was missing, a motive for murder.

"Don't tell anyone what you have told me," William said.

"Trust me, Doctor, I will not," Spaulding said. "It would no more be in my interest than in yours. This is dangerous knowledge I have shared with you, dangerous to me as well as you."

"But valuable to you, Master Spaulding. A juicy story about a maid poisoning her master is almost as good as yet another story of witches and their mischief."

"True, Doctor. But I assure you that what I have said is fact, not fiction. I am not making all this up for my benefit—or for yours, sir, but that the women might be freed from blame."

William said they would talk again, but then he thought to ask, "Tell me, Master Spaulding, what brought you to Chelmsford in the first place? Had you heard of the witch trial there?"

Spaulding laughed. "Hardly. In truth I am here because of the Reverend Doctor Culpeper. He has a book he wants me to publish."

"A book about witches?"

"Well, yes, about that and what he calls other moral enormities endangering the rule of law and the peace of the commonwealth."

"Then he's your patron," William said, suddenly suspicious.

"He's a customer, Doctor, no patron, Spaulding said. "I'd publish a book authored by the Devil, were I paid enough."

"I have no love for the man, but I doubt he's that," William said.

Spaulding laughed again. It was a boisterous, good-humored laugh. "Between you and me, Doctor, the Reverend is a blow-hard, a prattling fool who, having once read Holy Writ, believes he's the world's expert therein and loves God less than the sound of his own voice. But, as I say, his book will undoubtedly sell, there's a market for it, and I assure you I will profit thereby. I make no pretense to religiosity myself, you see. I am a writer, printer, a man of business. I am very much of this world, not the next—which I trust will see to itself in due course."

50

Alone in his room, William reviewed what he'd learned. He believed what Matthew Spaulding had heard from the maid he had once loved was probably true. That Agnes Robinson was the mother of Julian. But it was another thing to prove that she murdered her master's son so that her own could inherit. A legitimate daughter's right would come before a bastard's. That was the law as he understood it. Even if there were family covenants which dictated otherwise, they would hardly prevail against current custom. Which would mean Agnes Robinson would have to kill Clara as well as her brother to have her own son inherit—that is, if his bastardy were revealed. And perhaps even if it weren't. The thought of this chilled him. He went at once to Southcote's room.

Justice Southcote answered after the second knock, opened his door, and looked startled, as if William were a housebreaker and himself in danger. "What is it, Doctor, I pray there is no fire in the inn that you should wake me at so late an hour."

William had secured the pamphleteer's promise not to speak of what he knew about Agnes Robinson, but he had not promised to keep the information from others himself. He told the justice now what he had learned from Matthew Spaulding, that Agnes Robinson was possibly Julian Bascombe's mother, that her encouraging Clara to administer ceruse to her brother might have had the purpose to poison, not cure. Her motive, William said, was to make her son Julian, heir.

"If true," said the justice who was in his sleeping robe and night cap but now very much awake. "She would not be the first household servant to poison her master's family. The question, Doctor, is it true? Servant's

292

gossip cannot be relied on. I know that from my own experience. What other evidence is there?"

William was ready for Southcote's reservation. "Agnes obtained the ceruse from Hawkins, the apothecary. He told me before the trial began that when she would come to him, she would also buy ratsbane. The ceruse was for her mistress. The ratsbane was for the rats, which do abound in the Rise. He testified to the same in court this very day."

"My cook uses it for that same purpose in my London house," Southcote said. "I see nothing sinister in that."

"Ratsbane is a white powder. It poisons rats and other vermin and can poison a man, or woman, or child. It is made of arsenic, well known to kill. But I learned that Bascombe no longer uses ratsbane."

"Why not?" Southcote said. "Surely the Rise must be as besieged by the vermin as any other decent house in England."

"The ratsbane killed his favorite hound," William said. "After that, Sir Richard forbade its use in the house. They resorted to cats to keep the kitchens free. But Agnes acquired ratsbane only this week. I saw her buy it myself. What if Agnes mixed it with the ceruse? White lead, white powder. What if the Lady Clara is her next victim? Already Clara shows symptoms of the same malaise that killed her brother. Not witchcraft, Justice Southcote, but poison, by a poisoner, not a witch. A murder having nothing to do with breach of promise or the revenge of a wrong. I would have seen it before but only this night learned that Agnes had good reason to kill, not help, Thomas."

The justice shook his head. "The trial is virtually over, Doctor. Even if all this gossip is true, the jury is prepared to convict according to the indictment. Some of the jurymen have come to me. They ask, when it will be over? They grow weary of all the talk and wrangling. They want to go back to their lives. Back to their families. And their families want them back. Their minds are made up, were made up before the trial began. For them it all is theatre, a kind of formality for which they have little patience. They want to see justice done; the witches hanged."

"There will be no justice done if a poisoner goes free, lives to poison another. We are talking about Lady Clara Bascombe, Agnes Robinson's next victim."

"We cannot be sure she is in danger," Southcote said, shaking his head. "I doubt Sir Richard will allow us to exhume his son's body to examine it. No, I know that much of him. You have seen how he is in court. He's a

293

lord of the manor, which means he's a big frog in a little pond. He's used to throwing his weight around—even in my court. It was all I could do to shut him up."

"We need exhume no bodies, my lord," William said. "We could examine the ceruse Lady Clara applies to her face. If we find it contains ratsbane as well as the lead, Agnes Robinson's murderous intent will be clear. From there, it is no great step to infer she conveyed the same devilish concoction to Thomas Bascombe."

The justice thought about this, then said, "The lady is distraught, especially after your questioning of her today. She hates you, Doctor, but perhaps you missed that."

"With all due respect, I missed nothing, my lord."

"I doubt she would cooperate in any such examination of what is so personal to her. And especially if you were to suggest it or do the examination of her cosmetic."

"Then let the apothecary do it, my lord. He has been the supplier of her ceruse. It would be more difficult for her to deny him. Perhaps if she understood her own life might be in danger, say from a contaminated ceruse, she would be more agreeable to such an examination."

But then William had another idea. "What, my lord, if Master Apothecary visits the Rise, inquires into Lady Clara's supply, explaining that he fears he has made a mistake in the mixture. Surely, she would not object to his examination. She has nothing against Hawkins."

"And what if Hawkins were to agree to do this, she permitted it, and then found nothing but pure ceruse? What would you say then, Doctor? How could I justify postponing the verdict for that? I would be a laughingstock in the town, a hiss and byword to Sir Richard, who I am hesitant to offend more than I already have. He is not without friends at court. Remember, in accusing Agnes of murder for advancing her bastard son, you accuse at the same time Sir Richard of adultery. Parentage cannot be proven without question. It would be the word of a disgruntled servant against a knight of the realm. Easily dismissed. It would be slanderous. And think what that might mean for his lady wife, to learn of her husband's infidelity."

"It is possible she knows of it, my lord. It is possible she consented to it, for all we know. It is a strange household, made stranger by its history."

"What history is that?"

294

"Of dungeons, my lord. There is one beneath the house itself. A torture chamber. Lady Clara showed it to me during my visit there."

Southcote gave a heavy sigh and drew his hand across his brow. It was apparent to William that the justice was as weary of the Harkness case as the jury. "It is very late, Doctor. We reconvene at nine o'clock. As of now, I will put the matter to the jury before ten. Understand, I am not disputing anything you have said. But a trial must rely on proof, and much testimony has been offered—by the constable's wife and her friend who examined Ursula Harkness's body and found marks thereon, by the Reverend who was most eloquent in denouncing the women, and even by Master Julian Bascombe who left us all with a bad impression of the woman's character."

"You had my words, my lord. I related my experience with the Harkness family. My time at the Old Priory."

"Another mark against them, their association with Papist superstition and deviltry. Who could escape the accusation of satanic influence who chose to live in such a place?"

William was getting nowhere. He had thought the justice to be sympathetic to his cause, or at least objective. Now, he wasn't sure.

He said he was sorry for having awakened the justice so late at night. And he was. Southcote looked very tired and very worn by the trial.

Although not as tired and worn as the two women who were the subject of it.

51

Despite Southcote's reservations, William was now convinced the pamphleteer's evidence, such as it was, was worth pursuing. He returned to his room, disrobed, but before he blew out the candle by his bedside, he had a thought.

English juries, he knew from his father's accounts, were commissioned by law and tradition to do more than simply listen to the prosecutor and his witnesses, assess the facts, and render a verdict. They themselves might investigate a case, collectively or as individuals, summon witnesses, offer evidence themselves, or inspect crime scenes. If Southcote was reluctant to make trouble for the Bascombes, he doubted the Chelmsford jury was of the same mind. He knew from his conversations with Rafe Tuttle that there was considerable resentment of Bascombe pride and that Agnes Robinson herself was widely disliked in the town. Very possibly more than the Harknesses.

He fell asleep and dreamed. It was not a pleasant dream. In it he saw himself traveling to Mowbray Rise, knocking on the door, and Agnes Robinson answering. She looked at him as though he were a stranger to her, as though they had never met at the Rise or exchanged words along the road. She asked who he was and what he wanted of her, as though the Rise was her house, not her master's, as though he had come to see her and not the Bascombes.

In his dream he told her he wanted to see Clara, but the Agnes of her dream, a younger version of herself and one that Sir Richard might have found alluring twenty years before, blocked his way. In her hand she held a small book bound in black leather as though it were a weapon, as though it was this book that would keep him out, not merely the power of her will.

When he awoke in the morning, he remembered the dream. He remembered most particularly what the Agnes Robinson of his dreams had said to him. "My secret's here," she said, pointing to the slim volume in her hand.

He dressed quickly and went to find Rafe. The innkeeper was already about his day, hurrying to direct all who served there before he went to the Sessions House. William pulled him away. He told the innkeeper what he had learned from the pamphleteer the day before. He told him what the serving girl had heard and seen. He was disappointed when Rafe's reaction was similar to Southcote's.

"A servant's blather, motivated by malice. It's common, William. Even if Agnes is Julian Bascombe's mother, what of it? It's Thomas Bascombe who is dead, not Julian. It's his death we are called to render our verdict upon."

"Thomas Bascombe was his father's heir," William said. "Him dead, his place is taken by Julian. Though a bastard he may be, he may under some laws inherit, which would give his true mother reason to be rid of Thomas. Besides, all the world thinks he's Lady Margaret's son. Think of it, Rafe."

"I will think upon it, Doctor. But I must tell you we on the jury are eager to put the assizes behind us, hang the Wolf Maiden and her dame, and get back to our lives."

"Do you not want to do justly? William asked.

"Of course we do, and shall."

"It would be a shameful thing were the wrong person convicted and the true murderer go free," William said. "Not every evil doer lives in the forest, keeps company with a black dog, and bears a child out of wedlock. If witches be, then some may live in great houses and have ambitions beyond our thought, and murder with devices ready at hand. Men have no need of Satan to do evil. They can conceive it in their own dark hearts."

"Are you talking about Lady Clara?"

"I mean her maid, Agnes Robinson," William said.

Rafe laughed. "Well, I can easily believe she's a witch; haughty woman thinks she's better than everyone else in town. Still, Doctor, a serving girl's story of something she overheard, some brief exchange in a dark corner? I would there was a greater plenty of evidence."

"You may find it, if you have a warrant to search Mowbray Rise."

"Search the Rise, a knight's manor?" Rafe said, his eyes open in wonder. "No one has ever seen within that pile of stone and brick. Save you, Doctor, I should say. Tell me, is what they say true, that beneath the house there's a dungeon with instruments of torture from the old days?"

"With a warrant you and the jury can see for yourselves," William said. "As I have seen it, and it is a thing most wonderful to behold."

Rafe had to go. He was already late. He said the Justice wanted to meet with the jury before the trial began for the day.

"Just do the right thing," William called after him, although he wasn't sure Rafe had heard. The innkeeper was already out the door and probably halfway to the Sessions House.

52

The crowd was larger than any day before and more unruly. It filled the street. Word had spread that this was the day the jury would reach its verdict and the sentence handed down, and William reckoned more than three hundred persons were pressing to enter a courtroom that could contain but a hundred. The expectation was that the two women found guilty, they would both confess. They would give speeches, express contrition, describe their evil acts in rich detail, and plead for mercy from a forgiving God and from a less forgiving citizenry they had offended by being the kind they were.

But this was not to happen. By the time William found a place where the gentry had been seated, he could see already a bustle of conversation between Justice Southcote and the other officials and his friend the innkeeper who was the jury foreman. When the room was called to order, Justice Southcote spoke.

He said the proceedings of the trial would be postponed for a day, although he did not say why.

The surprise and disappointment at the announcement turned the chamber into a cacophony of unrest and protest. Justice Southcote ordered the defendants removed and the courtroom cleared, but this proved no easy task. The most unruly of the audience happened to be by the door the audience had entered, and they refused to leave, preventing those who were inclined to comply from leaving too. The constable and his hirelings waded into the multitude to disperse it and return the prisoners to their confinement. Southcote threatened to declare an unlawful assembly. No one seemed to be taking his threats seriously.

Meanwhile the justice had left along with the other officials of the court to escape the danger of an impending riot, and it was only when there seemed to be no purpose in remaining that the court cleared and William himself was able to escape the clamor and confusion.

On the High Street, Doctor Junius Culpeper stood upon a wagon and preached the evil of witchcraft, and suggested even the civil authorities were somehow implicated in the evil practice since so much time had been spent in a trial where the evidence of guilt was clear and danger to the public was obvious.

"And why has justice been delayed?" Culpeper cried. "Is there not something suspicious in that, does it not reek of the devil's work?"

There followed another diatribe against witchcraft, which was wildly approved by those listening as far as William could see. Since it was what the reverend had said before, William didn't stop to hear more. He feared it would only be a matter of time before he heard his own name among the list of enemies of the people. He envisioned an angry crowd turning on him, dragging him toward the scaffold that had already been set up at town's end in happy anticipation of the conviction.

Then he saw Rafe Tuttle struggling to make his way toward him.

"Doctor Gilbert, a minute of your time, sir."

William stopped. Behind the crowd was cheering something the reverend had said. It was an angry crowd, disappointed in the court's delay and now stirred to greater anger by fear that they were endangered by the witches. Culpeper was fanning the flames, his eyes alight with excitement, perhaps imagining already how this scene of which he was the principal actor might figure in the book Matthew Spalding had told Matthew of.

"Come, Doctor, I have news," Rafe said, taking William's arm. "You'll want to hear it."

William followed Rafe Tuttle down the High Street where they found refuge from the uproar in a narrow alley between two houses. Rafe said, "I am the reason the trial is postponed, if you're curious, Doctor."

"What do you mean, you're the reason?"

"Half of us on the jury were prepared to vote guilty. The other half not so certain. I am now of the latter opinion, if you must know."

William said he was glad to hear it.

"I went to Justice Southcote and said we wanted to question Lady Clara again, but more particularly her companion, the Robinson woman. It was your testimony, Doctor, that did it. I mean, we listened and it made sense, all that you said about the, the... what is the thing?"

"Ceruse, Venetian ceruse."

"Yes, Doctor, that's it."

"And we wondered about her maid who gave it to her. We all know her in the town, Agnes Robinson, and most of us don't like her."

"What did you say to the justice?"

"I told him the jury wasn't ready. I told him we wanted to go up to the Rise. He said he could try to summon Lady Clara again and her maid, too, but he wasn't sure they would answer the summons. He said Sir Richard forbade it. Sir Richard said his daughter had suffered enough. That he wouldn't put her through it a second time. But we said to Justice Southcote that we would render no verdict unless we could go talk to them ourselves. We told him we wanted to go up to the Rise. Look around for the ratsbane. We said it was our right as a jury to inquire of the truth as much as his."

"You spoke boldly to Justice Southcote," William said.

"Well, he knows me, Doctor. As I told you, I was juryman before and foreman as well at Mother Waterhouse's trial eight years past. I spoke with respect to his lordship, but I spoke firmly. Even the juryman leaning toward a guilty verdict for the women are for finding out more."

"What did he say to that?"

"He said that was true, that English juries had such power, although he wished they did not and that someday it might be otherwise. Then he thought a bit. He said to choose three of the jury, three only. He said I should be one, Hawkins the apothecary another, the grocer Dunning a third. He said you should go too, not only because of your testimony but because you are the only one of us who have been in the Rise and know your way about the house. The constable and two of his men as well. He said we should all go up to the Rise and we should have a warrant to do it. He said we should dig up the body of Thomas Bascombe and look in his stomach to see what was there. To see if he died as you said, from poison, or as the prosecutor said, from the curse of witches."

William could hardly believe it. He had thought he had failed with Southcote, but perhaps during the night the justice had reconsidered. At least he had conceded to the jury's demands. It was what he had hoped for, what he wanted.

"When, when shall we do this?" William said.

"At noon, his lordship says. We will gather at the inn and then go to the Rise as a company. The Justice said we should have a warrant and that Sir Richard won't stop us. Though he be a knight and no commoner, he is still subject to the law of man and of God and most particularly of England, as are we all."

They all met in Justice Southcote's room at the inn. To the company had been added the prosecutor Poole, who seemed more than ill at ease at what the Justice intended, but perhaps he was merely frustrated that his case against the Harknesses was now threatened by a new explanation of Thomas Bascombe's death.

To William, it was obvious why Rafe had been chosen. He was the foreman of the jury and was much respected in the town. The selection of the apothecary was obvious as well. His value was two-fold. It was he who had prepared the ceruse, sold the ratsbane. He was also someone who could determine whether the ceruse had been adulterated by some other element.

As to the selection of the grocer, William had no clue. At least at first, at least before Rafe Tuttle had told him that the grocer, a man past sixty named Roger Dunning, knew everyone in town, everyone's business, everyone's history. Dunning even remembered the nuns at the Old Priory, which may have been why he was selected for the jury in the first place. Everyone had expected the Priory's peculiar history would loom large in the trial, since the Harknesses persisted in living there, even though everyone knew the Bascombes had wanted the land back and had been prepared to pay more than it was worth to have it.

William wondered if Dunning had heard the gossip about Agnes Robinson, about her being Julian Bascombe's real mother. Maybe he would ask him, but the time was not now.

"I expect we shall not be welcome at the Rise," Justice Southcote said. "But there are Master Prosecutor and I, three jurymen, and the constable and his men, who will join us presently."

William wasn't sure about the constable and was surprised Southcote had chosen him to be a member of the party. Southcote said the constable was needed to make an arrest.

"Do you expect arrests to be made?" William asked.

"We shall see, Doctor. I don't want to invade a man's castle, find a guilty mind and hand, and merely discuss the matter with the perpetrator. So, yes, Doctor, if we find a murderer, we shall bring him back to town with us in irons if need be."

Southcote continued, "we shall lay out our plan, for we shall not suddenly appear, be rebuffed and then be sent packing. I want us to be able to go in and to justify what we intend."

53

It was less than an hour's ride from Chelmsford to Mowbray Rise. Along the way, little was said among the company, either by Justice Southcote, its commander or any of the three jurymen, or the constable and his men.

Sooner than William expected, the Rise appeared, its battlements stark and unwelcoming against the afternoon sky, as if the building itself was offended by the imminent invasion. William's original elation at the opportunity of finding evidence of Agnes Robinson's crime now had declined into an unsettling pessimism. He was sure that Sir Richard would defend his castle against them all, despite Justice Southcote's presence, despite William's conviction that Clara, too, was in danger. And as for the warrant, it was piece of paper, easily shredded or tossed in the fire. What could it mean to a man comfortable with the idea he was above the law?

The door to the Rise was answered by the sober-faced butler, who seeing the company of gentlemen, or at least some gentlemen, begged them to wait until Sir Richard was told. The butler said it was Sir Richard who must give them permission to enter, even though Southcote had shown them the warrant from the high sheriff. "I know nothing, my lord of warrants, but I do know I cannot admit you unless my master, Sir Richard, says that I may."

"Very well, fetch your master," Southcote barked. "And do it now."

The butler closed the door, scowling. William could hear the heavy bolt shot.

They waited. It must have been a quarter of an hour before the door was opened again. Yet it wasn't Sir Richard who appeared, but the butler. He said that his master was indisposed and asked what was wanted and if the gentlemen might postpone their business to another day.

"We must see Sir Richard today," Southcote said. "The matter is urgent and pertains to the trial of the Harkness women."

"The Harkness women?" The butler's confused expression suggested he had never heard of any women of that name, or the trial. He did not seem impressed. Even when William added that their concern was for the Lady Clara's health and that of others in the household, the butler's blank expression did not change.

"Do you know who I am?" Justice Southcote asked the butler.

The butler said he did not know who the gentleman was, and in a tone implying that he didn't care.

Southcote told him. He said, too, that obstructing the work of the queen's lawful authority was itself a crime. This seemed to have its intended effect.

"You do know who Lady Clara is, do you not?" Southcote asked the butler.

The question took the butler aback. "Yes, my lord, I do."

Southcote asked if Agnes Robinson was within.

"I do not know, sir, whether she be in or no." He said he had not seen her that day.

It was at that moment that Southcote beckoned the constable and his man to come forward and seize the butler. This move surprised William as much as it surprised the butler, who cried out piteously for mercy when he was dragged from the threshold and told to stand over by the horses and not move from that place on pain of arrest.

"We have danced enough with this prattling fool," Southcote cried. "By heaven, we shall enter, for we have a lawful warrant so to do." Southcote was not wearing a sword, but had he had one, he would have been brandishing it at this moment.

Of the company, only William had been in the Rise and knew the arrangement of the rooms—at least, most of them. He now acted as a guide through the house unto the drawing room where Sir Richard was found—not asleep at midday as the butler had falsely claimed, but very much awake and busy conversing with his lady wife and Clara, all of whom looked up with alarm to see such a large company suddenly crowding in like an invading army.

"What is the meaning of this, Justice Southcote?" Sir Richard bellowed, seeing the intruders. Others in the chamber said nothing but looked fearful of the company. It was clear this was the first news they had received that a company of officials and townspeople were demanding entrance.

"Did your man not say we waited without, and you did not come?"

"Why should I come? Bascombe responded angrily. "This is my home, sirs. I may come and go here as I please. None of you is welcome here, and especially this so-called doctor who so defamed my daughter."

Bascombe fixed his eyes on William as though he were the fomenter of the invasion. It was the response William fully expected, but he was beyond caring about the knight's responses. Southcote turned to the prosecutor Poole.

"Master Poole. I pray you read the warrant to these persons," Southcote said in a voice full of authority.

When the prosecutor had finished the reading, Sir Richard wanted to know the purpose of the search. "Are we on trial for some offense against the law and good order, that I and my family should be subjected to such indignity?"

"You are not on trial, Sir Richard, nor any in this house—at least, not at present. But we have reason to believe that one among your servants may have aided and abetted the poisoning of your son."

"Poisoning? Nonsense. My son was cursed by the Harkness women," he said.

"Perhaps yes, perhaps no, Sir Richard," Southcote said. "We are here to determine that. I'm sure you would want to know the truth about your son's death."

"I know the truth," Bascombe cried. "Ursula Harkness cursed him because she wrongly believed he was the father of her child and would not make an honest woman of her. The woman is mad to think my son would touch her, much less marry her."

Southcote said, "Tell me, Sir Richard, do you keep poison in the house?"

"We do not."

"Not even ratsbane for the rats in the kitchen?"

Sir Richard was calmer now. He said, "We used to. Until one of my dogs got into it. Since then, we have relied on cats. I presume there is no law in England against that?" He spoke with a sneer, turning first to Southcote, then to William, as though challenging each to say there was such a law.

"And when was that, the poisoning of your hound?" Southcote asked.

"Half a year ago. The cats are not as efficient as the ratsbane, but they present no threat to the household or my dogs."

"Nonetheless, we must search," Southcote said.

"Is my word not sufficient, my lord?"

306

"I am afraid it is not, Sir Richard. I am directed by the warrant to search the premises."

Clara also protested at this indignity. She said she was not used to such treatment and would protest to the authorities.

"We *are* the authorities, Lady Clara," Southcote said.

Clara dropped her hands to her side in resignation. It was clear that Southcote was to have his way.

"It is a big house, my lord justice. Will you search every inch thereof?" Bascombe asked, as though the magnitude of the task made any searching futile.

"Nonetheless, we will search." Southcote said. He motioned to William and the apothecary. "Find this Robinson woman," Southcote said. "Search her rooms. Search her person if you must." Southcote sent the prosecutor and constable and his men to inspect the kitchen and the outbuildings.

"Agnes Robinson is no longer here, my lord," Clara said. "She heard of how she was defamed in court and has quit service. She is no longer here."

"Be that as it may, lady, show Doctor Gilbert and Master Hawkins to her room," Southcote said, in a tone he might have used in commanding troops.

Clara rose from where she had been seated, cast a quick and disdainful glance at William and without further protest led the way up the stairs.

54

Agnes Robinson's chamber was adjacent to Clara's, so that she could come quickly to her mistress if needed. It was a more accommodating quarters than William would have expected for a servant; well furnished with a canopied bed, two straight-backed chairs, and a great chest in one of the corners. Everything was very clean and neat. There was also a little desk by the window upon which were a handful of personal articles.

William went over to take a look at these. He noticed a set of combs and brushes, a little hand mirror of silver—probably a gift from her mistress—a crucifix on a stand, and a prayer book with a red leather cover, very worn.

"Was she a religious woman?" William asked Clara, who had come into the room with the two men. He picked up the prayer book and showed it to her.

"She was," Clara said. "She was of the old faith. She prayed daily. I have heard her often at her prayers, Doctor, seen her as often on her knees. But what do you make of that? Does that make her guilty in your mind of some great offense? I would think her devotion to Our Lord would suggest quite the opposite."

"No, it does not make her guilty," William said. "At least not for that reason, although I must say that as much evil has been done in Christ's name as good, as history plainly teaches."

William remembered his meeting with Agnes Robinson along the road. It had been an awkward encounter, ending badly with hateful words and recrimination. She had not struck him then as a particularly pious woman, although perhaps she kept such feelings to herself, hidden under a stony exterior like the battlements of Mowbray Rise itself. Instead, he had come away with the same impression she had evidently given the townspeople. A haughty, arrogant servant with her nose in the air and leisure to scorn those below her in station.

He asked Clara, "Where did she keep the ointments and salves, she prepared for you?"

"In a small chest that she ever kept upon her desk, but I see she has taken it with her," Clara said, pointing to the desk. She has been my governess since my birth and served in this house before that. We shall all miss her. I regret she was dragged into this trial. She hardly deserved that, given her years of faithful service."

"It is strange she left her prayer book behind, and the crucifix I find within," William said. He held up a silver chain, at the end of which was a small cross.

"She used it as a placemark. It testifies to her devotion."

"Yet she left it behind her."

"She must have forgotten it in her haste to leave," Clara said, blaming him for that too if he read her expression right.

"Lady Clara, were you here when she left?"

"No, I was not. She left before I returned from the trial."

"Then how did you know she left the Rise if you didn't see her leave?"

"My father told me she left." Clara said. "And the reason for her flight. His word was enough for me."

William continued to page through the prayer book. Its worn leather cover bore witness to its age and frequent use. Then he found what he had not searched for. It was a circlet of human hair, bound with a thin gold thread. The hair was dark and thick and curled, like her own.

He made a guess at whose hair it was, placed there among the things Agnes Robinson revered, worshipped, but he said nothing to Clara about finding it or to Hawkins, who had been standing idly by during William's exchange with Clara, seemingly unnerved by the evident tension between them and still, William surmised, unhappy about William's dragging one of his best customers into the case.

William slipped the prayer book into his pocket when neither Clara nor the apothecary was looking. And then he remembered his dream of the night before. Had he really dreamed of a book in Agnes's hand, held like a token, a sign? Or was it only a false memory, imagined now, in these present circumstances? He had little faith in dreams as revelations of truth or future events despite scriptural accounts of such phenomena, but were evidence needed to affirm the contrary, that dreams were revelatory, surely this was it. The prayer book was not in Agnes Robinson's hand in any literal sense, but it was surely there in a figurative one, presenting at this moment physical evidence of the veracity of the otherwise unproven gossip about the family scandal.

He turned to the apothecary. "Master Hawkins, would you leave us for a few minutes? I have something to ask Lady Clara, something of a very personal nature."

Hawkins said he would, and looked relieved to escape the room.

When the apothecary closed the door behind him, William spoke. "I know you hate me, Lady Clara."

"I do," she said looking at him with scorn. "With all my heart. But the fault is yours that my love has turned to hate. You offended me in your defense of the women, the witches, and again humiliated me in court by making my ceruse a topic of your defense, humiliated me in front of a courtroom full of rustics and common tradesmen, an obnoxious rabble who cannot keep good order. You made me a figure of ridicule. Any lady would find it hard to forgive such disrespect."

"That was not my intention," William said.

"Your intention is not what matters, Doctor, but the consequences. And this business about my being sick, my health in danger? What nonsense, Doctor Gilbert. Do I look sick to you? Either in body or mind? When my lips pressed yours did you withdraw from me in disgust? Am I wasting away, going mad, poisoned by my cosmetic?"

He was sorely tempted to say yes. The truth was that that at the moment she did not look well to him. The ceruse on her face had been more heavily applied, he guessed because the skin beneath had begun to show the baleful effects of the lead and she wished to cover it. And her erratic behavior in court and earlier suggested that her mind had also been affected, but of course she would deny that, perhaps in another intemperate rant that would only confirm in him his suspicions that it was true.

"You have wronged me, Doctor," she declared, her eyes flashing with anger. "You have behaved despicably toward me. You have abused the hospitality I and my father showed you in admitting you to this house, feeding you, showing you about as though you were some person of importance, which you are not. And you have done more and worse, you abused the tender feelings I showed toward you, my intimate secrets I shared."

55

He bore her diatribe with stoic endurance, inured now to her vengefulness. It was no less than what he had expected, and perhaps he thought what he deserved, and when she had said what she wanted to say, what she was driven to say, she was breathless and close to tears. She slumped down on her bed as though the wind were knocked out of her, her slender arms extended toward her thighs to support her. She looked up at him wretchedly. "What will you have of me, Doctor? What more can you do to me to make me loathe you, the very sight of you?"

She looked surprised when he seemed to take her question seriously, unafraid of what might follow from his presumption.

"I want, I need, a sample of your ceruse."

"What do you mean, sample?"

"I mean a trace of it, Lady Clara, no more than a trace. That I might examine it for its purity."

She shook her head in bewilderment and looked away from him. She laughed. "I think, Doctor, it is you who are sick."

"Please," he said. "Indulge me, and then I will be gone out of your life forever."

"Is that a promise you will keep?"

"It is, Lady Clara."

For a few moments she was pensive, her head down as though she were considering his offer. He could see that her fury had exhausted her. Tears rolled down her cheeks and made streaks in her cosmetic. He felt a wave of pity for her and a corresponding guilt. He did not love her, it had never come to that, but neither would he hurt her. The question was, how could he avoid it?

"There is none to have, the ceruse," she said. She made a gesture of surrender. "You have searched this room, every shelf and drawer and closet. Agnes took her chest of medicaments and herbs with her when she left. There are none to be had."

"There is a sample to be had," he said. "That which you have applied to your face."

He thought for a moment she was going to strike him. Her slight body shook with rage. Her eyes blazed, but then her rage passed, turned to a smoldering resentment. "You have no decency, Doctor. What could I have found in you to admire, nay, to love? I must have been delusional."

"Will you give it to me? Use a cloth to rub it off?" he asked.

"I will not," she said.

"I pray you do so, for your good as well as the good of your brother."

"Not for my good, nor my brother's," she said, her eyes dull now, half closed as though on the verge of sleep. "Ursula Harkness killed my brother with a witch's curse, for which she will hang."

"If that be so, if Ursula Harkness is to blame for all this and her doom is fixed, what harm would there be in granting my request?"

"Why would you want such a sample? I grant it's ceruse. All the world knows now what it is and what it does, thanks to you, Doctor. Do you want it to whiten your own flesh, to cover some blemish perhaps? I see your face is bruised. That must hurt your vanity, supposing you men are as vain as we women are."

"Not for myself," he said, avoiding her question. "But for you. For your health and safety. To determine its purity."

"It is pure enough. I trust the apothecary, Master Hawkins. I trust Agnes. Neither would have mixed anything in it to my hurt, or to my brother's. Why should they? No one, not even my father, loves me as does Agnes, who has ever been a second mother to me."

"In which case then," William said. "You will make a fool of me for doubting them if the ceruse proves as pure and undefiled as you claim."

She thought about this for a while. Finally, she sighed heavily and stood. She went to the chest and withdrew a scarlet handkerchief. She returned to the bed, sat upon it, and began rubbing the ceruse from her face. She rubbed slowly at first, then rapidly, angrily using long strokes. As she did so, she kept her eyes fixed on him. He knew it was a look of reproach, of blame, for this most recent mortification.

When she had scrubbed her face clean, almost raw, she thrust the handkerchief at him. It was covered with a thin layer of the substance, chalky white.

He looked at her. Without the ceruse the pock marks on her cheeks were visible. They covered her reddened flesh like little pinpricks. He had seen worse in his medical practice, but knowing her vanity, he knew her pain. Her face still had fine shape, and her eyes, even in her hatred for him, were clear and quite beautiful.

He took the handkerchief, walked to the door, opened it, and called the apothecary back in. Hawkins looked from William to Clara. He seemed shocked at her transformation, as though the Lady Clara had been replaced by some more earthly woman, a woman without pretention or vanity, a woman shamed.

"Tell me, Master Apothecary. Is this ceruse what you sold to Agnes Robinson to give to her mistress?"

"It would appear so," the apothecary said, peering closely at the white substance. But then he walked to the window and held the handkerchief up to the light. He removed some of the substance and rubbed it between his fingers. His face changed its expression. "This is not what I sold to Mistress Robinson," he said. "It is different."

"How different?" William asked.

"If feels different. It is more… grainy. Something has been added to my composition. Fine ceruse is smooth, like a cream, like a paint. This is not so."

His statement caught Clara's attention. She looked at Hawkins, her face showing concern.

"What has been added, Master Apothecary?" she asked, her voice trembling. "I pray you say what has been added."

Hawkins raised his fingers to his mouth and sucked. "I don't know what has been added, Lady Clara, but I do know this is not the ceruse I made up for your use. The texture is not smooth but grainy. I can tell the difference."

"But how can that be?" she exclaimed. She looked from the apothecary to William and back again.

"You think Agnes did this?" she said to the apothecary.

"I know *I* did not do it, Lady Clara. Nor would I ever."

"There must be some mistake," she said, now looking at William.

313

"There is no mistake," William said. "The corruption of the ceruse was intended, and no doubt the ceruse you applied to your brother contained the same mixture."

"But why would Agnes do this?" Clara cried, burying her face in her hands. "She loves me. She loved my brother. I cannot believe this. It's a lie. It's a lie. The ceruse is pure, undefiled."

The apothecary shook his head. "You may secure a second opinion, my lady, or a third or fourth. There are as many apothecaries in Chelmsford, each of whom will doubtless affirm the same. You know I have made ceruse for you a dozen years or more. I know its feel, its texture. This is not the ceruse I prepared for you."

William picked up the handkerchief and examined the substance as the apothecary had done. He felt the grainy texture. He said he agreed with the apothecary. Something had been mixed with the ceruse to make it thicker, more like a heavy paste than a cream.

"Ratsbane," Hawkins said, after examining it again. "That what's added thereto. She bought it from me along with the ceruse. She did so regularly. For rats in the kitchens, she said."

Clara Bascombe trembled, then began to weep again. William ran to her and put his arm about her shoulders to stop her from shaking. It was not a thing he would ordinarily have done with a patient, but she was not his patient. She was not even a friend, given her loathing of him. But surprising to him, she did not resist his comfort. Her whole body shook until he feared for her life. She was seized by a spasm, a kind of fit. Her eyes rolled back into her head. For a few moments she seemed to lose consciousness. He called her name, shook her, bid her awake. Finally, she came to herself again. He held her head close to his chest. She said in a weak voice, "But why would she have done this? She had no reason."

"I believe she had, Lady Clara," William said.

She looked up at him. He reached into his pocket and pulled out the prayer book and handed it to her.

"It is hers. The truth is within," he said.

He opened the pages to where the circlet of hair lay like a bookmark.

"Do you recognize this?"

"It is like Agnes's hair."

"Could it be Julian's?"

314

"Perhaps it's her own hair," she repeated.

"Why would she keep among her treasured things strands of hair belonging to herself?" William asked. "It is customary to cherish a strand of hair belonging to another, is it not? Some person extraordinarily beloved—a husband, a wife, a cherished child?"

She said she supposed it was. It made little sense, she said, to cut a strand of one's hair since one carried about a head full of it at all hours.

"A lover's lock, a child's, or a dear friend's," William said.

"I grant you, Doctor," she said with some irritation in her voice. "But may it not be the hair of some lover she had, a lover she lost? She never married, but devoted all to this family."

"Is it like anyone else's?" he asked.

She did not answer quickly. She let out a breath of air as though she had been holding it in ever since he had shown her the hair. "My brother Julian's," she said as though she knew what name he sought.

"For whom doubtlessly she has great love," William said.

"So she has, for all three of us children."

He told her what the pamphleteer had told him. About the serving maid who had seen what she was not supposed to see, heard what she was not supposed to hear. The secret and intimate moment between mother and son. He was surprised when she did not interrupt with protest, with expressions of disbelief. Instead, she listened, her vision set in the middle distance.

When he was finished, she shook her head and said, "That is impossible. Julian is my mother's child, not Agnes's."

"Are you so sure? How old were you when Julian was born?"

"Two. Thomas and I were two."

"Do you remember when your mother was big with child with him?"

"We were two, as I said. She might have been twice her present size and we would not have taken notice. I was raised more by Agnes than my mother. In faith, I believe she has always loved me more than did she who gave me birth. You've seen my mother, what she's become. She is a quiet, submissive presence in this house. Submitting in all things to my father's strength of will and vigor."

For a moment she was silent, shaking her head to clear what fears she had. William could almost read her mind. She was now making the connections he had. Imagining how what she had moments before resolutely denied might be true.

315

"Agnes and my father?" she proposed, as much to herself as to him.

"So it would appear," William said. "You never noticed anything between them, anything more than a master and servant?"

She shook her head, but it was a tentative denial. He waited.

"My brother and I were twins, as you know," she said, more calmly now. "Born within minutes of one another, with I the elder of us. After us came Julian. My mother bore no more children after that, which was a great disappointment to my father, who wanted more sons, lest one or more die and he be left without an heir."

"But your mother had no more children?" he asked.

"She could not," Clara said. "Her body had been torn in the bearing of Thomas and me. It caused her great grief, that fault in her."

"It was hardly a fault, Lady Clara."

"She thought of it as such. As did my father."

"Yet she bore Julian, or so it is supposed."

"So it is supposed," she said. "But perhaps what you say is true. My father is a vigorous man. He wanted another son at least."

"Which son was born to Agnes."

She nodded her head, accepting it. Then she told a story. It was a memory she said she had not thought of for years, a thing she remembered now.

"Once, when a child, seven or eight or thereabouts, I stepped into my father's room. He lay abed, but not alone. I thought it was my mother he lay with. They were entwined, he sprawled atop her. I was young then, unaware of the way it was between man and woman, husband and wife. Indeed, in my innocence I supposed he was subduing her for some disobedient act or playing roughly with her, as did Thomas and I when young. I drew away and waited until they had finished their… intercourse, which I now realize it was."

She stopped her story here and stared far off as though she were seeing what she remembered, seeing it afresh, and understanding it now as she had not then in her childish innocence.

"I waited outside the chamber. Presently, someone came out."

"Who?"

"Not my mother. It was Agnes."

"Did she see you?"

"Yes, she saw me. She was surprised, I remember, and looked upon me and held her finger to her lips and said that my father was not well, and she had come to make him better. She told me, I remember, that I should not say anything to my mother about what I had seen, for she said it would make my mother sad that she was not able to nurse her husband herself. She made me promise."

"Did you keep that promise?"

"I did, then forgot all I had seen, until now."

"And your mother?"

"It was her practice to sleep in a different chamber. She was often sick, as you know."

"Did you believe what Agnes said?"

"I did. I was a child. I did not imagine another reason she might be in my father's bed. She had more than once had me in her bed when I was sick, Thomas too. We thought nothing of it but that she loved us both and wanted us to be well."

William asked if it had happened since, her father and Agnes. Clara didn't know. Her father and mother still slept in different beds, different rooms. Her father forbade anyone from entering his.

She didn't know whether he made an exception for Agnes Robinson.

"But why should she poison Thomas, or try to poison me?" Clara cried. "Perhaps the mixing of the ratsbane was unintended, an accident. I have heard of such cases. A woman in Chelmsford confused ratsbane with flour, baked it into bread, fed it to her husband, who grew sick thereby and died betimes. She was tried for murdering him, but the jury believed her account, that it was an accident."

"I do think in this case the poisoning was intended," William said. "Why else should she acquire the ratsbane and say it was for the rats when your father forbade its use because it killed his dog."

"Caesar," she said.

"Caesar?"

"The hound. He was a great tracker. My father loved him beyond measure and grieved mightily when the dog was dead."

But he knew Clara was unconvinced.

"Who inherits the Rise when your father dies?"

"Thomas would have done so. Julian succeeds."

"But if he is a bastard?" William said.

"Then it would be I. A daughter can inherit if there is no legitimate male heir."

"Yet who knows but ourselves his true parentage?"

"That's true," Clara said. Then her face fell. "I knew little about my brother's doings. He kept them to himself. I knew he delighted in women, women of every condition. It was Agnes, not William, who first told me about Ursula Harkness and her child. She told me that Ursula was a witch and had cast a spell on Thomas. I believed her."

"She had her own reasons for advancing that idea," William said.

"I see that now," Clara said.

She looked stricken. But she did not weep or sob or look to him for comfort. Her face slowly was frozen in hate, a fearsome transformation. It was a face that she had shown to him when she realized he was prepared to defend the witches of Chelmsford. He shuddered despite himself, almost afraid of her.

But now that enmity was directed to another, whose act of betrayal was worse than any witch's curse, or would-be suitor's indifference.

"Let's go to see Justice Southcote and your father and tell them what we've found," William aid to Clara. He motioned to Hawkins. "Come, too, Master Apothecary; your testimony as to the ingredients of Lady Clara's cosmetic is now essential to the case. I believe we are hard upon the end of things."

56

Downstairs, Bascombe and Southcote were still quarreling, the knight complaining of the warrant that had permitted the invasion of his house. Seeing William, he exploded in anger. "And what have you found, Doctor, to incriminate me or any in this house?"

"Sufficient to convict Agnes Robinson of murder, Sir Richard."

Bascombe laughed. He turned to Southcote and said, "I think our doctor here has lost his mind." And then to William, "And who did she murder, Doctor? Tell us please."

"Your son, Thomas. And she was well on her way to murder your daughter as well."

"Ridiculous," Bascombe said. He turned to Southcote again. "Is there not, my lord something that can be done to silence this man, his wild speculations and groundless charges against me and this household? Is there no justice, sir, no law?"

"There is law indeed," Southcote responded. He turned to William, "What, Doctor, have you found?

"My lord, I am told Agnes Robinson has left the house. Voluntarily, because she is embarrassed by what was said of her in court. But in truth she has left behind her what she would not have done, things dear to her such as this prayer book which I found within her room and is testimony to her daily devotion—but more. It is also a testimony to her devotion to Julian, who I have reason to believe is her natural son."

There was a moment of stunned silence in the room. Then Bascombe, seated before, leaped to his feet. His face, normally pallid, was flushed, his eyes hard with indignation and outrage. He glared at William, then glanced once at his wife to see her reaction to this. But Margaret

Bascombe had no reaction. She sat motionless, smiling as though she heard nothing, cared nothing, for what was going on about her.

"What are you saying, Doctor? Julian is my own son, my heir."

"But not by your lady wife, Sir Richard, by your daughter's former governess and servant, Agnes Robinson."

There was still no reaction from Bascombe's wife. She sat as though she were sitting for her portrait, motionless, a smile frozen on her face. Again, William asked himself: had the wife known all along, and suffered it?

Bascombe turned to Southcote. "This is base and vile slander, my lord justice. I demand this man be arrested that he not be allowed to defame me or my wife further. His words are naught but lies, born of resentment and a desire to revenge himself upon my family for some imagined grievance of his."

"The defense of slander is truth," Southcote replied calmly. "Be at ease, Sir Richard. If this accusation is untrue, then Doctor Gilbert must answer for it. But as for now, I will look at the evidence." He turned to William. "And if she is Julian's mother, what follows?"

"She mixed ratsbane with the ceruse, my lord, making a deadly concoction of lead and arsenic, which ratsbane is. The wonder, sir, is not that Thomas Bascombe died, but that he lived so long. His death was not witchcraft. It had nothing to do with Thomas Bascombe's rejection of a woman he had got with child. It had nothing to do with the Harkness women at all, or the Old Priory."

"The ceruse has been adulterated, my lord," Adam Hawkins said. "It is not my composition. And Agnes Robinson acquired ratsbane of me, after Sir Richard forbade its use."

"Are you sure of this, Master Hawkins?" Southcote asked.

To his point, Clara Bascombe had said nothing. She had stood slightly behind William as though he were her protector. Now she stepped forward and glared accusingly at her father. "My brother Julian is your son, father— not by my mother, but rather by Agnes. She is your lover and has been secretly so for many years."

William showed Southcote the prayer book and the rosette of hair. "See, my lord, it is like unto the hair of Julian, dark and thick. Agnes Robinson's hair is like unto it. It is a symbol of her special love for him."

"She gave it to Lady Clara," William said, "who earlier used it in an effort to heal her brother, all for the purpose of advancing her son as heir to Mowbray Rise. She also tried to poison Lady Clara."

Through all this Lady Bascombe sat wordless, her eyes fixed on her husband. Her thin innocuous smile had disappeared, been replaced with an icy glare. Now William was sure that her husband's infidelity was no new revelation. She had accommodated the lord of the manor as she had accommodated him in everything else. She had probably been pleased that he had begotten another son, even if not by her, but by a woman who had given her husband a son and pleasure that she could not, while not attempting to take her place.

William said, "We believe Agnes Robinson is still in this house, my lord. She is a prisoner of it, held against her will so that that the truth of all these matters may not be known."

"I say, sirs, that she has left the house," Bascombe said to Southcote.

"We shall see, Sir Richard," Southcote said.

"I think I know where she may be," William said. He exchanged a glance with Clara. "And I do as well," Clara said. "Follow me, my lord justice. If Agnes is where I think she is, she will, I think, confess all, if she has not already been made to do so."

Southcote said, "Lead the way, Lady Clara, and we all shall follow you, and I do hope we find this wretched woman, wherever she is. If we are wrong, we will apologize to your father and leave the house."

It was clear to William that Sir Richard Bascombe went unwillingly, insisting still that Agnes Robinson had gone away. He said she had told him she had to leave, to see her aging mother who lived in a distant village and was sick.

"Then she will visit a grave. Agnes's mother is dead, has been so for years," Clara said. "The woman has no relatives... save her son, Julian Bascombe, my half-brother."

57

Clara led the way to the chamber she had shown William before, content now that William and the apothecary should bear the flaming torches. Her mother, frozen now like a wax figure, remained in the drawing room. Clara opened the heavy door to what she herself had called the dungeon, and had no sooner done so than a piteous cry was heard from within.

William rushed forward with the others to see. It was Agnes. She was horrible to look upon. She wore only a short thin shift that clung to her damp body like a wet sheet, exposing her naked thighs and arms. Her thick hair had been close cropped and stood every which way, like a medusa, her face was bloody and bruised. She was confined within the iron crate, the one Clara had called the bird cage, the one Clara had said Alain Mowbray, the founder of the house, used to torture the enemies of the Norman king.

Seeing her, Clara cried out and turned to her father, an expression of disbelief on her face. "What have you done, Father? God in heaven, what have you done?"

Agnes was sobbing, muttering thanks for her deliverance. She looked at her master, Sir Richard, and then at the others, the justice, Clara, then at William and the apothecary. All were stunned at what they were seeing, hardly believing.

"How did you come here, woman?" Southcote asked.

Agnes nodded toward her employer, who stood ashen faced.

"I forced her that she might confess," Bascombe said defensively. "She murdered my son."

"And has she confessed?"

"She has, my lord."

322

"This is not your place to torture, Sir Richard," Southcote said, turning from the sight of Agnes to the knight standing next to him. "This wretched woman will be charged and tried by the court, not by private justice, though you be a knight of the realm."

"But she has confessed, my lord," Bascombe protested.

"Confessed? Southcote asked. "Under duress, I warrant."

"She has confessed to poisoning my son," Bascombe cried. "What difference does it make whether I forced it out of her, or she gave it up voluntarily?"

Southcote looked at Agnes. Her face was bloody. One arm hung at her side in such a way to suggest a bone or several had been broken. Her expression was lifeless. "What confession did you make, woman?" he asked.

When she made no answer, he asked again.

William listened while in a thin, weary voice, Agnes Robinson confessed what she had done.

Confined as she was, weakened by torture, Agnes Robinson had not held back. But now she told them what she had no need to confess to her torturer; what had been done to her. In doing so she seemed to want to include the man who had tortured her into a web of guilt. His had been the first sin, she said, raping her repeatedly until she became big with child, then taking that same child and pretending that it was born of his own wife, the passive, submissive woman who dared not object to the imposture because she would please her husband and she was deathly afraid of him. Because after giving birth to the twins, she knew she could provide him with no other sons, or daughters either.

"Julian is my child. My child by this man who has tortured me."

"You were lovers?" Southcote asked.

"Never *lovers*," she said in a thin, barely audible voice. "He ravished me, ravished me more than once."

"I never did!" Bascombe cried, turning to the justice. "She lies, Southcote, she lies in her teeth. She consented to it all. Delighted in it. She is a confessed murderer. Who can believe anything she says?"

"You might have taken you child and gone off with him," Southcote said to Agnes.

"Sir Richard would not have it," she answered. "I bore a son, which was what he wanted. The Lady Margaret knew of it but feared to deny

323

him what he wanted. She suffered him to pretend the child was born of her, not of me. The children, Thomas and Clara, never knew otherwise but that Julian was their full brother."

The rest of her story she told in bits and pieces. It was largely what William had surmised. Agnes had stayed to be near her son. She was ambitious for him. She said that when Thomas became sick, she told Clara that it was witchcraft caused by the Harknesses.

"I knew there was bad blood between the families... over the ownership of the Priory. I knew the witchcraft claim would be readily believed... by Clara, by her father, by everyone in the town."

She conceived of the plan to offer ceruse to Clara for her brother's recovery and then to mix ratsbane with it to make the concoction all the more deadly. Her aim was to make her son by Sir Richard his heir, which she believed she might achieve, since all thought he was the son of Sir Richard's lawful wife. She admitted the circlet of hair in her prayer book was Julian's, even as Willliam had supposed. She said she loved Julian, but hid their relationship. The circlet of hair made her feel close to him.

When she had said all this, Sir Richard said, "By Christ's blood, I swear I never abused her. She is lying about that. She gave herself to me. I do swear it. She seduced me, if the truth be known. The fault was hers, not mine."

Southcote wanted to know why, within the hour, Bascombe had lied about Agnes Robinson leaving the house when he knew well she languished in the dungeon. He replied that he wanted to punish her himself.

"It was my right," Bascombe declared. "I am lord of the manor. I rule over my servants as the queen rules the country, is that not right, sirs?"

He said he had suspected his former lover had used poison as soon as, in court, he heard the apothecary say that she had bought ratsbane along with the ceruse. Both were white in color, easily mixed. He said he had doubts about the danger of lead poisoning, but none about ratsbane. It had killed his dog, he complained again, which proved its efficacy for murder. Yes, he had beaten Agnes, hit her hard until she confessed, confined her in the cage. He said it was nothing more than what was done regularly to extract confessions from evildoers. He was citing examples of prisoners tortured in the tower of London when Southcote stopped him.

"Be silent, sir. You acted with no authority to torture this woman. You have abused her by your own admission, and you shall pay for it, I warrant you."

324

Then Southcote ordered the constable—who having learned that the justice and others had gone to the cellars had arrived in time to hear Agnes Robinson's confession—to release her from the cage that constrained her and place her in manacles, which the constable had brought with him at Southcote's orders.

Agnes Robinson did not resist. She had neither strength, nor will. She had been calm and articulate in her confession. Now she seemed so weak as to be unable to stand without the constable's support. Her eyelids fluttered as though she was about to faint. William wondered if Bascombe had thought to feed her or give her water during her confinement, which must have lasted for hours.

At that moment, voices could be heard from upstairs, descending. One William recognized as Julian Bascombe's, the other was the butler who had evidently told his young master where everyone had gone. When Julian saw Agnes, he stopped abruptly. His face registered his shock. He looked to his father as though to ask for an explanation.

"She betrayed me," Bascombe bellowed, when he saw the look on his son's face. "This evil woman murdered your brother Thomas and was in the way of doing the same to your sister Clara. Though she gave birth to you, yet she is a devil, a vicious witch. She confessed it before this company."

Julian stood motionless, surveying his mother's pitiful state; the bloody face, her nakedness. Tears welled in his eyes. He turned suddenly and glared at his father, a searing look far beyond anything he had ever given to William in their acrimonious encounters.

"How could you do this?" he hissed. He got no response.

Then, out of the corner of his eye, William caught the flash of steel. In an instant, Julian Bascombe had drawn his dagger from its sheath, rushed toward Sir Richard Bascombe and with a cry more animal than human, driven the blade into his father's heart.

It happened before anyone could expect or prevent it. Sir Richard Bascombe stumbled backward, falling to the floor, his mouth open in a wordless cry.

His son turned and ran from the cellar before any had presence of mind to stop him; before William could fully take in what he had just seen.

Now all around there were cries of alarm and horror; from Clara, even from Agnes, who may have hated her master for torturing her but could see what fate now awaited her son.

In the confusion, William rushed to give aid, knelt by the side of the fallen man, but he knew it was too late. Julian's aim had been true to his intent. The blood ceased to flow from the terrible wound.

Southcote, stunned like everyone else by what had happened with such suddenness, now asserted control. He ordered the constable and his men to pursue the assailant and asked William and the apothecary Hawkins to join them. "Stop him, hold him, the man must not escape!"

The constable and his men were armed, William and the apothecary were not, so the risk was greater for them. The last thing William saw, as he rushed with others to do his duty, was Clara, kneeling beside her dead father, pleading with him to live, although the lord of Mowbray Rise was unmistakably dead.

58

There was, William remembered, a large store of weapons in the house; hung upon walls, on display in glass cases, leaning against fireplaces and tucked away, doubtlessly in closets and cabinets. All testimonies to Sir Richard Bascombe's fascination with war and weaponry. Mowbray Rise was a virtual armory.

The apothecary Hawkins picked up a dagger, much like the weapon Julian Bascombe had used to kill his father. William found a pistol, a wheellock with an ivory handle, a quantity of lead balls, and though neither man was skilled or experienced in combat, they proceeded now from room to room looking for Julian Bascombe and not finding him.

In the great hall, there was more confusion. Already the word of what had happened in the bowels of the house had spread among the maid-servants, the groomsmen, the steward, the butlers, many of whom were weeping, and others were so terrorized by the news that son had murdered father, and the master of the house was dead or dying, they streamed from the house as though their very presence there was a danger to themselves. As though the enormity of patricide was such that surely the Rise would collapse upon itself, burying the scene of the crime and its ancient history beneath a mountain of rubble. Surely, God would do it, if man could not.

The servants had congregated in front of the house and stood staring up at the battlements and the towers as if expecting Julian Bascombe would presently appear there and perhaps account for his act with a splendid speech or leap to his death as an act of contrition. This proved to make the search for Julian Bascombe more difficult, for everyone was running to and fro, and William imagined it would be easy for the fugitive to escape in all such confusion. It was unlikely anyone would help him. He had made himself a hiss and a byword with the household—if not before, then now.

The search of the house and grounds continued for an hour or more without success. Southcote sent one of the constable's men into Chelmsford to raise the hue and cry, the ancient and mandatory summons of all able-bodied men to join in the pursuit. He would tell William later that he had sat in judgment of many a murderer but had never seen the act done before his eyes and it was truly terrible, he said, more so because it was no simple murder, but patricide, the most heinous of crimes.

After his futile search of the upper stories, William had returned to the dungeon where Clara still sat, cross-legged, by the body of her father.

He went over to her and said, "I'm sorry for you, my lady. May God console you in your loss."

His words were a poor mendicant for the grief he knew she felt. She had lost her beloved brother, now her father, her younger brother had committed murder, her maid and counselor proved faithless. Her life was in ruins. Who could bear such a loss? Who would not pity one that had suffered it?

At the sound of his voice, she looked up at him; unconcerned, it seemed, by the awkward position of her legs. She had wept hard and long, but did not do so now. She made no response to his attempt to console her, but turned back to where her father lay—on his back, his eyes open—as though still unbelieving what had happened to him and who had done it. Bascombe's chest was soaked with blood. His son's blade had not been withdrawn.

One of the maidservants had remained with her, the young girl Clara had chided for her color blindness. Otherwise, hers was a solitary vigil.

William decided he would not disturb her further. Nothing he could say would assuage her sorrow. He wouldn't try; at least, not now.

By late afternoon, more than a hundred men from Chelmsford and surrounding villages had arrived at the Rise and were assembled before the house. They stood restlessly, whispering among themselves, waiting for instructions. Most, if not all, were armed—at least with something. William saw staves, pitchforks, swords, knives, and clubs, and even a few pistols, although most of these were the old flintlock style requiring two hands to fire and not the more modern and easily handled and fired wheellock he had secured from a display case in Bascombe's library. They were men of all ages; some mere apprentice boys by their look, or farm

lads, others graybeards, reputable merchants or tradesmen, veterans of England's wars with other nations or with itself, eager by all signs to join in the chase, especially since their quarry was no common felon but the son and heir of the town's most prominent lord.

Southcote came out the main door of the house, stood upon the porch, and told them what had happened, although it was quickly obvious that the constable's man, who had called for the hue and cry, had already explained it. He was a little man named Fisher, who was clearly enjoying his celebrity as having been a witness to the crime itself, although as it turned out he had no notion of who the assailant was, having never met the man or heard his name. Southcote provided the fuller story.

"You are searching for Julian Bascombe," Southcote announced, once the crowd had quieted down. "Some of you may know him. He was a witness at the trial, was the brother of Thomas Bascombe, whose father he has slain."

The news of the knight's death by the hand of his son drew little grief from the citizenry assembled. William had already learned that Sir Richard was not well loved in the borough, was known to be a terror to his tenants and servants, and one, who only a knight, behaved as though he were an earl or duke. Among the English, William had observed, nothing was more common than social pretension, yet nothing was more mocked and despised.

Southcote said nothing about Agnes Robinson or why Julian Bascombe might have wanted to kill his father. William supposed the justice thought that that complex history would prove a distraction to the search party. The full account would be brought out later, when Julian Bascombe was found and brought to trial, and the townspeople would then judge, even though they might not serve on any jury.

William watched from the entry way to the Rise as Southcote went on to describe Julian Bascombe; but it was quickly evident that the description he offered would fit every other man of Julian's age and there was no guarantee that the fugitive would still be dressed as a gentleman. Indeed, Southcote admitted that he would likely have changed his clothes to fit in with the run of persons and appear as a servant or even a husbandman. He did tell those assembled that Bascombe was a practiced hunter, who knew the forest well, and that it was not unlikely that he should seek to hide in the forest around about the Rise.

One of the household servants, who had fled the house but remained in the garden, reported she had seen a cloaked figure, no one she recognized, making for the woods at a run. She had heard of her master's murder and thought the running figure suspicious. The runner—a woman, by her garb—had been alone, and the servant had called out to her, but the fleeing figure had not stopped, not even looked around to see who had hailed her. The servant had reported this to the lord justice.

"Might she not have been a fellow servant, too afraid to stop?" he had asked the girl, who could not have been above twelve or thirteen.

"Mayhaps, my lord. Yet he did run like a boy or man runs, no girl or woman."

"You know this, mistress?"

The girl said she had played many running games on feast days. She said she was a good runner herself and so were her sisters. She couldn't explain in words just how boys ran differently from girls, but she knew they did.

This conversation was reported to William by Southcote himself. The justice was convinced the mysterious runner was Julian Bascombe.

The news that the forest was to be searched caused some murmuring in the crowd of able-bodied citizens called to the hue and cry. Also, that the fugitive might be disguised as a woman. The forest had a bad reputation before the witch trial. The trial, with its attention to the Old Priory and the alleged influence of evil there, made it all the worse. Southcote had called for volunteers. One company to search the barns, outbuildings, and horse pasture. Another to search the woods. But when hands were raised for each company, almost all of those assembled chose the first and only a few the latter. Southcote decided to choose himself who should go where; a solution William approved of.

"Doctor Gilbert, you go with those that will search the woods. You know the lay of the land there, the rest do not. More important, you know the man we seek. and should any be wounded or injured in pursuit you can attend them."

William knew something of what Southcote had called the lay of the land. On the day Clara Bascombe had given him a tour of the estate, she had followed a path that wound its way toward the Old Priory, but she had stopped short of arriving there.

Of his group, Constable Pickney had been put in charge because as an officer of the town he was commissioned to make an arrest. Given his troubled history with the constable, William was not happy about this, but he understood why Southcote had made the decision he did. Only William and the constable were mounted and armed with weapons, expressly designed as such. The other men—townsmen and local farmers—brought pitchforks, staffs, and clubs and a variety of other tools that could cause hurt if they were used for that purpose.

To this there were two exceptions. He realized that he knew two of his party. As he surveyed the faces, he saw that his friend Rafe Tuttle had joined his group. But more to his surprise, he saw Matthew Spaulding, the pamphleteer, also among them. He approached Spaulding and said, "You are not a resident of Chelmsford, Master Spaulding. You need not have heeded the hue and cry. You might be safe at home, reading a book, or writing one."

"True, Doctor. So I might have done and be sitting in Master Tuttle's commodious tavern as we speak, musing over a tankard of his excellent ale instead of being out in the cold and very possibly in danger. But think of the opportunity for me, much more my readers, to have a first-hand account of this pursuit, the murderer himself, and—let us hope—his capture. Julian Bascombe might even confess his crime, in which case I may take all down in a notebook I have brought with me."

He pointed to a small satchel he carried by his side. "It contains all my worldly goods."

"You do travel light, sir. You are not armed? William said.

"Armed with a pen, Doctor. Were I armed as you," he said, nodding toward the pistol fixed in William's belt, "I know I should straightway shoot myself in the foot, or some less conspicuous but no less critical part of my anatomy. My wife wants more children from me."

William laughed.

Spaulding continued, "The story I seek would sell ten thousand copies, I believe. To see something for oneself is always to be preferred from hearing it from some other, who doubtless has his own reasons for enlarging the tale beyond belief. Besides, Doctor, you neither are of this town, yet you are here."

"Yes, by orders of Justice Southcote."

"Which, as a gentleman physician, you might well have ignored,' Spaulding said. "Your class has its privileges denied to common folk such as I and as you say, the hue and cry obligates citizens of the town, not random visitors thereto."

"True, perhaps, but like you, Master Pamphleteer, I have my own reasons for being here, ones you know not of but for me are compelling." He extended his hand to both Rafe and Spaulding. "I am glad to have friends with me, and not just strangers."

59

The little company began cheerfully, exchanging jokes and droll stories. Despite Justice Southcote's warning that Julian Bascombe was an experienced woodsman, it was generally thought that since their quarry was a gentleman, he would soon find himself lost in the woods or frightened, which would inhibit his flight and make him more vulnerable to capture. It was thought Julian Bascombe might even surrender. Either because he was faced with a superior force or because he was overcome with guilt for having murdered his father.

William knew better. His association with Julian Bascombe had been brief but revealing. Julian Bascombe had not struck him as the kind of man susceptible to a bad conscience, but assertive and selfish, devious and grasping, and doubtless fully aware of his mother's plotting. He knew from what Clara Bascombe told him that her younger brother was an experienced woodsman, a practiced hunter and because he was no respecter of property lines, he had often trespassed on the Harknesses' land not only in pursuit of game, but to assert his family's claim on the property.

Indeed, it occurred to William that if Julian Bascombe sought a hiding place it might well be in the Old Priory. Julian would know how the place was feared by the local inhabitants, know that Jacob Harkness was staying in Chelmsford during the trial to be near as possible to his wife and daughter, and that sheltering there would at least provide a roof over his head, unlike the gloomy forest. He might even secure a horse from Harkness's chapel-turned-barn.

William shared this idea with the constable, who agreed that Master Bascombe might well take refuge at the Old Priory. "Well, he might, Doctor," he said. "It might be a sanctuary for him, for they say the women who once lived there were ever allowing thieves and brigands to hide in their chapel to the detriment of law and order in the county."

Despite his agreement, William could see that the constable was unnerved by the prospect and would have preferred to look for Julian Bascombe any place else than the forest.

"And had he done so, what would he have found, Master Constable?"

The constable thought for a moment. He named a few villages that surrounded Chelmsford. And then there was Chelmsford itself.

"And think you he would have found refuge with some honest husbandman or tradesmen there, given word of the murder has surely spread as far as London by now? Julian Bascombe is a marked man. His attack on his father was witnessed by us all, we being nearly eight persons who will testify at his trial, if he comes to it, that he ended his father's life."

The business about London was, of course, an exaggeration. It was unlikely anyone in London had yet heard of the murder, and unlikely they would ever hear of it unless an industrious pamphleteer like Matthew Spaulding wrote and printed the story, which William fully expected he would. A detailed narrative of a son's murder of his father, occurring in a medieval dungeon amidst instruments of torture, while the murderer's mother was a half-naked prisoner, could easily compete with the story of a witch trial, with its inevitably trivial evidence of satanic possession.

"Master Bascombe might have gone east by south, along the forest edge, Doctor," the constable said.

"You are fearful of the forest, Constable, of the Old Priory and its ghosts?" William asked.

"I fear no such thing, Doctor," the constable declared, clearly offended by what he considered a slight on his manhood. He told William he was possessed of a charm that he had acquired to protect himself from witches and other supernatural beings. He pulled out an object that hung from a chain about his neck, and showed it to William. William could not see clearly what it was. He thought it first it might be simply a round medallion. When he looked closer, he saw that it was an old Roman coin. Someone had punched a hole in it that it might hang from a slender chain. To ward off evil, the constable said. The old woman who had sold it to him was most positive of its efficacy, she having used it many a time herself for the same purpose.

"If it protected her, it will protect me," the constable reasoned, although his eyes still betrayed his unease at being where he was, and for so dire a purpose.

William suspected the constable's feelings were in line with those of others in the party. Although the constable had been designated as leader, William's superior social status—William was gentry, the constable a mere tradesman—gave his suggestions more weight.

When they came to the edge of the forest, William showed the constable the trail that William and Clara had followed and where the single witness had seen the suspicious figure enter; the figure garbed as a woman but running like a man, the girl had said. It was neither wide nor even, but considering the denseness of the trees and bushes that grew on each side and especially because most of the search party were on foot, it was decided that the path would afford the best way to penetrate the forest. The plan would save the trouble of struggling though the underbrush and the trees and make it less likely that any of the party would get lost or injured. Besides, the constable noted, he supposed Julian Bascombe doubtless used the same route in his flight, and for the same reason. He said a storm was coming, and Bascombe would have no more reason to wander aimlessly among trees in a storm than did they who sought him.

Despite there being a path, it was slow going. The path was far from straight, but rather wound its way among old-growth trees and thickets, and at least one stream bed where but a few days before William and Clara had stopped to talk. The mounted men—William and the constable—could not move faster than the men on foot. They dismounted and walked the horses, the tree branches being too low to allow passage were a man astride.

After about an hour into the forest it began to rain. It was a slow, cold rain that diminished after a while into a drizzle, but provided no relief for that, for the trees about them were thoroughly dampened and the branches weighed down by the water. Already it was beginning to grow dark, and the men in the party, merry and talkative before, now seemed less eager to continue the pursuit. For all their walking and looking about, they had yet to see a sign of Bascombe or any other mortal. Several voiced the opinion that Bascombe had not gone into the forest at all and that further searching was futile. The constable heard all the murmuring behind him and bade the little company of searchers stop. He went up to William and bent close to him.

"Should we give heed to what they're saying, Doctor? Master Bascombe might well have taken flight another way. Some of the men want to go back. They're tired, wet, hungry, Doctor."

William looked back at where the men had gathered. Through the dripping trees, he could see that more than half the original company had deserted like timorous soldiers in the field. Those that remained grumbled among themselves, then two turned and ran, apparently following their friends. Suddenly, there were only two besides William and the constable: Rafe Tuttle and Matthew Spaulding.

William said, "Come, Rafe, Master Pamphleteer, both of you, come with us. Let us press on. If there is nothing at the Old Priory, we'll spend the night there, warm and dry our bones by the fire, and return in the morning. Take heart. I know the place well; it will present no danger to us in and of itself."

William and Clara had not gone farther than the spring, where they had stopped to talk about her brother and she had revealed her hatred for the Harknesses. He wasn't sure how far ahead the Old Priory lay or how far ahead of them Julian Bascombe might be, if he was there at all. Then, by the last rays of the sun, they came upon the gown Julian had used to disguise himself, discarded. They were on the right track.

It was now fully dark, and the moon was shrouded in heavy clouds that had brought the rain in the first place. In their haste, no one had thought to bring torches. The four men felt their way from tree to tree, barely able to see the path, and William remembered how lost he had become in the same dense forest in December and how it was only through Ursula's help that he had found his way back to the London road.

William estimated that they had walked for at least three hours, maybe four. Which meant they may have walked twice that in miles. Ursula Harkness had once told him that the Old Priory lay ten miles from the Rise. He was considering this when the constable cried out, "I see it, Doctor. Is that not it, just ahead of us and over beyond those trees?"

William looked in the direction the constable had pointed. He saw above the trees what seemed a shadow, a darker part of the sky quite dark enough as it was. It was what was left of the chapel tower, a pile of soulless stone, a monument to the old and discredited religion. While the Harknesses lived there, it was a habitation for man. Now who or what inhabited it, he could not know. Owls, bats, flying things without names. Even witches.

For a moment, he felt what the constable must have felt even before starting out on the search, an innate, primal terror of the forest, a place fit for devils and their works.

Did William, with all his university knowledge, believe that? He knew his ancestors had, dwelling in their primitive camps no better than caves, fearing the dark, fearing the forest, fearing the savage beasts that dwelt therein and even within themselves.

He put these visions aside. What else could he do? They could hardly go back now, having come so far and with evidence now that Julian had come the same way. He said to the remnant of their band, "Come, friends, our search is almost done. Pray to heaven we may find whom we seek and escape all danger to ourselves."

60

During the last hour, the clouds had cleared, leaving the land before them bathed in moonlight. This was better than the torches they left behind them. Julian could see the torches and would know he was being followed.

William could feel beneath his feet a harder surface, which he knew was the cobbled path that led from the Old Priory to where the cemetery was.

When the constable recognized where he stood, he stopped, groaned, and declared he would not go farther. He was of the queen's church, as were the four of them, but the constable raised his charm in one hand and the other made a quick succession of crosses, like an avid papist. Then he folded his arms across his thick chest and lifted his chin in defiance. He said to William, "I'll not budge from here, Doctor. You may tell the justice that I would not. He may remove me from my office, hang me from a tree, still I will not lose my soul by going further."

"Very well, Constable Pickney," William said, "But make yourself useful, will you? Stay here by the horses while the three of us go forward."

The constable seemed more than happy to accept the offer. He breathed a great sigh of relief but while he had stopped crossing himself, he held the charm in his fist to ward off any evil that he imagined might assail him.

"Come, friends," William said, finding himself in charge now. "Bascombe is either here or he is not. In either case, our work is nearly done."

Rafe Tuttle was more heavily built than either William or Matthew Spaulding with a strong arm and back made stronger by lifting casks at the inn and occasionally throwing troublemakers in the tavern into the street. He had brought from the Rise a sword, and had confessed to William along the way that he had never wielded one, but had seen the skill demonstrated many times at Chelmsford spring fair, sometimes by former soldiers, sometimes by puppets. He thought in combat he would surely be killed, but if Bascombe surrendered he could make himself useful by holding Julian Bascombe at sword point.

Matthew Spaulding had told William he had no skill in gunnery, but in a more candid mood admitted he had some military experience. He had been for a short time in Holland and had seen action in several battles. He had served there as a record keeper for an English lord William had never heard of, and once, when the English were in full retreat, he was obliged to pick up a sword to defend himself and his fellow soldiers. He said he had never killed a man, never wanted to, and would die before armoring himself in the queen's cause. Yet he was grateful for his military experience. It was there, he said, he had learned to write a good story, falsifying accounts of military engagements to make the commanders look good. It had been the foundation of his career as a printer and pamphleteer.

Likewise armed, but with a pistol rather than a blade, William admitted readily himself to a lack of skill. He had engaged in mock battles as a boy, with his friends and wooden swords and shields, and had enjoyed the exercise, but no one was ever hurt—except himself, when he received a hard blow to the ear that left him partially deaf for a week. "We three make a poor excuse for *a posse comitatus*," he told them. "Yet we have a duty and must go forward with it."

William removed his pistol from his belt and confirmed that it was charged. He had fired a pistol before, once at Cambridge in an experiment in combustion. The discharge had startled him, knocking him backward to land on his butt, much to the amusement of his fellow scholars looking on. If he needed to use it, he would have one chance. He might be able to reload, but he knew it was a cumbersome process that would give Julian ample time to strike back, should William come face to face with the murderer.

The walked through the graveyard, trying to avoid the toppled headstones, not so much out of respect for the dead as to their own safety. No one wanted to trip over one and break a leg or cry out. Then William looked down and saw at his feet the shoe tracks in the mud. He could see by moonlight that they were freshly made, perhaps within the very hour. Surely, they were no tracks of spirits haunting the cemetery, but of a man, a man in a hurry, if William read the tracks aright,

He signaled to his companions and showed them what he had found.

"You think that's Bascombe?" Rafe asked in a whisper.

"Likely so," William said. "Who else would be outside on a night such as it was? Harkness is in town, his wife and daughter imprisoned. Who else might be here but Julian Bascombe?"

There was agreement now that he whom they sought was close at hand and all that needed to be done was to follow his tracks to find him, but William feared that could be dangerous too. Bascombe surely knew he would be followed. He might even have spotted his pursuers at one time during their search of the woods. Bascombe would be like a cornered animal, twice, even thrice, as dangerous and concerned not only to flee his pursuers but kill them for daring to come after him. After all, he had nothing to lose. He had killed one man in front of witnesses. He could hang but once.

When they had come within a dozen feet of the priory itself, William told them it would be wise to divide up. The first one to spot Bascombe would alarm the others, and all would converge. It seemed to William a reasonable plan, indeed the only plan that might prevent Bascombe from simply moving around, avoiding the group of them, until weary of their search, they gave up and returned to Mowbray Rise or to Chelmsford.

William tried to remember the interior of the Priory, the location of the rooms, the refectory, the nuns' cells. Where might Bascombe hide? Certainly not in the refectory with its open space and high ceiling; where was there to conceal himself behind, beneath, atop? Perhaps not even in the old nun's quarters where he had lodged for those three days that now seemed to him a century past, though it was but six months. If Bascombe hid in these, when discovered, he would have no way out, William and his friends would need only block the door and wait for him to surrender. They would have no need of sword or pistol. Only patience. It might take time, perhaps a day or more but there would be no escape for him. He would have no food, no water, no hope. Julian Bascombe might as well be in a cell in Chelmsford, where he would be fed, at least until he was hanged.

There was only one other place, William thought, assuming Bascombe was somewhere in the Priory and not already fled to the forest again. And that place was the chapel. Harkness used it as a barn, a stable for his animals, a storage place for grain and farm equipment, old tools, barrels, and casks. William imagined it full of potential hiding places. He doubted that Bascombe, in his flight from the Rise, had found time to take a weapon with him. The dagger he carried habitually was still lodged in his dead father's heart.

But the barn would have tools, the same array of equipment brought to the hue and cry. Makeshift weapons; not swords, pistols, pikes other conventional weapons, but nonetheless deadly if wielded with skill, deadly even without skill, as the thousands of accidental deaths and other injuries on farmsteads and street corners testified.

William and Rafe Tuttle took the interior of the Old Priory. He knew it was unlikely Bascombe had taken refuge there. They had no light, no torches, but their use would have made them vulnerable, so it made no difference. The search took the two men no more than a few minutes. They found nothing, as William had supposed, although he knew it had to be done. The nuns' cells were empty. Now it was time for the chapel.

William had never been inside what Harkness had used as his barn and storage place. It shared a wall with the refectory and there was a door from it to the chapel itself. He knew there was a larger door on the opposite side, a main entrance with an ornate configuration of crosses and other symbols to identify its original use. A door through which the nuns would have filed for their devotions. Now Harkness brought his cattle in and out through that door, fed his swine in the sacristy, chickens and ducks came in and out, those he had seen whilst there. Harkness had kept horses, too. He remembered seeing them. If Bascombe had headed for the Old Priory and found one, he would be gone and their search would be over.

William went first, his heart racing. He knew his night vision was poor, and the blackness of the interior coupled with the sounds of animals alert to a stranger's scent and footfall diminished the little courage he had mustered before entering.

Spaulding had taken his sword and gone around to the main entrance. The animals were still there. It was black within, but William could smell and hear the cattle, breathing in their stalls, the chickens alarmed at the entrance of a stranger and flapping their wings, clucking hysterically, the ducks accompanying them. It was a racket that would have muffled any human movement, even if there were a human within.

He might as well have been blind, for all he could see. If Bascombe were here, he had chosen the securest of hiding places. Crouched behind some dumb animal, more at ease than the foul with a human presence, hardly visible in daylight, invisible in this fetid gloom.

Then, suddenly, William sensed a movement to his right. Instinctively, he leaped back. He heard a swishing sound, and then a crash within inches

341

of him, the sound of splintering wood. Behind him, Rafe Tuttle cried out in pain. William heard a thud, the sound of a body falling, he seized the pistol at his belt, felt for the trigger, aimed at the sound he had heard and fired blindly into the darkness.

The explosion elicited an even greater din of animal cries, fluttering wings, and movement. It deafened him, briefly lit up the space. He could see now what he had not seen before. It was Julian Bascombe, his face twisted in hatred, holding a bleeding shoulder with one hand and a pitchfork with the other. The pitchfork was aimed at William's chest.

By some accident, William's blind shot into the dark had hit its mark; it had not killed but wounded—yet not seriously enough to prevent a violent response from the man.

Suddenly Julian charged forward, the tines of the pitchfork still aimed at William, but William moved as quickly to avoid it, and the tines embedded themselves in a sack of grain. The counterattack failed, Julian ran toward the door of the chapel, howling like a wild man, or like some creature he might have, on another day, hunted for pleasure.

William yelled out to Spaulding to stop the fugitive, but the pamphleteer had been surprised by the shot and scream and stood immobilized, watching the fleeing form dash by him into the woods.

Without time to reload, William dropped his pistol, retrieved the pitchfork Julian had used to attack him, and ran to the doorway, grabbing the stunned pamphleteer's shoulder as he went.

"After him, Master Spaulding. Don't let him escape."

The forest began no more than a dozen feet before the chapel door. To William it seemed an impenetrable wall, especially in the dark, with branches intertwined so as to make a single organism. By the time William had come there, Julian Bascombe had already found a way through.

William went after him. He didn't know whether he would be able to use the pitchfork to subdue Bascombe. It was no small thing to pierce a man's flesh, to cause him to bleed, to squirm in agony, to cry out to heaven, to die. His medical training had not prepared him for bloody combat. But neither did he want yet another encounter without something to defend himself with.

He'd gone but a short way when he heard a fierce snarling noise and terrified screams.

In less than a dozen feet, he and Spaulding had come upon the scene, an opening in the trees providing full view of the spectacle. It was Bascombe, but also Vulcan, Ursula's dog, the dog Bascombe had hunted fruitlessly but the dog who had found him and was presently fixing his teeth into Bascombe's calf. The fugitive screamed with pain and tried to beat off the dog, but with one arm disabled by William's shot, he was no match for the dog's ferocity, which was intensified by Bascombe's futile efforts to fight back.

William didn't dare intervene. He knew he would not be able to curtail the dog's fury. He would only expose himself to attack. He watched helplessly as the dog mauled Julian. Julian kept screaming, he had stopped struggling. He was on the ground now, his eyes staring not at the dog but at William, as though he couldn't believe that William was not coming to help him, was not somehow restraining the beast. "For God's sake, help me!" he cried.

But then William could stand no more. He grabbed the pitchfork and thrust its tines into the dog's thick fur—not deeply, but enough to distract and discourage. He did not want to kill the animal that had saved his life, only to drive him off, to make him stop.

But then, as suddenly as it had begun, the dog gave up the attack, moved away from the fallen man, stared up briefly at William as though he recognized him, and disappeared into the dark forest from whence he had come.

Bascombe's wounds bled copiously, and William was at pains to stop the bleeding. He rushed back to the chapel, grabbed handfuls of straw, and returned to press them against the wounds on Bascombe's leg until the straw was soaked, He applied more. He removed his belt to serve as a tourniquet, tightened it on Julian's thigh. William knew that, at the moment, there was nothing more that he could do for the man. The first thing was to stop the bleeding. Later he would clean the wounds, apply herbs and salves to promote healing, to prevent the flesh from rotting, from turning black.

He was confident that Julian's bullet wound would heal. Despite the blood, it seemed only to have grazed Bascombe's shoulder, but the leg was so mangled, such a mess of ripped and torn tissue, that he doubted Bascombe would ever walk again. He might even lose the leg. If the dog had made for Bascombe's neck, these efforts would have been unnecessary.

Bascombe would have been dead, as dead as the father he had murdered mere hours before.

But for the moment, Bascombe was alive and conscious, although barely so. Delirious, he lay on his back on the damp forest floor, writhing in agony, holding on to what was left of his calf, gritting his teeth, panting heavily, mumbling something about the Wolf Maiden and her cursed dog. Tears ran down his eyes and into his beard. He looked at William. "Help me, Doctor. Help me," he said in a barely audible voice, as though only now was he recognizing who William was, who he had tried to run through in the chapel with the pitchfork and who now had taken him into custody and would presently deliver him up to the law.

61

It was a long night. None slept except the wounded man. Rafe had recovered from the blow Bascombe had given him, although with a sore head and shoulder, and the pamphleteer had managed to get Bascombe back into the refectory and light a fire in the hearth next to which William had slept months earlier, the dog by his side. William removed the blood-soaked straw and heated water to clean the wounds on Bascombe's shoulder and leg. He had found soap. Then he made a bandage from a fragment of his own shirt.

The constable, who out of fear had remained beyond the cemetery, had found courage enough to come forward when he heard gunfire and, moments after, cries of alarm and pain. When he realized Bascombe had been taken and was incapacitated by his wounds, he felt confident enough to join Rafe and William in the refectory but was disappointed upon finding no food there. William said he was welcome to milk one of the cows in the stall chapel if he was that hungry.

At dawn, William told the Constable Pickney to return to the Rise and report the events of the night. William, Rafe, and Spaulding would come later, bringing the prisoner with them.

"Inform Justice Southcote that Julian Bascombe is wounded severely, by ball and by mauling dog. If he asks what dog it was, tell him it was Ursula Harkness's dog, the one thought to be a wolf and her familiar, although it would seem in apprehending a murderer it is unlikely such a creature is employed by the Devil, but by God rather."

By midday, Julian seemed well enough to travel. William and Rafe put him up onto one of the horses, groaning still with pain but able to sit upright. During his recovery, he had refused to speak as if, deprived of the strength to resist, he still maintained a perverse integrity. He would not confess to his crime, although it had been committed before witnesses, nor would he speak ill of his father, or even inquire if his mother, Agnes Robinson, still lived.

When William asked if the bandages were too tight upon his leg, Julian Bascombe would not answer. When asked if he wanted water to drink, he shook his head like a petulant child. It was as though he were punishing his captors, enveloping them in his own silence, his own obdurate resistance.

When they returned to the Rise several hours later, Justice Southcote and the citizenry of the hue and cry had gone and only the constable and a handful of his men remained. William was told that Agnes Robinson had revived from her swoon and had been conveyed to Chelmsford, to be imprisoned until she should be tried for murder. He was told that her fall from grace was as welcomed by her fellow servants at the Rise as by the townspeople. The household servants, having first fled the house in fear, had slowly returned and were taking care of their master's body and under direction of the master's butler were continuing their household duties.

Sir Richard's widow, Lady Margaret Bascombe, was reported to be devastated by her husband's death. Whether this was true or whether the poor woman secretly celebrated her release from marital bondage, William was unsure. She had broken down under the strain and been taken to the rooms she had occupied, alone, for years. Unlike her husband, she was regarded as a tragic figure, a hapless victim of her husband's indifference, brutality, and infidelity. All the servants in the house believed this, and William heard many expressions of sympathy for her, but no condemnation of her husband. It was too soon for that. The man was dead, but that didn't mean his spirit didn't linger to eavesdrop on idle gossip and punish it accordingly.

There would be, in due course, an inquest, although the cause of death having been witnessed by a half-dozen or more, including a doctor and apothecary, the constable and Justice Southcote, verdict of death by murder was a foregone conclusion. Besides, on the way back, Julian Bascombe, having apparently reassessed his position, decided to talk. He confessed it in front of both William and the pamphleteer, who had written down every word in a little notebook he carried with him.

In his confession, he admitted he had stabbed his father when he realized Sir Richard had tortured his birth mother. He had done so on an impulse, he said, in a moment of passion, perhaps even madness, for what son would not avenge his mother so? And who could blame him, seeing her bleeding, half-naked, her attacker admitting to the act, indeed boasting of it?

William had not answered that question. He expected that he was hearing what would become Julian Bascombe's defense at his trial. He thought that it might sway many a juryman devoted to his mother, or resentful of his father, or simply impressed by the defendant's status as gentry, the son of a knight, though a bastard after all. If he could convince the court that he was mad when he acted, he might escape punishment entirely. And yet the defense would require Julian's admission that he was a bastard, and that might put him at considerable disadvantage. Legally, at least, if not monetarily.

William gave Julian over to the constable, who had apparently told everyone including Justice Southcote that it had been he who had subdued the fugitive, and watched as he was put into a cart with two of the constable's men to guard him and conveyed toward town. "A mother and a son both accused of murder," the pamphleteer marveled. "An ancient pile more castle than manor. It will make a wonderful story with the most perfect setting. I know none like it."

William asked after Lady Clara and was told she had retired to her rooms and had not answered her door when they had come to see to her wants and needs. She had locked the door from within, they said, and recognizing she was grieving for her dead father they had dared not disturb her. The house was in mourning, they all said. Death had visited it. Betrayal, too. There was a great deal of whispering about Agnes Robinson, expressions of horror and dismay that a servant should seek to murder her mistress and her mistress's half-brother. Some of this, William imagined, was stoked by the dislike for Agnes among her fellow servants.

But when he could, he stole up the stairs to Clara's chamber, knocked softly at the door, and when he whispered his name, she opened it at once as though she had been standing on the other side, waiting for him to come.

Clara stood before him almost a different woman than he had known before. She was wearing a thin silk nightgown, loose upon her shoulders, and her face, whitened before by the painted ceruse, was scrubbed clean revealing the pitted cheeks that had marred her idea of herself. Her hair hung loose and unruly on her shoulders. Her eyes were red with weeping, and she trembled as she stood before him. William had rarely seen a woman look so stricken. It was evident that her grief and sense of betrayal had overwhelmed her, infecting her body as well as her mind.

She took a chair and invited him to sit in another. Facing her, he wondered if there would be more acrimony, or if her father's murder had put an end to it.

"Your brother, Julian, has been taken," he said. "He'll be conveyed to Chelmsford and stand trial for your father's murder."

She said she'd heard it. She said hanging was the least that Julian deserved. And then she added, "You will be happy to learn, Doctor, that before Justice Southcote left for Chelmsford I asked him to withdraw my complaint against Ursula Harkness and her mother, and begged him to tell the jury so. I have no reason to believe now that my brother Thomas died from any other cause than the ceruse and the evil additive that I ignorantly applied to him, believing that it would restore him to health."

"Ceruse and ratsbane. Lead paint and arsenic. That's a most deadly combination," William said.

"That woman must not suffer because of my own action, nor must her mother," Clara said. "It would be wrong of me. It *was* wrong of me, but Agnes Robinson was she who first put it in my mind that witchcraft was the cause of Thomas's illness."

"I know it, Lady Clara. She has confessed to it."

"Then may she burn in hell for her treason, for that is what it is, to poison one's master, to attempt to poison one's mistress who loved her dearly and would have died for her."

She meant, of course, herself. She was finally realizing the full enormity of Agnes Robinson's ambitions, the depth of her wickedness. She said she had thought the worst of witches was at the Old Priory. But, as it fell out, the worst was at Mowbray Rise.

She asked him to tell her what had really happened in the forest. She said the constable had returned boasting that he had come upon her brother Julian and forced him to submit by the threat of his sword.

"It was not quite like that, my lady."

William proceeded to tell her the real story. He also told her about the dog, that all in the town thought was a wolf.

"The dog that was Ursula Harkness's dog, the dog my brother Julian tried to hunt and kill?"

"The dog nearly killed him," William said. He decided not to tell her the nature of the wounds. He did not tell her that he had fired a ball at Julian's shoulder and wounded him. This was not a thing doctors were supposed to do. He had been caught up in an action contrary to his nature and training and it did not set well with him even though he would not have wanted Julian to escape and in retrospect would have done nothing other than he did.

"I have much abused you, Doctor," she said quietly. "For which I am most sorry."

"You bore many burdens, Lady Clara. Of grief and regret."

"And if I did?" she asked. "Others bear such burdens and remain themselves. They do not change as did I, become another person than I am, than I wish to be."

She looked away from him and began to weep softly again. He told her he needed to go. She asked him if he must.

"The trial of the Harknesses is not over," he said. "I have a duty not yet fulfilled."

He told her what he had not told her before, how they had saved his life, nurtured him to health, led him from the forest. All this he had said in court. He had not said it directly to her, and he could see in her eyes that, unlike her late father, she believed him.

"Then you must go, Doctor Gilbert," Clara said. "God be with you and with the women."

He wished her well and said he might see her another time before he returned to London. But he could tell from her eyes that she didn't believe him, and he knew himself that it wasn't true. He would not see her again. They had no future together. Too much had happened between them, and not enough.

62

When William returned to Chelmsford later that afternoon, he learned that the witch trial had been suspended for that day, and almost everyone in the town had heard of the murders and the capture of them who had done them. There was talk of little else, according to Rafe Tuttle, who having been an instrument in the capture of Julian Bascombe, was now holding court at the Blue Board and standing drinks all round to celebrate his own courage.

Nor was there great sadness at the news that Sir Richard Bascombe was dead. William was not surprised. He knew his countrymen paid homage to the high and mighty that governed them, but save for their adulation of her majesty he believed that much of that was false, and that the discovery of adultery and treachery in their landlords only confirmed their ill opinion of them.

Of the murders, that of Thomas Bascombe drew the most attention. Although patricide was abhorrent, there was a certain manliness in assault by knife, or so it was supposed. What son, at some ill-tempered moment, had not wished to kill his father? Many had doubtless tried, before they were subdued by a stronger hand.

Poison was another matter altogether. It was widely believed to be a peculiarly feminine undertaking that deserved the worst of punishments; not a hanging, but a burning. It was thought not merely violent, but sinister and underhanded and treacherous, because the victim might never know his enemy but be dead and prostrate at the throne of God before he understood what had happened to him.

Surely, the death of Thomas Bascombe was a case in point, as William knew the townspeople would see it. Poor Thomas thought he was being helped while he was in fact being poisoned. He would have blessed his sister for her ministrations while she unknowingly painted his body with a white death. What had Agnes Robinson called it, angel white?

The trial resumed the next day, with those attending a larger multitude than before for it had drawn observers from villages thereabout and more than a few persons, it was said, from London itself. But before anything else Justice Southcote rose from his place and announced that Lady Clara Bascombe had withdrawn her charge against the defendants and was now pleading for their release. This drew cries of surprise and confusion from those assembled who remembered Clara Bascombe's virulent accusations against the two women only days before, but not from the jury, who William understood had been told all by Rafe and the apothecary regarding what had been discovered at the Rise. "Agnes Robinson has confessed that she mixed the poison that killed Thomas Bascombe and caused him to waste away. Moreover, the dog, thought to be Ursula Harkness's familiar, was he who allowed the murderer Julian Bascombe to be apprehended."

The news about the dog also caused a stir. For days, the people of Chelmsford had lived in terror of it, keeping their children indoors at nights and blaming it for killing chickens, smaller dogs, and house cats.

The justice proceeded to describe the action as he had heard it from William and reasoned that no imp of Satan would have aided in the apprehension of a murderer and thus the dog, like its owner, should be regarded as innocent of any suspicion.

Which left the other evidence against Ursula: her marked child. Therein, Justice Southcote's comments were a help. He said he knew a half dozen men, men of good report, who were likewise birthmarked, if not upon their faces, then upon other parts of their body, and that he himself had such a stain upon his thigh, although he admitted it had faded in color in his later manhood. And, no, he was not prepared to expose his thigh to the public eye, a remark that caused laughter in the court. It was neither more nor less what William had testified to in court two days before, but coming from Justice Southcote the commonsensical observation had more credibility.

Having concluded his comments, the justice then ordered the bailiff to ask the jury to retire to an adjoining chamber to consider their verdict, but the jury declined to do so. Rafe, the foreman, said he was satisfied that the evidence against the women of witchcraft was trivial stuff not to be credited now that Agnes Robinson had confessed. He said he himself had seen the dog act righteously, as he called it, and that it was a damned poor cause to hang a person because her son had a birthmark. He said all the jury agreed, and the jury was polled by the bailiff and all said they agreed to a man with what Rafe had said.

At this, Ursula and her mother, who had been abused in body and soul before and during the trial and looked near death's door for it, broke into uncontrollable weeping and praising of God for their deliverance. They were freed to go home.

And then the Justice announced that because both Agnes Robinson and her son, Julian, had confessed to their murders he thought their trials might proceed at once since there was no other business scheduled for this session, whereupon there was a great roar of approval from those assembled, for the interest in the alleged witches had waned and they were eager to hear more of the Bascombe scandal and murder by poison and blade.

63

After the trial, William returned to the inn to pack his things. He was dirty, exhausted, and saddened. He was unsure why, for he had, after all, accomplished his purpose in coming to Chelmsford in the first place. The Harknesses had been exonerated, two murderers brought to account, and his own reputation, for all his father's warnings, had remained unsullied because of his part in it all. At least as far as he knew. But before he had done much more than find his satchel, he had two visitors. The first was Jacob Harkness, who had come to thank him for saving his family.

"It was only right," William said to the farmer, who looked as pale and haggard as if he himself had escaped the rope. "You and your good wife and daughter played the Good Samaritan in my time of need. But for you, I would have surely died."

"It was the dog that found you," Harkness reminded him.

"And the dog that helped me capture Julian Bascombe who killed his father."

"What shall you do now, Master Harkness?" William asked.

"We shall leave the county, Doctor. You were there, I understand. You saw how little remains, only the livestock and the fowl and these I am arranging to sell to a distant neighbor."

"And where will you go?"

He said he didn't know, only that it be far off where none had heard of the trial, or the accusations made. "That my wife and daughter were acquitted means little, if we are talking about how they are regarded in the town and thereabouts. Once accused, always suspected, they do say where I am from. We might well be accused a second time and not be so lucky as to have someone like you to aid us. In a trial, as you have seen, no one speaks for him or her who is accused, only for the prosecution. Every bit of gossip is credited though it were Gospel truth. In Chelmsford, witches are the great thing. There are folks there who think of little else but who they might profitably accuse. Besides that, because of what Julian Bascombe said at the trial, my daughter is now considered a whore. Her reputation is ruined. How might she find a decent husband and father for her innocent child?"

William could not argue differently. He had heard on his way back to the inn the reverend holding forth to the crowd who passed, faulting the jury and their verdict and claiming that the women freed were what they were alleged to be, enemies of the people, and that Ursula Harkness was nothing but a slattern, offering herself to anyone for money.

"How will you live, Master Harkness, wherever you go?" William asked.

"I'll sell the Old Priory if I can find someone with the courage to buy it. I'll sell it even to Lady Clara Bascombe, if I must. The Bascombes have wanted it for years. Well, Doctor, they are welcome to it and my curse upon them, for the Bascombes started this business that has ruined our lives, and may the property prove a curse to them, as it has proved to be to me."

"Do you need money in the meantime?" William asked.

Harkness thought about this for a moment, then said, "No, Doctor. No need of that, but many thanks anyway. You have done enough for us, more than any other person would. You were our only help, save heaven."

Despite Harkness's refusal, William pressed him further. Harkness finally took a handful of silver, which William thought might help the family survive for several months, at least until they could reestablish themselves.

But then he remembered what he had sworn not to forget, but had anyway until that very moment.

"Wait, before you leave, Master Harkness… Jacob."

"Doctor?"

William went to his desk and brought to Harkness a small package carefully wrapped in gold cloth and twine, like a present. "Give this to your daughter, if you will. They are hers."

He had planned to say no more than that, but he saw in the eyes of her father a questioning look that deserved an answer. William said, "They are letters your daughter wrote to Thomas Bascombe. He saved them. I found where he had concealed them at his own room at the Rise. Against the prying eyes of his sister, brother. Evidently, they were precious to him. Tell her that, will you? She should know he prized them if she ever doubts his love for her, or for the son he never saw."

William's second visitor was Matthew Spaulding, the printer and pamphleteer. He looked not merely happy, but joyful.

"I have news."

"Share it, if be good. Save it for another day, if it isn't." William said.

"I just left the Sessions House where Bascombe has been indicted for his father's murder. You will not believe this, but he is prepared to claim he acted in self-defense."

"I'm not surprised, not at all. By what Jesuitical reasoning? William asked, although he thought he knew. He remembered that Julian was already building his case on the way back to the Rise the morning after he was captured.

"He says that when he saw his mother had been tortured by Sir Richard, his father, he supposed he might next be seized, so that he wielded his dagger to protect himself from this supposed attack."

"From his father?"

"Yes."

"One must give him credit for inventiveness," William said.

"For little else," Spaulding said.

William said, "There were a half dozen of us standing by, including Justice Southcote, the constable and two of his men, myself, and Lady Clara. Does he truly suppose that his father would have seized him with such a cloud of witnesses to the act? His defense is absurd."

"He also says he struck to protect his mother," Spaulding said.

"Hardly better. The man's mad if he believes a jury will buy this," William said.

"Well, Doctor, some juries have had mad men amongst themselves and rendered verdicts as mad as themselves. While other juries lack a good man like unto Justice Southcote to preside over them. In any case, Julian Bascombe is prepared to plead not guilty to the charge."

They reminisced about their time in the forest, the encounter with Julian Bascombe in the chapel-turned-barn, the attack of the dog named Vulcan, the ride back to Mowbray Rise with the manor's supposed heir in custody.

William asked Spaulding if he had written his pamphlet. Spaulding said it was in progress. "This is no simple story of witchcraft, Doctor. It entails, as well, scandal and murder in a prominent family. I expect to sell several thousand copies the first week at a shilling each. I may have competitors for my tale, but only I can claim to know much of the story's details firsthand."

"Do me a favor, will you, Master Spaulding?"

"With all my heart, Doctor Gilbert."

"Leave me out of your pamphlet, if you will. My role will lend me little credit among my medical colleagues or enhance my reputation as a physician. And as in your experience, it may make me enemies here in Chelmsford, at least among those who are not my enemies already."

"But what of the capture of Bascombe? I can't merely write that he was captured without saying by whom and under what circumstances. It's the best part of the story."

"Take credit for it yourself, then, Master Spaulding. I understand the constable has already done that himself without an iota of justification. You, at least, were by my side when I wounded him and drove off the dog that attacked him."

"And what of Lady Clara?"

"I pray you be gentle in writing of her, Master Spaulding. She has lost much in these events of late; two brothers, a father, a trusted servant. There's no reason to subject her to more public humiliation, which telling her story certainly would."

Spaulding protested. "But I must tell of the ceruse she painted her face with and administered to her brother, or the means of her brother's murder would make no sense."

"Mercy is often better than accuracy, my friend," William said. "Use your judgment. You are the writer of this work for good or ill, not I or any other man. But, by all means, tell the truth. Do not invent or elaborate but tell the story straight."

"Upon my oath, Doctor. I will do it," Spaulding said, slapping his knee for emphasis.

He turned to go, but then hesitated, turned back, and said, "Doctor, I have a question about the Bascombe scandal. It's been bothering me since I first was told the details."

"And what is that?" William asked.

"Sir Richard claimed Agnes seduced him, claimed they mated by consent, but she said he abused her, forced her into the act. Which is true?"

William thought he knew the answer. He remembered what Clara said she observed as a child, a tussle in the sheets, Agnes emerging from her father's bedroom, seeing the child Clara was then and swearing her to secrecy to spare her mother's feelings of inadequacy. It hadn't sounded like a rape.

But Clara had told him that in confidence. It seemed a private memory, not to become a detail in anyone's tale of scandal. William had revealed too many of Clara Bascombe's secrets already. He would not reveal this one.

"God knows which is true, Master Spaulding, not I."

Spaulding shrugged. "Oh well, then I may just make something up. The rape makes a better story, don't you think, Doctor?"

64

A month after, when William was busy again at his true calling, he came across Matthew Spaulding's pamphlet about the Chelmsford murders in an unusual way. One morning his servant at Wingfield House found it folded and stuck in the door and remembering that his master the doctor had spent a week in Chelmsford some time earlier that summer he brought it to William straightway, thinking it was something the Doctor might read with interest.

William took it and read the lengthy title with some amusement: *A True and Veritable Account of the Recent Trial of the Wolf Maiden of Chelmsford and the devilish Poisoning of Thomas Bascombe of Mowbray Rise, Wherein the true breadth and depth of Evil be Exposed.*

William noticed that the author of the pamphlet was not named, and he remembered that Spaulding had explained that identifying himself might subject him to harassment or revenge from those mentioned in the story. But William did notice that written in hand on the title page were the initials M. S. For Matthew Spaulding.

Spaulding's pamphlet contained a dozen pages of closely printed script coupled with several illustrations. One was of Agnes Robinson standing before a table and mixing ingredients, presumably ceruse and ratsbane. The person depicted looked nothing like Agnes Robinson, who was a woman of middling age, forty or forty-five William judged, a woman whose features must have at some earlier time been pleasing, poisoner though she was. The depiction in the illustration showed an aged hag, bent over, with sharply pointed nose and chin that almost met, and unnaturally long fingernails.

The second illustration, situated toward the end of the pamphlet, was of Ursula Harkness's dog. The dog the family had called Vulcan. The dog, depicted as twice its actual size, was clearly more wolf than dog and had his teeth fixed in a man's leg while the man screamed in agony. The man, not surprisingly, looked nothing like Julian Bascombe although it was clear that it was intended to be he. Julian Bascombe was not a handsome man, but the figure in the illustration looked vicious, more animal than human himself, his fingers like claws, the nails extended like knives.

William read the pamphlet from beginning to end. There was no mention of himself in it. Spaulding had kept his promise to that extent, but the scene of the capture of Julian Bascombe at the Old Priory was elaborated upon excessively, with a lengthy passage of description of the ruined priory, emphasizing its sinister connection with papistry and presenting Spaulding himself as the one who had successfully dragged the dog from the mutilated body of the fugitive, slain the beast, and presented the patricide to the arms of the law. William noticed with amusement that Spaulding had described Constable Pickney's conduct as cowardly and insignificant, clearly giving the lie to the constable's own account of his heroic actions which he given upon returning to the Rise.

Spaulding had also succeeded in treating Lady Clara Bascombe's part in the story with some delicacy. He represented her as being a good and beautiful young woman unduly influenced by her old servant in accusing the Harknesses, and tragically misled in the nature of the substances with which she had treated her brother. She was, in a word, a victim, a conclusion with which William could not disagree.

There was in addition to all this an extravagantly written passage denouncing the use of poison and condemning any servant who might think to use such against his or her master. The tone of the pamphlet was dignified, measured, and moral, and even the details Spaulding had made up had at least the appearance of plausibility.

William had no doubt it would be widely read and put many a penny in its author's pocket.

65

In September of that same year, Jerome Gilbert paid another visit to London. As usual, he stayed with William at Wingfield House.

His father's first comment was about Clara.

"I do think, son," Jerome Gilbert said, making himself comfortable by the library fire, that you were well advised not to pursue the lady. I mean in light of the family scandal, the bastard brother, what's his name?"

"Julian Bascombe," William said, smiling to himself since his father had given him no such advice, but quite the contrary.

"The family is unsound," his father murmured, nodding his head. "I think I always knew it. That his bastard son should have killed him did not surprise me. I knew Bascombe, as you know, we were friends long ago, but I knew nothing about his mistress, the poisoner, nor knew she was the mother of his bastard son, whom I remember as a nasty little boy with a cruel streak."

"That would be Julian Bascombe," William said.

But his father also had news of Chelmsford, where he had many friends and legal connections.

"And what of Lady Clara?" William asked.

"Ah, she has married at last," his father said.

"A gentleman of her station?" William asked, surprised but not displeased with this news.

"She has married a man named Anthony Poole, a lawyer."

"The queen's counsel at the witch trial," William said, laughing. "That's where they met. It was plain he was infatuated with her, during her testimony. He could not keep his eyes off her. Do you know him?"

"Never heard of him, but then lawyers are tuppence each about the court these days."

William imagined Clara and Poole together, joined in holy matrimony. It was not easy. She had married down, a mere lawyer, no titled gentleman. Agnes Robinson would not have approved. Well, love does make strange bedfellows, he thought. Still, he wished them well. He had no animus against either, not after so long a time, and no regrets either.

"And what of the Old Priory?" William remembered to ask.

"Ah, thereby hangs a tale," his father said. "I got this from our friend Rafe Tuttle at the inn. Rafe says Jacob Harkness sold it to Lady Clara for half of what he thought it worth, along with all his livestock. But before he left it, he set fire to the place, and it burned to the ground. Only the chapel stands, and it is no more than a pile of blackened stones. There is little there now that the forest will not cover within the next few years. In a dozen more, no one in Chelmsford will remember its name or what was done there."

"No loss," William observed, thinking of the nun's graveyard and the bodies buried there, the lingering monument of papistry in a town that had no tolerance for it. But the bones, he knew, were still there. Unless they were exhumed, they would always be there, even when they were dust, even when weeds and thistles, vines and branches and roots of mighty trees had obscured the headstones. The dead would not be moved.

"And what of Julian Bascombe?"

"Hanged. Along with his mother. The jury had little patience with a son who kills his father, public morals haven't sunk that low. They rejected the self-defense argument; thought he might have just run away instead. The killing smelled like old-fashioned revenge to them. He was a bastard anyway, the son of a treacherous servant, a poisoner. No, there was little sympathy there. More for the mother, oddly. Women who poison are usually burned. She escaped that at least."

"Did they say anything before they were hanged?"

"Julian Bascombe stood there scowling at the multitude as though they were the malefactors and not he. He cursed the town and all therein, said he was glad he'd killed his father and would do so again. At least, that's what I've heard. I wasn't there."

"And Agnes Robinson?"

"She spoke at length, I understand, confessed all, begged forgiveness for her crimes and prayed for those assembled and for the queen. It was a good death, as they say. Dignified, although she was no more than a servant in a rich man's house."

"She had been ill used too," William said.

"Hardly a justification for murder, my son."

"No, I suppose not."

William received a letter after Christmas, one year to the day of his ordeal at the Old Priory. It was from Ursula Harkness; he recognized her hand. She said she and the family were settled in Norfolk, along with the dog who had saved William's life and mangled Julian Bascombe's leg. She said she had met a local farmer, an honest man and widower with two sons of his own. They were to be wed in a month. She said they were happy, all of them, and prospering. They wanted to leave their dark past behind them.

They had changed their name to Harker.

Ursula said she would never forget him for what he had done.

Nor would he, it turned out, forget her. In years to come he would sometimes dream of being lost in the forest, finding himself again in the Old Priory, and there would be an image of the hard-featured girl—the Wolf Maiden, as she had been called—bending over him, the wolf dog by her side. William would feel the rough tongue of the creature lick his face. He would smell the sour canine breath, see with horror the sharp teeth ready to sink into his own vulnerable flesh.

The vision would come to him just moments before sleep, just moments before the dream turned into something else, something less strange and fearful.